THE BLACK ROBE

Lewis Romayne is handsome and rich, but he is also a recluse, pursuing a life of academic research in the isolated Vange Abbey, his North Riding country seat. Forced from this life by the dying call of his aunt in Paris, he there, becomes involved in a duel and returns to London a broken man. At the house of loyal friends, he meets Stella Eyrecourt and marriage looks a possibility. But Father Benwell, a Jesuit priest, is determined that the abbey and its riches will be returned to the Church. He instructs his assistant, to make Romayne convert. And so begins a battle for Romayne's soul . . .

WILKIE COLLINS

THE
BLACK ROBE

Complete and Unabridged

CHARNWOOD
Leicester

First published in Great Britain in 1994

First Charnwood Edition
published 2001

British Library CIP Data

Collins, Wilkie, *1824 – 1889*
 The black robe.—Large print ed.—
 Charnwood library series
 1. Large type books
 I. Title
 823.8 [F]

 ISBN 0–7089–9212–9

F

1383523

Published by
F. A. Thorpe (Publishing)
Anstey, Leicestershire
Set by Words & Graphics Ltd.
Anstey, Leicestershire
Printed and bound in Great Britain by
T. J. International Ltd., Padstow, Cornwall

This book is printed on acid-free paper

Biographical Introduction

William Wilkie Collins was born in Marylebone on 8 January 1824. He died sixty-five years later in Wimpole Street, little more than three blocks away, and lived most of his life in that central part of London. Yet from that narrow base he managed to live as colourful a life as any other Victorian and wrote some of the most gripping novels of the nineteenth century. He is still regarded as 'the father of the detective story' and 'the novelist who invented sensation'. He himself put it more modestly. He was, he said, just a simple story teller.

Such stories, however, included *The Moonstone* and *The Woman in White*. His first published novel, *Antonina*, appeared in 1851, and his last, *Blind Love*, had to be finished by an old friend, Walter Besant, in 1889. In the intervening years Collins wrote over thirty novels and collections of stories, as well as a biography of his father William Collins. The manuscript of the first novel he actually wrote, though it was turned down by every publisher he approached and vanished for nearly 150 years, finally surfaced in New York in 1990. Entitled *Iolani; Or Tahiti as it Was*, its somewhat belated publication is now planned. Collins himself was remarkably frank about that early failure. 'My youthful imagination ran riot among the noble savages, in scenes which caused the respectable

British publisher [actually Chapman and Hall] to declare that it was impossible to put his name on the title page of such a novel'.

It was during the writing of that first, unsuccessful, novel that Collins' parents first became fully aware that all their assumptions about 'Willy's future' (as he was known in the family) were quite wrong. His father, William Collins, already an RA, with a string of wealthy clients, including the late George IV, was a leading landscape artist and had readily assumed that both sons (Charles Allston Collins was two years younger than Wilkie) would also take up painting. William's own father, another William, was a picture dealer and Harriet, Wilkie Collins' mother, came from a family of painters. Both Constable and Linnell were close friends of the family as the boys grew up in Hampstead, and sketching became second nature to them both.

Yet it was the written word and a good story well told that tugged at Wilkie Collins. He later described how at his second school at Highbury, where he was a boarder, he was regularly bullied at night by the head boy. 'You will go to sleep, Collins', he was apparently told, 'when you have told me a story'. Quite an incentive. 'It was this brute who first awakened in me, his poor little victim, a power of which but for him I might never have been aware . . . When I left school I continued story telling for my own pleasure'.

The occasions when he could do so were varied indeed. His school days were remarkably interrupted by his father's decision to take the family to Italy for two years, an extended visit

that gave Collins not only visual stimuli but provided the background for what would be his first published novel, *Antonina*. It was also in Italy that, according to Dickens, Collins experienced his 'first love adventure'. As Dickens explained the affair to his sister-in-law later, it 'had proceeded, if I may be allowed the expression, to the utmost extremities'. Collins was thirteen at the time. Perhaps more important, for his writing if not his character, it was probably in Italy that his attraction to the visual began to seek an alternative outlet to painting, and where the embryo writer began to emerge from the family of artists.

When, a few years later, his father was considering whether Wilkie should be entered at art school, prior to applying to the Royal Academy, it was already clear that his interests lay elsewhere. One idea was that he should go to Oxford, before entering the Church. But William was eventually persuaded that a spell in a tea merchant's office would at least provide Wilkie with a more secure income than the desultory writing that seemed to attract him. It did not last, though since the office in the Strand was near all the publishers it at least allowed him to trail round them with his articles in spare moments. He had his first short story, *The Last Stage Coachman*, published under his name in *The Illuminated Magazine* at this time. His father's next initiative was to arrange for Wilkie to enter Lincoln's Inn and to read for the Bar, again on the assumption that it might provide

a better source of income than writing. It was to be one of William's last family concerns, for he died the following year, in 1847.

Collins managed to sustain his legal studies, or at least his necessary attendances, sufficiently over the next few years to be finally called to the Bar in 1851. It may not have been a particularly attractive calling, in his eyes, but it was later to serve its purpose. Eight of his novels have lawyers as prominent characters and the drawing up of wills was crucial to several of his later plots, including *The Woman in White*. When his father died, Collins, though still ostensibly studying for the Bar, had reached the third chapter of the second volume of *Antonina*, and had already read the bulk of the first volume to his father. Thereafter he immediately laid the novel aside and took up the preparations for a memoir of his father. It was thus a biographical work, *The Life of William Collins*, and not a novel that in 1848 became his first published work and established his name in the publishing world.

With the death of William Collins his family, though saddened by his suffering, were soon showing a new kind of independence. His love for them had never been in doubt, but William had early acquired a streak of moral rectitude which over the years irritated his friends and restricted his family. Wilkie had probably felt the heavy hand more than his brother Charles, but had chosen to ride the storms when they occurred, while pursuing his personal inclinations as best he could. Once

the memoirs were completed, Harriet and her two sons settled down in an imposing house overlooking Regents Park, where she was happy to play host to her sons' younger friends from the artistic and literary worlds. It was here that Wilkie came under the wing of Charles Dickens and his brother befriended John Millais, William Holman-Hunt and other Pre-Raphaelites.

It was in this period that Wilkie Collins extended the range of his writing, providing leading articles for *The Leader*, short stories and essays for *Bentley's Miscellany*, a travel book about Cornwall entitled *Rambles Beyond Railways*, as well as dramatic criticisms and a short play. Charles Dickens had already enticed him to participate in the private theatricals he was developing and within eighteen months Wilkie had performed, in a small part, at a Dickens-directed charity performance in the presence of Queen Victoria. It was a short step from this to a joint production of Wilkie's first play, *The Lighthouse*, and a later commercial production at the Olympic Theatre. Soon they were co-operating on Dickens' journal *Household Words* and, with Wilkie in the lead, nicely egged on by Dickens, sharing colourful entertainments and distractions together in London and Paris.

It was a time when Collins began to write the kind of novels that were always to be identified with him, combining well-constructed plots with strong characters, beginning with *Basil* in the early fifties, followed by *Hide and Seek, After Dark* (short stories) and *The Dead Secret*, and

culminating in *The Woman in White* in 1860. It was also the time when he met the two women — Caroline Graves and Martha Rudd — who were to weave in and out of his life for the next thirty years.

Caroline Graves appeared first, dramatically if Collins himself is to be believed, in much the same way as the mysterious lady in St John's Wood at the outset of *The Woman in White*. The story goes that the woman in distress gave a piercing scream one moonlit night as Wilkie and his brother were accompanying John Millais back to his lodgings. Millais simply exclaimed 'What a lovely woman'. Wilkie followed her into the darkness and later told them that she was a lady of good birth who had fallen into the clutches of a man who was threatening her life.

An element of truth perhaps, but it was tinged with Collins' undoubted storytelling ability. We now know that Caroline came from a humble family in the west country, had been married young, had a child and had been left a widow. It was not long before Collins was sharing lodgings with her, even answering letters openly from the various addresses they occupied in and around Marylebone. He even put her down as his wife, quite inaccurately, in the Census of 1861. He shared his triumphs with her, from *The Woman in White* onwards, but in spite of her obvious wishes, he was determined not to marry her.

These were the years of Collins' best-known novels. *The Woman in White* was followed by *Armadale* (for which he received the, then

record, sum of £5,000 before a word had been written), *No Name* and *The Moonstone*. It was the preparation of *Armadale* and the writing of *The Moonstone*, however, that were to produce such dramatic upheavals in his private life and, to some extent, account for what many critics have detected as a relative falling off in his narrative power as a novelist.

His search for background for *Armadale* took him to the Norfolk Broads and to the small coastal village of Winterton. There, or nearby, he met Martha Rudd, the nineteen-year-old daughter of a large, though poor, family. Her parents and relations have been traced (their graves are still in the local churchyard), but the timing of Martha's move to be closer to Collins in London remains obscure. What we do know is that only a few years later, when Collins was writing instalments of *The Moonstone*, already laid low by an acute attack of rheumatic gout and grieving over the death of his mother, Caroline decided to leave him and to marry a much younger man. Dickens felt that she had tried to bluff Collins into marriage and had failed. It could also have been Martha's appearance in London that proved to be the last straw.

Collins was devastated and finished *The Moonstone* in a haze of pain and with increasing doses of laudanum. It was a habit he was to follow for the rest of his life, his intake of opium eventually reaching remarkable levels, with inevitable repercussions on his writing ability. The domestic drama, however, was

not yet over. Within nine months of Caroline's marriage, Martha, living in lodgings in Bolsover Street, was to bear Collins his first child and within another two years Caroline had left her husband and returned to Collins in Gloucester Place and Martha was pregnant with his second child.

And so it continued for the rest of his life, with Caroline once more established in Gloucester Place, though probably as housekeeper and hostess rather than mistress, and Martha and his 'morganatic' family (eventually two girls and a boy: Marian, Harriet and William Charles) not far away. When he visited Martha he became William Dawson, Barrister-at-Law, and she was known as Mrs Dawson. His male friends readily accepted these arrangements, though their wives were rarely, if ever, invited to Gloucester Place or, later, Wimpole Street.

His two families, basically Caroline's grand-children and Martha's children, happily mingled together on holiday in Ramsgate and even occasionally in Gloucester Place, but Martha and Caroline never met. It was against this domestic background, with a host of literary and theatrical friends, that he pursued the last decade and a half of his life, completing some of his more socially conscious novels, such as *Heart and Science*, as well as his more recognizable suspense novels, like *Poor Miss Finch, The Haunted Hotel, The New Magdalen, The Black Robe*, and *Jezebel's Daughter*.

He died in Wimpole Street in September 1889, and was buried at Kensal Green

Cemetery. Caroline was eventually buried with him and Martha continued to tend the grave until she left London. She died in Southend in 1919. The gold locket Wilkie gave Martha in 1868, marking the death of his mother, is still in the possession of my wife, Faith, their great-granddaughter.

WILLIAM M. CLARKE

Before the Story

First Scene

Boulogne-sur-Mer — The Duel

I

The doctors could do no more for the Dowager
Lady Berrick.

When the medical advisers of a lady who
has reached seventy years of age recommend
the mild climate of the South of France, they
mean in plain language that they have arrived at
the end of their resources. Her ladyship gave the
mild climate a fair trial, and then decided (as she
herself expressed it) to 'die at home.' Travelling
slowly, she had reached Paris at the date when
I last heard of her. It was then the beginning of
November. A week later, I met with her nephew,
Lewis Romayne, at the club.

'What brings you to London at this time of
year?' I asked.

'The fatality that pursues me,' he answered
grimly. 'I am one of the unluckiest men living.'

He was thirty years old; he was not married;
he was the enviable possessor of the fine old
country seat, called Vange Abbey; he had
no poor relations; and he was one of the
handsomest men in England. When I add that
I am, myself, a retired army officer, with a

1

wretched income, a disagreeable wife, four ugly children, and a burden of fifty years on my back, no one will be surprised to hear that I answered Romayne, with bitter sincerity, in these words:

'I wish to Heaven I could change places with you!'

'I wish to Heaven you could!' he burst out, with equal sincerity, on his side. 'Read that.'

He handed me a letter addressed to him by the travelling medical attendant of Lady Berrick. After resting in Paris, the patient had continued her homeward journey as far as Boulogne. In her suffering condition, she was liable to sudden fits of caprice. An insurmountable horror of the Channel passage had got possession of her: she positively refused to be taken on board the steamboat. In this difficulty, the lady who held the post of her 'companion' had ventured on a suggestion. Would Lady Berrick consent to make the Channel passage if her nephew came to Boulogne expressly to accompany her on the voyage? The reply had been so immediately favourable, that the doctor lost no time in communicating with Mr Lewis Romayne. This was the substance of the letter.

It was needless to ask any more questions — Romayne was plainly on his way to Boulogne. I gave him some useful information. 'Try the oysters,' I said, 'at the restaurant on the pier.'

He never even thanked me. He was thinking entirely of himself.

'Just look at my position,' he said. 'I detest Boulogne; I cordially share my aunt's horror of the Channel passage; I had looked forward to

2

some months of happy retirement in the country among my books — and what happens to me? I am brought to London in this season of fogs, to travel by the tidal train at seven to-morrow morning — and all for a woman with whom I have no sympathies in common. If I am not an unlucky man — who is?'

He spoke in a tone of vehement irritation which seemed to me, under the circumstances, to be simply absurd. But *my* nervous system is not the irritable system — sorely tried by night study and strong tea — of my friend Romayne. 'It's only a matter of two days,' I remarked, by way of reconciling him to his situation.

'How do I know that?' he retorted. 'In two days the weather may be stormy. In two days she may be too ill to be moved. Unfortunately, I am her heir; and I am told I must submit to any whim that seizes her. I'm rich enough already; I don't want her money. Besides, I dislike all travelling — and especially travelling alone. You are an idle man. If you were a good friend, you would offer to go with me.' He added, with the delicacy which was one of the redeeming points in his wayward character, 'Of course as my guest.'

I had known him long enough not to take offence at his reminding me, in this considerate way, that I was a poor man. The proposed change of scene tempted me. What did I care for the Channel passage? Besides, there was the irresistible attraction of getting away from home. The end of it was that I accepted Romayne's invitation.

3

II

Shortly after noon, on the next day, we were established at Boulogne — near Lady Berrick, but not at her hotel. 'If we live in the same house,' Romayne reminded me, 'we shall be bored by the companion and the doctor. Meetings on the stairs, you know, and exchanging bows and small talk.' He hated those trivial conventionalities of society, in which other people delight. When somebody once asked him in what company he felt most at ease? he made a shocking answer — he said, 'In the company of dogs.'

I waited for him on the pier while he went to see her ladyship. He joined me again, with his bitterest smile. 'What did I tell you? She is not well enough to see me to-day. The doctor looks grave, and the companion puts her handkerchief to her eyes. We may be kept in this place for weeks to come.'

The afternoon proved to be rainy. Our early dinner was a bad one. This last circumstance tried his temper sorely. He was no gourmand; the question of cookery was (with him) purely a matter of digestion. Those late hours of study, and that abuse of tea to which I have already alluded, had sadly injured his stomach. The doctors warned him of serious consequences to his nervous system, unless he altered his habits. He had little faith in medical science, and he greatly overrated the restorative capacity of his constitution. So far as I know, he had always neglected the doctors' advice.

The weather cleared towards evening, and we went out for a walk. We passed a church — a Roman Catholic church, of course — the doors of which were still open. Some poor women were kneeling at their prayers in the dim light. 'Wait a minute,' said Romayne, 'I am in a vile temper. Let me try to put myself into a better frame of mind.'

I followed him into the church. He knelt down in a dark corner by himself. I confess I was surprised. He had been baptised in the Church of England; but, so far as outward practice was concerned, he belonged to no religious community. I had often heard him speak with sincere reverence and admiration of the spirit of Christianity — but he never, to my knowledge, attended any place of public worship. When we met again outside the church, I asked if he had been converted to the Roman Catholic faith.

'No,' he said. 'I hate the inveterate striving of that priesthood after social influence and political power as cordially as the fiercest Protestant living. But let us not forget that the Church of Rome has great merits to set against great faults. Its system is administered with an admirable knowledge of the higher needs of human nature. Take as one example what you have just seen. The solemn tranquillity of that church, the poor people praying near me, the few words of prayer by which I silently united myself to my fellow-creatures have calmed me, and done me good. In *our* country I should have found the church closed, out of service hours.' He took my arm, and abruptly changed

the subject. 'How will you occupy yourself,' he asked, 'if my aunt receives me to-morrow?'

I assured him that I should easily find ways and means of getting through the time. The next morning a message came from Lady Berrick, to say that she would see her nephew after breakfast. Left by myself, I walked towards the pier, and met with a man who asked me to hire his boat. He had lines and bait, at my service. Most unfortunately, as the event proved, I decided on occupying an hour or two by sea fishing.

The wind shifted while we were out, and before we could get back to the harbour, the tide had turned against us. It was six o'clock when I arrived at the hotel. A little open carriage was waiting at the door. I found Romayne impatiently expecting me, and no signs of dinner on the table. He informed me that he had accepted an invitation, in which I was included, and promised to explain everything in the carriage.

Our driver took the road that led towards the High Town. I subordinated my curiosity to my sense of politeness, and asked for news of his aunt's health.

'She is seriously ill, poor soul,' he said. 'I am sorry I spoke so petulantly and so unfairly, when we met at the club. The near prospect of death has developed qualities in her nature which I ought to have seen before this. No matter how it may be delayed, I will patiently wait her time for the crossing to England.'

So long as he believed himself to be in the

right, he was, as to his actions and opinions, one of the most obstinate men I ever met with. But once let him be convinced that he was wrong, and he rushed into the other extreme — became needlessly distrustful of himself, and needlessly eager in seizing his opportunity of making atonement. In this latter mood he was capable (with the best intentions) of committing acts of the most childish imprudence. With some misgivings, I asked how he had amused himself in my absence.

'I waited for you,' he said, 'till I lost all patience, and went out for a walk. First, I thought of going to the beach, but the smell of the harbour drove me back into the town; and there, oddly enough, I met with a man, a certain Captain Peterkin, who had been a friend of mine at college.'

'A visitor to Boulogne?' I inquired.

'Not exactly.'

'A resident?'

'Yes. The fact is, I lost sight of Peterkin when I left Oxford — and since that time he seems to have drifted into difficulties. We had a long talk. He is living here, he tells me, until his affairs are settled.'

I needed no further enlightenment — Captain Peterkin stood as plainly revealed to me as if I had known him for years. 'Isn't it a little imprudent,' I said, 'to renew your acquaintance with a man of that sort? Couldn't you have passed him, with a bow?'

Romayne smiled uneasily. 'I dare say you're right,' he answered. 'But, remember, I had left

7

my aunt, feeling ashamed of the unjust way in which I had thought and spoken of her. How did I know that I mightn't be wronging an old friend next, if I kept Peterkin at a distance? His present position may be as much his misfortune, poor fellow, as his fault. I was half inclined to pass him, as you say — but I distrusted my own judgment. He held out his hand, and he was so glad to see me. It can't be helped now. I shall be anxious to hear your opinion of him.'

'Are we going to dine with Captain Peterkin?'

'Yes. I happened to mention that wretched dinner yesterday at our hotel. He said, 'Come to my boarding-house. Out of Paris, there isn't such a table d'hôte in France.' I tried to get off it — not caring, as you know, to go among strangers — I said I had a friend with me. He invited you most cordially to accompany me. More excuses on my part only led to a painful result. I hurt Peterkin's feelings. 'I'm down in the world,' he said, 'and I'm not fit company for you and your friends. I beg your pardon for taking the liberty of inviting you!' He turned away with the tears in his eyes. What could I do?'

I thought to myself, 'You could have lent him five pounds, and got rid of his invitation without the slightest difficulty.' If I had returned in reasonable time to go out with Romayne, we might not have met the captain — or, if we had met him, my presence would have prevented the confidential talk and the invitation that followed. I felt I was to blame — and yet, how could I help

it? It was useless to remonstrate: the mischief was done.

We left the Old Town on our right hand, and drove on, past a little colony of suburban villas, to a house standing by itself, surrounded by a stone wall. As we crossed the front garden on our way to the door, I noticed against the side of the house two kennels, inhabited by two large watch-dogs. Was the proprietor afraid of thieves?

III

The moment we were introduced to the drawing-room, my suspicions of the company we were likely to meet with were fully confirmed.

'Cards, billiards, and betting' — there was the inscription legibly written on the manner and appearance of Captain Peterkin. The bright-eyed yellow old lady who kept the boarding-house would have been worth five thousand pounds in jewellery alone, if the ornaments which profusely covered her had been genuine precious stones. The younger ladies present had their cheeks as highly rouged and their eyelids as elaborately pencilled in black as if they were going on the stage, instead of going to dinner. We found these fair creatures drinking Madeira as a whet to their appetites. Among the men, there were two who struck me as the most finished and complete blackguards whom I had ever met with in all my experience, at home and abroad. One, with a brown face and a broken nose, was presented to us by the title

9

of 'Commander,' and was described as a person of great wealth and distinction in Peru, travelling for amusement. The other wore a military uniform and decorations, and was spoken of as 'the General.' A bold bullying manner, a fat sodden face, little leering eyes, and greasy-looking hands, made this man so repellent to me that I privately longed to kick him. Romayne had evidently been announced, before our arrival, as a landed gentleman with a large income. Men and women vied in servile attentions to him. When we went into the dining-room, the fascinating creature who sat next to him held her fan before her face, and so made a private interview of it between the rich Englishman and herself. With regard to the dinner, I shall only report that it justified Captain Peterkin's boast, in some degree at least. The wine was good, and the conversation became gay to the verge of indelicacy. Usually the most temperate of men, Romayne was tempted by his neighbours into drinking freely. I was unfortunately seated at the opposite extremity of the table, and I had no opportunity of warning him.

The dinner reached its conclusion, and we all returned together, on the foreign plan, to coffee and cigars in the drawing-room. The women smoked, and drank liqueurs as well as coffee, with the men. One of them went to the piano, and a little impromptu ball followed, the ladies dancing with their cigarettes in their mouths. Keeping my eyes and ears on the alert, I saw an innocent-looking table, with a surface of rosewood, suddenly develop a substance of green

10

cloth. At the same time, a neat little roulette-table made its appearance from a hiding-place in a sofa. Passing near the venerable landlady, I heard her ask the servant, in a whisper, 'if the dogs were loose?' After what I had observed, I could only conclude that the dogs were used as a patrol, to give the alarm in case of a descent of the police. It was plainly high time to thank Captain Peterkin for his hospitality, and to take our leave.

'We have had enough of this,' I whispered to Romayne in English. 'Let us go.'

In these days it is a delusion to suppose that you can speak confidentially in the English language, when French people are within hearing. One of the ladies asked Romayne, tenderly, if he was tired of her already. Another reminded him that it was raining heavily (as we could all hear), and suggested waiting until it cleared up. The hideous General waved his greasy hand in the direction of the card table, and said, 'The game is waiting for us.'

Romayne was excited, but not stupefied, by the wine he had drunk. He answered, discreetly enough, 'I must beg you to excuse me; I am a poor card player.'

The General suddenly looked grave. 'You are speaking, sir, under a strange misapprehension,' he said. 'Our game is lansquenet — essentially a game of chance. With luck, the poorest player is a match for the whole table.'

Romayne persisted in his refusal. As a matter of course, I supported him, with all needful care to avoid giving offence. The General took

offence, nevertheless. He crossed his arms on his breast, and looked at us fiercely.

'Does this mean, gentlemen, that you distrust the company?' he asked.

The broken-nosed Commander, hearing the question, immediately joined us, in the interests of peace — bearing with him the elements of persuasion, under the form of a lady on his arm.

The lady stepped briskly forward, and tapped the General on the shoulder with her fan. '*I* am one of the company,' she said, 'and I am sure Mr Romayne doesn't distrust *me*.' She turned to Romayne with her most irresistible smile. 'A gentleman always plays cards,' she resumed, 'when he has a lady for a partner. Let us join our interests at the table — and, dear Mr Romayne, don't risk too much!' She put her pretty little purse into his hand, and looked as if she had been in love with him for half her lifetime.

The fatal influence of the sex, assisted by wine, produced the inevitable result. Romayne allowed himself to be led to the card table. For a moment, the General delayed the beginning of the game. After what had happened, it was necessary that he should assert the strict sense of justice that was in him. 'We are all honourable men,' he began.

'And brave men,' the Commander added, admiring the General.

'And brave men,' the General admitted, admiring the Commander. 'Gentlemen, if I have been led into expressing myself with unnecessary warmth of feeling, I apologise, and regret it.'

'Nobly spoken!' the Commander pronounced. The General put his hand on his heart and bowed. The game began.

As the poorest man of the two, I had escaped the attentions lavished by the ladies on Romayne. At the same time, I was obliged to pay for my dinner, by taking some part in the proceedings of the evening. Small stakes were allowed, I found, at roulette; and, besides, the heavy chances in favour of the table made it hardly worth while to run the risk of cheating in this case. I placed myself next to the least rascally-looking man in the company, and played roulette.

For a wonder, I was successful at the first attempt. My neighbour handed me my winnings. 'I have lost every farthing I possess,' he whispered to me, piteously, 'and I have a wife and children at home.' I lent the poor wretch five francs. He smiled faintly as he looked at the money. 'It reminds me,' he said, 'of my last transaction, when I borrowed of that gentleman there, who is betting on the General's luck at the card table. Beware of employing him as I did. What do you think I got for my note of hand of four thousand francs? A hundred bottles of champagne, fifty bottles of ink, fifty bottles of blacking, three dozen handkerchiefs, two pictures by unknown masters, two shawls, one hundred maps, *and* — five francs.'

We went on playing. My luck deserted me; I lost, and lost, and lost again. From time to time I looked round at the card table. The 'deal' had fallen early to the General, and it seemed to

13

be indefinitely prolonged. A heap of notes and gold (won mainly from Romayne, as I afterwards discovered) lay before him. As for my neighbour, the unhappy possessor of the bottles of blacking, the pictures by unknown masters, and the rest of it, he won, and then rashly presumed on his good fortune. Deprived of his last farthing, he retired into a corner of the room, and consoled himself with a cigar. I had just risen, to follow his example, when a furious uproar burst out at the card table.

I saw Romayne spring up, and snatch the cards out of the General's hand. 'You scoundrel!' he shouted, 'you are cheating!' The General started to his feet in a fury. 'You lie!' he cried. I attempted to interfere, but Romayne had already seen the necessity of controlling himself. 'A gentleman doesn't accept an insult from a swindler,' he said, coolly. 'Accept this, then!' the General answered — and spat on him. In an instant Romayne knocked him down.

The blow was dealt straight between his eyes: he was a gross big-boned man, and he fell heavily. For the time he was stunned. The women ran, screaming, out of the room. The peaceable Commander trembled from head to foot. Two of the men present, who, to give them their due, were no cowards, locked the doors. 'You don't go,' they said, 'till we see whether he recovers or not.' Cold water, assisted by the landlady's smelling salts, brought the General to his senses after a while. He whispered something to one of his friends, who immediately turned to me. 'The General challenges Mr Romayne,'

he said. 'As one of his seconds, I demand an appointment for to-morrow morning.' I refused to make any appointment unless the doors were first unlocked, and we were left free to depart. 'Our carriage is waiting outside,' I added. 'If it returns to the hotel without us, there will be an inquiry.' This latter consideration had its effect. On their side, the doors were opened. On our side, the appointment was made. We left the house.

IV

In consenting to receive the General's representatives, it is needless to say that I merely desired to avoid provoking another quarrel. If those persons were really impudent enough to call at the hotel, I had arranged to threaten them with the interference of the police, and so to put an end to the matter. Romayne expressed no opinion on the subject, one way or the other. His conduct inspired me with a feeling of uneasiness. The filthy insult of which he had been made the object seemed to be rankling in his mind. He went away thoughtfully to his own room. 'Have you nothing to say to me?,' I asked. He only answered, 'Wait till to-morrow.'

The next day the seconds appeared.

I had expected to see two of the men with whom we had dined. To my astonishment, the visitors proved to be officers of the General's regiment. They brought proposals for a hostile meeting the next morning; the choice of weapons being left to Romayne as the challenged man.

It was now quite plain to me that the General's peculiar method of card-playing had, thus far, not been discovered and exposed. He might keep doubtful company, and might (as I afterwards heard) be suspected in certain quarters. But that he still had, formally-speaking, a reputation to preserve, was proved by the appearance of the two gentlemen present as his representatives. They declared, with evident sincerity, that Romayne had made a fatal mistake; had provoked the insult offered to him; and had resented it by a brutal cowardly outrage. As a man and a soldier, the General was doubly bound to insist on a duel. No apology would be accepted, even if an apology were offered.

In this emergency, as I understood it, there was but one course to follow. I refused to receive the challenge.

Being asked for my reasons, I found it necessary to speak within certain limits. Though we knew the General to be a cheat, it was a delicate matter to dispute his right to claim satisfaction, when he had found two officers to carry his message. I produced the seized cards (which Romayne had brought away with him in his pocket), and offered them as a formal proof that my friend had not been mistaken.

The seconds — evidently prepared for this circumstance by their principal — declined to examine the cards. In the first place, they said, not even the discovery of foul play (supposing the discovery to have been really made) could justify Romayne's conduct. In the second place, the General's high character made

16

it impossible, under any circumstances, that *he* could be responsible. Like ourselves, he had rashly associated with bad company; and he had been the innocent victim of an error or a fraud, committed by some other person present at the table.

Driven to my last resource, I could now only base my refusal to receive the challenge on the ground that we were Englishmen, and that the practice of duelling had been abolished in England. Both the seconds at once declined to accept this statement in justification of my conduct.

'You are now in France,' said the elder of the two, 'where a duel is the established remedy for an insult, among gentlemen. You are bound to respect the social laws of the country in which you are for the time residing. If you refuse to do so, you lay yourselves open to a public imputation on your courage, of a nature too degrading to be more particularly alluded to. Let us adjourn this interview for three hours on the ground of informality. We ought to confer with *two* gentlemen, acting on Mr Romayne's behalf. Be prepared with another second to meet us, and reconsider your decision before we call again.'

The Frenchmen had barely taken their departure by one door, when Romayne entered by another.

'I have heard it all,' he said quietly. 'Accept the challenge.'

I declare solemnly that I left no means untried of opposing my friend's resolution. No

man could have felt more strongly convinced than I did, that nothing could justify the course he was taking. My remonstrances were completely thrown away. He was deaf to sense and reason, from the moment when he had heard an imputation on his courage suggested as a possible result of any affair in which he was concerned.

'With your views,' he said, 'I won't ask you to accompany me to the ground. I can easily find French seconds. And mind this, if you attempt to prevent the meeting, the duel will take place elsewhere — and our friendship is at an end from that moment.'

After this, I suppose it is needless to add that I accompanied him to the ground the next morning as one of his seconds.

V

We were punctual to the appointed hour — eight o'clock.

The second who acted with me was a French gentleman, a relative of one of the officers who had brought the challenge. At his suggestion, we had chosen the pistol as our weapon. Romayne, like most Englishmen at the present time, knew nothing of the use of the sword. He was almost equally inexperienced with the pistol.

Our opponents were late. They kept us waiting for more than ten minutes. It was not pleasant weather to wait in. The day had dawned damp and drizzling. A thick white fog was slowly rolling in on us from the sea.

When they did appear, the General was not among them. A tall, well-dressed young man saluted Romayne with stern courtesy, and said to a stranger who accompanied him, 'Explain the circumstances.'

The stranger proved to be a surgeon. He entered at once on the necessary explanation. The General was too ill to appear. He had been attacked that morning by a fit — the consequence of the blow that he had received. Under these circumstances, his eldest son (Maurice) was now on the ground to fight the duel, on his father's behalf; attended by the General's seconds, and with the General's full approval.

We instantly refused to allow the duel to take place; Romayne loudly declaring that he had no quarrel with the General's son. Upon this, Maurice broke away from his seconds; drew off one of his gloves; and stepping close up to Romayne, struck him on the face with the glove. 'Have you no quarrel with me now?' the young Frenchman asked. 'Must I spit on you, as my father did?' His seconds dragged him away, and apologised to us for the outbreak. But the mischief was done. Romayne's fiery temper flashed in his eyes. 'Load the pistols,' he said. After the insult publicly offered to him, and the outrage publicly threatened, there was no other course to take.

It had been left to us to produce the pistols. We therefore requested the seconds of our opponent to examine, and to load them. While this was being done, the advancing sea-fog so

19

completely enveloped us, that the duellists were unable to see each other. We were obliged to wait for the chance of a partial clearing in the atmosphere. Romayne's temper had become calm again. The generosity of his nature spoke in the words which he now addressed to his seconds.

'After all,' he said, 'the young man is a good son — he is bent on redressing what he believes to be his father's wrong. Does his flipping his glove in my face matter to me? I think I shall fire in the air.'

'I shall refuse to act as your second if you do,' answered the French gentleman who was assisting us. 'The General's son is famous for his skill with the pistol. If you didn't see it in his face just now, I did — he means to kill you. Defend your life, sir!' I spoke quite as strongly, to the same purpose, when my turn came. Romayne yielded — he placed himself unreservedly in our hands.

In a quarter of an hour the fog lifted a little. We measured the distance, having previously arranged (at my suggestion) that the two men should both fire at the same moment, at a given signal. Romayne's composure, as they faced each other, was, in a man of his irritable nervous temperament, really wonderful. I placed him sideways, in a position which in some degree lessened his danger, by lessening the surface exposed to the bullet. My French colleague put the pistol into his hand, and gave him the last word of advice. 'Let your arm hang loosely down, with the barrel of the pistol

pointing straight to the ground. When you hear the signal, only lift your arm as far as the elbow; keep the elbow pressed against your side — and fire.' We could do no more for him. As we drew aside — I own it — my tongue was like a cinder in my mouth, and a horrid inner cold crept through me to the marrow of my bones.

The signal was given, and the two shots were fired at the same time.

My first look was at Romayne. He took off his hat, and handed it to me with a smile. His adversary's bullet had cut a piece out of the brim of his hat, on the right side. He had literally escaped by a hairbreadth.

While I was congratulating him, the fog gathered again more thickly than ever. Looking anxiously towards the ground occupied by our adversaries, we could only see vague, shadowy forms hurriedly crossing and re-crossing each other in the mist. Something had happened! My French colleague took my arm and pressed it significantly. 'Leave *me* to inquire,' he said. Romayne tried to follow; I held him back — we neither of us exchanged a word.

The fog thickened and thickened, until nothing was to be seen. Once we heard the surgeon's voice, calling impatiently for a light to help him. No light appeared that *we* could see. Dreary as the fog itself, the silence gathered round us again. On a sudden it was broken, horribly broken, by another voice, strange to both of us, shrieking hysterically through the impenetrable mist. 'Where is he?' the voice cried,

in the French language. 'Assassin! Assassin! where are you?' Was it a woman? or was it a boy? We heard nothing more. The effect upon Romayne was terrible to see. He who had calmly confronted the weapon lifted to kill him, shuddered dumbly like a terror-stricken animal. I put my arm round him, and hurried him away from the place.

We waited at the hotel until our French friend joined us. After a brief interval he appeared, announcing that the surgeon would follow him.

The duel had ended fatally. The chance course of the bullet, urged by Romayne's unpractised hand, had struck the General's son just above the right nostril — had penetrated to the back of his neck — and had communicated a fatal shock to the spinal marrow. He was a dead man before they could take him back to his father's house.

So far, our fears were confirmed. But there was something else to tell, for which our worst presentiments had not prepared us.

A younger brother of the fallen man (a boy of thirteen years old) had secretly followed the duelling party, on their way from his father's house — had hidden himself — and had seen the dreadful end. The seconds only knew of it when he burst out of his place of concealment, and fell on his knees by his dying brother's side. His were the frightful cries which we had heard from invisible lips. The slayer of his brother was the 'assassin' whom he had vainly tried to discover through the fathomless obscurity of the mist.

We both looked at Romayne. He silently looked back at us, like a man turned to stone. I tried to reason with him.

'Your life was at your opponent's mercy,' I said. 'It was *he* who was skilled in the use of the pistol; your risk was infinitely greater than his. Are you responsible for an accident? Rouse yourself, Romayne! Think of the time to come, when all this will be forgotten.'

'Never,' he said, 'to the end of my life.'

He made that reply in dull monotonous tones. His eyes looked wearily and vacantly straight before him. I spoke to him again. He remained impenetrably silent; he appeared not to hear, or not to understand me. The surgeon came in, while I was still at a loss what to say or do next. Without waiting to be asked for his opinion, he observed Romayne attentively, and then drew me away into the next room.

'Your friend is suffering from a severe nervous shock,' he said. 'Can you tell me anything of his habits of life?'

I mentioned the prolonged night studies, and the excessive use of tea. The surgeon shook his head.

'If you want my advice,' he proceeded, 'take him home at once. Don't subject him to further excitement, when the result of the duel is known in the town. If it ends in our appearing in a court of law, it will be a mere formality in this case, and you can surrender when the time comes. Leave me your address in London.'

I felt that the wisest thing I could do was to follow his advice. The boat crossed to Folkestone

at an early hour that day — we had no time to lose. Romayne offered no objection to our return to England; he seemed perfectly careless what became of him. 'Leave me quiet,' he said; 'and do as you like.' I wrote a few lines to Lady Berrick's medical attendant, informing him of the circumstances. A quarter of an hour afterwards we were on board the steamboat.

There were very few passengers. After we had left the harbour, my attention was attracted by a young English lady — travelling, apparently, with her mother. As we passed her on the deck she looked at Romayne, with compassionate interest so vividly expressed in her beautiful face, that I imagined they might be acquainted. With some difficulty, I prevailed sufficiently over the torpor that possessed him to induce him to look at our fellow-passenger.

'Do you know that charming person?' I asked.

'No,' he replied, with the weariest indifference. 'I never saw her before. I'm tired — tired — tired! Don't speak to me; leave me by myself.'

I left him. His rare personal attractions — of which, let me add, he never appeared to be conscious — had evidently made their natural appeal to the interest and admiration of the young lady who had met him by chance. The expression of resigned sadness and suffering, now visible in his face, added greatly no doubt to the influence that he had unconsciously exercised over the sympathies of a delicate and sensitive woman. It was no uncommon

circumstance in his past experience of the sex — as I myself well knew — to be the object, not of admiration only, but of true and ardent love. He had never reciprocated the passion — had never even appeared to take it seriously. Marriage might, as the phrase is, be the salvation of him. Would he ever marry?

Leaning over the bulwark, idly pursuing this train of thought, I was recalled to present things by a low sweet voice — the voice of the lady of whom I had been thinking.

'Excuse me for disturbing you,' she said; 'I think your friend wants you.'

She spoke with the modesty and self-possession of a highly-bred woman. A little heightening of her colour made her, to my eyes, more beautiful than ever. I thanked her, and hastened back to Romayne.

He was standing by the barred skylight which guarded the machinery. I instantly noticed a change in him. His eyes wandering here and there, in search of me, had more than recovered their animation — there was a wild look of terror in them. He seized me roughly by the arm, and pointed down to the engine-room.

'What do you hear there?' he asked.

'I hear the thump of the engines.'

'Nothing else?'

'Nothing. What do *you* hear?'

He suddenly turned away.

'I'll tell you,' he said, 'when we get on shore.'

Second Scene

Vange Abbey — The Forewarnings

VI

As we approached the harbour at Folkestone, Romayne's agitation appeared to subside. His head drooped; his eyes half closed — he looked like a weary man quietly falling asleep.

On leaving the steamboat, I ventured to ask our charming fellow-passenger if I could be of any service in reserving places in the London train for her mother and herself. She thanked me, and said they were going to visit some friends at Folkestone. In making this reply, she looked at Romayne. 'I am afraid he is very ill?' she said, in gently lowered tones. Before I could answer, her mother turned to her with an expression of surprise, and directed her attention to the friends whom she had mentioned, waiting to greet her. Her last look, as they took her away, rested tenderly and sorrowfully on Romayne. He never returned it — he was not even aware of it. As I led him to the train he leaned more and more heavily on my arm. Seated in the carriage, he sank at once into profound sleep.

We drove to the hotel at which my friend was accustomed to reside when he was in London. His long sleep on the journey seemed, in some degree, to have relieved him. We dined together

in his private room. When the servants had withdrawn, I found that the unhappy result of the duel was still preying on his mind.

'The horror of having killed that man,' he said, 'is more than I can bear alone. For God's sake, don't leave me!'

I had received letters at Boulogne, which informed me that my wife and family had accepted an invitation to stay with some friends at the sea-side. Under these circumstances, I was entirely at his service. Having quieted his anxiety on this point, I reminded him of what had passed between us on board the steamboat. He tried to change the subject. My curiosity was too strongly aroused to permit this; I persisted in helping his memory.

'We were looking into the engine-room,' I said; 'and you asked me what I heard there. You promised to tell me what *you* heard, as soon as we got on shore — '

He stopped me, before I could say more.

'I begin to think it was a delusion,' he answered. 'You ought not to interpret too literally what a person in my dreadful situation may say. The stain of another man's blood is on me — '

I interrupted him in my turn. 'I refuse to hear you speak of yourself in that way,' I said. 'You are no more responsible for the Frenchman's death than if you had been driving, and had accidentally run over him in the street. I am not the right companion for a man who talks as you do. The proper person to be with you is a doctor.' I really felt irritated with him — and

I saw no reason for concealing it.

Another man, in his place, might have been offended with me. There was a native sweetness in Romayne's disposition, which asserted itself even in his worst moments of nervous irritability. He took my hand.

'Don't be hard on me,' he pleaded. 'I will try to think of it as you do. Make some little concession on your side. I want to see how I get through the night. We will return to what I said to you on board the steamboat to-morrow morning. Is it agreed?'

It was agreed, of course. There was a door of communication between our bedrooms. At his suggestion it was left open. 'If I find I can't sleep,' he explained, 'I want to feel assured that you can hear me if I call to you.'

Three times in the night I woke, and, seeing the light burning in his room, looked in at him. He always carried some of his books with him when he travelled. On each occasion when I entered the room, he was reading quietly. 'I suppose I forestalled my night's sleep on the railway,' he said. 'It doesn't matter; I am content. Something that I was afraid of has not happened. I am used to wakeful nights. Go back to bed, and don't be uneasy about me.'

The next morning the deferred explanation was put off again.

'Do you mind waiting a little longer?' he asked.

'Not if you particularly wish it.'

'Will you do me another favour? You know that I don't like London. The noise in the streets

28

is distracting. Besides, I may tell you I have a sort of distrust of noise, since — ' He stopped, with an appearance of confusion.

'Since I found you looking into the engine-room?' I asked.

'Yes. I don't feel inclined to trust the chances of another night in London. I want to try the effect of perfect quiet. Do you mind going back with me to Vange? Dull as the place is, you can amuse yourself. There is good shooting, as you know.'

In an hour more we had left London.

VII

Vange Abbey is, as I suppose, the most solitary country house in England. If Romayne wanted quiet, it was exactly the place for him.

On the rising ground of one of the wildest moors in the North Riding of Yorkshire, the ruins of the old monastery are visible from all points of the compass. There are traditions of thriving villages clustering about the Abbey, in the days of the monks, and of hostelries devoted to the reception of pilgrims from every part of the Christian world. Not a vestige of these buildings is left. They were deserted by the pious inhabitants, it is said, at the time when Henry the Eighth suppressed the monasteries, and gave the Abbey and the broad lands of Vange to his faithful friend and courtier, Sir Miles Romayne. In the next generation, the son and heir of Sir Miles built the dwelling-house, helping himself liberally from the solid stone

walls of the monastery. With some unimportant alterations and repairs, the house stands, defying time and weather, to the present day.

At the last station on the railway, the horses were waiting for us. It was a lovely moonlight night, and we shortened the distance considerably by taking the bridle path over the moor. Between nine and ten o'clock we reached the Abbey.

Years had passed since I had last been Romayne's guest. Nothing, out of the house or in the house, seemed to have undergone any change in the interval. Neither the good North-country butler, nor his buxom Scotch wife, skilled in cookery, looked any older: they received me as if I had left them a day or two since, and had come back again to live in Yorkshire. My well-remembered bedroom was waiting for me; and the matchless old Madeira welcomed us when my host and I met in the inner-hall, which was the ordinary dining-room of the Abbey.

As we faced each other at the well-spread table, I began to hope that the familiar influences of his country home were beginning already to breathe their blessed quiet over the disturbed mind of Romayne. In the presence of his faithful old servants, he seemed to be capable of controlling the morbid remorse that oppressed him. He spoke to them composedly and kindly; he was affectionately glad to see his old friend once more in the old house.

When we were near the end of our meal, something happened that startled me. I had just

handed the wine to Romayne, and he had filled his glass — when he suddenly turned pale, and lifted his head like a man whose attention is unexpectedly roused. No person but ourselves was in the room; I was not speaking to him at the time. He looked round suspiciously at the door behind him, leading into the library, and rang the old-fashioned handbell which stood by him on the table. The servant was directed to close the door.

'Are you cold?' I asked.

'No.' He reconsidered that brief answer, and contradicted himself. 'Yes — the library fire has burnt low, I suppose.'

In my position at the table, I had seen the fire: the grate was heaped with blazing coals and wood. I said nothing. The pale change in his face, and his contradictory reply, roused doubts in me which I had hoped never to feel again.

He pushed away his glass of wine, and still kept his eyes fixed on the closed door. His attitude and expression were plainly suggestive of the act of listening. Listening to what?

After an interval, he abruptly addressed me. 'Do you call it a quiet night?' he said.

'As quiet as quiet can be,' I replied. 'The wind has dropped — and even the fire doesn't crackle. Perfect stillness, indoors and out.'

'Out?' he repeated. For a moment, he looked at me intently, as if I had started some new idea in his mind. I asked as lightly as I could, if I had said anything to surprise him. Instead of answering me, he sprang to his feet with a cry of terror, and left the room.

I hardly knew what to do. It was impossible, unless he returned immediately, to let this extraordinary proceeding pass without notice. After waiting for a few minutes, I rang the bell.

The old butler came in. He looked in blank amazement at the empty chair. 'Where's the master?' he asked.

I could only answer that he had left the table suddenly, without a word of explanation. 'He may perhaps be ill,' I added. 'As his old servant, you can do no harm if you go and look for him. Say that I am waiting here, if he wants me.'

The minutes passed slowly and more slowly. I was left alone for so long a time that I began to feel seriously uneasy. My hand was on the bell again, when there was a knock at the door. I had expected to see the butler. It was the groom who entered the room.

'Garthwaite can't come down to you sir,' said the man. 'He asks if you will please go up to the master on the Belvidere.'

The house — extending round three sides of a square — was only two stories high. The flat roof, accessible through a species of hatchway, and still surrounded by its sturdy stone parapet, was called 'The Belvidere,' in reference as usual to the fine view which it commanded. Fearing I knew not what, I mounted the ladder which led to the roof. Romayne received me with a harsh outburst of laughter — that saddest false laughter which is true trouble in disguise.

'Here's something to amuse you!' he cried. 'I believe old Garthwaite thinks I am drunk — he

won't leave me up here by myself.'

Letting this strange assertion remain unanswered, the butler withdrew. As he passed me on his way to the ladder, he whispered, 'Be careful of the master! I tell you, sir, he has a bee in his bonnet this night.'

Although not of the north country myself, I knew the meaning of the phrase. Garthwaite suspected that the master was nothing less than mad!

Romayne took my arm when we were alone — we walked slowly from end to end of the Belvidere. The moon was, by this time, low in the heavens; but her mild mysterious light still streamed over the roof of the house and the high heathy ground round it. I looked attentively at Romayne. He was deadly pale; his hand shook as it rested on my arm — and that was all. Neither in look nor manner did he betray the faintest sign of mental derangement. He had perhaps needlessly alarmed the faithful old servant by something that he had said or done. I determined to clear up that doubt immediately.

'You left the table very suddenly,' I said. 'Did you feel ill?'

'Not ill,' he replied. 'I was frightened. Look at me — I'm frightened still.'

'What do you mean?'

Instead of answering, he repeated the strange question which he had put to me downstairs.

'Do you call it a quiet night?'

Considering the time of year, and the exposed situation of the house, the night was almost

preternaturally quiet. Throughout the vast open country all around us, not even a breath of air could be heard. The nightbirds were away, or were silent at the time. But one sound was audible, when we stood still and listened — the cool quiet bubble of a little stream, lost to view in the valley-ground to the south.

'I have told you already,' I said. 'So still a night I never remember on this Yorkshire moor.'

He laid one hand heavily on my shoulder. 'What did the poor boy say of me, whose brother I killed?' he asked. 'What words did we hear through the dripping darkness of the mist?'

'I won't encourage you to think of them. I refuse to repeat the words.'

He pointed over the northward parapet.

'It doesn't matter whether you accept or refuse,' he said, 'I hear the boy at this moment — there!'

He repeated the horrid words — marking the pauses in the utterance of them with his finger, as if they were sounds that he heard: —

'Assassin! Assassin! where are you?'

'Good God!' I cried. 'You don't mean that you really *hear* the voice?'

'Do you hear what I say? I hear the boy as plainly as you hear me. The voice screams at me through the clear moonlight, as it screamed at me through the sea-fog. Again and again. It's all round the house. *That* way now, where the light just touches on the tops of the heather. Tell the servants to have the horses ready the first

thing in the morning. We leave Vange Abbey to-morrow.'

These were wild words. If he had spoken them wildly, I might have shared the butler's conclusion that his mind was deranged. There was no undue vehemence in his voice or his manner. He spoke with a melancholy resignation — he seemed like a prisoner submitting to a sentence that he had deserved. Remembering the cases of men suffering from nervous disease who had been haunted by apparitions, I asked if he saw any imaginary figure under the form of a boy.

'I see nothing,' he said; 'I only hear. Look yourself. It is in the last degree improbable — but let us make sure that nobody has followed me from Boulogne, and is playing me a trick.'

We made the circuit of the Belvidere. On its eastward side, the house wall was built against one of the towers of the old Abbey. On the westward side, the ground sloped steeply down to a deep pool or tarn. Northward and southward, there was nothing to be seen but the open moor. Look where I might, with the moonlight to make the view plain to me, the solitude was as void of any living creature as if we had been surrounded by the awful dead world of the moon.

'Was it the boy's voice that you heard on the voyage across the Channel?' I asked.

'Yes, I heard it for the first time — down in the engine-room; rising and falling, rising and falling, like the sound of the engines themselves.'

'And when did you hear it again?'

'I feared to hear it in London. It left me, I should have told you, when we stepped ashore out of the steamboat. I was afraid that the noise of the traffic in the streets might bring it back to me. As you know, I passed a quiet night. I had the hope that my imagination had deceived me — that I was the victim of a delusion, as people say. It is no delusion. In the perfect tranquility of this place the voice has come back to me. While we were at table I heard it again — behind me, in the library. I heard it still, when the door was shut. I ran up here to try if it would follow me into the open air. It *has* followed me. We may as well go down again into the hall. I know now that there is no escaping from it. My dear old home has become horrible to me. Do you mind returning to London to-morrow?'

What I felt and feared in this miserable state of things matters little. The one chance I could see for Romayne was to obtain the best medical advice. I sincerely encouraged his idea of going back to London the next day.

We had sat together by the hall fire for about ten minutes, when he took out his handkerchief, and wiped away the perspiration from his forehead, drawing a deep breath of relief. 'It has gone!' he said faintly.

'When you hear the boy's voice,' I asked, 'do you hear it continuously?'

'No, at intervals; sometimes longer, sometimes shorter.'

'And thus far, it comes to you suddenly, and leaves you suddenly?'

'Yes.'

'Do my questions annoy you?'

'I make no complaint,' he said sadly. 'You can see for yourself — I patiently suffer the punishment that I have deserved.'

I contradicted him at once. 'It is nothing of the sort! It's a nervous malady, which medical science can control and cure. Wait till we get to London.'

This expression of opinion produced no effect on him.

'I have taken the life of a fellow-creature,' he said. 'I have closed the career of a young man who, but for me, might have lived long and happily and honourably. Say what you may, I am of the race of Cain. *He* had the mark set on his brow. I have *my* ordeal. Delude yourself, if you like, with false hopes. I can endure — and hope for nothing. Good-night.'

VIII

Early the next morning, the good old butler came to me, in great perturbation, for a word of advice.

'Do come, sir, and look at the master! I can't find in my heart to wake him.'

It was time to wake him, if we were to go to London that day. I went into the bedroom. Although I was no doctor, the restorative importance of that profound and quiet sleep impressed itself on me so strongly, that I took the responsibility of leaving him undisturbed. The event proved that I had acted wisely. He

slept until noon. There was no return of 'the torment of the voice' — as he called it, poor fellow. We passed a quiet day, excepting one little interruption, which I am warned not to pass over without a word of record in this narrative.

We had returned from a ride. Romayne had gone into the library to read; and I was just leaving the stables, after a look at some recent improvements, when a pony-chaise with a gentleman in it drove up to the door. He asked politely if he might be allowed to see the house. There were some fine pictures at Vange, as well as many interesting relics of antiquity; and the rooms were shown, in Romayne's absence, to the very few travellers who were adventurous enough to cross the heathy desert that surrounded the Abbey. On this occasion, the stranger was informed that Mr Romayne was at home. He at once apologised — with an appearance of disappointment, however, which induced me to step forward and speak to him.

'Mr Romayne is not very well,' I said; 'and I cannot venture to ask you into the house. But you will be welcome, I am sure, to walk round the grounds, and to look at the ruins of the Abbey.'

He thanked me, and accepted the invitation. I find no great difficulty in describing him, generally. He was elderly fat and cheerful; buttoned up in a long black frock coat, and presenting that closely shaven face and that inveterate expression of watchful humility about the eyes, which we all associate with the reverend

personality of a priest.

To my surprise, he seemed, in some degree at least, to know his way about the place. He made straight for the dreary little lake which I have already mentioned, and stood looking at it with an interest which was so incomprehensible to me, that I own I watched him.

He ascended the slope of the moorland, and entered the gate which led to the grounds. All that the gardeners had done to make the place attractive failed to claim his attention. He walked past lawns, shrubs, and flowerbeds, and only stopped at an old stone fountain, which tradition declared to have been one of the ornaments of the garden in the time of the monks. Having carefully examined this relic of antiquity, he took a sheet of paper from his pocket, and consulted it attentively. It might have been a plan of the house and grounds, or it might not — I can only report that he took the path which led him, by the shortest way, to the ruined Abbey church.

As he entered the roofless enclosure, he reverently removed his hat. It was impossible for me to follow him any further, without exposing myself to the risk of discovery. I sat down on one of the fallen stones, waiting to see him again. It must have been at least half an hour before he appeared. He thanked me for my kindness, as composedly as if he had quite expected to find me in the place that I occupied.

'I have been deeply interested in all that I have seen,' he said. 'May I venture to ask, what is perhaps an indiscreet question on the part of a stranger?'

I ventured, on my side, to inquire what the question might be.

'Mr Romayne is indeed fortunate,' he resumed, 'in the possession of this beautiful place. He is a young man, I think?'

'Yes.'

'Is he married?'

'No.'

'Excuse my curiosity. The owner of Vange Abbey is an interesting person to all good antiquaries like myself. Many thanks again. Good-day.'

His pony-chaise took him away. His last look rested — not on me — but on the old Abbey.

IX

My record of events approaches its conclusion.

On the next day we returned to the hotel in London. At Romayne's suggestion, I sent the same evening to my own house for any letters which might be waiting for me. His mind still dwelt on the duel: he was morbidly eager to know if any communication had been received from the French surgeon.

When the messenger returned with my letters, the Boulogne postmark was on one of the envelopes. At Romayne's entreaty, this was the letter that I opened first. The surgeon's signature was at the end.

One motive for anxiety — on my part — was set at rest in the first lines. After an official inquiry into the circumstances, the French authorities had decided that it was

not expedient to put the survivor of the duellists on his trial before a court of law. No jury, hearing the evidence, would find him guilty of the only charge that could be formally brought against him — the charge of 'homicide by premeditation.' Homicide by misadventure, occurring in a duel, was not a punishable offence by the French law. My correspondent cited many cases in proof of it, strengthened by the publicly-expressed opinion of the illustrious Berryer himself. In a word, we had nothing to fear.

The next page of the letter informed us that the police had surprised the card-playing community with whom we had spent the evening at Boulogne, and that the much-bejewelled old landlady had been sent to prison for the offence of keeping a gambling-house. It was suspected in the town that the General was more or less directly connected with certain disreputable circumstances discovered by the authorities. In any case, he had retired from active service. He and his wife and family had left Boulogne, and had gone away in debt. No investigation had thus far succeeded in discovering the place of their retreat.

Reading this letter aloud to Romayne, I was interrupted by him at the last sentence.

'The inquiries must have been carelessly made,' he said. 'I will see to it myself.'

'What interest can *you* have in the inquiries?' I exclaimed.

'The strongest possible interest,' he answered. 'It has been my one hope to make some little

atonement to the poor people whom I have so cruelly wronged. If the wife and children are in distressed circumstances (which seems to be only too likely) I may place them beyond the reach of anxiety — anonymously, of course. Give me the surgeon's address. I shall write instructions for tracing them at my expense — merely announcing that an Unknown Friend desires to be of service to the General's family.'

This appeared to me to be a most imprudent thing to do. I said so plainly — and quite in vain. With his customary impetuosity, he wrote the letter at once, and sent it to the post that night.

X

On the question of submitting himself to medical advice (which I now earnestly pressed upon him), Romayne was disposed to be equally unreasonable. But in this case, events declared themselves in my favour.

Lady Berrick's last reserves of strength had given way. She had been brought to London in a dying state while we were at Vange Abbey. Romayne was summoned to his aunt's bedside on the third day of our residence at the hotel, and was present at her death. The impression produced on his mind roused the better part of his nature. He was more distrustful of himself, more accessible to persuasion than usual. In this gentler frame of mind he received a welcome visit from an old friend, to whom he was sincerely attached. The visit — of no great

42

importance in itself — led, as I have since been informed, to very serious events in Romayne's later life. For this reason, I briefly relate what took place within my own hearing.

Lord Loring — well known in society as the head of an old English Catholic family, and the possessor of a magnificent gallery of pictures — was distressed by the change for the worse which he perceived in Romayne when he called at the hotel. I was present when they met, and rose to leave the room, feeling that the two friends might perhaps be embarrassed by the presence of a third person. Romayne called me back. 'Lord Loring ought to know what has happened to me,' he said. 'I have no heart to speak of it myself. Tell him everything, and if he agrees with you, I will submit to see the doctors.' With those words, he left us together.

It is almost needless to say that Lord Loring did agree with me. He was himself disposed to think that the moral remedy, in Romayne's case, might prove to be the best remedy.

'With submission to what the doctors may decide,' his lordship said, 'the right thing to do, in my opinion, is to divert our friend's mind from himself. I see a plain necessity for making a complete change in the solitary life that he has been leading for years past. Why shouldn't he marry? A woman's influence, by merely giving a new turn to his thoughts, might charm away that horrible voice which haunts him. Perhaps you think this a merely sentimental view of the case? Look at it practically, if you like, and you come to the same conclusion. With that fine

43

estate — and with the fortune which he has now inherited from his aunt — it is his duty to marry. Don't you agree with me?'

'I agree most cordially. But I see serious difficulties in your lordship's way. Romayne dislikes society; and, as to marrying, his coldness towards women seems (so far as I can judge) to be one of the incurable defects of his character.'

Lord Loring smiled. 'My dear sir, nothing of that sort is incurable, if we can only find the right woman.'

The tone in which he spoke suggested to me that he had got 'the right woman' — and I took the liberty of saying so. He at once acknowledged that I had guessed right.

'Romayne is, as you say, a difficult subject to deal with,' he resumed. 'If I commit the slightest imprudence, I shall excite his suspicion — and there will be an end of my hope of being of service to him. I shall proceed carefully, I can tell you. Luckily, poor dear fellow, he is fond of pictures! It's quite natural that I should ask him to see some recent additions to my gallery — isn't it? There is the trap that I set! I have a sweet girl to tempt him, staying at my house, who is a little out of health and spirits herself. At the right moment, I shall send word upstairs. She may well happen to look in at the gallery (by the merest accident) just at the time when Romayne is looking at my new pictures. The rest depends, of course, on the effect she produces. If you knew her, I believe you would agree with me that the experiment is worth trying.'

Not knowing the lady, I had little faith in the success of the experiment. No one, however, could doubt Lord Loring's admirable devotion to his friend — and with that I was fain to be content.

When Romayne returned to us, it was decided to submit his case to a consultation of physicians at the earliest possible moment. When Lord Loring took his departure, I accompanied him to the door of the hotel, perceiving that he wished to say a word more to me in private. He had, it seemed, decided on waiting for the result of the medical consultation before he tried the effect of the young lady's attractions; and he wished to caution me against speaking prematurely of visiting the picture gallery to our friend.

Not feeling particularly interested in these details of the worthy nobleman's little plot, I looked at his carriage, and privately admired the two splendid horses that drew it. The footman opened the door for his master, and I became aware, for the first time, that a gentleman had accompanied Lord Loring to the hotel, and had waited for him in the carriage. The gentleman bent forward, and looked up from a book that he was reading. To my astonishment, I recognised the elderly fat and cheerful priest who had shown such a knowledge of localities, and such an extraordinary interest in Vange Abbey!

It struck me as an odd coincidence that I should see the man again in London, so soon after I had met with him in Yorkshire. This was all I thought about it, at the time. If I had known then, what I know now, I might

have dreamed, let us say, of throwing that priest into the lake at Vange, and might have reckoned the circumstance among the wisely-improved opportunities of my life.

To return to the serious interests of the present narrative, I may now announce that my evidence as an eye-witness of events has come to an end. The day after Lord Loring's visit, domestic troubles separated me, to my most sincere regret, from Romayne. I have only to add, that the foregoing narrative of personal experience has been written with a due sense of responsibility, and that it may be depended on throughout as an exact statement of the truth.

JOHN PHILIP HYND
(late Major, 110th Regiment).

The Story

Book the First

1

The Confidences

In an upper room of one of the palatial houses which are situated on the north side of Hyde Park, two ladies sat at breakfast, and gossiped over their tea.

The elder of the two was Lady Loring — still in the prime of life; possessed of the golden hair and the clear blue eyes, the delicately-florid complexion, and the freely developed figure, which are among the favourite attractions popularly associated with the beauty of Englishwomen. Her younger companion was the unknown lady admired by Major Hynd on the sea passage from France to England. With hair and eyes of the darkest brown; with a pure pallor of complexion, only changing to a faint rose tint in moments of agitation; with a tall grateful figure, incompletely developed in substance and strength — she presented an almost complete contrast to Lady Loring. Two more opposite types of beauty it would have been hardly possible to place at the same table. The servant brought in the letters of the

47

morning. Lady Loring ran through her correspondence rapidly, pushed away the letters in a heap, and poured herself out a second cup of tea.

'Nothing interesting this morning for me,' she said. 'Any news of your mother, Stella?'

The young lady handed an open letter to her hostess, with a faint smile. 'See for yourself, Adelaide,' she answered, with the tender sweetness of tone which made her voice irresistibly charming — 'and tell me if there were ever two women so utterly unlike each other as my mother and myself.'

Lady Loring ran through the letter, as she had run through her own correspondence. 'Never, dearest Stella, have I enjoyed myself as I do in this delightful country house, — twenty-seven at dinner every day, without including the neighbours — a little carpet dance every evening — we play billiards, and go into the smoking room — the hounds meet three times a week — all sorts of celebrities among the company, famous beauties included — such dresses! such conversation! — and serious duties, my dear, not neglected — high church and choral service in the town on Sundays — recitations in the evening from Paradise Lost, by an amateur elocutionist — oh, you foolish, headstrong child! why did you make excuses and stay in London, when you might have accompanied me to this earthly Paradise? — are you really ill? — my love to Lady Loring — and of course, if you *are* ill, you must have medical advice — they ask after you so kindly here — the first dinner

bell is ringing, before I have half done my letter
— what *am* I to wear? — why is my daughter
not here to advise me,' &c., &c., &c.

'There is time to change your mind and advise
your mother,' Lady Loring remarked with grave
irony as she returned the letter.

'Don't even speak of it!' said Stella. 'I really
know no life that I should not prefer to the
life that my mother is enjoying at this moment.
What should I have done, Adelaide, if you had
not offered me a happy refuge in your house? *My*
'earthly Paradise' is here, where I am allowed to
dream away my time over my drawings and my
books, and to resign myself to poor health and
low spirits, without being dragged into society,
and (worse still) threatened with that 'medical
advice' in which, when she isn't threatened
with it herself, my poor dear mother believes
so implicitly. I wish you would hire me as your
'companion,' and let me stay here for the rest
of my life.'

Lady Loring's bright face became grave while
Stella was speaking.

'My dear,' she said kindly, 'I know well how
you love retirement, and how differently you
think and feel from other young women of
your age. And I am far from forgetting what
sad circumstances have encouraged the natural
bent of your disposition. But, since you have
been staying with me this time, I see something
in you which my intimate knowledge of your
character fails to explain. We have been friends
since we were together at school — and, in those
old days, we never had any secrets from each

other. You are feeling some anxiety, or brooding over some sorrow, of which I know nothing. I don't ask for your confidence; I only tell you what I have noticed — and I say with all my heart, Stella, I am sorry for you.'

She rose, and, with intuitive delicacy, changed the subject. 'I am going out earlier than usual this morning,' she resumed. 'Is there anything I can do for you?' She laid her hand tenderly on Stella's shoulder, waiting for the reply. Stella lifted the hand and kissed it with passionate fondness.

'Don't think me ungrateful,' she said; 'I am only ashamed.' Her head sank on her bosom; she burst into tears.

Lady Loring waited by her in silence. She well knew the girl's self-contained nature, always shrinking, except in moments of violent emotion, from the outward betrayal of its trials and its sufferings to others. The true depth of feeling which is marked by this inbred modesty is most frequently found in men. The few women who possess it are without the communicative consolations of the feminine heart. They are the noblest — and but too often the unhappiest of their sex.

'Will you wait a little before you go out?' Stella asked softly.

Lady Loring returned to the chair that she had left — hesitated for a moment — and then drew it nearer to Stella. 'Shall I sit by you?' she said.

'Close by me. You spoke of our school days just now, Adelaide. There was some difference

between us. Of all the girls, I was the youngest — and you were the eldest, or nearly the eldest, I think?'

'Quite the eldest, my dear. There is a difference of ten years between us. But why do you go back to that?'

'It's only a recollection. My father was alive then. I was at first homesick and frightened in the strange place, among the big girls. You used to let me hide my face on your shoulder, and tell me stories. May I hide in the old way, and tell *my* story?'

She was now the calmest of the two. The elder woman turned a little pale, and looked down in silent anxiety at the darkly beautiful head that rested on her shoulder.

'After such an experience as mine has been,' said Stella, 'would you think it possible that I could ever again feel my heart troubled by a man — and that man a stranger?'

'My dear! I think it quite possible. You are only now in your twenty-third year. You were innocent of all blame at that wretched bygone time which you ought never to speak of again. Love and be happy, Stella — if you can only find the man who is worthy of you. But you frighten me when you speak of a stranger. Where did you meet with him?'

'On our way back from Paris.'

'Travelling in the same carriage with you?'

'No — it was in crossing the Channel. There were few travellers in the steamboat, or I might never have noticed him.'

'Did he speak to you?'

'I don't think he even looked at me.'

'That doesn't say much for his taste, Stella.'

'You don't understand. I mean, I have not explained myself properly. He was leaning on the arm of a friend; weak and worn and wasted, as I supposed, by some long and dreadful illness. There was an angelic sweetness in his face — such patience! such resignation! For Heaven's sake keep my secret. One hears of men falling in love with women at first sight. But a woman who looks at a man, and feels — oh, it's shameful! I could hardly take my eyes off him. If he had looked at me in return, I don't know what I should have done — I burn when I think of it. He was absorbed in his suffering and his sorrow. My last look at his beautiful face was on the pier, before they took me away. The perfect image of him has been in my heart ever since. In my dreams, I see him as plainly as I see you now. Don't despise me, Adelaide!'

'My dear, you interest me indescribably. Do you suppose he was in our rank of life? I mean, of course, did he look like a gentleman?'

'There could be no doubt of it.'

'Do try to describe him, Stella. Was he tall and well dressed?'

'Neither tall nor short — rather thin — quiet and graceful in all his movements — dressed plainly, in perfect taste. How can I describe him? When his friend brought him on board, he stood at the side of the vessel, looking out thoughtfully towards the sea. Such eyes I never saw before, Adelaide, in any human face — so divinely tender and sad — and the colour of

them that dark violet blue, so uncommon and so beautiful — too beautiful for a man. I may say the same of his hair. I saw it completely. For a minute or two he removed his hat — his head was fevered, I think — and he let the sea breeze blow over it. The pure light brown of his hair was just warmed by a lovely reddish tinge. His beard was of the same colour; short and curling, like the beards of the Roman heroes one sees in pictures. I shall never see him again — and it is best for me that I shall not. What can I hope from a man who never once noticed me? But I *should* like to hear that he had recovered his health and his tranquillity, and that his life was a happy one. It has been a comfort to me, Adelaide, to open my heart to you. I am getting bold enough to confess everything. Would you laugh at me, I wonder, if I — ?'

She stopped. Her pale complexion softly glowed into colour; her grand dark eyes brightened — she looked her loveliest at that moment.

'I am far more inclined, Stella, to cry over you than to laugh at you,' said Lady Loring. 'There is something, to my mind, very sad about this adventure of yours. I wish I could find out who the man is. Even the best description of a person falls so short of the reality!'

'I thought of showing you something,' Stella continued, 'which might help you to see him as I saw him. It's only making one more acknowledgement of my own folly.'

'You don't mean a portrait of him!' Lady Loring exclaimed.

'The best that I could do from recollection,' Stella answered sadly.

'Bring it here directly!'

Stella left the room and returned with a little drawing in pencil. The instant Lady Loring looked at it, she recognised Romayne, and started excitedly to her feet.

'You know him!' cried Stella.

Lady Loring had placed herself in an awkward position. Her husband had described to her his interview with Major Hynd, and had mentioned his project for bringing Romayne and Stella together, after first exacting a promise of the strictest secrecy from his wife. She felt herself bound — doubly bound, after what she had now discovered — to respect the confidence placed in her; and this at the time when she had betrayed herself to Stella! With a woman's feline fineness of perception, in all cases of subterfuge and concealment, she picked a part of the truth out of the whole, and answered harmlessly without a moment's hesitation.

'I have certainly seen him,' she said — 'probably at some party. But I see so many people, and I go to so many places, that I must ask for time to consult my memory. My husband might help me, if you don't object to my asking him,' she added slily.

Stella snatched the drawing away from her, in terror. 'You don't mean that you will tell Lord Loring?' she said.

'My dear child! how can you be so foolish? Can't I show him the drawing without mentioning who it was done by? His memory is

a much better one than mine. If I say to him, 'Where did we meet that man?' — he may tell me at once — he may even remember the name. Of course, if you like to be kept in suspense, you have only to say so. It rests with you to decide.'

Poor Stella gave way directly. She returned the drawing, and affectionately kissed her artful friend. Having now secured the means of consulting her husband without exciting suspicion, Lady Loring left the room.

At that time in the morning, Lord Loring was generally to be found either in the library or the picture gallery. His wife tried the library first.

On entering the room, she found but one person in it — not the person of whom she was in search. There, buttoned up in his long frock coat, and surrounded by books of all sorts and sizes, sat the plump elderly priest who had been the especial object of Major Hynd's aversion.

'I beg your pardon, Father Benwell,' said Lady Loring; 'I hope I don't interrupt your studies?'

Father Benwell rose and bowed, with a pleasant paternal smile. 'I am only trying to organise an improved arrangement of the library,' he said simply. 'Books are companionable creatures — members, as it were, of his family, to a lonely old priest like myself. Can I be of any service to your ladyship?'

'Thank you, Father. If you can kindly tell me where Lord Loring is — '

'To be sure! His lordship was here five minutes since — he is now in the picture gallery. Pray permit me!'

With a remarkably light and easy step for a man of his age and size, he advanced to the further end of the library, and opened a door which led into the gallery.

'Lord Loring is among the pictures,' he announced. 'And alone.' He laid a certain emphasis on the last word, which might or might not (in the case of a spiritual director of the household) invite a word of explanation.

Lady Loring merely said, 'Just what I wanted; thank you once more, Father Benwell' — and passed into the picture gallery.

Left by himself again in the library, the priest walked slowly to and fro, thinking. His latent power and resolution began to show themselves darkly in his face. A skilled observer would now have seen plainly revealed in him the habit of command, and the capacity for insisting on his right to be obeyed. From head to foot, Father Benwell was one of those valuable soldiers of the Church who acknowledge no defeat, and who improve every victory.

After a while, he returned to the table at which he had been writing when Lady Loring entered the room. An unfinished letter lay open on the desk. He took up his pen and completed it in these words: 'I have therefore decided on trusting this serious matter in the hands of Arthur Penrose. I know he is young — but we have to set against the drawback of his youth, the counter-merits of his incorruptible honesty and his true religious zeal. No better man is just now within my reach — and there is no time to lose. Romayne has recently inherited a

large increase of fortune. He will be the object of the basest conspiracies — conspiracies of men to win his money, and (worse still) of women to marry him. Even these contemptible efforts may be obstacles in the way of our righteous purpose, unless we are first in the field. Penrose left Oxford last week. I expect him here this morning, by my invitation. When I have given him the necessary instructions, and have found the means of favourably introducing him to Romayne, I shall have the honour of forwarding a statement of our prospects so far.'

Having signed these lines, he addressed the letter to 'The Reverend the Secretary, Society of Jesus, Rome.' As he closed and sealed the envelope, a servant opened the door communicating with the hall, and announced:

'Mr Arthur Penrose.'

2

The Jesuits

Father Benwell rose, and welcomed the visitor with his paternal smile. 'I am heartily glad to see you,' he said — and held out his hand with a becoming mixture of dignity and cordiality. Penrose lifted the offered hand respectfully to his lips. As one of the 'Provincials' of the Order, Father Benwell occupied a high place among the English Jesuits. He was accustomed to acts of homage offered by his younger brethren to their spiritual chief. 'I fear you are not well,' he proceeded gently. 'Your hand is feverish, Arthur.'

'Thank you, Father — I am as well as usual.'

'Depression of spirits, perhaps?' Father Benwell persisted.

Penrose admitted it with a passing smile. 'My spirits are never very lively,' he said.

Father Benwell shook his head in gentle disapproval of a depressed state of spirits in a young man. 'This must be corrected,' he remarked. 'Cultivate cheerfulness, Arthur. I am myself, thank God, a naturally cheerful man. My mind reflects, in some degree (and reflects gratefully), the brightness and beauty which are part of the great scheme of creation. A similar disposition is to be cultivated — I know

instances of it in my own experience. Add one more instance, and you will really gratify me. In its seasons of rejoicing, our Church is eminently cheerful. Shall I add another encouragement? A great trust is about to be placed in you. Be socially agreeable, or you will fail to justify the trust. This is Father Benwell's little sermon. I think it has a merit, Arthur — it is a sermon soon over.'

Penrose looked up at his superior, eager to hear more.

He was a very young man. His large, thoughtful, well-opened grey eyes, and his habitual refinement and modesty of manner, gave a certain attraction to his personal appearance, of which it stood in some need. In stature he was little and lean; his hair had become prematurely thin over his broad forehead; there were hollows already in his cheeks, and marks on either side of his thin delicate lips. He looked like a person who had passed many miserable hours in needlessly despairing of himself and his prospects. With all this, there was something in him so irresistibly truthful and sincere — so suggestive, even where he might be wrong, of a purely conscientious belief in his own errors — that he attached people to him without an effort, and often without being aware of it himself. What would his friends have said if they had been told that the religious enthusiasm of this gentle, self-distrustful, melancholy man, might, in its very innocence of suspicion and self-seeking, be perverted to dangerous uses in unscrupulous

hands? His friends would, one and all, have received the scandalous assertion with contempt; and Penrose himself, if he had heard of it, might have failed to control his temper for the first time in his life.

'May I ask a question, without giving offence?' he said, timidly.

Father Benwell took his hand. 'My dear Arthur, let us open our minds to each other without reserve. What is your question?'

'You have spoken, Father, of a great trust that is about to be placed in me.'

'Yes. You are anxious, no doubt, to hear what it is?'

'I am anxious to know, in the first place, if it requires me to go back to Oxford.'

Father Benwell dropped his young friend's hand. 'Do you dislike Oxford?' he asked, observing Penrose attentively.

'Bear with me, Father, if I speak too confidently. I dislike the deception which has obliged me to conceal that I am a Catholic and a priest.'

Father Benwell set this little difficulty right, with the air of a man who could make benevolent allowance for unreasonable scruples. 'I think, Arthur, you forget two important considerations,' he said. 'In the first place, you have a dispensation from your superiors, which absolves you of all responsibility in respect of the concealment that you have practised. In the second place, we could only obtain information of the progress which our Church is silently making at the University by employing you in

the capacity of — let me say, an independent observer. However, if it will contribute to your ease of mind, I see no objection to informing you that you will *not* be instructed to return to Oxford. Do I relieve you?'

There could be no question of it. Penrose breathed more freely, in every sense of the word.

'At the same time,' Father Benwell continued, 'let us not misunderstand each other. In the new sphere of action which we design for you, you will not only be at liberty to acknowledge that you are a Catholic, it will be absolutely necessary that you should do so. But you will continue to wear the ordinary dress of an English gentleman, and to preserve the strictest secrecy on the subject of your admission to the priesthood, until you are further advised by myself. Now, dear Arthur, read that paper. It is the necessary preface to all that I have yet to say to you.'

The 'paper' contained a few pages of manuscript, relating the early history of Vange Abbey, in the days of the monks, and the circumstances under which the property was confiscated to lay uses in the time of Henry the Eighth. Penrose handed back the little narrative, vehemently expressing his sympathy with the monks, and his detestation of the King.

'Compose yourself, Arthur,' said Father Benwell, smiling pleasantly. 'We don't mean to allow Henry the Eighth to have it all his own way for ever.'

Penrose looked at his superior in blank bewilderment. His superior withheld any further

information for the present.

'Everything in its turn,' the discreet Father resumed; 'the turn of explanation has not come yet. I have something else to show you first. One of the most interesting relics in England. Look here.'

He unlocked a flat mahogany box, and displayed to view some writings on vellum, evidently of great age.

'You have had a little sermon already,' he said. 'You shall have a little story now. No doubt you have heard of Newstead Abbey — famous among the readers of poetry as the residence of Byron? King Henry treated Newstead exactly as he treated Vange Abbey! Many years since, the lake at Newstead was dragged, and the brass eagle which had served as the lectern in the old church was rescued from the waters in which it had lain for centuries. A secret receptacle was discovered in the body of the eagle, and the ancient title-deeds of the Abbey were found in it. The monks had taken that method of concealing the legal proof of their rights and privileges, in the hope — a vain hope, I need hardly say — that a time might come when Justice would restore to them the property of which they had been robbed. Only last summer, one of our bishops, administering a northern diocese, spoke of these circumstances to a devout Catholic friend, and said he thought it possible that the precaution taken by the monks at Newstead might also have been taken by the monks at Vange. The friend, I should tell you, was an enthusiast. Saying nothing to the bishop (whose

position and responsibilities he was bound to respect), he took into his confidence persons whom he could trust. One night — in the absence of the present proprietor, or I should rather say, the present usurper, of the estate — the lake at Vange was privately dragged, with a result that proved the bishop's conjecture to be right. Read those valuable documents. Knowing your strict sense of honour, my son, and your admirable tenderness of conscience, I wish you to be satisfied of the title of the Church to the lands of Vange, by evidence which is beyond dispute.'

With this little preface, he waited while Penrose read the title-deeds. 'Any doubt on your mind?' he asked, when the reading had come to an end.

'Not the shadow of a doubt.'

'Is the Church's right to the property clear?'

'As clear, Father, as words can make it.'

'Very good. We will lock up the documents. Arbitrary confiscation, Arthur, even on the part of a king, cannot override the law. What the Church once lawfully possessed, the Church has a right to recover. Any doubt about that in your mind?'

'Only the doubt of *how* the Church can recover. Is there anything in this particular case to be hoped from the law?'

'Nothing whatever.'

'And yet, Father, you speak as if you saw some prospect of the restitution of the property. By what means can the restitution be made?'

'By peaceful and worthy means,' Father

Benwell answered. 'By honourable restoration of the confiscated property to the Church, on the part of the person who is now in possession of it.'

Penrose was surprised and interested. 'Is the person a Catholic?' he asked, eagerly.

'Not yet.' Father Benwell laid a strong emphasis on those two little words. His fat fingers drummed restlessly on the table; his vigilant eyes rested expectantly on Penrose. 'Surely you understand me, Arthur?' he added, after an interval.

The colour rose slowly in the worn face of Penrose. 'I am afraid to understand you,' he said.

'Why?'

'I am not sure that it is my better sense which understands. I am afraid, Father, it may be my vanity and presumption.'

Father Benwell leaned back luxuriously in his chair. 'I like that modesty,' he said, with a relishing smack of his lips as if modesty was as good as a meal to him. 'There is power of the right sort, Arthur, hidden under the diffidence that does you honour. I am more than ever satisfied that I have been right in reporting you as worthy of this most serious trust. I believe the conversion of the owner of Vange Abbey is — in your hands — no more than a matter of time.'

'May I ask what his name is?'

'Certainly. His name is Lewis Romayne.'

'When do you introduce me to him?'

'Impossible to say. I have not yet been introduced myself.'

'You don't know Mr Romayne?'

'I have never even seen him.'

These discouraging replies were made with the perfect composure of a man who saw his way clearly before him. Sinking from one depth of perplexity to another, Penrose ventured on putting one last question. 'How am I to approach Mr Romayne?' he asked.

'I can only answer that, Arthur, by admitting you still further into my confidence. It is disagreeable to me,' said the reverend gentleman, with the most becoming humility, 'to speak of myself. But it must be done. Shall we have a little coffee to help us through the coming extract from Father Benwell's autobiography? Don't look so serious, my son! When the occasion justifies it, let us take life lightly.' He rang the bell and ordered the coffee, as if he was the master of the house. The servant treated him with the most scrupulous respect. He hummed a little tune, and talked at intervals of the weather, while they were waiting. 'Plenty of sugar, Arthur?' he inquired, when the coffee was brought in. 'No! Even in trifles, I should have been glad to feel that there was perfect sympathy between us. I like plenty of sugar myself.'

Having sweetened his coffee with the closest attention to the process, he was at liberty to enlighten his young friend. He did it so easily and so cheerfully that a far less patient man than Penrose would have listened to him with interest.

3

The Introduction to Romayne

'Excepting my employment here in the library,' Father Benwell began, 'and some interesting conversation with Lord Loring, to which I shall presently allude, I am almost as great a stranger in this house, Arthur, as yourself. When the object which we now have in view was first taken seriously into consideration, I had the honour of being personally acquainted with Lord Loring. I was also aware that he was an intimate and trusted friend of Romayne. Under these circumstances, his lordship presented himself to our point of view as a means of approaching the owner of Vange Abbey without exciting distrust. I was charged accordingly with the duty of establishing myself on terms of intimacy in this house. By way of making room for me, the spiritual director of Lord and Lady Loring was removed to a cure of souls in Ireland. And here I am in his place! By-the-way, don't treat me (when we are in the presence of visitors) with any special marks of respect. I am not Provincial of our Order in Lord Loring's house — I am one of the inferior clergy.'

Penrose looked at him with admiration. 'It is a great sacrifice to make, Father, in your position and at your age.'

'Not at all, Arthur. A position of authority

involves certain temptations to pride. I feel this change as a lesson in humility which is good for me. For example, Lady Loring (as I can plainly see) dislikes and distrusts me. Then, again, a young lady has recently arrived here on a visit. She is a Protestant, with all the prejudices incident to that way of thinking — avoids me so carefully, poor soul, that I have never seen her yet. These rebuffs are wholesome reminders of his fallible human nature, to a man who has occupied a place of high trust and command. Besides, there have been obstacles in my way which have had an excellent effect in rousing my energies. How do you feel, Arthur, when you encounter obstacles?'

'I do my best to remove them, Father. But I am sometimes conscious of a sense of discouragement.'

'Curious,' said Father Benwell, 'I am only conscious, myself, of a sense of impatience. What right has an obstacle to get in *my* way? — that is how I look at it. For example, the first thing I heard, when I came here, was that Romayne had left England. My introduction to him was indefinitely delayed: I had to look to Lord Loring for all the information I wanted relating to the man and his habits. There was another obstacle! Not living in the house, I was obliged to find an excuse for being constantly on the spot, ready to take advantage of his lordship's leisure moments for conversation. I sat down in this room, and I said to myself, 'Before I get up again, I mean to brush these impertinent obstacles out of my way!' The state

of the books suggested the idea of which I was in search. Before I left the house, I was charged with the re-arrangement of the library. From that moment I came and went as often as I liked. Whenever Lord Loring was disposed for a little talk, there I was, to lead the talk in the right direction. And what is the result? On the first occasion when Romayne presents himself, I can place you in a position to become his daily companion. All due, Arthur, in the first instance, to my impatience of obstacles. Amusing, isn't it?'

Penrose was perhaps deficient in the sense of humour. Instead of being amused, he appeared to be anxious for more information.

'In what capacity am I to be Mr Romayne's companion?' he asked.

Father Benwell poured himself out another cup of coffee.

'Suppose I tell you first,' he suggested, 'how circumstances present Romayne to us as a promising subject for conversion. He is young; still a single man; not compromised by any illicit connection; romantic, sensitive, highly cultivated. No near relations are alive to influence him; and, to my certain knowledge, his estate is not entailed. He has devoted himself for years past to books, and is collecting materials for a work of immense research, on the Origin of Religions. Some great sorrow or remorse — Lord Loring did not mention what it was — has told seriously on his nervous system, already injured by night study. Add to this, that he is now within our reach. He has lately returned to London, and

is living quite alone at a private hotel. For some reason which I am not acquainted with, he keeps away from Vange Abbey — the very place, as I should have thought, for a studious man.'

Penrose began to be interested. 'Have you been to the Abbey?' he said.

'I made a little excursion to that part of Yorkshire, Arthur, not long since. A very pleasant trip — apart from the painful associations connected with the ruin and profanation of a sacred place. There is no doubt about the revenues. I know the value of that productive part of the estate which stretches southward, away from the barren region round the house. Let us return for a moment to Romayne, and to your position as his future companion. He has had his books sent to him from Vange, and has persuaded himself that continued study is the one remedy for his troubles, whatever they may be. At Lord Loring's suggestion, a consultation of physicians was held on his case the other day.'

'Is he so ill as that!' Penrose exclaimed.

'So it appears,' Father Benwell replied. 'Lord Loring is mysteriously silent about the illness. One result of the consultation I extracted from him, in which you are interested. The doctors protested against his employing himself on his proposed work. He was too obstinate to listen to them. There was but one concession that they could gain from him — he consented to spare himself, in some small degree, by employing an amanuensis. It was left to Lord Loring to find the man. I was consulted by his lordship;

69

I was even invited to undertake the duty myself. Each one in his proper sphere, my son! The person who converts Romayne must be young enough and pliable enough to be his friend and companion. Your part is there, Arthur — you are the future amanuensis. How does the prospect strike you now?'

'I beg your pardon, Father! I fear I am unworthy of the confidence which is placed in me.'

'In what way?'

Penrose answered with unfeigned humility.

'I am afraid I may fail to justify your belief in me,' he said, 'unless I can really feel that I am converting Mr Romayne for his own soul's sake. However righteous the cause may be, I cannot find, in the restitution of the Church property, a sufficient motive for persuading him to change his religious faith. There is something so serious in the responsibility which you lay on me, that I shall sink under the burden unless my whole heart is in the work. If I feel attracted towards Mr Romayne when I first see him; if he wins upon me, little by little, until I love him like a brother — then, indeed, I can promise that his conversion shall be the dearest object of my life. But if there is not this intimate sympathy between us — forgive me if I say it plainly — I implore you to pass me over, and to commit the task to the hands of another man.'

His voice trembled; his eyes moistened. Father Benwell handled his young friend's rising emotion with the dexterity of a skilled angler humouring the struggles of a lively fish.

'Good Arthur!' he said. 'I see much — too much, dear boy — of self-seeking people. It is as refreshing to me to hear you, as a draught of water to a thirsty man. At the same time, let me suggest that you are innocently raising difficulties, where no difficulties exist. I have already mentioned as one of the necessities of the case that you and Romayne should be friends. How can that be, unless there is precisely that sympathy between you which you have so well described? I am a sanguine man, and I believe you will like each other. Wait till you see him.'

As the words passed his lips, the door that led to the picture gallery was opened. Lord Loring entered the library.

He looked quickly round him — apparently in search of some person who might, perhaps, be found in the room. A shade of annoyance showed itself in his face, and disappeared again, as he bowed to the two Jesuits.

'Don't let me disturb you,' he said, looking at Penrose. 'Is this the gentleman who is to assist Mr Romayne?'

Father Benwell presented his young friend. 'Arthur Penrose, my lord. I ventured to suggest that he should call here to-day, in case you wished to put any questions to him.'

'Quite needless, after your recommendation,' Lord Loring answered, graciously. 'Mr Penrose could not have come here at a more appropriate time. As it happens, Mr Romayne has paid us a visit to-day — he is now in the picture gallery.'

The priests looked at each other. Lord Loring left them as he spoke. He walked to the opposite door of the library — opened it — glanced round the hall, and at the stairs — and returned again, with the passing expression of annoyance visible once more. 'Come with me to the gallery, gentlemen,' he said; 'I shall be happy to introduce you to Mr Romayne.'

Penrose accepted the proposal. Father Benwell pointed with a smile to the books scattered about him. 'With permission, I will follow your lordship,' he said.

'Who was my lord looking for?' That was the question in Father Benwell's mind, while he put some of the books away on the shelves, and collected the scattered papers on the table, relating to his correspondence with Rome. It had become a habit of his life to be suspicious of any circumstances occurring within his range of observation, for which he was unable to account. He might have felt some stronger emotion, on this occasion, if he had known that the conspiracy in the library to convert Romayne was matched by the conspiracy in the picture gallery to marry him.

Lady Loring's narrative of the conversation which had taken place between Stella and herself had encouraged her husband to try his proposed experiment without delay. 'I shall send a letter at once to Romayne's hotel,' he said.

'Inviting him to come here to-day?' her ladyship inquired.

'Yes. I shall say I particularly wish to consult

him about a picture. Are we to prepare Stella to see him? or would it be better to let the meeting take her by surprise?'

'Certainly not!' said Lady Loring. 'With her sensitive disposition, I am afraid of taking Stella by surprise. Let me only tell her that Romayne is the original of her portrait, and that he is likely to call on you to see the picture to-day — and leave the rest to me.'

Lady Loring's suggestion was immediately carried out. In the first fervour of her agitation, Stella had declared that her courage was not equal to a meeting with Romayne on that day. Becoming more composed, she yielded to Lady Loring's persuasion so far as to promise that she would at least make the attempt to follow her friend to the gallery. 'If I go down with you,' she said, 'it will look as if we had arranged the thing between us. I can't bear even to think of that. Let me look in by myself, as if it was by accident.' Consenting to this arrangement, Lady Loring had proceeded alone to the gallery, when Romayne's visit was announced. The minutes passed, and Stella did not appear. It was quite possible that she might shrink from openly presenting herself at the main entrance to the gallery, and might prefer — especially if she was not aware of the priest's presence in the room — to slip in quietly by the library door. Failing to find her, on putting this idea to the test, Lord Loring had discovered Penrose, and had so hastened the introduction of the younger of the two Jesuits to Romayne.

Having gathered his papers together, Father Benwell crossed the library to the deep bow-window which lighted the room, and opened his despatch-box, standing on a small table in the recess. Placed in this position, he was invisible to any person entering the room by the hall door. He had secured his papers in the despatch-box, and had just closed and locked it, when he heard the door cautiously opened.

The instant afterwards the rustling of a woman's dress over the carpet caught his ear. Other men might have walked out of the recess and shown themselves. Father Benwell stayed where he was, and waited until the lady crossed his range of view.

The priest observed with cold attention her darkly-beautiful eyes and hair, her quickly-changing colour, her modest grace of movement. Slowly, and in evident agitation, she advanced to the door of the picture gallery — and paused, as if she was afraid to open it. Father Benwell heard her sigh to herself softly, 'Oh, how shall I meet him?' She turned aside to the looking-glass over the fireplace. The reflection of her charming face seemed to rouse her courage. She retraced her steps, and timidly opened the door. Lord Loring must have been close by at the moment. His voice immediately made itself heard in the library.

'Come in, Stella — come in! Here is a new picture for you to see; and a friend whom I want to present to you, who must be your friend too — Mr Lewis Romayne.'

The door was closed again. Father Benwell

stood still as a statue in the recess, with his head down, deep in thought. After awhile he roused himself, and rapidly returned to the writing table. With a roughness strangely unlike his customary deliberation of movement, he snatched a sheet of paper out of the case, and, frowning heavily, wrote these lines on it: — 'Since my letter was sealed, I have made a discovery which must be communicated without the loss of a post. I greatly fear there may be a woman in our way. Trust me to combat this obstacle as I have combated other obstacles. In the meantime, the work goes on. Penrose has received his first instructions, and has to-day been presented to Romayne.'

He addressed this letter to Rome, as he had addressed the letter preceding it. 'Now for the woman!' he said to himself — and opened the door of the picture gallery.

4

Father Benwell Hits

Art has its trials as well as its triumphs. It is powerless to assert itself against the sordid interests of everyday life. The greatest book ever written, the finest picture ever painted, appeals in vain to minds preoccupied by selfish and secret cares. On entering Lord Loring's gallery, Father Benwell found but one person who was not looking at the pictures under false pretences.

Innocent of all suspicion of the conflicting interests whose struggle now centred in himself, Romayne was carefully studying the picture which had been made the pretext for inviting him to the house. He had bowed to Stella, with a tranquil admiration of her beauty; he had shaken hands with Penrose, and had said some kind words to his future secretary — and then he had turned to the picture, as if Stella and Penrose had ceased from that moment to occupy his mind.

'In your place,' he said quietly to Lord Loring, 'I should not buy this work.'

'Why not?'

'It seems to me to have the serious defect of the modern English school of painting. A total want of thought in the rendering of the subject, disguised under dexterous technical tricks of the

brush. When you have seen one of that man's pictures, you have seen all. He manufactures — he doesn't paint.'

Father Benwell came in while Romayne was speaking. He went through the ceremonies of introduction to the master of Vange Abbey with perfect politeness, but a little absently. His mind was bent on putting his suspicion of Stella to the test of confirmation. Not waiting to be presented, he turned to her with the air of fatherly interest and chastened admiration which he well knew how to assume in his intercourse with women.

'May I ask if you agree with Mr Romayne's estimate of the picture?' he said, in his gentlest tones.

She had heard of him, and of his position in the house. It was quite needless for Lady Loring to whisper to her, 'Father Benwell, my dear!' Her antipathy identified him as readily as her sympathy might have identified a man who had produced a favourable impression on her. 'I have no pretension to be a critic,' she answered, with frigid politeness. 'I only know what I personally like or dislike.'

The reply exactly answered Father Benwell's purpose. It diverted Romayne's attention from the picture to Stella. The priest had secured his opportunity of reading their faces while they were looking at each other.

'I think you have just stated the true motive for all criticism,' Romayne said to Stella. 'Whether we only express our opinions of pictures or books in the course of conversation, or whether we

assert them at full length, with all the authority of print, we are really speaking, in either case, of what personally pleases or repels us. My poor opinion of that picture means that it says nothing to Me. Does it say anything to You?'

He smiled gently as he put the question to her, but there was no betrayal of emotion in his eyes or in his voice. Relieved of anxiety, so far as Romayne was concerned, Father Benwell looked at Stella.

Steadily as she controlled herself, the confession of her heart's secret found its way into her face. The coldly-composed expression which had confronted the priest when she spoke to him, melted away softly under the influence of Romayne's voice and Romayne's look. Without any positive change of colour, her delicate skin glowed faintly, as if it felt some animating inner warmth. Her eyes and lips brightened with a new vitality; her frail elegant figure seemed insensibly to strengthen and expand, like the leaf of a flower under a favouring sunny air. When she answered Romayne (agreeing with him, it is needless to say), there was a tender persuasiveness in her tones, shyly inviting him still to speak to her and still to look at her, which would in itself have told Father Benwell the truth, even if he had not been in a position to see her face. Confirmed in his doubts of her, he looked, with concealed suspicion, at Lady Loring next. Sympathy with Stella was undisguisedly expressed to him in the honest blue eyes of Stella's faithful friend.

The discussion on the subject of the unfortunate

picture was resumed by Lord Loring, who thought the opinions of Romayne and Stella needlessly severe. Lady Loring, as usual, agreed with her husband. While the general attention was occupied in this way, Father Benwell said a word to Penrose — thus far, a silent listener to the discourse on Art.

'Have you seen the famous portrait of the first Lady Loring, by Gainsborough?' he asked. Without waiting for a reply, he took Penrose by the arm, and led him away to the picture — which had the additional merit, under present circumstances, of hanging at the other end of the gallery.

'How do you like Romayne?' Father Benwell put the question in low peremptory tones, evidently impatient for a reply.

'He interests me already,' said Penrose. 'He looks so ill and so sad, and he spoke to me so kindly — '

'In short,' Father Benwell interposed, 'Romayne has produced a favourable impression on you. Let us get on to the next thing. You must produce a favourable impression on Romayne.'

Penrose sighed. 'With the best will to make myself agreeable to people whom I like,' he said, 'I don't always succeed. They used to tell me at Oxford that I was shy — and I am afraid that is against me. I wish I possessed some of your social advantages, Father!'

'Leave it to me, son! Are they still talking about the picture?'

'Yes.'

'I have something more to say to you. Have

you noticed the young lady?'

'I thought her beautiful — but she looks a little cold.'

Father Benwell smiled. 'When you are as old as I am,' he said, 'you will not believe in appearances where women are concerned. Do you know what *I* think of her? Beautiful, if you like — and dangerous as well.'

'Dangerous! In what way?'

'This is for your private ear, Arthur. She is in love with Romayne. Wait a minute! And Lady Loring — unless I am entirely mistaken in what I observed — knows it and favours it. The beautiful Stella may be the destruction of all our hopes, unless we keep Romayne out of her way.'

These words were whispered with an earnestness and agitation which surprised Penrose. His superior's equanimity was not easily overthrown. 'Are you sure, Father, of what you say?' he asked.

'I am quite sure — or I should not have spoken.'

'Do you think Mr Romayne returns the feeling?'

'Not yet, luckily. You must use your first friendly influence over him — what is her name? Her surname, I mean.'

'Eyrecourt. Miss Stella Eyrecourt.'

'Very well. You must use your influence (when you are quite sure that it *is* an influence) to keep Mr Romayne away from Miss Eyrecourt.'

Penrose looked embarrassed. 'I am afraid I should hardly know how to do that,' he

said. 'But I should naturally, as his assistant, encourage him to keep to his studies.'

Whatever Arthur's superior might privately think of Arthur's reply, he received it with outward indulgence. 'That will come to the same thing,' he said. 'Besides, when I get the information I want — this is strictly between ourselves — I may be of some use in placing obstacles in the lady's way.'

Penrose started. 'Information!' he repeated. 'What information?'

'Tell me something before I answer you,' said Father Benwell. 'How old do you take Miss Eyrecourt to be?'

'I am not a good judge in such matters. Between twenty and twenty-five, perhaps?'

'We will take her age at that estimate, Arthur. In former years, I have had opportunities of studying women's characters in the confessional. Can you guess what my experience tells me of Miss Eyrecourt?'

'No, indeed!'

'A lady is not in love for the first time when she is between twenty and twenty-five years old — that is my experience,' said Father Benwell. 'If I can find a person capable of informing me, I may make some valuable discoveries in the earlier history of Miss Eyrecourt's life. No more, now. We had better return to our friends.'

5

Father Benwell Misses

The group before the picture which had been the subject of dispute was broken up. In one part of the gallery, Lady Loring and Stella were whispering together on a sofa. In another part, Lord Loring was speaking privately to Romayne.

'Do you think you will like Mr Penrose?' his lordship asked.

'Yes — so far as I can tell at present. He seems to be modest and intelligent.'

'You are looking ill, my dear Romayne. Have you again heard the voice that haunts you?'

Romayne answered with evident reluctance. 'I don't know why,' he said — 'but the dread of hearing it again has oppressed me all this morning. To tell you the truth, I came here in the hope that the change might relieve me.'

'Has it done so?'

'Yes — thus far.'

'Doesn't that suggest, my friend, that a greater change might be of use to you?'

'Don't ask me about it, Loring! I can go through my ordeal — but I hate speaking of it.'

'Let us speak of something else then,' said Lord Loring. 'What do you think of Miss Eyrecourt?'

'A very striking face; full of expression and character. Leonardo would have painted a noble portrait of her. But there is something in her manner — ' He stopped, unwilling or unable to finish the sentence.

'Something you don't like?' Lord Loring suggested.

'No; something I don't quite understand. One doesn't expect to find any embarrassment in the manner of a well-bred woman. And yet she seemed to be embarrassed when she spoke to me. Perhaps I produced an unfortunate impression on her.'

Lord Loring laughed. 'In any man but you, Romayne, I should call that affectation.'

'Why?' Romayne asked sharply.

Lord Loring looked unfeignedly surprised. 'My dear fellow, do you really think you are the sort of man who impresses a woman unfavourably at first sight? For once in your life, indulge in the amiable weakness of doing yourself justice — and find a better reason for Miss Eyrecourt's embarrassment.'

For the first time since he and his friend had been talking together, Romayne turned towards Stella. He innocently caught her in the act of looking at him. A younger woman, or a woman of weaker character, would have looked away again. Stella's noble head drooped; her eyes sank slowly, until they rested on her long white hands crossed upon her lap. For a moment more Romayne looked at her with steady attention. He roused himself, and spoke to Lord Loring in lowered tones.

'Have you known Miss Eyrecourt for a long time?'

'She is my wife's oldest and dearest friend. I think, Romayne, you would feel interested in Stella, if you saw more of her.'

Romayne bowed in silent submission to Lord Loring's prophetic remark. 'Let us look at the pictures,' he said quietly.

As he moved down the gallery, the two priests met him. Father Benwell saw his opportunity of helping Penrose to produce a favourable impression.

'Forgive the curiosity of an old student, Mr Romayne,' he said in his pleasant cheerful way. 'Lord Loring tells me you have sent to the country for your books. Do you find a London hotel favourable to study?'

'It is a very quiet hotel,' Romayne answered; 'and the people know my ways.' He turned to Arthur. 'I have my own set of rooms, Mr Penrose,' he continued — 'with a room at your disposal. I used to enjoy the solitude of my house in the country. My tastes have lately changed — there are times now when I want to see the life in the streets, as a relief. Though we are in an hotel, I can promise that you will not be troubled by interruptions, when you kindly lend me the use of your pen.'

Father Benwell answered before Penrose could speak. 'You may perhaps find my young friend's memory of some use to you, Mr Romayne, as well as his pen. Penrose has studied in the Vatican Library. If your reading leads you that way, he knows more than most men of the rare

old manuscripts which treat of the early history of Christianity.'

This delicately managed reference to the projected work on 'The Origin of Religions' produced its effect.

'I should like very much, Mr Penrose, to speak to you about those manuscripts,' Romayne said. 'Copies of some of them may perhaps be in the British Museum. Is it asking too much to inquire if you are disengaged this morning?'

'I am entirely at your service, Mr Romayne.'

'If you will kindly call at my hotel in an hour's time, I shall have looked over my notes, and shall be ready for you with a list of titles and dates. There is the address.'

With those words, he advanced to take his leave of Lady Loring and Stella.

Father Benwell was a man possessed of extraordinary power of foresight — but he was not infallible. Seeing that Romayne was on the point of leaving the house, and feeling that he had paved the way successfully for Romayne's amanuensis, he too readily assumed that there was nothing further to be gained by remaining in the gallery. Moreover, the interval before Penrose called at the hotel might be usefully filled up by some wise words of advice, relating to the religious uses to which he might turn his intercourse with his employer. Making one of his ready and plausible excuses, he accordingly returned with Penrose to the library — and so committed (as he himself discovered at a later time) one of the few mistakes in the long record of his life.

In the meanwhile, Romayne was not permitted to bring his visit to a conclusion without hospitable remonstrance on the part of Lady Loring. She felt for Stella, with a woman's enthusiastic devotion to the interests of true love; and she had firmly resolved that a matter so trifling as the cultivation of Romayne's mind should not be allowed to stand in the way of the far more important enterprise of opening his heart to the influence of the sex.

'Stay, and lunch with us,' she said, when he held out his hand to bid her goodbye.

'Thank you, Lady Loring, I never take lunch.'

'Well, then, come and dine with us — no party: only ourselves. Tomorrow, and next day, we are disengaged. Which day shall it be?'

Romayne still resisted. 'You are very kind. In my state of health, I am unwilling to make engagements which I may not be able to keep.'

Lady Loring was just as resolute on her side. She appealed to Stella. 'Mr Romayne persists, my dear, in putting me off with excuses. Try if *you* can persuade him.'

'*I* am not likely to have any influence, Adelaide.'

The tone in which she replied struck Romayne. He looked at her. Her eyes, gravely meeting his eyes, held him with a strange fascination. She was not herself conscious how openly all that was noble and true in her nature, all that was most deeply and sensitively felt in her aspirations, spoke at that moment in her look. Romayne's face changed: he turned pale

under the new emotion that she had roused in him. Lady Loring observed him attentively.

'Perhaps you underrate your influence, Stella?' she suggested.

Stella remained impenetrable to persuasion. 'I have only been introduced to Mr Romayne half an hour since,' she said. 'I am not vain enough to suppose that I can produce a favourable impression on anyone in so short a time.'

She had expressed, in other words, Romayne's own idea of himself, in speaking of her to Lord Loring. He was struck by the coincidence.

'Perhaps we have begun, Miss Eyrecourt, by misinterpreting one another,' he said. 'We may arrive at a better understanding when I have the honour of meeting you again.'

He hesitated, and looked at Lady Loring. She was not the woman to let a fair opportunity escape her. 'We will say to-morrow evening,' she resumed, 'at seven o'clock.'

'To-morrow,' said Romayne. He shook hands with Stella, and left the picture gallery.

Thus far, the conspiracy to marry him promised even more hopefully than the conspiracy to convert him. And Father Benwell, carefully instructing Penrose in the next room, was not aware of it!

But the hours, in their progress, mark the march of events as surely as they mark the march of time. The day passed, the evening came — and, with its coming, the prospects of the conversion brightened in their turn.

Let Father Benwell himself relate how it

happened — in an extract from his report to Rome, written the same evening.

' . . . I had arranged with Penrose that he should call at my lodgings, and tell me how he had prospered at the first performance of his duties as secretary to Romayne.

'The moment he entered the room, the signs of disturbance in his face told me that something serious had happened. I asked directly if there had been any disagreement between Romayne and himself.

'He repeated the word with every appearance of surprise. 'Disagreement?' he said. 'No words can tell how sincerely I feel for Mr Romayne. I cannot express to you, Father, how eager I am to be of service to him!'

'Relieved so far, I naturally asked what had happened. Penrose betrayed a marked embarrassment in answering my question.

' 'I have innocently surprised a secret,' he said, 'on which I had no right to intrude. All that I can honourably tell you, shall be told. Add one more to your many kindnesses — don't command me to speak, when it is my duty towards a sorely-tried man to be silent, even to you.'

'It is needless to say that I abstained from directly answering this strange appeal. 'Let me hear what you *can* tell,' I replied, 'and then we shall see.'

'Upon this, he spoke. I need hardly recall to your memory how careful we were, in first planning the attempt to recover the Vange property, to assure ourselves of the promise

of success which the peculiar character of the present owner held out to us. In reporting what Penrose said, I communicate a discovery, which I venture to think will be as welcome to you, as it was to me.

'He began by reminding me of what I had myself told him in speaking of Romayne. 'You mentioned having heard from Lord Loring of a great sorrow or remorse from which he was suffering,' Penrose said. 'I know what he suffers and why he suffers, and with what noble resignation he submits to his affliction. We were sitting together at the table, looking over his notes and memoranda, when he suddenly dropped the manuscript from which he was reading to me. A ghastly paleness overspread his face. He started up, and put both his hands to his ears as if he heard something dreadful, and was trying to deafen himself to it. I ran to the door to call for help. He stopped me; he spoke in faint gasping tones, forbidding me to call anyone in to witness what he suffered. It was not the first time, he said; it would soon be over. If I had not courage to remain with him I could go, and return when he was himself again. I so pitied him that I found the courage to remain. When it was over he took me by the hand, and thanked me. I had stayed by him like a friend, he said, and like a friend he would treat me. Sooner or later (those were his exact words) I must be taken into his confidence — and it should be now. He told me his melancholy story. I implore you, Father, don't ask me to repeat it! Be content if I tell you the effect of it on myself.

The one hope, the one consolation for him, is in our holy religion. With all my heart I devote myself to his conversion — and, in my inmost soul, I feel the conviction that I shall succeed!'

'To this effect, and in this tone, Penrose spoke. I abstained from pressing him to reveal Romayne's confession. The confession is of no consequence to *us*. You know how the moral force of Arthur's earnestness and enthusiasm fortifies his otherwise weak character. I, too, believe he will succeed.

'To turn for a moment to another subject. You are already informed that there is a woman in our way. I have my own idea of the right method of dealing with this obstacle when it shows itself more plainly. For the present, I need only assure you that neither this woman nor any woman shall succeed in her designs on Romayne, if I can prevent it.'

Having completed his report in these terms, Father Benwell reverted to the consideration of his proposed inquiries into the past history of Stella's life.

Reflection convinced him that it would be unwise to attempt, no matter how guardedly, to obtain the necessary information from Lord Loring or his wife. If he assumed, at his age, to take a strong interest in a Protestant young lady, who had notoriously avoided him, they would certainly feel surprise — and surprise might, in due course of development, turn to suspicion.

There was but one other person under Lord Loring's roof, to whom he could address himself — and that person was the housekeeper. As

an old servant, possessing Lady Loring's confidence, she might prove a source of information on the subject of Lady Loring's fair friend; and, as a good Catholic, she would feel flattered by the notice of the spiritual director of the household.

'It may not be amiss,' thought Father Benwell, 'if I try the housekeeper.'

6

The Order of the Dishes

When Miss Notman assumed the post of housekeeper in Lady Loring's service, she was accurately described as 'a competent and respectable person;' and was praised, with perfect truth, for her incorruptible devotion to the interests of her employers. On its weaker side, her character was represented by the wearing of a youthful wig, and the erroneous conviction that she still possessed a fine figure. The ruling idea in her narrow little mind was the idea of her own dignity. Any offence offered in this direction oppressed her memory for days together, and found its way outwards in speech to any human being whose attention she could secure.

At five o'clock, on the day which followed his introduction to Romayne, Father Benwell sat drinking his coffee in the housekeeper's room — to all appearances as much at his ease as if he had known Miss Notman from the remote days of her childhood. A new contribution to the housekeeper's little library of devotional works lay on the table, and bore silent witness to the means by which he had made those first advances which had won him his present position. Miss Notman's sense of dignity was doubly flattered. She had a priest for her guest,

92

and a new book with the reverend gentleman's autograph inscribed on the title page.

'Is your coffee to your liking, Father?'

'A little more sugar, if you please.'

Miss Notman was proud of her hand, viewed as one of the meritorious details of her figure. She took up the sugar-tongs with suavity and grace; she dropped the sugar into the cup with a youthful pleasure in ministering to the minor desires of her illustrious guest. 'It is so good of you, Father, to honour me in this way,' she said — with the appearance of sixteen superinduced upon the reality of sixty.

Father Benwell was an adept at moral disguises of all kinds. On this occasion he wore the disguise of pastoral simplicity. 'I am an idle old man at this hour of the afternoon,' he said. 'I hope I am not keeping you from any household duties?'

'I generally enjoy my duties,' Miss Notman answered. 'To-day, they have not been so agreeable as usual: it is a relief to me to have done with them. Even my humble position has its trials.'

Persons acquainted with Miss Notman's character, hearing these last words, would have at once changed the subject. When she spoke of 'her humble position,' she invariably referred to some offence offered to her dignity, and she was invariably ready to state the grievance at full length. Ignorant of this peculiarity, Father Benwell committed a fatal error. He inquired, with courteous interest, what the housekeeper's 'trials' might be.

'Oh, sir, they are beneath your notice!' said Miss Notman, modestly. 'At the same time, I should feel it an honour to have the benefit of your opinion — I should so like to know that you do not altogether disapprove of my conduct, under some provocation. You see, Father, the whole responsibility of ordering the dinners falls on me. And, when there is company, as there is this evening, the responsibility is particularly trying to a timid person like myself.'

'A large dinner party, Miss Notman?'

'Oh, dear, no! Quite the reverse. Only one gentleman — Mr Romayne.'

Father Benwell set down his cup of coffee, half way to his lips. He at once drew the correct conclusion that the invitation to Romayne must have been given and accepted after he had left the picture gallery. That the object was to bring Romayne and Stella together, under circumstances which would rapidly improve their acquaintance, was as plain to him as if he had heard it confessed in so many words. If he had only remained in the gallery, he might have become acquainted with the form of persuasion used to induce a man so unsocial as Romayne to accept an invitation. 'I have myself to blame,' he thought bitterly, 'for being left in the dark.'

'Anything wrong with the coffee?' Miss Notman asked anxiously.

He rushed on his fate. He said, 'Nothing whatever. Pray go on.'

Miss Notman went on.

'You see, Father, Lady Loring was unusually particular about the dinner on this occasion.

She said, 'Lord Loring reminds me that Mr Romayne is a very little eater, and yet very difficult to please in what he does eat.' Of course I consulted my experience, and suggested exactly the sort of dinner that was wanted under the circumstances. I wish to do her ladyship the utmost justice. She made no objection to the dinner in itself. On the contrary, she complimented me on what she was pleased to call my ready invention. But when we came next to the order in which the dishes were to be served — ' Miss Notman paused in the middle of the sentence, and shuddered over the private and poignant recollections which the order of the dishes called up.

By this time Father Benwell had discovered his mistake. He took a mean advantage of Miss Notman's susceptibilities to slip his own private inquiries into the interval of silence.

'Pardon my ignorance,' he said; 'my own poor dinner is a matter of ten minutes, and one dish. I don't understand a difference of opinion on a dinner for three people only: Lord and Lady Loring, two; Mr Romayne, three — oh! perhaps I am mistaken? Perhaps Miss Eyrecourt makes a fourth?'

'Certainly, Father!'

'A very charming person, Miss Notman. I only speak as a stranger. You, no doubt, are much better acquainted with Miss Eyrecourt?'

'Much better, indeed — if I may presume to say so,' Miss Notman replied. 'She is my lady's intimate friend; we have often talked of Miss Eyrecourt during the many years of my

residence in this house. On such subjects, her ladyship treats me quite on the footing of an humble friend. A complete contrast to the tone she took, Father, when we came to the order of the dishes. We agreed, of course, about the soup and the fish; but we had a little, a very little, divergence of opinion, as I may call it, on the subject of the dishes to follow. Her ladyship said, 'First the sweetbreads, and then the cutlets.' I ventured to suggest that the sweetbreads, as white meat, had better not immediately follow the turbot, as white fish. 'The brown meat, my lady,' I said, 'as an agreeable variety presented to the eye, and then the white meat, recalling pleasant remembrances of the white fish.' You see the point, Father?'

'I see, Miss Notman, that you are a consummate mistress of an art which is quite beyond poor me. Was Miss Eyrecourt present at the little discussion?'

'Oh, no! Indeed, I should have objected to her presence; I should have said she was a young lady out of her proper place.'

'Yes, yes; I understand. Is Miss Eyrecourt an only child?'

'She had two sisters, Father Benwell. One of them is in a convent.'

'Ah, indeed?'

'And the other is dead.'

'Sad for the father and mother, Miss Notman!'

'Pardon me, sad for the mother, no doubt. The father died long since.'

'Aye? aye? A sweet woman, the mother? At least, I think I have heard so.'

96

Miss Notman shook her head. 'I should wish to guard myself against speaking unjustly of anyone,' she said; 'but when you talk of 'a sweet woman,' you imply (as it seems to me) the domestic virtues. Mrs Eyrecourt is essentially a frivolous person.'

A frivolous person is, in the vast majority of cases, a person easily persuaded to talk, and not disposed to be reticent in keeping secrets. Father Benwell began to see his way already to the necessary information. 'Is Mrs Eyrecourt living in London?' he inquired.

'Oh, dear, no! At this time of year she lives entirely in other people's houses — goes from one country seat to another, and only thinks of amusing herself. No domestic qualities, Father. *She* would know nothing of the order of the dishes! Lady Loring, I should have told you, gave way in the matter of the sweetbread. It was only at quite the latter part of my 'Menoo' (as the French call it) that she showed a spirit of opposition — well! well! I won't dwell on that. I will only ask *you*, Father, at what part of a dinner an oyster-omelette ought to be served?'

Father Benwell seized his opportunity of discovering Mrs Eyrecourt's present address. 'My dear lady,' he said, 'I know no more when the omelette ought to be served than Mrs Eyrecourt herself! It must be very pleasant, to a lady of her way of thinking, to enjoy the beauties of Nature inexpensively — as seen in other people's houses, from the point of view of a welcome guest. I wonder whether she is

staying at any country seat which I happen to have seen?'

'She may be in England, Scotland, or Ireland, for all I know,' Miss Notman answered, with an unaffected ignorance which placed her good faith beyond doubt. 'Consult your own taste, Father. After eating jelly, cream, and ice-pudding, could you even *look* at an oyster-omelette without shuddering? Would you believe it? Her ladyship proposed to serve the omelette with the cheese. Oysters, after sweets! I am not (as yet) a married woman — '

Father Benwell made a last desperate effort to pave the way for one more question before he submitted to defeat. 'That must be *your* fault, my dear lady!' he interposed, with his persuasive smile.

Miss Notman simpered. 'You confuse me, Father!' she said softly.

'I speak from inward conviction, Miss Notman. To a looker-on, like myself, it is sad to see how many sweet women, who might be angels in the households of worthy men, prefer to lead a single life. The Church, I know, exalts the single life to the highest place. But even the Church allows exceptions to its rule. Under this roof, for example, I think I see two exceptions. One of them my unfeigned respect' (he bowed to Miss Notman) 'forbids me to indicate more particularly. The other seems, to my humble view, to be the young lady of whom we have been speaking. Is it not strange that Miss Eyrecourt has never been married?'

The trap had been elaborately set; Father

Benwell had every reason to anticipate that Miss Notman would walk into it. The disconcerting housekeeper walked up to it — and then proved unable to advance a step farther.

'I once made the same remark myself to Lady Loring,' she said.

Father Benwell's pulse began to quicken its beat. 'Yes?' he murmured, in tones of the gentlest encouragement.

'And her ladyship,' Miss Notman proceeded, 'did not encourage me to go on. 'There are reasons for not pursuing that subject,' she said; 'reasons into which, I am sure, you will not expect me to enter.' She spoke with a flattering confidence in my prudence, which I felt gratefully. Such a contrast to her tone when the omelette presented itself in the order of the dishes! As I said just now, I am not a married woman. But if I proposed to my husband to give him an oyster-omelette after his puddings and his pies, I should not be surprised if he said to me, 'My dear, have you taken leave of your senses?' I reminded Lady Loring (most respectfully) that a *cheese*-omelette might be in its proper place if it followed the sweets. 'An *oyster*-omelette,' I suggested, 'surely comes after the birds?' I should be sorry to say that her ladyship lost her temper — I will only mention that I kept mine. Let me repeat what she said, and leave you, Father, to draw your own conclusions. She said, 'Which of us is mistress in this house, Miss Notman? I order the oyster-omelette to come in with the cheese.' There was not only irritability,

99

there was contempt — oh, yes! contempt in her tone. Out of respect for myself, I made no reply. As a Christian, I can forgive; as a wounded gentlewoman, I may not find it so easy to forget.'

Miss Notman laid herself back in her easy chair — she looked as if she had suffered martyrdom, and only regretted having been obliged to mention it. Father Benwell surprised the wounded gentlewoman by rising to his feet.

'You are not going away already, Father?'

'Time flies fast in your society, dear Miss Notman. I have an engagement — and I am late for it already.'

The housekeeper smiled sadly. 'At least let me hear that you don't disapprove of my conduct under trying circumstances,' she said.

Father Benwell took her hand. 'A true Christian only feels offences to pardon them,' he remarked, in his priestly and paternal character. 'You have shown me, Miss Notman, that *you* are a true Christian. My evening has indeed been well spent. God bless you!'

He pressed her hand; he shed on her the light of his fatherly smile; he sighed, and took his leave. Miss Notman's eyes followed him out with devotional admiration.

Father Benwell still preserved his serenity of temper when he was out of the housekeeper's sight. One important discovery he had made, in spite of the difficulties placed in his way. A compromising circumstance had unquestionably occurred in Stella's past life; and, in all

probability, a man was in some way connected with it. 'My evening has not been entirely thrown away,' he thought, as he ascended the stairs which led from the housekeeper's room to the hall.

7

The Influence of Stella

Entering the hall, Father Benwell heard a knock at the house door. The servants appeared to recognise the knock — the porter admitted Lord Loring.

Father Benwell advanced and made his bow. It was a perfect obeisance of its kind — respect for Lord Loring, unobtrusively accompanied by respect for himself. 'Has your lordship been walking in the park?' he inquired.

'I have been out on business,' Lord Loring answered; 'and I should like to tell you about it. If you can spare me a few minutes, come into the library. Some time since,' he resumed, when the door was closed, 'I think I mentioned that my friends had been speaking to me on a subject of some importance — the subject of opening my picture gallery occasionally to the public.'

'I remember,' said Father Benwell. 'Has your lordship decided what to do?'

'Yes. I have decided (as the phrase is) to 'go with the times,' and follow the example of other owners of picture galleries. Don't suppose I ever doubted that it is my duty to extend, to the best of my ability, the civilising influences of Art. My only hesitation in the matter arose from a dread of some accident happening, or some

injury being done, to the pictures. Even now, I can only persuade myself to try the experiment under certain restrictions.'

'A wise decision, undoubtedly,' said Father Benwell. 'In such a city as this, you could hardly open your gallery to anybody who happens to pass the house-door.'

'I am glad you agree with me, Father. The gallery will be opened for the first time on Monday. Any respectably-dressed person, presenting a visiting card at the offices of the librarians in Bond Street and Regent Street, will receive a free ticket of admission; the number of the tickets, it is needless to say, being limited, and the gallery being only opened to the public two days in the week. You will be here, I suppose, on Monday?'

'Certainly. My work in the library, as your lordship can see, has only begun.'

'I am very anxious about the success of this experiment,' said Lord Loring. 'Do look in at the gallery once or twice in the course of the day, and tell me what your own impression is.'

Having expressed his readiness to assist 'the experiment' in every possible way, Father Benwell still lingered in the library. He was secretly conscious of a hope that he might, at the eleventh hour, be invited to join Romayne at the dinner-table. Lord Loring only looked at the clock on the mantelpiece: it was nearly time to dress for dinner. The priest had no alternative but to take the hint, and leave the house.

Five minutes after he had withdrawn, a messenger delivered a letter for Lord Loring,

in which Father Benwell's interests were directly involved. The letter was from Romayne; it contained his excuses for breaking his engagement, literally at an hour's notice.

'Only yesterday,' he wrote, 'I had a return of what you, my dear friend, call 'the delusion of the voice.' The nearer the hour of your dinner approaches, the more keenly I fear that the same thing may happen in your house. Pity me, and forgive me.'

Even good-natured Lord Loring felt some difficulty in pitying and forgiving, when he read these lines. 'This sort of caprice might be excusable in a woman,' he thought. 'A man ought really to be capable of exercising some self-control. Poor Stella! And what will my wife say?'

He walked up and down the library, with Stella's disappointment and Lady Loring's indignation prophetically present in his mind. There was, however, no help for it — he must accept his responsibility, and be the bearer of the bad news.

He was on the point of leaving the library, when a visitor appeared. The visitor was no less a person than Romayne himself. 'Have I arrived before my letter?' he asked eagerly.

Lord Loring showed him the letter.

'Throw it into the fire,' he said, 'and let me try to excuse myself for having written it. You remember the happier days when you used to call me the creature of impulse? An impulse produced that letter. Another impulse brings me here to disown it. I can only explain my strange

104

conduct by asking you to help me at the outset. Will you carry your memory back to the day of the medical consultation on my case? I want you to correct me, if I inadvertently misrepresent my advisers. Two of them were physicians. The third, and last, was a surgeon, a personal friend of yours; and *he*, as well as I recollect, told you how the consultation ended?'

'Quite right, Romayne — so far.'

'The first of the two physicians,' Romayne proceeded, 'declared my case to be entirely attributable to nervous derangement, and to be curable by purely medical means. I speak ignorantly; but, in plain English, that, I believe, was the substance of what he said?'

'The substance of what he said,' Lord Loring replied, 'and the substance of his prescriptions — which, I think, you afterwards tore up?'

'If you have no faith in a prescription,' said Romayne, 'that is, in my opinion, the best use to which you can put it. When it came to the turn of the second physician, he differed with the first, as absolutely as one man can differ with another. The third medical authority, your friend the surgeon, took a middle course, and brought the consultation to an end by combining the first physician's view and the second physician's view, and mingling the two opposite forms of treatment in one harmonious result?'

Lord Loring remarked that this was not a very respectful way of describing the conclusion of the medical proceedings. That it *was* the conclusion, however, he could not honestly deny.

'As long as I am right,' said Romayne,

'nothing else appears to be of much importance. As I told you at the time, the second physician appeared to me to be the only one of the three authorities who really understood my case. Do you mind giving me, in few words, your own impression of what he said?'

'Are you sure that I shall not distress you?'

'On the contrary, you may help me to hope.'

'As I remember it,' said Lord Loring, 'the doctor did not deny the influence of the body over the mind. He was quite willing to admit that the state of your nervous system might be one, among other predisposing causes, which led you — I really hardly like to go on.'

'Which led me,' Romayne continued, finishing the sentence for his friend, 'to feel that I never shall forgive myself — accident or no accident — for having taken that man's life. Now go on.'

'The delusion that you still hear the voice,' Lord Loring proceeded, 'is, in the doctor's opinion, the moral result of the morbid state of your mind at the time when you really heard the voice on the scene of the duel. The influence acts physically, of course, by means of certain nerves. But it is essentially a moral influence; and its power over you is greatly maintained by the self-accusing view of the circumstances which you persist in taking. That, in substance, is my recollection of what the doctor said.'

'And when he was asked what remedies he proposed to try,' Romayne inquired, 'do you remember his answer? 'The mischief which

moral influences have caused, moral influences alone can remedy.' '

'I remember,' said Lord Loring. 'And he mentioned, as examples of what he meant, the occurrence of some new and absorbing interest in your life, or the working of some complete change in your habits of thought — or perhaps some influence exercised over you by a person previously unknown, appearing under unforeseen circumstances, or in scenes quite new to you.'

Romayne's eyes sparkled.

'Now you are coming to it!' he cried. 'Now I feel sure that I recall correctly the last words the doctor said: — 'If my view is the right one, I should not be surprised to hear that the recovery which we all wish to see had found its beginning in such apparently trifling circumstances as the tone of some other person's voice or the influence of some other person's look.' That plain expression of his opinion only occurred to my memory after I had written my foolish letter of excuse. I spare you the course of other recollections that followed, to come at once to the result. For the first time I have the hope, the faint hope, that the voice which haunts me has been once already controlled by one of the influences of which the doctor spoke — the influence of a look.'

If he had said this to Lady Loring, instead of to her husband, she would have understood him at once. Lord Loring asked for a word more of explanation.

'I told you yesterday,' Romayne answered,

107

'that a dread of the return of the voice had been present to me all the morning, and that I had come to see the picture with an idea of trying if change would relieve me. While I was in the gallery I was free from the dread, and free from the voice. When I returned to the hotel it tortured me — and Mr Penrose, I grieve to say, saw what I suffered. You and I attributed the remission to the change of scene. I now believe we were both wrong. Where was the change? In seeing you and Lady Loring, I saw the two oldest friends I have. In visiting your gallery, I only revived the familiar associations of hundreds of other visits. To what influence was I really indebted for my respite? Don't try to dismiss the question by laughing at my morbid fancies. Morbid fancies are realities to a man like me. Remember the doctor's words, Loring. Think of a new face, seen in your house! Think of a look that searched my heart for the first time!'

Lord Loring glanced once more at the clock on the mantelpiece. The hands pointed to the dinner hour.

'Miss Eyrecourt?' he whispered.

'Yes; Miss Eyrecourt.'

The library door was thrown open by a servant. Stella herself entered the room.

8

The Priest or the Woman?

Lord Loring hurried away to his dressing-room. 'I won't be more than ten minutes,' he said — and left Romayne and Stella together.

She was attired with her customary love of simplicity. White lace was the only ornament on her dress of delicate silvery grey. Her magnificent hair was left to plead its own merits, without adornment of any sort. Even the brooch which fastened her lace pelerine was of plain gold only. Conscious that she was showing her beauty to the greatest advantage in the eyes of a man of taste, she betrayed a little of the embarrassment which Romayne had already noticed at the moment when she gave him her hand. They were alone, and it was the first time she had seen him in evening dress.

It may be that women have no positive appreciation of what is beautiful in form and colour — or it may be that they have no opinions of their own when the laws of fashion have spoken. This at least is certain, that not one of them in a thousand sees anything objectionable in the gloomy and hideous evening costume of a gentleman in the nineteenth century. A handsome man is, to their eyes, more seductive than ever in the contemptible black coat and the stiff white cravat which

he wears in common with the servant who waits on him at table. After a stolen glance at Romayne, Stella lost all confidence in herself — she began turning over the photographs on the table.

The momentary silence which followed their first greeting became intolerable to her. Rather than let it continue, she impulsively confessed the uppermost idea in her mind when she entered the room.

'I thought I heard my name when I came in,' she said. 'Were you and Lord Loring speaking of me?'

Romayne owned without hesitation that they had been speaking of her.

She smiled, and turned over another photograph. But when did sun-pictures ever act as a restraint on a woman's curiosity? The words passed her lips in spite of her. 'I suppose I mustn't ask what you were saying?'

It was impossible to answer this plainly without entering into explanations from which Romayne shrank. He hesitated.

She turned over another photograph. 'I understand,' she said. 'You were talking of my faults.' She paused, and stole another look at him. 'I will try to correct my faults, if you will tell me what they are.'

Romayne felt that he had no alternative but to tell the truth — under certain reserves. 'Indeed you are wrong,' he said. 'We were talking of the influence of a tone or a look on a sensitive person.'

'The influence on Me?' she asked.

'No. The influence which You might exercise on another person.'

She knew perfectly well that he was speaking of himself. But she was determined to feel the pleasure of making him own it.

'If I have any such influence as you describe,' she began, 'I hope it is for good?'

'Certainly for good.'

'You speak positively, Mr Romayne. Almost as positively — only that can hardly be — as if you were speaking from experience.'

He might still have evaded a direct reply, if she had been content with merely saying this. But she looked at him while she spoke. He answered the look.

'Shall I own that you are right?' he said. 'I was thinking of my own experience yesterday.'

She returned to the photographs. 'It sounds impossible,' she rejoined softly. There was a pause. 'Was it anything I said?' she asked.

'No. It was only when you looked at me. But for that look, I don't think I should have been here to-day.'

She shut up the photographs on a sudden, and drew her chair a little away from him.

'I hope,' she said, 'you have not so poor an opinion of me as to think I like to be flattered?'

Romayne answered with an earnestness that instantly satisfied her.

'I should think it an act of insolence to flatter you,' he said. 'If you knew the true reason why I hesitated to accept Lady Loring's invitation — if I could own to you the new hope for

111

myself that has brought me here — you would feel, as I feel, that I have been only speaking the truth. I daren't say yet that I owe you a debt of gratitude for such a little thing as a look. I must wait till time puts certain strange fancies of mine to the proof.'

'Fancies about me, Mr Romayne?'

Before he could answer, the dinner bell rang. Lord and Lady Loring entered the library together.

The dinner having pursued its appointed course (always excepting the case of the omelette), the head servant who had waited at table was graciously invited to rest, after his labours, in the housekeeper's room. Having additionally conciliated him by means of a glass of rare liqueur, Miss Notman, still feeling her grievance as acutely as ever, ventured to inquire, in the first place, if the gentlefolks upstairs had enjoyed their dinner. So far the report was, on the whole, favourable. But the conversation was described as occasionally flagging. The burden of the talk had been mainly borne by my lord and my lady, Mr Romayne and Miss Eyrecourt contributing but little to the social enjoyment of the evening. Receiving this information without much appearance of interest, the housekeeper put another question, to which, judging by her manner, she attached a certain importance. She wished to know if the oyster-omelette (accompanying the cheese) had been received as a welcome dish, and treated with a just recognition of its merits. The answer to this

was decidedly in the negative. Mr Romayne and Miss Eyrecourt had declined to taste it. My lord had tried it, and had left it on his plate. My lady alone had really eaten her share of the misplaced dish. Having stated this apparently trivial circumstance, the head servant was surprised by the effect which it produced on the housekeeper. She leaned back in her chair and closed her eyes, with an appearance of unutterable enjoyment. That night there was one supremely happy woman in London. And her name was Miss Notman.

Ascending from the housekeeper's room to the drawing-room, it is to be further reported that music was tried, as a means of getting through the time, in the absence of general conversation. Lady Loring sat down at the piano, and played as admirably as usual. At the other end of the room Romayne and Stella were together, listening to the music. Lord Loring walking backwards and forwards, with a restlessness which was far from being characteristic of him in his after-dinner hours, was stopped when he reached the neighbourhood of the piano by a private signal from his wife.

'What are you walking about for?' Lady Loring asked in a whisper, without interrupting her musical performance.

'I'm not quite easy, my dear.'

'Turn over the music. Indigestion?'

'Good heavens, Adelaide, what a question.'

'Well, what is it then?'

Lord Loring looked towards Stella and her

companion. 'They don't seem to get on together as well as I had hoped,' he said.

'I should think not — when you are walking about and disturbing them! Sit down there behind me.'

'What am I to do?'

'Am I not playing? Listen to me.'

'My dear, I don't understand modern German music.'

'Then read the evening paper.'

The evening paper had its attractions. Lord Loring took his wife's advice.

Left entirely by themselves, at the other end of the room, Romayne and Stella justified Lady Loring's belief in the result of reducing her husband to a state of repose. Stella ventured to speak first, in a discreet undertone.

'Do you pass most of your evenings alone, Mr Romayne?'

'Not quite alone. I have the company of my books.'

'Are your books the companions that you like best?'

'I have been true to those companions, Miss Eyrecourt, for many years. If the doctors are to be believed, my books have not treated me very well in return. They have broken down my health, and have made me, I am afraid, a very unsocial man.' He seemed about to say more, and suddenly checked the impulse. 'Why am I talking of myself?' he resumed with a smile. 'I never do it at other times. Is this another result of your influence over me?'

He put the question with an assumed gaiety. Stella made no effort, on her side, to answer him in the same tone.

'I almost wish I really had some influence over you,' she said gravely and sadly.

'Why?'

'I should try to induce you to shut up your books, and choose some living companion who might restore you to your happier self.'

'It is already done,' said Romayne; 'I have a new companion in Mr Penrose.'

'Penrose?' she repeated. 'He is the friend — is he not — of the priest here, whom they call Father Benwell?'

'Yes.'

'I don't like Father Benwell.'

'Is that a reason for disliking Mr Penrose?'

'Yes,' she said boldly, 'because he is Father Benwell's friend.'

'Indeed you are mistaken, Miss Eyrecourt. Mr Penrose only entered yesterday on his duties as my secretary, and I have already had reason to think highly of him. Many men, after *that* experience of me,' he added, speaking more to himself than to her, 'might have asked me to find another secretary.'

Stella heard those last words, and looked at him in astonishment. 'Were you angry with Mr Penrose?' she asked innocently. 'Is it possible that *you* could speak harshly to any person in your employment?'

Romayne smiled. 'It was not what I said,' he answered. 'I am subject to attacks — to sudden attacks of illness. I am sorry I alarmed

115

Mr Penrose by letting him see me under those circumstances.'

She looked at him; hesitated; and looked away again. 'Would you be angry with me if I confessed something?' she said timidly.

'It is impossible I can be angry with you!'

'Mr Romayne, I think I have seen what your secretary saw. I know how you suffer, and how patiently you bear it.'

'You!' he exclaimed.

'I saw you with your friend, when you came on board the steamboat at Boulogne. Oh, no, you never noticed me! You never knew how I pitied you. And afterwards, when you moved away by yourself, and stood by the place in which the engines work — you are sure you won't think the worse of me, if I tell it?'

'No! no!'

'Your face frightened me — I can't describe it — I went to your friend and took it on myself to say that you wanted him. It was an impulse — I meant well.'

'I am sure you meant well.' As he spoke, his face darkened a little, betraying a momentary feeling of distrust. Had she put indiscreet questions to his travelling companion; and had the Major, under the persuasive influence of her beauty, been weak enough to answer them? 'Did you speak to my friend?' he asked.

'Only when I told him that he had better go to you. And I think I said afterwards I was afraid you were very ill. We were in the confusion of arriving at Folkestone — and, even

116

if I had thought it right to say more, there was no opportunity.'

Romayne felt ashamed of the suspicion by which he had wronged her. 'You have a generous nature,' he said earnestly. 'Among the few people whom I know, how many would feel the interest in me that you felt?'

'Don't say that, Mr Romayne! You could have had no kinder friend than the gentleman who took care of you on your journey. Is he with you now, in London?'

'No.'

'I am sorry to hear it. You ought to have some devoted friend always near you.'

She spoke very earnestly. Romayne shrank, with a strange shyness, from letting her see how her sympathy affected him. He answered lightly. 'You go almost as far as my good friend there reading the newspaper,' he said. 'Lord Loring doesn't scruple to tell me that I ought to marry. I know he speaks with a sincere interest in my welfare. He little thinks how he distresses me.'

'Why should he distress you?'

'He reminds me — live as long as I may — that I must live alone. Can I ask a woman to share such a dreary life as mine? It would be selfish, it would be cruel; I should deservedly pay the penalty of allowing my wife to sacrifice herself. The time would come when she would repent having married me.'

Stella rose. Her eyes rested on him with a look of gentle remonstrance. 'I think you hardly do women justice,' she said softly. 'Perhaps some day a woman may induce you to change your

117

opinion.' She crossed the room to the piano. 'You must be tired of playing, Adelaide,' she said, putting her hand caressingly on Lady Loring's shoulder.

'Will you sing, Stella?'

She sighed, and turned away. 'Not to-night,' she answered.

Romayne took his leave rather hurriedly. He seemed to be out of spirits and eager to get away. Lord Loring accompanied his guest to the door. 'You look sad and careworn,' he said. 'Do you regret having left your books to pass an evening with us?'

Romayne looked up absently, and answered, 'I don't know yet.'

Returning to report this extraordinary reply to his wife and Stella, Lord Loring found the drawing-room empty. Eager for a little private conversation, the two ladies had gone upstairs.

'Well?' said Lady Loring, as they sat together over the fire. 'What did he say?'

Stella only repeated what he had said before she rose and left him. 'What is there in Mr Romayne's life,' she asked, 'which made him say that he would be selfish and cruel if he expected a woman to marry him? It must be something more than mere illness. If he had committed a crime, he could not have spoken more strongly. Do you know what it is?'

Lady Loring looked uneasy. 'I promised my husband to keep it a secret from everybody,' she said.

'It is nothing degrading, Adelaide — I am sure of that.'

'And you are right, my dear. I can understand that he has surprised and disappointed you; but, if you knew his motives — ' she stopped, and looked earnestly at Stella. 'They say,' she went on, 'the love that lasts longest is the love of slowest growth. This feeling of yours for Romayne is of sudden growth. Are you very sure that your whole heart is given to a man of whom you know little?'

'I know that I love him,' said Stella simply.

'Even though he doesn't seem, as yet, to love *you*?' Lady Loring asked.

'All the more *because* he doesn't. I should be ashamed to make the confession to anyone but you. It is useless to say any more. Good-night.'

Lady Loring allowed her to get as far as the door, and then suddenly called her back. Stella returned unwillingly and wearily. 'My head aches and my heart aches,' she said. 'Let me go away to my bed.'

'I don't like you to go away, wronging Romayne perhaps in your thoughts,' said Lady Loring. 'And, more than that, for the sake of your own happiness, you ought to judge for yourself if this devoted love of yours may ever hope to win its reward. It is time, and more than time, that you should decide whether it is good for you to see Romayne again. Have you courage enough to do that?'

'Yes — if I am convinced that it ought to be done.'

'Nothing would make *me* so happy,' Lady Loring resumed, 'as to know that you were one day, my dear, to be his wife. But I am not a prudent person — I can never look, as you can, to consequences. You won't betray me, Stella? If I am doing wrong in telling a secret which has been trusted to me, it is my fondness for you that misleads me. Sit down again. You shall know what the misery of Romayne's life really is.'

With those words, she told the terrible story of the duel, and of all that had followed it.

'It is for you to say,' she concluded, 'whether Romayne is right. Can any woman hope to release him from the torment that he suffers, with nothing to help her but love? Determine for yourself.'

Stella answered instantly.

'I determine to be his wife!'

With the same pure enthusiasm, Penrose had declared that he too devoted himself to the deliverance of Romayne. The loving woman was not more resolved to give her whole life to him, than the fanatical man was resolved to convert him. On the same common battle-ground the two were now to meet in unconscious antagonism. Would the priest or the woman win the day?

9

The Public and the Pictures

On the memorable Monday, when the picture gallery was opened to the public for the first time, Lord Loring and Father Benwell met in the library.

'Judging by the number of carriages already at the door,' said Father Benwell, 'your lordship's kindness is largely appreciated by the lovers of Art.'

'All the tickets were disposed of in three hours,' Lord Loring answered. 'Everybody (the librarians tell me) is eager to see the pictures. Have you looked in yet?'

'Not yet. I thought I would get on first with my work among the books.'

'I have just come from the gallery,' Lord Loring continued. 'And here I am, driven out of it again by the remarks of some of the visitors. You know my beautiful copies of Raphael's Cupid and Psyche designs? The general impression, especially among the ladies, is that they are disgusting and indecent. That was enough for me. If you happen to meet Lady Loring and Stella, kindly tell them that I have gone to the club.'

'Do the ladies propose paying a visit to the gallery?'

'Of course — to see the people! I have

recommended them to wait until they are ready to go out for their drive. In their indoor costume they might become the objects of general observation, as the ladies of the house. I shall be anxious to hear, Father, if you can discover the civilising influences of Art among my guests in the gallery. Good morning.'

Father Benwell rang the bell when Lord Loring had left him.

'Do the ladies drive out to-day at their usual hour?' he inquired, when the servant appeared. The man answered in the affirmative. The carriage was ordered at three o'clock.

At half-past two Father Benwell slipped quietly into the gallery. He posted himself midway between the library door and the grand entrance; on the watch, not for the civilising influences of Art, but for the appearance of Lady Loring and Stella. He was still of opinion that Stella's 'frivolous' mother might be turned into a source of valuable information, on the subject of her daughter's earlier life. The first step towards attaining this object was to discover Mrs Eyrecourt's present address. Stella would certainly know it — and Father Benwell felt a just confidence in his capacity to make the young lady serviceable, in this respect, to the pecuniary interests of the Church.

After an interval of a quarter of an hour, Lady Loring and Stella entered the gallery by the library door. Father Benwell at once advanced to pay his respects.

For some little time he discreetly refrained from making any attempt to lead the conversation

to the topic that he had in view. He was too well acquainted with the insatiable interest of women in looking at other women to force himself into notice. The ladies made their remarks on the pretensions to beauty and to taste in dress among the throng of visitors — and Father Benwell waited by them, and listened, with the resignation of a modest young man. Patience, being a virtue, is sometimes its own reward. Two gentlemen, evidently interested in the pictures, approached the priest. He drew back, with his ready politeness, to let them see the picture before which he happened to be standing.

The movement disturbed Stella. She turned sharply — noticed one of the gentlemen, the taller of the two — became deadly pale — and instantly quitted the gallery. Lady Loring, looking where Stella had looked, frowned angrily, and followed Miss Eyrecourt into the library. Wise Father Benwell let them go, and concentrated his attention on the person who had been the object of this startling recognition.

Unquestionably a gentleman — with light hair and complexion — with a bright benevolent face, and keen intelligent blue eyes — apparently still in the prime of life. Such was Father Benwell's first impression of the stranger. He had evidently seen Miss Eyrecourt at the moment when she first noticed him; and he too showed signs of serious agitation. His face flushed deeply, and his eyes expressed, not merely surprise, but distress. He turned to his friend. 'This place is hot,' he said; 'let us get out of it!'

'My dear Winterfield!' the friend remonstrated,

'we haven't seen half the pictures yet.'

'Excuse me if I leave you,' the other replied. 'I am used to the free air of the country. Let us meet again this evening. Come and dine with me. The same address as usual — Derwent's Hotel.'

With those words he hurried out, making his way, without ceremony, through the crowd in the picture gallery.

Father Benwell returned to the library. It was quite needless to trouble himself further about Mrs Eyrecourt or her address. 'Thanks to Lord Loring's picture gallery,' he thought, 'I have found the man!'

He took up his pen and made a little memorandum — 'Winterfield. Derwent's Hotel.'

10

Father Benwell's Correspondence

I

To Mr Bitrake. Private and Confidential.

Sir, — I understand that your connection with the law does not exclude your occasional superintendence of confidential inquiries, which are not of a nature to injure your professional position. The enclosed letter of introduction will satisfy you that I am incapable of employing your experience in a manner unbecoming to you, or to myself.

The inquiry that I propose to you relates to a gentleman named Winterfield. He is now staying in London, at Derwent's Hotel, and is expected to remain there for a week from the present date. His place of residence is on the North Devonshire coast, and is well known in that locality by the name of Beaupark House.

The range of my proposed inquiry dates back over the last four or five years — certainly not more. My object is to ascertain, as positively as may be, whether, within this limit of time, events in Mr Winterfield's life have connected him with a young lady named Miss Stella Eyrecourt. If this proves to be the case, it is essential that I should be made acquainted with the whole of the circumstances.

I have now informed you of all that I want to know. Whatever the information may be, it is most important that it shall be information which I can implicitly trust. Please address to me, when you write, under cover to the friend whose letter I enclose.

I beg your acceptance — as time is of importance — of a cheque for preliminary expenses, and remain, sir, your faithful servant,

AMBROSE BENWELL.

II

To the Secretary, Society of Jesus, Rome.

I enclose a receipt for the remittance which your last letter confides to my care. Some of the money has been already used in prosecuting inquiries, the result of which will, as I hope and believe, enable me to effectually protect Romayne from the advances of the woman who is bent on marrying him.

You tell me that our Reverend Fathers, lately sitting in council on the Vange Abbey affair, are anxious to hear if any positive steps have yet been taken towards the conversion of Romayne. I am happily able to gratify their wishes, as you shall now see.

Yesterday, I called at Romayne's hotel to pay one of those occasional visits which help to keep up our acquaintance. He was out, and Penrose (for whom I asked next) was with him. Most fortunately, as the event proved, I had not seen Penrose, or heard from him, for some little time; and I thought it desirable to judge for

myself of the progress that he was making in the confidence of his employer. I said I would wait. The hotel servant knows me by sight. I was shown into Romayne's waiting-room.

This room is so small as to be a mere cupboard. It is lit by a glass fanlight over the door which opens from the passage, and is supplied with air (in the absence of a fireplace) by a ventilator in a second door, which communicates with Romayne's study. Looking about me, so far, I crossed to the other end of the study, and discovered a dining-room and two bedrooms beyond — the set of apartments being secluded, by means of a door at the end of the passage, from the other parts of the hotel. I trouble you with these details in order that you may understand the events that followed.

I returned to the waiting-room, not forgetting of course to close the door of communication.

Nearly an hour must have passed before I heard footsteps in the passage. The study door was opened, and the voices of persons entering the room reached me through the ventilator. I recognised Romayne, Penrose — and Lord Loring.

The first words exchanged among them informed me that Romayne and his secretary had overtaken Lord Loring in the street, as he was approaching the hotel door. The three had entered the house together — at a time, probably, when the servant who had admitted me was out of the way. However it may have happened, there I was, forgotten in the waiting-room!

Could I intrude myself (on a private conversation perhaps) as an unannounced and unwelcome visitor? And could I help it, if the talk found its way to me through the ventilator, along with the air that I breathed? If our Reverend Fathers think I was to blame, I bow to any reproof which their strict sense of propriety may inflict on me. In the meantime I beg to repeat the interesting passages in the conversation, as nearly word for word as I can remember them.

His lordship, as the principal personage in social rank, shall be reported first. He said, 'More than a week has passed, Romayne, and we have neither seen you nor heard from you. Why have you neglected us?'

Here, judging by certain sounds that followed, Penrose got up discreetly, and left the room. Lord Loring went on.

He said to Romayne, 'Now we are alone, I may speak to you more freely. You and Stella seemed to get on together admirably that evening when you dined with us. Have you forgotten what you told me of her influence over you? or have you altered your opinion — and is that the reason why you keep away from us?'

Romayne answered, 'My opinion remains unchanged. All that I said to you of Miss Eyrecourt, I believe as firmly as ever.'

His lordship remonstrated, naturally enough. 'Then why remain away from the good influence? Why — if it really *can* be controlled — risk another return of that dreadful nervous delusion?'

'I have had another return.'

128

'Which, as you yourself believe, might have been prevented! Romayne, you astonish me.'

There was a time of silence, before Romayne answered this. He was a little mysterious when he did reply. 'You know the old saying, my good friend — of two evils, choose the least. I bear my sufferings as one of two evils, and the least of the two.'

Lord Loring appeared to feel the necessity of touching a delicate subject with a light hand. He said, in his pleasant way, 'Stella isn't the other evil, I suppose?'

'Most assuredly not.'

'Then what is it?'

Romayne answered, almost passionately, 'My own weakness and selfishness! Faults which I must resist, or become a mean and heartless man. For me, the worst of the two evils is there. I respect and admire Miss Eyrecourt — I believe her to be a woman in a thousand — don't ask me to see her again! Where is Penrose? Let us talk of something else.'

Whether this wild way of speaking offended Lord Loring, or only discouraged him, I cannot say. I heard him take his leave in these words: — 'You have disappointed me, Romayne. We will talk of something else the next time we meet.' The study door was opened and closed. Romayne was left by himself.

Solitude was apparently not to his taste just then. I heard him call to Penrose. I heard Penrose ask, 'Do you want me?'

Romayne answered, 'God knows I want a friend — and I have no friend near me but

you! Major Hynd is away, and Lord Loring is offended with me.'

Penrose asked why.

Romayne, thereupon, entered on the necessary explanation. As a priest, writing to priests, I pass over details utterly uninteresting to *us*. The substance of what he said amounted to this: — Miss Eyrecourt had produced an impression on him which was new to him in his experience of women. If he saw more of her, it might end — I ask your pardon for repeating the ridiculous expression — in his 'falling in love with her.' In this condition of mind or body, whichever it may be, he would probably be incapable of the self-control which he had hitherto practised. If she consented to devote her life to him, he might accept the cruel sacrifice. Rather than do this, he would keep away from her, for her dear sake — no matter what he might suffer, or whom he might offend.

Imagine any human being, out of a lunatic asylum, talking in this way. Shall I own to you, my reverend colleague, how this curious self-exposure struck me? As I listened to Romayne, I felt grateful to the famous Council which definitely forbade the priests of the Catholic Church to marry. *We* might otherwise have been morally enervated by the weakness which degrades Romayne — and priests might have become instruments in the hands of women.

But you will be anxious to hear what Penrose did under the circumstances. For the moment, I can tell you this, he startled me.

Instead of seizing the opportunity, and

directing Romayne's mind to the consolations of religion, Penrose actually encouraged him to reconsider his decision. All the weakness of my poor little Arthur's character showed itself in his next words.

He said to Romayne, 'It may be wrong in me to speak to you as freely as I wish to speak. But you have so generously admitted me to your confidence — you have been so considerate and so kind towards me — that I feel an interest in your happiness, which perhaps makes me over bold. Are you very sure that some such entire change in your life as your marriage might not end in delivering you from your burden? If such a thing could be, is it wrong to suppose that your wife's good influence over you might be the means of making your marriage a happy one? I must not presume to offer an opinion on such a subject. It is only my gratitude, my true attachment to you, that ventures to put the question. Are you conscious of having given this matter — so serious a matter for you — sufficient thought?'

Make your mind easy, reverend sir! Romayne's answer set everything right.

He said, 'I have thought of it till I could think no longer. I still believe that sweet woman might control the torment of the voice. But could she deliver me from the remorse perpetually gnawing at my heart? I feel as murderers feel. In taking another man's life — a man who had not even injured me! — I have committed the one unatonable and unpardonable sin. Can any human creature's influence make me forget that?

131

No more of it — no more. Come! Let us take refuge in our books.'

Those words touched Penrose in the right place. Now, as I understand his scruples, he felt that he might honourably speak out. His zeal more than balanced his weakness, as you will presently see.

He was loud, he was positive, when I heard him next. 'No!' he burst out, 'your refuge is not in books, and not in the barren religious forms which call themselves Protestant. Dear master, the peace of mind, which you believe you have lost for ever, you will find again in the divine wisdom and compassion of the holy Catholic Church. There is the remedy for all that you suffer! There is the new life that will yet make you a happy man!'

I repeat what he said, so far, merely to satisfy you that we can trust his enthusiasm, when it is once roused. Nothing will discourage, nothing will defeat him now. He spoke with all the eloquence of conviction — using the necessary arguments with a force and feeling which I have rarely heard equalled. Romayne's silence vouched for the effect on him. He is not the man to listen patiently to reasoning which he thinks he can overthrow.

Having heard enough to satisfy me that Penrose had really begun the good work, I quietly slipped out of the waiting-room, and left the hotel.

To-day being Sunday, I shall not lose a post if I keep my letter open until to-morrow. I have already sent a note to Penrose, asking him to call

on me at his earliest convenience. There may be more news for you before post time.

<p align="right">*Monday*, 10 A.M.</p>

There *is* more news. Penrose has just left me.

His first proceeding, of course, was to tell me what I had already discovered for myself. He is modest, as usual, about the prospect of success which awaits him. But he has induced Romayne to suspend his historical studies for a few days, and to devote his attention to the books which we are accustomed to recommend for perusal in such cases as his. This is unquestionably a great gain at starting.

But my news is not at an end yet. Romayne is actually playing our game — he has resolved definitely to withdraw himself from the influence of Miss Eyrecourt! In another hour, he and Penrose will have left London. Their destination is kept a profound secret. All letters addressed to Romayne are to be sent to his bankers.

The motive for this sudden resolution is directly traceable to Lady Loring.

Her ladyship called at the hotel yesterday evening, and had a private interview with Romayne. Her object, no doubt, was to shake his resolution, and to make him submit himself again to Miss Eyrecourt's fascinations. What means of persuasion she used to effect this purpose is of course unknown to us. Penrose saw Romayne after her ladyship's departure, and describes him as violently agitated. I can quite understand it. His resolution to take refuge in

secret flight (it is really nothing less) speaks for itself as to the impression produced on him, and the danger from which, for the time at least, we have escaped.

Yes! I say 'for the time at least.' Don't let our reverend fathers suppose that the money expended on my private inquiries has been money thrown away. Where these miserable love affairs are concerned, women are daunted by no adverse circumstances and warned by no defeat. Romayne has left London, in dread of his own weakness — we must not forget that. The day may yet come when nothing will interpose between us and failure but my knowledge of events in Miss Eyrecourt's life.

For the present, there is no more to be said.

11

Stella Asserts Herself

Two days after Father Benwell had posted his letter to Rome, Lady Loring entered her husband's study, and asked eagerly if he had heard any news of Romayne.

Lord Loring shook his head. 'As I told you yesterday,' he said, 'the proprietor of the hotel can give me no information. I went myself this morning to the bankers, and saw the head partner. He offered to forward letters, but he could do no more. Until further notice, he was positively enjoined not to disclose Romayne's address to anybody. How does Stella bear it?'

'In the worst possible way,' Lady Loring answered. 'In silence.'

'Not a word even to you?'

'Not a word.'

At that reply, the servant interrupted them by announcing the arrival of a visitor, and presenting his card. Lord Loring started, and handed it to his wife. The card bore the name of 'Major Hynd,' and this line was added in pencil: — 'On business connected with Mr Romayne.'

'Show him in directly!' cried Lady Loring.

Lord Loring remonstrated. 'My dear! perhaps I had better see this gentleman alone?'

'Certainly not — unless you wish to drive me into committing an act of the most revolting

135

meanness! If you send me away I shall listen at the door.'

Major Hynd was shown in, and was duly presented to Lady Loring. After making the customary apologies, he said, 'I returned to London last night, expressly to see Romayne on a matter of importance. Failing to discover his present address at the hotel, I had the hope that your lordship might be able to direct me to our friend.'

'I am sorry to say I know no more than you do,' Lord Loring replied. 'Romayne's present address is a secret confided to his bankers, and to no one else. I will give you their names, if you wish to write to him.'

Major Hynd hesitated. 'I am not quite sure that it would be discreet to write to him, under the circumstances.'

Lady Loring could no longer keep silence. 'Is it possible, Major Hynd, to tell us what the circumstances are?' she asked. 'I am almost as old a friend of Romayne as my husband — and I am very anxious about him.'

The Major looked embarrassed. 'I can hardly answer your ladyship,' he said, 'without reviving painful recollections — '

Lady Loring's impatience interrupted the Major's apologies. 'Do you mean the duel?' she inquired.

Lord Loring interposed. 'I should tell you, Major Hynd, that Lady Loring is as well informed as I am of what happened at Boulogne, and of the deplorable result, so far as Romayne is concerned. If you still wish to speak to me

privately, I will ask you to accompany me into the next room.'

Major Hynd's embarrassment vanished. 'After what you tell me,' he said, 'I hope to be favoured with Lady Loring's advice. You both know that Romayne fought the fatal duel with a son of the French General who had challenged him. When we returned to England, we heard that the General and his family had been driven away from Boulogne by pecuniary difficulties. Romayne, against my advice, wrote to the surgeon who had been present at the duel, desiring that the General's place of retreat might be discovered, and expressing his wish to assist the family anonymously, as their Unknown Friend. The motive, of course, was, in his own words, 'to make some little atonement to the poor people whom he had wronged.' I thought it a rash proceeding at the time; and I am confirmed in my opinion by a letter from the surgeon, received yesterday. Will you kindly read it to Lady Loring?'

He handed the letter to Lord Loring. Translated from the French, it ran as follows: —

'Sir, — I am at last able to answer Mr Romayne's letter definitely, with the courteous assistance of the French Consul in London, to whom I applied when other means of investigation had produced no result.

'A week since, the General died. Circumstances connected with the burial expenses informed the Consul that he had taken refuge from his creditors, not in Paris as we supposed, but in

137

London. The address is, Number 10, Camp's Hill, Islington. I should also add that the General, for obvious reasons, lived in London under the assumed name of Marillac. It will be necessary, therefore, to inquire for his widow by the name of Madame Marillac.

'You will perhaps be surprised to find that I address these lines to you, instead of to Mr Romayne. The reason is soon told.

'I was acquainted with the late General — as you know — at a time when I was not aware of the company that he kept, or of the deplorable errors into which his love of gambling had betrayed him. Of his widow and his children I know absolutely nothing. Whether they have resisted the contaminating influence of the head of the household — or whether poverty and bad example combined have hopelessly degraded them — I cannot say. There is at least a doubt whether they are worthy of Mr Romayne's benevolent intentions towards them. As an honest man, I cannot feel this doubt, and reconcile it to my conscience to be the means, however indirectly, of introducing them to Mr Romayne. To your discretion I leave it to act for the best, after this warning.'

Lord Loring returned the letter to Major Hynd. 'I agree with you,' he said. 'It is more than doubtful whether you ought to communicate this information to Romayne.'

Lady Loring was not quite of her husband's opinion. 'While there is a doubt about these people,' she said, 'it seems only just to find

out what sort of character they bear in the neighbourhood. In your place, Major Hynd, I should apply to the person in whose house they live, or to the tradespeople whom they have employed.'

'I am obliged to leave London again to-day,' the Major replied; 'but on my return I will certainly follow your ladyship's advice.'

'And you will let us know the result?'

'With the greatest pleasure.'

Major Hynd took his leave. 'I think you will be responsible for wasting the Major's time,' said Lord Loring, when the visitor had retired.

'I think not,' said Lady Loring.

She rose to leave the room. 'Are you going out?' her husband asked.

'No. I am going upstairs to Stella.'

Lady Loring found Miss Eyrecourt in her own room. The little portrait of Romayne which she had drawn from recollection lay on the table before her. She was examining it with the closest attention.

'Well, Stella, and what does the portrait tell you?'

'What I knew before, Adelaide. There is nothing false and nothing cruel in that face.'

'And does the discovery satisfy you? For my part, I despise Romayne for hiding himself from us. Can you excuse him?'

Stella locked up the portrait in her writing-case. 'I can wait,' she said quietly.

This assertion of patience seemed to irritate Lady Loring. 'What is the matter with you this

morning?' she asked. 'You are more reserved than ever.'

'No; I am only out of spirits, Adelaide. I can't help thinking of that meeting with Winterfield. I feel as if some misfortune was hanging over my head.'

'Don't speak of that hateful man!' her ladyship exclaimed. 'I have something to tell you about Romayne. Are you completely absorbed in your presentiments of evil? or do you think you can listen to me?'

Stella's face answered for her. Lady Loring described the interview with Major Hynd in the minutest detail — including, by way of illustration, the Major's manners and personal appearance. 'He and Lord Loring,' she added, 'both think that Romayne will never hear the last of it if he allows these foreigners to look to him for money. Until something more is known about them, the letter is not to be forwarded.'

'I wish I had the letter!' cried Stella.

'Would you forward it to Romayne?'

'Instantly! Does it matter whether these poor French people are worthy of his generosity? If it restores his tranquillity to help them, who cares whether they deserve the help? They are not even to know who it is that assists them — Romayne is to be their unknown friend. It is he, not they, whom we have to think of — his peace of mind is everything; their merit is nothing. I say it's cruel to *him* to keep him in ignorance of what has happened. Why didn't you take the letter away from Major Hynd?'

'Gently, Stella! The Major is going to make

inquiries about the widow and children when he returns to London.'

'When he returns!' Stella repeated indignantly 'Who knows what the poor wretches may be suffering in the interval, and what Romayne may feel if he ever hears of it? Tell me the address again — it was somewhere in Islington, you said.'

'Why do you want to know it?' Lady Loring asked. 'You are not going to write to Romayne yourself?'

'I am going to think, before I do anything. If you can't trust my discretion, Adelaide, you have only to say so!'

It was spoken sharply. Lady Loring's reply betrayed a certain loss of temper on her side. 'Manage your own affairs, Stella — I have done meddling with them.' Her unlucky visit to Romayne at the hotel had been a subject of dispute between the two friends — and this referred to it. 'You shall have the address,' my lady added in her grandest manner. She wrote it on a piece of paper, and left the room.

Easily irritated, Lady Loring had the merit of being easily appeased. That meanest of all vices, the vice of sulkiness, had no existence in her nature. In five minutes she regretted her little outburst of irritability. For five minutes more she waited, on the chance that Stella might be the first to seek a reconciliation. The interval passed, and nothing happened. 'Have I really offended her?' Lady Loring asked herself. The next moment she was on her way back to Stella.

The room was empty. She rang the bell for the maid.

'Where is Miss Eyrecourt?'

'Gone out, my lady.'

'Did she leave no message?'

'No, my lady. She went away in a great hurry.'

Lady Loring at once drew the conclusion that Stella had rashly taken the affair of the General's family into her own hands. Was it possible to say how this most imprudent proceeding might end? After hesitating and reflecting, and hesitating again, Lady Loring's anxiety got beyond her control. She not only decided on following Stella, but, in the excess of her nervous apprehension, she took one of the men-servants with her, in case of emergency!

12

The General's Family

Not always remarkable for arriving at just
conclusions, Lady Loring had drawn the right
inference this time. Stella had stopped the first
cab that passed her, and had directed the driver
to Camp's Hill, Islington.

The aspect of the miserable little street, closed
at one end, and swarming with dirty children
quarrelling over their play, daunted her for the
moment. Even the cabman, drawing up at the
entrance to the street, expressed his opinion that
it was a queer sort of place for a young lady to
venture into alone. Stella thought of Romayne.
Her firm persuasion that she was helping him
to perform an act of mercy, which was (to his
mind) an act of atonement as well, roused her
courage. She boldly approached the open door of
No. 10, and knocked on it with her parasol.

The tangled grey hair and grimy face of a
hideous old woman showed themselves slowly
at the end of the passage, rising from the
strong-smelling obscurity of the kitchen regions.
'What do you want?' said the half-seen witch
of the London slums. 'Does Madame Marillac
live here?' Stella asked. 'Do you mean the
foreigner?' 'Yes.' 'Second floor.' With those
instructions the upper half of the witch sank
and vanished. Stella gathered her skirts together,

and ascended a filthy flight of stairs for the first time in her life.

Coarse voices, shameless language, gross laughter behind the closed doors of the first floor hurried her on her way to the rooms on the higher flight. Here there was a change for the better — here, at least, there was silence. She knocked at the door on the landing of the second floor. A gentle voice answered, in French, 'Entrez' — then quickly substituted the English equivalent, 'Come in.' Stella opened the door.

The wretchedly furnished room was scrupulously clean. Above the truckle-bed, a cheap little image of the Virgin was fastened to the wall, with some faded artificial flowers arranged above it in the form of a wreath. Two women, in dresses of coarse black stuff, sat at a small round table, working at the same piece of embroidery. The elder of the two rose when the visitor entered the room. Her worn and weary face still showed the remains of beauty in its finely proportioned parts — her dim eyes rested on Stella with an expression of piteous entreaty. 'Have you come for the work, madam?' she asked, in English, spoken with a strong foreign accent. 'Pray forgive me; I have not finished it yet.'

The second of the two workwomen suddenly looked up.

She, too, was wan and frail; but her eyes were bright; her movements still preserved the elasticity of youth. Her likeness to the elder woman proclaimed their relationship, even before she spoke. 'Ah! it's my fault!' she burst out passionately in French. 'I was

144

hungry and tired, and I slept hours longer than I ought. My mother was too kind to wake me and set me to work. I am a selfish wretch — and my mother is an angel!' She dashed away the tears gathering in her eyes, and proudly, fiercely, resumed her work.

Stella hastened to reassure them, the moment she could make herself heard. 'Indeed, I have nothing to do with the work,' she said, speaking in French, so that they might the more readily understand her. 'I came here, Madame Marillac — if you will not be offended with me, for plainly owning it — to offer you some little help.'

'Charity?' asked the daughter, looking up again sternly from her needle.

'Sympathy,' Stella answered gently.

The girl resumed her work. 'I beg your pardon,' she said; 'I shall learn to submit to my lot in time.'

The quiet long-suffering mother placed a chair for Stella. 'You have a kind beautiful face, Miss,' she said; 'and I am sure you will make allowances for my poor girl. I remember the time when I was as quick to feel as she is. May I ask how you came to hear of us?'

'I hope you will excuse me,' Stella replied. 'I am not at liberty to answer that question.'

The mother said nothing. The daughter asked sharply, 'Why not?'

Stella addressed her answer to the mother. 'I come from a person who desires to be of service to you as an unknown friend,' she said.

The wan face of the widow suddenly

145

brightened. 'Oh!' she exclaimed, 'has my brother heard of the General's death? and has he forgiven me my marriage at last?'

'No, no!' Stella interposed; 'I must not mislead you. The person whom I represent is no relation of yours.'

Even in spite of this positive assertion, the poor woman held desperately to the hope that had been roused in her. 'The name by which you know me may mislead you,' she suggested anxiously. 'My late husband assumed the name in his exile here. Perhaps, if I told you — '

The daughter stopped her there. 'My dear mother, leave this to me.' The widow sighed resignedly, and resumed her work. 'Madame Marillac will do very well as a name,' the girl continued, turning to Stella, 'until we know something more of each other. I suppose you are well acquainted with the person whom you represent?'

'Certainly, or I should not be here.'

'You know the person's family connections, in that case?' and you can say for certain whether they are French connections or not?'

'I can say for certain,' Stella answered, 'that they are English connections. I represent a friend who feels kindly towards Madame Marillac; nothing more.'

'You see, mother, you were mistaken. Bear it as bravely, dear, as you have borne other trials.' Saying this very tenderly, she addressed herself once more to Stella, without attempting to conceal the accompanying change in her manner to coldness and distrust. 'One of us

must speak plainly,' she said. 'Our few friends are nearly as poor as we are, and they are all French. I tell you positively that we have no English friends. How has this anonymous benefactor been informed of our poverty? You are a stranger to us — *you* cannot have given the information?'

Stella's eyes were now opened to the awkward position in which she had placed herself. She met the difficulty boldly, still upheld by the conviction that she was serving a purpose cherished by Romayne. 'You had good reasons, no doubt, mademoiselle, when you advised your mother to conceal her true name,' she rejoined. 'Be just enough to believe that your 'anonymous benefactor' has good reasons for concealment too.'

It was well said, and it encouraged Madame Marillac to take Stella's part. 'My dear Blanche, you speak rather harshly to this good young lady,' she said to her daughter. 'You have only to look at her, and to see that she means well.'

Blanche took up her needle again, with dogged submission. 'If we *are* to accept charity, mother, I should like to know the hand that gives it,' she answered. 'I will say no more.'

'When you are as old as I am, my dear,' rejoined Madame Marillac, 'you will not think quite so positively as you think now. I have learnt some hard lessons,' she proceeded, turning to Stella, 'and I hope I am the better for them. My life has not been a happy one — '

'Your life has been a martydom!' said the girl, breaking out again in spite of herself. 'Oh, my

147

father! my father!' She pushed aside the work, and hid her face in her hands.

The gentle mother spoke severely for the first time. 'Respect your father's memory!' she said. Blanche trembled and kept silence. 'I have no false pride,' Madame Marillac continued. 'I own that we are miserably poor; and I thank you, my dear young lady, for your kind intentions towards us, without embarrassing you by any inquiries. We manage to live. While my eyes last, our work helps to support us. My good eldest daughter has some employment as a teacher of music, and contributes her little share to assist our poor household. I don't distrust you — I only say, let us try a little longer if we cannot help ourselves.'

She had barely pronounced the last words, when a startling interruption led to consequences which the persons present had not foreseen. A shrill wailing voice suddenly pierced through the flimsy partition which divided the front room and the back room. 'Bread!' cried the voice in French; 'I'm hungry. Bread! bread!'

The daughter started to her feet. 'Think of his betraying us at this moment!' she exclaimed indignantly. The mother rose in silence, and opened a cupboard. Its position was opposite to the place in which Stella was sitting. She saw two or three knives and forks, some cups and saucers and plates, and a folded table-cloth. Nothing else appeared on the shelves; not even the stray crust of bread for which the poor woman had been looking. 'Go, my dear, and quiet your brother,' she said — and closed the

cupboard door again as patiently as ever.

Stella opened her pocket-book when Blanche had left the room. 'For God's sake, take something!' she cried. 'I offer it with the sincerest respect — I offer it as a loan.'

Madame Marillac gently signed to Stella to close the pocket-book again. 'That kind heart of yours must not be distressed about trifles,' she said. 'The baker will trust us until we get the money for our work — and my daughter knows it. If you can tell me nothing else, my dear, will you tell me your Christian name? It is painful to me to speak to you quite as a stranger.'

Stella at once complied with the request. Madame Marillac smiled as she repeated the name.

'There is almost another tie between us,' she said. 'We have your name in France — it speaks with a familiar sound to me in this strange place. Dear Miss Stella, when my poor boy startled you by that cry for food he recalled to me the saddest of all my anxieties. When I think of *him*, I should be tempted if my better sense did not restrain me — No! no! put back the pocket-book. I am incapable of the shameless audacity of borrowing a sum of money which I could never repay. Let me tell you what my trouble is, and you will understand that I am in earnest. I had two sons, Miss Stella. The elder — the most lovable, the most affectionate of my children — was killed in a duel.'

The sudden disclosure drew a cry of sympathy from Stella, which she was not mistress enough of herself to repress. Now for the first time she

understood the remorse that tortured Romayne, as she had not understood it when Lady Loring had told her the terrible story of the duel. Attributing the effect produced on her to the sensitive nature of a young woman, Madame Marillac innocently added to Stella's distress by making excuses.

'I am sorry to have frightened you, my dear,' she said. 'In your happy country such a dreadful death as my son's is unknown. I am obliged to mention it, or you might not understand what I have still to say. Perhaps I had better not go on?'

Stella roused herself. 'Yes! yes!' she answered eagerly. 'Pray go on!'

'My son in the next room,' the widow resumed, 'is only fourteen years old. It has pleased God sorely to afflict a harmless creature. He has not been in his right mind since — since the miserable day when he followed the duellists, and saw his brother's death. Oh! you are turning pale! How thoughtless, how cruel of me! I ought to have remembered that such horrors as these have never overshadowed your happy life!'

Struggling to recover her self-control, Stella tried to reassure Madame Marillac by a gesture. The voice which she had heard in the next room was — as she now knew — the voice that haunted Romayne. Not the words that had pleaded hunger and called for bread — but those other words, 'Assassin! assassin! where are you?' — rang in her ears. She entreated Madame Marillac to break the unendurable interval of silence. The widow's calm voice had a soothing

influence which she was eager to feel. 'Go on!' she repeated. 'Pray go on!'

'I ought not to lay all the blame of my boy's affliction on the duel,' said Madame Marillac. 'In childhood, his mind never grew with his bodily growth. His brother's death may have only hurried the result which was sooner or later but too sure to come. You need feel no fear of him. He is never violent — and he is the most beautiful of my children. Would you like to see him?'

'No! I would rather hear you speak of him. Is he not conscious of his own misfortune?'

'For weeks together, Stella — I am sure I may call you Stella? — he is quite calm; you would see no difference outwardly between him and other boys. Unhappily, it is just at those times that a spirit of impatience seems to possess him. He watches his opportunity, and, however careful we may be, he is cunning enough to escape our vigilance.'

'Do you mean that he leaves you and his sisters?'

'Yes, that is what I mean. For nearly two months past he has been away from us. Yesterday only, his return relieved us from a state of suspense which I cannot attempt to describe. We don't know where he has been, or in the company of what persons he has passed the time of his absence. No persuasion will induce him to speak to us on the subject. This morning we listened while he was talking to himself.'

Was it part of the boy's madness to repeat the words which still tormented Romayne? Stella

151

asked if he ever spoke of the duel.

'Never! He seems to have lost all memory of it. We only heard, this morning, one or two unconnected words — something about a woman, and then more that appeared to allude to some person's death. Last night I was with him when he went to bed, and I found that he had something to conceal from me. He let me fold all his clothes, as usual, except his waistcoat — and that he snatched away from me, and put it under his pillow. We have no hope of being able to examine the waistcoat without his knowledge. His sleep is like the sleep of a dog; if you only approach him, he wakes instantly. Forgive me for troubling you with these trifling details, only interesting to ourselves. You will at least understand the constant anxiety that we suffer.'

'In your unhappy position,' said Stella, 'I should try to resign myself to parting with him — I mean to placing him under medical care.'

The mother's face saddened. 'I have inquired about it,' she answered. 'He must pass a night in the workhouse before he can be received as a pauper lunatic in a public asylum. Oh, my dear, I am afraid there is some pride still left in me! He is my only son now; his father was a General in the French army; I was brought up among people of good blood and breeding — I can't take my own boy to the workhouse!'

Stella understood her. 'I feel for you with all my heart,' she said. 'Place him privately, dear Madame Marillac, under skilful and kind

control — and let me, do let me, open the pocket-book again.'

The widow steadily refused even to look at the pocket-book. 'Perhaps,' Stella persisted, 'you don't know of a private asylum that would satisfy you?'

'My dear, I do know of such a place! The good doctor who attended my husband in his last illness told me of it. A friend of his receives a certain number of poor people into his house, and charges no more than the cost of maintaining them. An unattainable sum to *me!* There is the temptation that I spoke of. The help of a few pounds I might accept, if I fell ill, because I might afterwards pay it back. But a larger sum — never!'

She rose, as if to end the interview. Stella tried every means of persuasion that she could think of, and tried in vain. The friendly dispute between them might have been prolonged, if they had not both been silenced by another interruption from the next room.

This time, it was not only endurable, it was even welcome. The poor boy was playing the air of a French vaudeville on a pipe or flageolet. 'Now he is happy!' said the mother. 'He is a born musician; do come and see him!' An idea struck Stella. She overcame the inveterate reluctance in her to see the boy so fatally associated with the misery of Romayne's life. As Madame Marillac led the way to the door of communication between the rooms, she quickly took from her pocket-book the bank-notes with which she had provided herself, and folded

them so that they could be easily concealed in her hand.

She followed the widow into the little room.

The boy was sitting on his bed. He laid down his flageolet and bowed to Stella. His long silky hair flowed to his shoulders. But one betrayal of a deranged mind presented itself in his delicate face — his large soft eyes had the glassy vacant look which it is impossible to mistake. 'Do you like music, mademoiselle?' he asked gently. Stella asked him to play his little vaudeville air again. He proudly complied with the request. His sister seemed to resent the presence of a stranger. 'The work is at a standstill,' she said — and passed into the front room. Her mother followed her as far as the door, to give her some necessary directions. Stella seized her opportunity. She put the bank-notes into the pocket of the boy's jacket, and whispered to him, 'Give them to your mother when I have gone away.' Under those circumstances, she felt sure that Madame Marillac would yield to the temptation. She could resist much — but she could not resist her son.

The boy nodded, to show that he understood her. The moment after, he laid down his flageolet with an expression of surprise.

'You are trembling!' he said. 'Are you frightened?'

She *was* frightened. The mere sense of touching him had made her shudder. Did she feel a vague presentiment of some evil to come from that momentary association with him?

Madame Marillac, turning away again from

her daughter, noticed Stella's agitation. 'Surely, my poor boy doesn't alarm you?' she said. Before Stella could answer, some one outside knocked at the door. Lady Loring's servant appeared, charged with a carefully-worded message. 'If you please, Miss, a friend is waiting for you below.' Any excuse for departure was welcome to Stella at that moment. She promised to call at the house again in a few days. Madame Marillac kissed her on the forehead as she took leave. Her nerves were still shaken by that momentary contact with the boy. Descending the stairs, she trembled so that she was obliged to hold by the servant's arm. She was not naturally timid. What did it mean?

Lady Loring's carriage was waiting at the entrance of the street, with all the children in the neighbourhood assembled to admire it. She impulsively forestalled the servant in opening the carriage door. 'Come in!' she cried. 'Oh, Stella, you don't know how you have frightened me! Good heavens, you look frightened yourself! From what wretches have I rescued you? Take my smelling bottle, and tell me all about it.'

The fresh air, and the reassuring presence of her old friend, revived Stella. She was able to describe her interview with the General's family, and to answer the inevitable inquiries which the narrative called forth. Lady Loring's last question was the most important of the series:- 'What are you going to do about Romayne?'

'I am going to write to him the moment we get home.'

The answer seemed to alarm Lady Loring. 'You won't betray me?' she said.

'What do you mean?'

'You won't let Romayne discover that I have told you about the duel?'

'Certainly not. You shall see my letter before I send it to be forwarded.'

Tranquillised so far, Lady Loring bethought herself next of Major Hynd. 'Can we tell him what you have done?' her ladyship asked.

'Of course we can tell him,' Stella replied. 'I shall conceal nothing from Lord Loring, and I shall beg your good husband to write to the Major. He need only say that I have made the necessary inquiries, after being informed of the circumstances by you, and that I have communicated the favourable result to Mr Romayne.'

'It's easy enough to write the letter, my dear. But it's not so easy to say what Major Hynd may think of you.'

'Does it matter to me what Major Hynd thinks?'

Lady Loring looked at Stella with a malicious smile. 'Are you equally indifferent,' she said, 'to what Romayne's opinion of your conduct may be?'

Stella's colour rose. 'Try to be serious, Adelaide, when you speak to me of Romayne,' she answered gravely. 'His good opinion of me is the breath of my life.'

An hour later, the important letter to Romayne was written. Stella scrupulously informed him of all that had happened — with two necessary

omissions. In the first place, nothing was said of the widow's reference to her son's death, and of the effect produced by it on his younger brother. The boy was simply described as being of weak intellect, and as requiring to be kept under competent control. In the second place, Romayne was left to infer that ordinary motives of benevolence were the only motives, on his part, known to Miss Eyrecourt.

The letter ended in these lines:-

'If I have taken an undue liberty in venturing, unasked, to appear as your representative, I can only plead that I meant well. It seemed to me to be hard on these poor people, and not just to you in your absence, to interpose any needless delays in carrying out those kind intentions of yours, which had no doubt been properly considered beforehand. In forming your opinion of my conduct, pray remember that I have been careful not to compromise you in any way. You are only known to Madame Marillac as a compassionate person who offers to help her, and who wishes to give that help anonymously. If, notwithstanding this, you disapprove of what I have done, I must not conceal that it will grieve and humiliate me — I have been so eager to be of use to you, when others appeared to hesitate. I must find my consolation in remembering that I have become acquainted with one of the sweetest and noblest of women, and that I have helped to preserve her afflicted son from dangers in the future which I cannot presume to estimate. You will complete what I have only begun. Be forbearing and kind to me if I have innocently

157

offended in this matter — and I shall gratefully remember the day when I took it on myself to be Mr Romayne's almoner.'

Lady Loring read these concluding sentences twice over.

'I think the end of your letter will have its effect on him,' she said.

'If it brings me a kind letter in reply,' Stella answered, 'it will have all the effect I hope for.'

'If it does anything,' Lady Loring rejoined, 'it will do more than that.'

'What more can it do?'

'My dear, it can bring Romayne back to you.'

Those hopeful words seemed rather to startle Stella than to encourage her.

'Bring him back to me?' she repeated. 'Oh, Adelaide, I wish I could think as you do!'

'Send the letter to the post,' said Lady Loring, 'and we shall see.'

13

Father Benwell's Correspondence

I

Arthur Penrose to Father Benwell.

Reverend and Dear Father, — When I last had the honour of seeing you, I received your instructions to report, by letter, the result of my conversations on religion with Mr Romayne.

As events have turned out, it is needless to occupy your time by dwelling at any length on this subject, in writing. Mr Romayne has been strongly impressed by the excellent books which I have introduced to his notice. He raises certain objections, which I have done my best to meet; and he promises to consider my arguments with his closest attention, in the time to come. I am happier in the hope of restoring his mental tranquillity — in other and worthier words, of effecting his conversion — than I can tell you in any words of mine. I respect and admire, I may almost say I love, Mr Romayne.

The details which are wanting in this brief report of progress I shall have the privilege of personally relating to you. Mr Romayne no longer desires to conceal himself from his friends. He received a letter this morning which has changed all his plans, and has decided him on immediately returning to London. I am not

acquainted with the contents of the letter, or with the name of the writer; but I am pleased, for Mr Romayne's sake, to see that the reading of it has made him happy.

By to-morrow evening I hope to present my respects to you.

II

Mr Bitrake to Father Benwell.

Sir, — The inquiries which I have instituted at your request have proved successful in one respect.

I am in a position to tell you that events in Mr Winterfield's life have unquestionably connected him with the young lady named Miss Stella Eyrecourt.

The attendant circumstances, however, are not so easy to discover. Judging by the careful report of the person whom I employ, there must have been serious reasons, in this case, for keeping facts secret and witnesses out of the way. I mention this, not to discourage you, but to prepare you for delays that may occur on our way to discovery.

Be pleased to preserve your confidence in me, and to give me time — and I answer for the result.

Book The Second

1

The Sandwich Dance

A fine spring, after a winter of unusual severity, promised well for the prospects of the London season.

Among the social entertainments of the time, general curiosity was excited, in the little sphere which absurdly describes itself under the big name of Society, by the announcement of a party to be given by Lady Loring, bearing the quaint title of a Sandwich Dance. The invitations were issued at an unusually early hour; and it was understood that nothing so solid and so commonplace as the customary supper was to be offered to the guests. In a word, Lady Loring's ball was designed as a bold protest against late hours and heavy mid-night meals. The younger people were all in favour of the proposed reform. Their elders declined to give an opinion before-hand.

In the small inner circle of Lady Loring's most intimate friends, it was whispered that an innovation in the matter of refreshments was contemplated, which would put the tolerant principles of the guests to a severe test. Miss Notman, the housekeeper, politely threatening

161

retirement on a small annuity, since the memorable affair of the oyster omelette, decided on carrying out her design, when she heard that there was to be no supper. 'My attachment to the family can bear a great deal,' she said. 'But when Lady Loring deliberately gives a ball, without a supper, I must hide my head somewhere — and it had better be out of the house!' Taking Miss Notman as representative of a class, the reception of the coming experiment looked, to say the least of it, doubtful.

On the appointed evening, the guests made one agreeable discovery when they entered the reception rooms. They were left perfectly free to amuse themselves as they liked.

The drawing-rooms were given up to dancing; the picture gallery was devoted to chamber music. Chess-players and card-players found remote and quiet rooms especially prepared for them. People who cared for nothing but talking were accommodated to perfection in a sphere of their own. And lovers (in earnest or not in earnest) discovered, in a dimly-lit conservatory with many recesses, that ideal of discreet retirement which combines solitude and society under one roof.

But the ordering of the refreshments failed, as had been foreseen, to share in the approval conferred on the arrangement of the rooms. The first impression was unfavourable. Lady Loring, however, knew enough of human nature to leave results to two potent allies — experience and time.

Excepting the conservatory, the astonished

guests could go nowhere without discovering tables prettily decorated with flowers, and bearing hundreds of little pure white china plates, loaded with nothing but sandwiches. All varieties of opinion were consulted. People of ordinary tastes, who liked to know what they were eating, could choose conventional beef or ham, encased in thin slices of bread of a delicate flavour quite new to them. Other persons, less easily pleased, were tempted by sandwiches of *pâté de foie gras*, and by exquisite combinations of chicken and truffles, reduced to a creamy pulp which clung to the bread like butter. Foreigners, making experiments, and not averse to garlic, discovered the finest sausages of Germany and Italy transformed into English sandwiches. Anchovies and sardines appealed, in the same unexpected way, to men who desired to create an artificial thirst — after having first ascertained that the champagne was something to be fondly remembered and regretted, at other parties, to the end of the season. The hospitable profusion of the refreshments was all-pervading and inexhaustible. Wherever the guests might be, or however they were amusing themselves, there were the pretty little white plates perpetually tempting them. People eat as they had never eaten before, and even the inveterate English prejudice against anything new was conquered at last. Universal opinion declared the Sandwich Dance to be an admirable idea, perfectly carried out.

Many of the guests paid their hostess the compliment of arriving at the early hour

mentioned in the invitations. One of them was Major Hynd. Lady Loring took her first opportunity of speaking to him apart.

'I hear you were a little angry,' she said, 'when you were told that Miss Eyrecourt had taken your inquiries out of your hands.'

'I thought it rather a bold proceeding, Lady Loring,' the Major replied. 'But as the General's widow turned out to be a lady, in the best sense of the word, Miss Eyrecourt's romantic adventure has justified itself. I wouldn't recommend her to run the same risk a second time.'

'I suppose you know what Romayne thinks of it?'

'Not yet. I have been too busy to call on him since I have been in town. Pardon me, Lady Loring, who is that beautiful creature in the pale yellow dress? Surely I have seen her somewhere before?'

'That beautiful creature, Major, is the bold young lady of whose conduct you don't approve.'

'Miss Eyrecourt?'

'Yes.'

'I retract everything I said!' cried the Major, quite shamelessly. 'Such a woman as that may do anything. She is looking this way. Pray introduce me.'

The Major was introduced, and Lady Loring returned to her guests.'I think we have met before, Major Hynd,' said Stella.

Her voice supplied the missing link in the Major's memory of events. Remembering how

164

she had looked at Romayne on the deck of the steamboat, he began dimly to understand Miss Eyrecourt's otherwise incomprehensible anxiety to be of use to the General's family. 'I remember perfectly,' he answered. 'It was on the passage from Boulogne to Folkestone — and my friend was with me. You and he have no doubt met since that time?' He put the question as a mere formality. The unexpressed thought in him was, 'Another of them in love with Romayne! and nothing, as usual, likely to come of it.'

'I hope you have forgiven me for going to Camp's Hill in your place,' said Stella.

'I ought to be grateful to you,' the Major rejoined. 'No time has been lost in relieving these poor people — and your powers of persuasion have succeeded, where mine might have failed. Has Romayne been to see them himself since his return to London?'

'No. He desires to remain unknown; and he is kindly content, for the present, to be represented by me.'

'For the present?' Major Hynd repeated.

A faint flush passed over her delicate complexion. 'I have succeeded,' she resumed, 'in inducing Madame Marillac to accept the help offered through me to her son. The poor creature is safe, under kind superintendence, in a private asylum. So far, I can do no more.'

'Will the mother accept nothing?'

'Nothing, either for herself or her daughter, so long as they can work. I cannot tell you how patiently and beautifully she speaks of her hard lot. But her health may give way — and it is

165

possible, before long, that I may leave London.'
She paused; the flush deepened on her face. 'The
failure of the mother's health may happen in my
absence,' she continued; 'and Mr Romayne will
ask you to look after the family, from time to
time, while I am away.'

'I will do it with pleasure, Miss Eyrecourt. Is
Romayne likely to be here tonight?'

She smiled brightly, and looked away. The
Major's curiosity was excited — he looked in the
same direction. There was Romayne, entering
the room, to answer for himself.

What was the attraction which drew the
unsocial student to an evening party? Major
Hynd's eyes were on the watch. When Romayne
and Stella shook hands, the attraction stood self-
revealed to him, in Miss Eyrecourt. Recalling the
momentary confusion which she had betrayed,
when she spoke of possibly leaving London, and
of Romayne's plans for supplying her place as his
almoner, the Major, with military impatience of
delays, jumped to a conclusion. 'I was wrong,'
he thought; 'my impenetrable friend is touched
in the right place at last. When the splendid
creature in yellow leaves London, the name on
her luggage will be Mrs Romayne.'

'You are looking quite another man, Romayne!'
he said mischievously, 'since we met last.'

Stella gently moved away, leaving them to
talk freely. Romayne took no advantage of
the circumstance to admit his old friend to
his confidence. Whatever relations might really
exist between Miss Eyrecourt and himself were
evidently kept secret thus far. 'My health has

been a little better lately,' was the only reply he made.

The Major dropped his voice to a whisper.

'Have you not had any return — ?' he began.

Romayne stopped him there. 'I don't want my infirmities made public,' he whispered back irritably. 'Look at the people all round us! When I tell you I have been better lately, *you* ought to know what it means.'

'Any discoverable reason for the improvement?' persisted the Major, still bent on getting evidence in support of his own private conclusions.

'None!' Romayne answered sharply.

But Major Hynd was not to be discouraged by sharp replies. 'Miss Eyrecourt and I have been recalling our first meeting on board the steamboat,' he went on. 'Do you remember how indifferent you were to that beautiful person when I asked you if you knew her? I'm glad to see that you show better taste to-night. I wish *I* knew her well enough to shake hands as you did.'

'Hynd! When a young man talks nonsense, his youth is his excuse. At your time of life, you have passed the excusable age — even in the estimation of your friends.'

With those words Romayne turned away. The incorrigible Major instantly met the reproof inflicted on him with a smart answer. 'Remember,' he said, 'that I was the first of your friends to wish you happiness!' He, too, turned away — in the direction of the champagne and the sandwiches.

Meanwhile, Stella had discovered Penrose, lost in the brilliant assemblage of guests, standing alone in a corner. It was enough for her that Romayne's secretary was also Romayne's friend. Passing by titled and celebrated personages, all anxious to speak to her, she joined the shy, nervous, sad-looking little man, and did all she could to set him at his ease.

'I am afraid, Mr Penrose, this is not a very attractive scene to you.' Having said those kind words, she paused. Penrose was looking at her confusedly, but with an expression of interest which was new to her experience of him. 'Has Romayne told him?' she wondered inwardly.

'It is a very beautiful scene, Miss Eyrecourt,' he said, in his low quiet tones.

'Did you come here with Mr Romayne?' she asked.

'Yes. It was by his advice that I accepted the invitation with which Lady Loring has honoured me. I am sadly out of place in such an assembly as this — but I would make far greater sacrifices to please Mr Romayne.'

She smiled kindly. Attachment so artlessly devoted to the man she loved, pleased and touched her. In her anxiety to discover a subject which might interest him, she overcame her antipathy to the spiritual director of the household. 'Is Father Benwell coming to us to-night?' she inquired.

'He will certainly be here, Miss Eyrecourt, if he can get back to London in time.'

'Has he been long away?'

'Nearly a week.'

Not knowing what else to say, she still paid Penrose the compliment of feigning an interest in Father Benwell.

'Has he a long journey to make in returning to London?' she asked.

'Yes — all the way from Devonshire.'

'From South Devonshire?'

'No. North Devonshire — Clovelly.'

The smile suddenly left her face. She put another question — without quite concealing the effort that it cost her, or the anxiety with which she waited for the reply.

'I know something of the neighbourhood of Clovelly,' she said. 'I wonder whether Father Benwell is visiting any friends of mine there?'

'I am not able to say, Miss Eyrecourt. The reverend Father's letters are forwarded to the hotel — I know no more than that.'

With a gentle inclination of her head, she turned towards other guests — looked back — and, with a last little courteous attention offered to him, said, 'If you like music, Mr Penrose, I advise you to go to the picture gallery. They are going to play a Quartette by Mozart.'

Penrose thanked her, noticing that her voice and manner had become strangely subdued. She made her way back to the room in which the hostess received her guests. Lady Loring was, for the moment, alone, resting on a sofa. Stella stooped over her, and spoke in cautiously-lowered tones.

'If Father Benwell comes here to-night,' she

169

said, 'try to find out what he has been doing at Clovelly.'

'Clovelly?' Lady Loring repeated. 'Is that the village near Winterfield's house?'

'Yes.'

2

The Question of Marriage

As Stella answered Lady Loring, she was smartly tapped on the shoulder by an eager guest with a fan.

The guest was a very little woman, with twinkling eyes and a perpetual smile. Nature, corrected by powder and paint, was liberally displayed in her arms, her bosom, and the upper part of her back. Such clothes as she wore, defective perhaps in quantity, were in quality absolutely perfect. More adorable colour, shape, and workmanship never appeared, even in a milliner's picture-book. Her light hair was dressed with a fringe and ringlets, on the pattern which the portraits of the time of Charles the Second have made familiar to us. There was nothing exactly young or exactly old about her except her voice, which betrayed a faint hoarseness, attributable possibly to exhaustion produced by untold years of incessant talking. It might be added that she was as active as a squirrel and as playful as a kitten. But the lady must be treated with a certain forbearance of tone, for this good reason — she was Stella's mother.

Stella turned quickly at the tap of the fan. 'Mamma!' she exclaimed, 'how you startle me!'

'My dear child,' said Mrs Eyrecourt, 'you are

constitutionally indolent, and you want startling. Go into the next room directly. Mr Romayne is looking for you.'

Stella drew back a step, and eyed her mother in blank surprise. 'Is it possible that you know him?' she asked.

'Mr Romayne doesn't go into society, or we should have met long since,' Mrs Eyrecourt replied. 'He is a striking person — and I noticed him when he shook hands with you. That was quite enough for me. I have just introduced myself to him as your mother. He was a little stately and stiff, but most charming when he knew who I was. I volunteered to find you. He was quite astonished. I think he took me for your elder sister. Not the least like each other — are we, Lady Loring? She takes after her poor dear father. *He* was constitutionally indolent. My sweet child, rouse yourself. You have drawn a prize in the great lottery at last. If ever a man was in love, Mr Romayne is that man. I am a physiognomist, Lady Loring, and I see the passions in the face. Oh, Stella, what a property! Vange Abbey. I once drove that way when I was visiting in the neighbourhood. Superb! And another fortune (twelve thousand a year and a villa at Highgate) since the death of his aunt. And my daughter may be mistress of this if she only plays her cards properly. What a compensation after all that we suffered through that monster, Winterfield!'

'Mamma! Pray don't — !'

'Stella, I will *not* be interrupted, when I am speaking to you for your own good. I don't

know a more provoking person, Lady Loring, than my daughter — on certain occasions. And yet I love her. I would go through fire and water for my beautiful child. Only last week I was at a wedding, and I thought of Stella. The church was crammed to the doors! A hundred at the wedding breakfast! The bride's lace — there! no language can describe it. Ten bridesmaids, in blue and silver. Reminded me of the ten virgins. Only the proportion of foolish ones, this time, was certainly more than five. However, they looked well. The Archbishop proposed the health of the bride and bridegroom; so sweetly pathetic. Some of us cried. I thought of my daughter. Oh, if I could live to see Stella the central attraction, so to speak, of such a wedding as that. Only I would have twelve bridesmaids at least, and beat the blue and silver with green and gold. Trying to the complexion, you will say. But there are artificial improvements. At least, I am told so. What a house this would be — a broad hint, isn't it, dear Lady Loring? — what a house for a wedding, with the drawing-room to assemble in and the picture gallery for the breakfast. I know the Archbishop. My darling, he shall marry you. Why *don't* you go into the next room? Ah, that constitutional indolence. If you only had my energy, as I used to say to your poor father. *Will* you go? Yes, dear Lady Loring, I should like a glass of champagne, and another of those delicious chicken sandwiches. If you don't go, Stella, I shall forget every consideration of propriety, and, big as you are, I shall push you out.'

173

Stella yielded to necessity. 'Keep her quiet, if you can,' she whispered to Lady Loring, in the moment of silence that followed. Even Mrs Eyrecourt was not able to talk while she was drinking champagne.

In the next room Stella found Romayne. He looked careworn and irritable, but brightened directly when she approached him.

'My mother has been speaking to you,' she said. 'I am afraid — '

He stopped her there. 'She *is* your mother,' he interposed kindly. 'Don't think that I am ungrateful enough to forget that.'

She took his arm, and looked at him with all her heart in her eyes. 'Come into a quieter room,' she whispered.

Romayne led her away. Neither of them noticed Penrose as they left the room.

He had not moved since Stella had spoken to him. There he remained in his corner, absorbed in thought — and not in happy thought, as his face would have plainly betrayed to anyone who had cared to look at him. His eyes sadly followed the retiring figures of Stella and Romayne. The colour rose on his haggard cheeks. Like most men who are accustomed to live alone, he had the habit, when he was strongly excited, of speaking to himself. 'No,' he said, as the unacknowledged lovers disappeared through the door, 'it is an insult to ask me to do it!' He turned the other way, escaped Lady Loring's notice in the reception-room, and left the house.

Romayne and Stella passed through the card-room and the chess-room, turned into a corridor,

174

and entered the conservatory.

For the first time the place was a solitude. The air of a newly-invented dance, faintly audible through the open windows of the ball-room above, had proved an irresistible temptation. Those who knew the dance were eager to exhibit themselves. Those who had only heard of it were equally anxious to look on and learn. Even towards the latter end of the nineteenth century the youths and maidens of Society can still be in earnest — when the object in view is a new dance.

What would Major Hynd have said if he had seen Romayne turn into one of the recesses of the conservatory, in which there was a seat which just held two? But the Major had forgotten his years and his family, and he too was one of the spectators in the ball-room.

'I wonder,' said Stella, 'whether you know how I feel those kind words of yours when you spoke of my mother. Shall I tell you?'

She put her arm round his neck and kissed him. He was a man new to love, in the nobler sense of the word. The exquisite softness in the touch of her lips, the delicious fragrance of her breath, intoxicated him. Again and again he returned the kiss. She drew back; she recovered her self-possession with a suddenness and a certainty incomprehensible to a man. From the depths of tenderness she passed to the shallows of frivolity. In her own defence she was almost as superficial as her mother, in less than a moment.

'What would Mr Penrose say if he saw you?' she whispered.

'Why do you speak of Penrose? Have you seen him to-night?'

'Yes — looking sadly out of his element, poor man. I did my best to set him at his ease — because I know *you* like him.'

'Dear Stella!'

'No, not again! I am speaking seriously now. Mr Penrose looked at me with a strange kind of interest — I can't describe it. Have you taken him into our confidence?'

'He is so devoted — he has such a true interest in me,' said Romayne — 'I really felt ashamed to treat him like a stranger. On our journey to London I did own that it was your charming letter which had decided me on returning. I did say, 'I must tell her myself how well she has understood me, and how deeply I feel her kindness.' Penrose took my hand, in his gentle considerate way. 'I understand you, too,' he said — and that was all that passed between us.'

'Nothing more, since that time?'

'Nothing.'

'Not a word of what we said to each other when we were alone last week in the picture gallery?'

'Not a word. I am self-tormentor enough to distrust myself, even now. God knows, I have concealed nothing from you; and yet — Am I not selfishly thinking of my own happiness, Stella, when I ought to be thinking only of you? You know, my angel, with what a life you must associate yourself if you marry me. Are you really sure that you have love enough and courage enough to be my wife?'

She rested her head caressingly on his shoulder, and looked up at him with her charming smile.

'How many times must I say it,' she asked, 'before you will believe me? Once more — I have love enough and courage enough to be your wife; and I knew it, Lewis, the first time I saw you! Will *that* confession satisfy your scruples? And will you promise never again to doubt yourself or me?'

Romayne promised, and sealed the promise — unresisted this time — with a kiss. 'When are we to be married?' he whispered.

She lifted her head from his shoulder with a sigh. 'If I am to answer you honestly,' she replied, 'I must speak of my mother, before I speak of myself.'

Romayne submitted to the duties of his new position, as well as he understood them. 'Do you mean that you have told your mother of our engagement?' he said. 'In that case, is it my duty or yours — I am very ignorant in these matters — to consult her wishes? My own idea is, that I ought to ask her if she approves of me as her son-in-law, and that you might then speak to her of the marriage.'

Stella thought of Romayne's tastes, all in favour of modest retirement, and of her mother's tastes, all in favour of ostentation and display. She frankly owned the result produced in her own mind. 'I am afraid to consult my mother about our marriage,' she said.

Romayne looked astonished. 'Do you think Mrs Eyrecourt will disapprove of it?' he asked.

Stella was equally astonished on her side. 'Disapprove of it?' she repeated. 'I know for certain that my mother will be delighted.'

'Then where is the difficulty?'

There was but one way of definitely answering that question. Stella boldly described her mother's idea of a wedding — including the Archbishop, the twelve bridesmaids in green and gold, and the hundred guests at breakfast in Lord Loring's picture gallery. Romayne's consternation literally deprived him, for the moment, of the power of speech. To say that he looked at Stella, as a prisoner in 'the condemned cell' might have looked at the sheriff, announcing the morning of his execution, would be to do injustice to the prisoner. He receives *his* shock without flinching; and, in proof of his composure, celebrates his wedding with the gallows by a breakfast which he will not live to digest.

'If you think as your mother does,' Romayne began, as soon as he had recovered his self-possession, 'no opinion of mine shall stand in the way — ' He could get no further. His vivid imagination saw the Archbishop and the bridesmaids, heard the hundred guests and their dreadful speeches: his voice faltered, in spite of himself.

Stella eagerly relieved him. 'My darling, I don't think as my mother does,' she interposed tenderly. 'I am sorry to say we have very few sympathies in common. Marriages, as I think, ought to be celebrated as privately as possible — the near and dear relations present, and

no one else. If there must be rejoicings and banquets, and hundreds of invitations, let them come when the wedded pair are at home after the honeymoon, beginning life in earnest. These are odd ideas for a woman to have — but they *are* my ideas, for all that.'

Romayne's face brightened. 'How few women possess your fine sense and your delicacy of feeling!' he exclaimed. 'Surely your mother must give way, when she hears we are both of one mind about our marriage?'

Stella knew her mother too well to share the opinion thus expressed. Mrs Eyrecourt's capacity for holding to her own little ideas, and for persisting (where her social interests were concerned) in trying to insinuate those ideas into the minds of other persons, was a capacity which no resistance, short of absolute brutality, could overcome. She was perfectly capable of worrying Romayne (as well as her daughter) to the utmost limits of human endurance; in the firm conviction that she was bound to convert all heretics, of their way of thinking, to the orthodox faith in the matter of weddings. Putting this view of the case with all possible delicacy, in speaking of her mother, Stella expressed herself plainly enough, nevertheless, to enlighten Romayne.

He made another suggestion. 'Can we marry privately,' he said, 'and tell Mrs Eyrecourt of it afterwards?'

This essentially masculine solution of the difficulty was at once rejected. Stella was too good a daughter to suffer her mother to be treated with even the appearance of

179

disrespect. 'Oh,' she said, 'think how mortified and distressed my mother would be! She *must* be present at my marriage.'

An idea of a compromise occurred to Romayne. 'What do you say,' he proposed, 'to arranging for the marriage privately — and then telling Mrs Eyrecourt only a day or two beforehand, when it would be too late to send out invitations? If your mother would be disappointed — '

'She would be angry,' Stella interposed.

'Very well — lay all the blame on me. Besides, there might be two other persons present, whom I am sure Mrs Eyrecourt is always glad to meet. You don't object to Lord and Lady Loring?'

'Object? They are my dearest friends, as well as your's!'

'Anyone else, Stella?'

'Anyone, Lewis, whom *you* like.'

'Then I say — no one else. My own love, when may it be? My lawyers can get the settlements ready in a fortnight, or less. Will you say in a fortnight?'

His arm was round her waist; his lips were touching her lovely neck. She was not a woman to take refuge in the common-place coquetries of the sex. 'Yes,' she said softly, 'if you wish it.' She rose, and withdrew herself from him. 'For my sake, we must not be here together any longer, Lewis.' As she spoke, the music in the ball-room ceased. Stella ran out of the conservatory.

The first person she encountered, on returning to the reception-room, was Father Benwell.

3

The End of the Ball

The priest's long journey did not appear to have fatigued him. He was as cheerful and as polite as ever — and so paternally attentive to Stella that it was quite impossible for her to pass him with a formal bow.

'I have come all the way from Devonshire,' he said. 'The train has been behind time as usual, and I am one of the late arrivals in consequence. I miss some familiar faces at this delightful party. Mr Romayne, for instance. Perhaps he is not one of the guests?'

'Oh, yes.'

'Has he gone away?'

'Not that I know of.'

The tone of her replies warned Father Benwell to let Romayne be. He tried another name. 'And Arthur Penrose?' he inquired next.

'I think Mr Penrose has left us.'

As she answered she looked towards Lady Loring. The hostess was the centre of a circle of ladies and gentlemen. Before she was at liberty, Father Benwell might take his departure. Stella resolved to make the attempt for herself which she had asked Lady Loring to make for her. It was better to try, and to be defeated, than not to try at all.

'I asked Mr Penrose what part of Devonshire

you were visiting,' she resumed, assuming her more gracious manner. 'I know something myself of the north coast, especially the neighbourhood of Clovelly.'

Not the faintest change passed over the priest's face; his fatherly smile had never been in a better state of preservation.

'Isn't it a charming place?' he said with enthusiasm. 'Clovelly is the most remarkable and most beautiful village in England. I have so enjoyed my little holiday — excursions by sea and excursions by land — do you know I feel quite young again!'

He lifted his eyebrows playfully, and rubbed his plump hands one over the other with such an intolerably innocent air of enjoyment that Stella positively hated him. She felt her capacity for self-restraint failing her. Under the influence of strong emotion her thoughts lost their customary discipline. In attempting to fathom Father Benwell, she was conscious of having undertaken a task which required more pliable moral qualities than she possessed. To her own unutterable annoyance, she was at a loss what to say next. At that critical moment her mother appeared — eager for news of the conquest of Romayne.

'My dear child, how pale you look!' said Mrs Eyrecourt. 'Come with me directly — you must have a glass of wine.'

This dexterous device for entrapping Stella into a private conversation failed. 'Not now, Mamma, thank you,' she said.

Father Benwell, on the point of discreetly

withdrawing, stopped, and looked at Mrs Eyrecourt with an appearance of respectful interest. As things were, it might not have been worth his while to take the trouble of discovering her. But when she actually placed herself in his way, the chance of turning Mrs Eyrecourt to useful account was not a chance to be neglected. 'Your mother?' he said to Stella. 'I should feel honoured if you will introduce me.'

Having (not very willingly) performed the ceremony of presentation, Stella drew back a little. She had no desire to take any part in the conversation that might follow — but she had her own reasons for waiting near enough to hear it.

In the meanwhile, Mrs Eyrecourt turned on her inexhaustible flow of small-talk with her customary facility. No distinction of persons troubled her; no convictions of any sort stood in her way. She was equally ready (provided she met him in good society) to make herself agreeable to a Puritan or a Papist.

'Delighted to make your acquaintance, Father Benwell. Surely I met you at that delightful evening at the Duke's? I mean when we welcomed the Cardinal back from Rome. Dear old man — if one may speak so familiarly of a Prince of the Church. How charmingly he bears his new honours. Such patriarchal simplicity, as everyone remarked. Have you seen him lately?'

The idea of the Order to which he belonged feeling any special interest in a Cardinal (except when they made him of some use to them), privately amused Father Benwell. 'How wise

the Church was,' he thought, 'in inventing a spiritual aristocracy. Even this fool of a woman is impressed by it.' His spoken reply was true to his assumed character as one of the inferior clergy. 'Poor priests like me, madam, see but little of Princes of the Church in the houses of Dukes.' Saying this with the most becoming humility, he turned the talk in a more productive direction, before Mrs Eyrecourt could proceed with her recollections of 'the evening at the Duke's.'

'Your charming daughter and I have been talking about Clovelly,' he continued. 'I have just been spending a little holiday in that delightful place. It was a surprise to me, Mrs Eyrecourt, to see so many really beautiful country seats in the neighbourhood. I was particularly struck — you know it, of course? — by Beaupark House.'

Mrs Eyrecourt's little twinkling eyes suddenly became still and steady. It was only for a moment. But that trifling change boded ill for the purpose which the priest had in view. Even the wits of a fool can be quickened by contact with the world. For many years Mrs Eyrecourt had held her place in society; acting under an intensely selfish sense of her own interests, fortified by those cunning instincts which grow best in a barren intellect. Perfectly unworthy of being trusted with secrets which only concerned other people, this frivolous creature could be the unassailable guardian of secrets which concerned herself. The instant the priest referred indirectly to Winterfield, by speaking of Beaupark House, her instincts warned her, as if in words: — Be

184

careful for Stella's sake!

'Oh, yes;' said Mrs Eyrecourt. 'I know Beaupark House; but — may I make a confession?' she added, with her sweetest smile.

Father Benwell caught her tone, with his customary tact. 'A confession at a ball is a novelty; even in my experience,' he answered with *his* sweetest smile.

'How good of you to encourage me!' proceeded Mrs Eyrecourt. 'No, thank you, I don't want to sit down. My confession won't take long — and I really must give that poor pale daughter of mine a glass of wine. A student of human nature like you — they say all priests are students of human nature; accustomed of course to be consulted in difficulties, and to hear *real* confessions — must know that we poor women are sadly subject to whims and caprices. We can't resist them as men do; and the dear good men generally make allowances for us. Well, do you know that place of Mr Winterfield's is one of my caprices? Oh, dear, I speak carelessly; I ought to have said the place *represents* one of my caprices. In short, Father Benwell, Beaupark House is perfectly odious to me, and I think Clovelly the most overrated place in the world. I haven't the least reason to give, but so it is. Excessively foolish of me. It's like hysterics, I can't help it; I'm sure you will forgive me. There isn't a place on the habitable globe that I am not ready to feel interested in, except detestable Devonshire. I am so sorry you went there. The next time you have a holiday,

185

take my advice. Try the Continent.'

'I should like it of all things,' said Father Benwell. 'Only I don't speak French. Allow me to get Miss Eyrecourt a glass of wine.'

He spoke with the most perfect temper and tranquillity. Having paid his little attention to Stella, and having relieved her of the empty glass, he took his leave, with a parting request thoroughly characteristic of the man.

'Are you staying in town, Mrs Eyrecourt?' he asked.

'Oh, of course, at the height of the season!'

'May I have the honour of calling on you — and talking a little more about the Continent?'

If he had said it in so many words, he could hardly have informed Mrs Eyrecourt more plainly that he thoroughly understood her, and that he meant to try again. Strong in the worldly training of half a lifetime, she at once informed him of her address, with the complimentary phrases proper to the occasion. 'Five o'clock tea on Wednesdays, Father Benwell. Don't forget!'

The moment he was gone, she drew her daughter into a quiet corner. 'Don't be frightened, Stella. That sly old person has some interest in trying to find out about Winterfield. Do you know why?'

'Indeed I don't, mamma. I hate him!'

'Oh, hush! hush! Hate him as much as you like; but always be civil to him. Tell me — have you been in the conservatory with Romayne?'

'Yes.'

'All going on well?'

'Yes.'

'My sweet child! Dear, dear me, the wine has done you no good; you're as pale as ever. Is it that priest? Oh, pooh, pooh, leave Father Benwell to me.'

4

In the Small Hours

When Stella left the conservatory, the attraction of the ball for Romayne was at an end. He went back to his rooms at the hotel.

Penrose was waiting to speak to him. Romayne noticed signs of suppressed agitation in his secretary's face. 'Has anything happened?' he inquired.

'Nothing of any importance,' Penrose answered, in sad, subdued tones. 'I only wanted to ask you for leave of absence.'

'Certainly. Is it for a long time?'

Penrose hesitated. 'You have a new life opening before you,' he said. 'If your experience of that life is — as I hope and pray it may be — a happy one, you will need me no longer; we may not meet again.' His voice began to tremble; he could say no more.

'Not meet again?' Romayne repeated. 'My dear Penrose, if *you* forget how many happy days I owe to your companionship, *my* memory is to be trusted. Do you really know what my new life is to be? Shall I tell you what I have said to Stella tonight?'

Penrose lifted his hand with a gesture of entreaty.

'Not a word!' he said, eagerly. 'Do me one more kindness — leave me to be prepared (as

I *am* prepared) for the change that is to come, without any confidence on your part to enlighten me further. Don't think me ungrateful. I have reasons for saying what I have just said — I cannot mention what they are — I can only tell you they are serious reasons. You have spoken of my devotion to you. If you wish to reward me a hundredfold more than I deserve, bear in mind our conversations on religion, and keep the books I asked you to read as gifts from a friend who loves you with his whole heart. No new duties that you can undertake are incompatible with the higher interests of your soul. Think of me sometimes. When I leave you I go back to a lonely life. My poor heart is full of your brotherly kindness at this last moment when I may be saying good-bye for ever. And what is my one consolation? What helps me to bear my hard lot? The Faith that I hold! Remember that, Romayne. If there comes a time of sorrow in the future, remember that.'

Romayne was more than surprised, he was shocked. 'Why must you leave me?' he asked.

'It is best for you and for *her*,' said Penrose, 'that I should withdraw myself from your new life.'

He held out his hand. Romayne refused to let him go. 'Penrose!' he said, 'I can't match your resignation. Give me something to look forward to. I must and will see you again.'

Penrose smiled sadly. 'You know that my career in life depends wholly on my superiors,' he answered. 'But if I am still in England — and if you have sorrows in the future that I can share

and alleviate — only let me know it. There is nothing within the compass of my power which I will not do for your sake. God bless and prosper you! Good-bye!'

In spite of his fortitude, the tears rose in his eyes. He hurried out of the room.

Romayne sat down at his writing-table, and hid his face in his hands. He had entered the room with the bright image of Stella in his mind. The image had faded from it now — the grief that was in him not even the beloved woman could share. His thoughts were wholly with the brave and patient Christian who had left him — the true man, whose spotless integrity no evil influence could corrupt. By what inscrutable fatality do some men find their way into spheres that are unworthy of them? Oh, Penrose, if the priests of your Order were all like you, how easily I should be converted! These were Romayne's thoughts, in the stillness of the first hours of the morning. The books of which his lost friend had spoken were close by him on the table. He opened one of them, and turned to a page marked by pencil lines. His sensitive nature was troubled to its inmost depths. The confession of that Faith which had upheld Penrose was before him in words. The impulse was strong in him to read those words, and think over them again.

He trimmed his lamp, and bent his mind on his book. While he was still reading, the ball at Lord Loring's house came to its end. Stella and Lady Loring were alone together, talking of him, before they retired to their rooms.

'Forgive me for owning it plainly,' said Lady Loring — 'I think you and your mother are a little too ready to suspect Father Benwell without any discoverable cause. Thousands of people go to Clovelly, and Beaupark House is one of the show-places in the neighbourhood. Is there a little Protestant prejudice in this new idea of yours?'

Stella made no reply; she seemed to be lost in her own thoughts.

Lady Loring went on.

'I am open to conviction, my dear. If you will only tell me what interest Father Benwell can have in knowing about you and Winterfield — '

Stella suddenly looked up. 'Let us speak of another person,' she said; 'I own I don't like Father Benwell. As you know, Romayne has concealed nothing from me. Ought I to have any concealments from *him*? Ought I not to tell him about Winterfield?'

Lady Loring started. 'You astonish me,' she said. 'What right has Romayne to know it?'

'What right have I to keep it a secret from him?'

'My dear Stella! if you had been in any way to blame, in that miserable matter, I should be the last person in the world to advise you to keep it a secret. But you are innocent of all blame. No man — not even the man who is soon to be your husband — has a right to know what you have so unjustly suffered. Think of the humiliation of even speaking of it to Romayne!'

'I daren't think of it,' cried Stella passionately. 'But if it is my duty — '

'It is your duty to consider the consequences,' Lady Loring interposed. 'You don't know how such things sometimes rankle in a man's mind. He may be perfectly willing to do you justice — and yet, there may be moments when he would doubt if you had told him the whole truth. I speak with the experience of a married woman. Don't place yourself in *that* position towards your husband, if you wish for a happy married life.'

Stella was not quite convinced yet. 'Suppose Romayne finds it out?' she said.

'He can't possibly find it out. I detest Winterfield, but let us do him justice. He is no fool. He has his position in the world to keep up — and that is enough of itself to close his lips. And as for others, there are only three people now in England who *could* betray you. I suppose you can trust your mother, and Lord Loring, and me?'

It was needless to answer such a question as that. Before Stella could speak again, Lord Loring's voice was audible outside the door. 'What! talking still,' he exclaimed. 'Not in bed yet?'

'Come in!' cried his wife. 'Let us hear what my husband thinks,' she said to Stella.

Lord Loring listened with the closest attention while the subject under discussion was communicated to him. When the time came to give his opinion, he sided unhesitatingly with his wife.

'If the fault was yours, even in the slightest degree,' he said to Stella, 'Romayne would have

192

a right to be taken into your confidence. But, my dear child, we, who know the truth, know you to be a pure and innocent woman. You go to Romayne in every way worthy of him, and you know that he loves you. If you did tell him that miserable story, he could only pity you. Do you want to be pitied?'

Those last unanswerable words brought the debate to an end. From that moment the subject was dropped.

There was still one other person among the guests at the ball who was waking in the small hours of the morning. Father Benwell, wrapped comfortably in his dressing gown, was too hard at work on his correspondence to think of his bed.

With one exception, all the letters that he had written thus far were closed, directed, and stamped for the post. The letter that he kept open he was now engaged in reconsidering and correcting. It was addressed as usual to the Secretary of the Order at Rome; and, when it had undergone the final revision, it contained these lines:-

My last letter informed you of Romayne's return to London and to Miss Eyrecourt. Let me entreat our reverend brethren to preserve perfect tranquillity of mind, in spite of this circumstance. The owner of Vange Abbey is not married yet. If patience and perseverance on my part win their fair reward, Miss Eyrecourt shall never be his wife.

But let me not conceal the truth. In the

uncertain future that lies before us, I have no one to depend on but myself. Penrose is no longer to be trusted: and the exertions of the agent to whom I committed my inquiries are exertions that have failed.

I will dispose of the case of Penrose first.

The zeal with which this young man has undertaken the work of conversion entrusted to him has, I regret to say, not been fired by devotion to the interests of the Church, but by a dog-like affection for Romayne. Without waiting for my permission, Penrose has revealed himself in his true character as a priest. And, more than this, he has not only refused to observe the proceedings of Romayne and Miss Eyrecourt — he has deliberately closed his ears to the confidence which Romayne wished to repose in him, on the ground that I might have ordered him to repeat that confidence to me.

To what use can we put this poor fellow's ungovernable sense of honour and gratitude? Under present circumstances, he is clearly of little use to us. I have therefore given him time to think. That is to say, I have not opposed his leaving London, to assist in the spiritual care of a country district. It will be a question for the future, whether we may not turn his enthusiasm to good account in a foreign mission. However, as it is always possible that his influence may still be of use to us, I venture to suggest keeping him within our reach until Romayne's conversion has actually taken place. Don't suppose that the present separation between them is final; I will answer for their meeting again.

I may now proceed to the failure of my agent, and to the course of action that I have adopted in consequence.

The investigations appear to have definitely broken down at the seaside village of Clovelly, in the neighbourhood of Mr Winterfield's country seat. Knowing that I could depend upon the information which associated this gentleman with Miss Eyrecourt, under compromising circumstances of some sort, I decided on seeing Mr Winterfield, and judging for myself.

The agent's report informed me that the person who had finally baffled his inquiries was an aged Catholic priest, long resident at Clovelly. His name is Newbliss, and he is much respected among the Catholic gentry in that part of Devonshire. After due consideration, I obtained a letter of introduction to my reverend colleague, and travelled to Clovelly — telling my friends here that I was taking a little holiday, in the interests of my health.

I found Father Newbliss a venerable and reticent son of the Church — with one weak point, however, to work on, which was entirely beyond the reach of the otherwise astute person charged with my inquiries. My reverend friend is a scholar, and is inordinately proud of his learning. I am a scholar too. In that capacity I first found my way to his sympathies, and then gently encouraged his pride. The result will appear in certain discoveries, which I number as follows:-

1. The events which connect Mr Winterfield with Miss Eyrecourt happened about two years

since, and had their beginning at Beaupark House.

2. At this period, Miss Eyrecourt and her mother were staying at Beaupark House. The general impression in the neighbourhood was that Mr Winterfield and Miss Eyrecourt were engaged to be married.

3. Not long afterwards, Miss Eyrecourt and her mother surprised the neighbourhood by suddenly leaving Beaupark House. Their destination was supposed to be London.

4. Mr Winterfield himself next left his country seat for the Continent. His exact destination was not mentioned to anyone. The steward, soon afterwards, dismissed all the servants, and the house was left empty for more than a year.

5. At the end of that time Mr Winterfield returned alone to Beaupark House, and told nobody how, or where, he had passed the long interval of his absence.

6. Mr Winterfield remains, to the present day, an unmarried man.

Having arrived at these preliminary discoveries, it was time to try what I could make of Mr Winterfield next.

Among the other good things which this gentleman has inherited is a magnificent library collected by his father. That one learned man should take another learned man to see the books was a perfectly natural proceeding. My introduction to the master of the house followed my introduction to the library almost as a matter of course.

I am about to surprise you, as I was myself

surprised. In all my long experience, Mr Winterfield is, I think, the most fascinating person I ever met with. Genial, unassuming manners, a prepossessing personal appearance, a sweet temper, a quaint humour delightfully accompanied by natural refinement — such are the characteristic qualities of the man from whom I myself saw Miss Eyrecourt (accidentally meeting him in public) recoil with dismay and disgust! It is absolutely impossible to look at him, and to believe him to be capable of a cruel or dishonourable action. I never was so puzzled in my life.

You may be inclined to think that I am misled by a false impression, derived from the gratifying welcome that I received as a friend of Father Newbliss. I will not appeal to my knowledge of human nature — I will refer to the unanswerable evidence of Mr Winterfield's poorer neighbours. Wherever I went, in the village or out of it, if I mentioned his name, I produced a universal outburst of admiration and gratitude. 'There never was such a friend to poor people, and there never can be such another to the end of the world.' Such was a fisherman's description of him; and the one cry of all the men and women near us answered, 'That's the truth!'

And yet there is something wrong — for this plain reason, that there is something to be concealed in the past lives of Mr Winterfield and Miss Eyrecourt.

Under these perplexing circumstances, what use have I made of my opportunities? I am going to surprise you again — I have mentioned

Romayne's name to Mr Winterfield; and I have ascertained that they are, so far, perfect strangers to one another — and that is all.

The little incident of mentioning Romayne arose out of my examination of the library. I discovered certain old volumes, which may one day be of use to him, if he continues his contemplated work on the Origin of Religions. Hearing me express myself to this effect, Mr Winterfield replied with the readiest kindness.

'I can't compare myself to my excellent Father,' he said; 'but I have at least inherited his respect for the writers of books. My library is a treasure which I hold in trust for the interests of literature. Pray say so, from me, to your friend Mr Romayne.'

And what does this amount to? — you will ask. My reverend friend, it offers me an opportunity, in the future, of bringing Romayne and Winterfield together. Do you see the complications which may ensue? If I can put no other difficulty in Miss Eyrecourt's way, I think there is fruitful promise of a scandal of some kind arising out of the introduction to each other of those two men. You will agree with me that a scandal may prove a valuable obstacle in the way of a marriage.

Mr Winterfield has kindly invited me to call on him when he is next in London. I may then have opportunities of putting questions which I could not venture to ask on a short acquaintance.

In the meantime, I have obtained another introduction since my return to town. I have

been presented to Miss Eyrecourt's mother, and I am invited to drink tea with her on Wednesday. My next letter may tell you — what Penrose ought to have discovered — whether Romayne has been already entrapped into a marriage engagement or not.

Farewell for the present. Remind the reverend Fathers, with my respects, that I possess one of the valuable qualities of an Englishman — I never know when I am beaten.

Book The Third

1

The Honeymoon

More than six weeks had passed. The wedded lovers were still enjoying their honeymoon at Vange Abbey.

Some offence had been given, not only to Mrs Eyrecourt, but to friends of her way of thinking, by the strictly private manner in which the marriage had been celebrated. The event took everybody by surprise when the customary advertisement appeared in the newspapers. Foreseeing the unfavourable impression that might be produced in some quarters, Stella had pleaded for a timely retreat to the seclusion of Romayne's country house. The will of the bride being, as usual, the bridegroom's law, to Vange they retired accordingly.

On one lovely moonlight night, early in July, Mrs Romayne left her husband on the Belvidere, described in Major Hynd's narrative, to give the housekeeper certain instructions relating to the affairs of the household. Half an hour later, as she was about to ascend again to the top of the house, one of the servants informed her that 'the master had just left the Belvidere, and had gone into his study.'

Crossing the inner hall, on her way to the study, Stella noticed an unopened letter, addressed to Romayne, lying on a table in a corner. He had probably laid it aside and forgotten it. She entered his room with the letter in her hand.

The only light was a reading lamp, with the shade so lowered that the corners of the study were left in obscurity. In one of these corners Romayne was dimly visible, sitting with his head sunk on his breast. He never moved when Stella opened the door. At first she thought he might be asleep.

'Do I disturb you, Lewis?' she asked softly.

'No, my dear.'

There was a change in the tone of his voice, which his wife's quick ear detected. 'I am afraid you are not well,' she said anxiously.

'I am a little tired after our long ride to-day. Do you want to go back to the Belvidere?'

'Not without you. Shall I leave you to rest here?'

He seemed not to hear the question. There he sat, with his head hanging down, the shadowy counterfeit of an old man. In her anxiety, Stella approached him, and put her hand caressingly on his head. It was burning hot. 'Oh!' she cried, 'you *are* ill, and you are trying to hide it from me.'

He put his arm round her waist, and made her sit on his knee. 'Nothing is the matter with me,' he said, with an uneasy laugh. 'What have you got in your hand? A letter?'

'Yes. Addressed to you, and not opened yet.'

He took it out of her hand, and threw it carelessly on a sofa near him. 'Never mind that now! Let us talk.' He paused, and kissed her, before he went on. 'My darling, I think you must be getting tired of Vange?'

'Oh, no! I can be happy anywhere with you — and especially at Vange. You don't know how this noble old house interests me, and how I admire the glorious country all round it.'

He was not convinced. 'Vange is very dull,' he said, obstinately; 'and your friends will be wanting to see you. Have you heard from your mother lately?'

'No. I am surprised she has not written.'

'She has not forgiven us for getting married so quietly,' he went on. 'We had better go back to London and make our peace with her. Don't you want to see the house my aunt left me at Highgate?'

Stella sighed. The society of the man she loved was society enough for her. Was he getting tired of his wife already? 'I will go with you wherever you like.' She said those words in tones of sad submission, and gently got up from his knee.

He rose also, and took from the sofa the letter which he had thrown on it. 'Let us see what our friends say,' he resumed. 'The address is in Loring's handwriting.'

As he approached the table on which the lamp was burning, she noticed that he moved with a languor that was new in her experience of him. He sat down and opened the letter. She watched him with an anxiety which had now become intensified to suspicion. The shade of the lamp

still prevented her from seeing his face plainly. 'Just what I told you,' he said; 'the Lorings want to know when they are to see us in London; and your mother says she 'feels like that character in Shakespeare who was cut by his own daughters.' Read it.'

He handed her the letter. In taking it, she contrived to touch the lamp shade, as if by accident, and tilted it so that the full flow of the light fell on him. He started back — but not before she had seen the ghastly pallor on his face. She had not only heard it from Lady Loring, she knew from his own unreserved confession to her what that startling change really meant. In an instant she was on her knees at his feet. 'Oh, my darling,' she cried, 'it was cruel to keep *that* secret from your wife! You have heard it again!'

She was too irresistibly beautiful, at that moment, to be reproved. He gently raised her from the floor — and owned the truth.

'Yes,' he said; 'I heard it after you left me on the Belvidere — just as I heard it on another moonlight night, when Major Hynd was here with me. Our return to this house is perhaps the cause. I don't complain; I have had a long release.'

She threw her arms round his neck. 'We will leave Vange to-morrow,' she said.

It was firmly spoken. But her heart sank, as the words passed her lips. Vange Abbey had been the scene of the most unalloyed happiness in her life. What destiny was waiting for her when she returned to London?

2

Events at Ten Acres

There was no obstacle to the speedy departure of Romayne and his wife from Vange Abbey. The villa at Highgate — called Ten Acres Lodge, in allusion to the measurement of the grounds surrounding the house — had been kept in perfect order by the servants of the late Lady Berrick, now in the employment of her nephew.

On the morning after their arrival at the villa, Stella sent a note to her mother. The same afternoon, Mrs Eyrecourt arrived at Ten Acres — on her way to a garden party. Finding the house, to her great relief, a modern building, supplied with all the newest comforts and luxuries, she at once began to plan a grand party, in celebration of the return of the bride and bridegroom.

'I don't wish to praise myself,' Mrs Eyrecourt said; 'but if ever there was a forgiving woman, I am that person. We will say no more, Stella, about your truly contemptible wedding — five people altogether, including ourselves and the Lorings. A grand ball will set you right with society, and that is the one thing needful. Tea and coffee, my dear Romayne, in your study; Coote's quadrille band; the supper from Gunter's; the grounds illuminated with coloured

lamps; Tyrolese singers among the trees, relieved by military music — and, if there *are* any African or other savages now in London, there is room enough in these charming grounds for encampments, dances, squaws, scalps, and all the rest of it, to end in a blaze of fireworks.'

A sudden fit of coughing seized her, and stopped the further enumeration of attractions at the contemplated ball. Stella had observed that her mother looked unusually worn and haggard, through the disguises of paint and powder. This was not an uncommon result of Mrs Eyrecourt's devotion to the demands of society; but the cough was something new, as a symptom of exhaustion.

'I am afraid, mamma, you have been over-exerting yourself,' said Stella. 'You go to too many parties.'

'Nothing of the sort, my dear; I am as strong as a horse. The other night, I was waiting for the carriage in a draught (one of the most perfect private concerts of the season, ending with a delightfully naughty little French play) — and I caught a slight cold. A glass of water is all I want. Thank you. Romayne, you are looking shockingly serious and severe; our ball will cheer you. If you would only make a bonfire of all those horrid books, you don't know how it would improve your spirits. Dearest Stella, I will come and lunch here to-morrow — you are within such a nice easy drive from town — and I'll bring my visiting-book, and settle about the invitations and the day. Oh, dear me, how late it is. I have nearly an hour's drive before I get

to my garden party. Good-bye, my turtle doves, good-bye.'

She was stopped, on the way to her carriage, by another fit of coughing. But she still persisted in making light of it. 'I'm as strong as a horse,' she repeated, as soon as she could speak — and skipped into the carriage like a young girl.

'Your mother is killing herself,' said Romayne.

'If I could persuade her to stay with us a little while,' Stella suggested, 'the rest and quiet might do wonders for her. Would you object to it, Lewis?'

'My darling, I object to nothing — except giving a ball and burning my books. If your mother will yield on these two points, my house is entirely at her disposal.'

He spoke playfully — he looked his best, since he had separated himself from the painful associations that were now connected with Vange Abbey. Had 'the torment of the Voice' been left far away in Yorkshire? Stella shrank from approaching the subject in her husband's presence, knowing that it must remind him of the fatal duel. To her surprise, Romayne himself referred to the General's family.

'I have written to Hynd,' he began, 'Do you mind his dining with us to-day?'

'Of course not!'

'I want to hear if he has anything to tell me — about those French ladies. He undertook to see them, in your absence, and to ascertain — ' He was unable to overcome his reluctance to pronounce the next words. Stella was quick to

206

understand what he meant. She finished the sentence for him.

'Yes,' he said, 'I wanted to hear how the boy is getting on, and if there is any hope of curing him. Is it — ' he trembled as he put the question — 'Is it hereditary madness?'

Feeling the serious importance of concealing the truth, Stella only replied that she had hesitated to ask if there was a taint of madness in the family. 'I suppose,' she added, 'you would not like to see the boy, and judge of his chances of recovery for yourself?'

'You suppose?' he burst out, with sudden anger. 'You might be sure. The bare idea of seeing him turns me cold. Oh, when shall I forget! when shall I forget! Who spoke of him first?' he said, with renewed irritability, after a moment of silence. 'You or I?'

'It was my fault, love — he is so harmless and so gentle, and he has such a sweet face — I thought it might soothe you to see him. Forgive me; we will never speak of him again. Have you any notes for me to copy? You know, Lewis, I am your secretary now.'

So she led Romayne away to his study and his books. When Major Hynd arrived, she contrived to be the first to see him. 'Say as little as possible about the General's widow and her son,' she whispered.

The Major understood her. 'Don't be uneasy, Mrs Romayne,' he answered. 'I know your husband well enough to know what you mean. Besides, the news I bring is good news.'

Romayne came in before he could speak more

particularly. When the servants had left the room, after dinner, the Major made his report.

'I am going to agreeably surprise you,' he began. 'All responsibility towards the General's family is taken off our hands. The ladies are on their way back to France.'

Stella was instantly reminded of one of the melancholy incidents associated with her visit to Camp's Hill. 'Madame Marillac spoke of a brother of hers who disapproved of the marriage,' she said. 'Has he forgiven her?'

'That is exactly what he has done, Mrs Romayne. Naturally enough, he felt the disgrace of his sister's marriage to such a man as the General. Only the other day he heard for the first time that she was a widow — and he at once travelled to England. I bade them good-bye yesterday — most happily reunited — on their journey home again. Ah, I thought you would be glad, Mrs Romayne, to hear that the poor widow's troubles are over. Her brother is rich enough to place them all in easy circumstances — he is as good a fellow as ever lived.'

'Have you seen him?' Stella asked eagerly.

'I have been with him to the asylum.'

'Does the boy go back to France?'

'No. We took the place by surprise, and saw for ourselves how well conducted it was. The boy has taken a strong liking to the proprietor — a bright, cheerful old man, who is teaching him some of our English games, and has given him a pony to ride on. He burst out crying, poor creature, at the idea of going away — and his mother burst out crying at the idea of leaving

him. It was a melancholy scene. You know what a good mother is — no sacrifice is too great for her. The boy stays at the asylum, on the chance that his healthier and happier life there may help to cure him. By-the-way, Romayne, his uncle desires me to thank you — '

'Hynd! you didn't tell the uncle my name?'

'Don't alarm yourself. He is a gentleman, and when I told him I was pledged to secrecy, he made but one inquiry — he asked if you were a rich man. I told him you had eighteen thousand a year.'

'Well?'

'Well, he set that matter right between us with perfect taste. He said, 'I cannot presume to offer repayment to a person so wealthy. We gratefully accept our obligation to our kind unknown friend. For the future, however, my nephew's expenses must be paid from my purse.' Of course I could only agree to that. From time to time the mother is to hear, and I am to hear, how the boy goes on. Or, if you like, Romayne — now that the General's family have left England — I don't see why the proprietor might not make his report directly to yourself.'

'No!' Romayne rejoined, positively. 'Let things remain as they are.'

'Very well. I can send you any letters that I may receive from the asylum. Will you give us some music, Mrs Romayne? Not to-night? Then let us go to the billiard-room; and as I am the worst of bad players, I will ask you to help me to beat your accomplished husband.'

On the afternoon of the next day, Mrs Eyrecourt's maid arrived at Ten Acres with a note from her mistress.

'Dearest Stella, — Matilda must bring you my excuses for to-day. I don't in the least understand it, but I seem to have turned lazy. It is most ridiculous — I really cannot get out of bed. Perhaps I did do just a little too much yesterday. The opera after the garden party, and a ball after the opera, and this tiresome cough all night after the ball. Quite a series, isn't it? Make my apologies to our dear dismal Romayne — and if you drive out this afternoon, come and have a chat with me. Your affectionate mother, Emily Eyrecourt. P.S. — You know what a fidget Matilda is. If she talks about me, don't believe a word she says to you.'

Stella turned to the maid with a sinking heart. 'Is my mother very ill?' she asked.

'So ill, ma'am, that I begged and prayed her to let me send for a doctor. You know what my mistress is. If you would please to use your influence — '

'I will order the carriage instantly, and take you back with me.'

Before she dressed to go out, Stella showed the letter to her husband. He spoke with perfect kindness and sympathy, but he did not conceal that he shared his wife's apprehensions. 'Go at once, were his last words to her; and, if I can be of any use, send for me.'

It was late in the evening before Stella returned. She brought sad news.

The physician consulted told her plainly that

the neglected cough, and the constant fatigue, had together made the case a serious one. He declined to say that there was any absolute danger as yet, or any necessity for her remaining with her mother at night. The experience of the next twenty-four hours, at most, would enable him to speak positively. In the meantime the patient insisted that Stella should return to her husband. Even under the influence of opiates, Mrs Eyrecourt was still drowsily equal to herself. 'You are a fidget, my dear, and Matilda is a fidget — I can't have two of you at my bedside. Good-night.' Stella stooped over her and kissed her. She whispered, 'Three weeks' notice, remember, for the party!'

By the next evening the malady had assumed so formidable an aspect, that the doctor had his doubts of the patient's chance of recovery. With her husband's full approval, Stella remained night and day at her mother's bedside.

Thus, in little more than a month from the day of his marriage, Romayne was, for the time, a lonely man again.

The illness of Mrs Eyrecourt was unexpectedly prolonged. There were intervals, during which her vigorous constitution rallied, and resisted the progress of the disease. On these occasions, Stella was able to return to her husband for a few hours — subject always to a message which recalled her to her mother when the chances of life or death appeared to be equally balanced. Romayne's one resource was in his books and his pen. For the first time since his union with Stella he opened the portfolios in which Penrose

had collected the first introductory chapters of his historical work. Almost at every page the familiar handwriting of his secretary and friend met his view. It was a new trial to his resolution to be working alone; never had he felt the absence of Penrose as he felt it now. He missed the familiar face, the quiet pleasant voice, and, more than both, the ever-welcome sympathy with his work. Stella had done all that a wife could do to fill the vacant place; and her husband's fondness had accepted the effort as adding another charm to the lovely creature who had opened a new life to him. But where is the woman who can intimately associate herself with the hard brain-work of a man devoted to an absorbing intellectual pursuit? She can love him, admire him, serve him, believe in him beyond all other men — but (in spite of exceptions which only prove the rule) she is out of her place when she enters the study while the pen is in his hand. More than once, when he was at work, Romayne closed the page bitterly; the sad thought came to him, 'Oh, if I only had Penrose here!' Even other friends were not available as a resource in the solitary evening hours. Lord Loring was absorbed in social and political engagements. And Major Hynd — true to the principle of getting away as often as possible from his disagreeable wife and his ugly children — had once more left London.

One day, while Mrs Eyrecourt still lay between life and death, Romayne found his historical labours suspended by the want of a certain volume which it was absolutely necessary to

consult. He had mislaid the references written for him by Penrose, and he was at a loss to remember whether the book was in the British Museum, in the Bodleian Library, or in the Bibliothèque at Paris. In this emergency a letter to his former secretary would furnish him with the information that he required. But he was ignorant of Penrose's present address. The Lorings might possibly know it — so to the Lorings he resolved to apply.

3

Father Benwell and the Book

Romayne's first errand in London was to see his wife, and to make inquiries at Mrs Eyrecourt's house. The report was more favourable than usual. Stella whispered, as she kissed him, 'I shall soon come back to you, I hope!'

Leaving the horses to rest for awhile, he proceeded to Lord Loring's residence on foot. As he crossed a street in the neighbourhood, he was nearly run over by a cab, carrying a gentleman and his luggage. The gentleman was Mr Winterfield, on his way to Derwent's Hotel.

Lady Loring very kindly searched her card basket, as the readiest means of assisting Romayne. Penrose had left his card, on his departure from London, but no address was written on it. Lord Loring, unable himself to give the required information, suggested the right person to consult.

'Father Benwell will be here later in the day,' he said. 'If you will write to Penrose at once, he will add the address. Are you sure, before the letter goes, that the book you want is not in my library?'

'I think not,' Romayne answered; 'but I will write down the title, and leave it here with my letter.'

The same evening he received a polite note from Father Benwell, informing him that the letter was forwarded, and that the book he wanted was not in Lord Loring's library. 'If there should be any delay or difficulty in obtaining this rare volume,' the priest added, 'I only wait the expression of your wishes, to borrow it from the library of a friend of mine, residing in the country.'

By return of post the answer, affectionately and gratefully written, arrived from Penrose. He regretted that he was not able to assist Romayne personally. But it was out of his power (in plain words, he had been expressly forbidden by Father Benwell) to leave the service on which he was then engaged. In reference to the book that was wanted, it was quite likely that a search in the catalogues of the British Museum might discover it. He had only met with it himself in the National Library at Paris.

This information led Romayne to London again, immediately. For the first time he called at Father Benwell's lodgings. The priest was at home, expecting the visit. His welcome was the perfection of unassuming politeness. He asked for the last news of 'poor Mrs Eyrecourt's health,' with the sympathy of a true friend.

'I had the honour of drinking tea with Mrs Eyrecourt, some little time since,' he said. 'Her flow of conversation was never more delightful — it seemed impossible to associate the idea of illness with so bright a creature. And how well she kept the secret of your contemplated marriage! May I offer my humble

215

congratulations and good wishes?'

Romayne thought it needless to say that Mrs Eyrecourt had not been trusted with the secret until the wedding day was close at hand. 'My wife and I agreed in wishing to be married as quietly as possible,' he answered, after making the customary acknowledgements.

'And Mrs Romayne?' pursued Father Benwell. 'This is a sad trial for her. She is in attendance on her mother, I suppose?'

'In constant attendance; I am quite alone now. To change the subject, may I ask you to look at the reply which I have received from Penrose? It is my excuse for troubling you with this visit.'

Father Benwell read the letter with the closest attention. In spite of his habitual self-control, his vigilant eyes brightened as he handed it back.

Thus far, the priest's well-planned scheme (like Mr Bitrake's clever inquiries) had failed. He had not even entrapped Mrs Eyrecourt into revealing the marriage engagement. Her unconquerable small talk had foiled him at every point. Even when he had deliberately kept his seat after the other guests at the tea-table had taken their departure, she rose with the most imperturbable coolness, and left him. 'I have a dinner and two parties to-night, and this is just the time when I take my little restorative nap. Forgive me — and do come again!' When he sent the fatal announcement of the marriage to Rome, he had been obliged to confess that he was indebted for the discovery to the newspaper. He had accepted the humiliation; he had accepted the defeat — but he was not

beaten yet. 'I counted on Romayne's weakness, and Miss Eyrecourt counted on Romayne's weakness; and Miss Eyrecourt has won. So let it be. My turn will come.' In that manner he had reconciled himself to his position. And now — he knew it when he handed back the letter to Romayne — his turn *had* come!

'You can hardly go to Paris to consult the book,' he said, 'in the present state of Mrs Eyrecourt's health.'

'Certainly not!'

'Perhaps you will send somebody to search the catalogue at the British Museum?'

'I should have done that already, Father Benwell, but for the very kind allusion in your note to your friend in the country. Even if the book is in the Museum Library, I shall be obliged to go to the Reading Room to get my information. It would be far more convenient to me to have the volume at home to consult, if you think your friend will trust me with it.'

'I am certain he will trust you with it. My friend is Mr Winterfield, of Beaupark House, North Devon. Perhaps you may have heard of him?'

'No; the name is quite new to me.'

'Then come and see the man himself. He is now in London — and I am entirely at your service.'

In half an hour more, Romayne was presented to a well-bred amiable gentleman in the prime of life; smoking, and reading the newspaper. The bowl of his long pipe rested on the floor, on one side of him, and a handsome

red and white spaniel reposed on the other. Before his visitors had been two minutes in the room, he understood the motive which had brought them to consult him, and sent for a telegraphic form.

'My steward will find the book and forward it to your address by passenger train this afternoon,' he said. 'I will tell him to put my printed catalogue of the library into the parcel, in case I have any other books which may be of use to you.'

With those words, he despatched the telegram to the office. Romayne attempted to make his acknowledgments. Mr Winterfield would hear no acknowledgments.

'My dear sir,' he said, with a smile that brightened his whole face, 'you are engaged in writing a great historical work; and I am an obscure country gentleman, who is lucky enough to associate himself with the production of a new book. How do you know that I am not looking forward to a complimentary line in the preface? I am the obliged person, not you. Pray consider me as a handy little boy who runs on errands for the Muse of History. Do you smoke?'

Not even tobacco would soothe Romayne's wasted and irritable nerves. Father Benwell — 'all things to all men' — cheerfully accepted a cigar from the box on the table.

'Father Benwell possesses all the social virtues,' Mr Winterfield ran on. 'He shall have his coffee, and the largest sugar-basin that the hotel can produce. I can quite understand that your literary labours have tried your nerves,'

he said to Romayne, when he had ordered the coffee. 'The mere title of your work overwhelms an idle man like me. 'The Origin of Religions' — what an immense subject! How far must we look back to find out the first worshippers of the human family? Where are the hieroglyphics, Mr Romayne, that will give you the earliest information? In the unknown centre of Africa, or among the ruined cities of Yucatan? My own idea, as an ignorant man, is that the first of all forms of worship must have been the worship of the sun. Don't be shocked, Father Benwell — I confess I have a certain sympathy with sun-worship. In the East especially, the rising of the sun is surely the grandest of all objects — the visible symbol of a beneficent Deity, who gives life, warmth, and light to the world of his creation.'

'Very grand, no doubt,' remarked Father Benwell, sweetening his coffee. 'But not to be compared with the noble sight at Rome, when the Pope blesses the Christian world from the balcony of St Peter's.'

'So much for professional feeling!' said Mr Winterfield. 'But, surely, something depends on what sort of man the Pope is. If we had lived in the time of Alexander the Sixth, would you have called *him* a part of that noble sight?'

'Certainly — at a proper distance,' Father Benwell briskly replied. 'Ah, you heretics only know the worst side of that most unhappy pontiff! Mr Winterfield, we have every reason to believe that he felt (privately) the truest remorse.'

219

'I should require very good evidence to persuade me of it.'

This touched Romayne on a sad side of his own personal experience. 'Perhaps,' he said, 'you don't believe in remorse.'

'Pardon me,' Mr Winterfield rejoined, 'I only distinguish between false remorse and true remorse. We will say no more of Alexander the Sixth, Father Benwell. If we want an illustration, I will supply it, and give no offence. True remorse depends, to my mind, on a man's accurate knowledge of his own motives — far from a common knowledge, in my experience. Say, for instance, that I have committed some serious offence — '

Romayne could not resist interrupting him. 'Say you have killed one of your fellow-creatures,' he suggested.

'Very well. If I know that I really meant to kill him, for some vile purpose of my own; and if (which by no means always follows) I am really capable of feeling the enormity of my own crime — that is, as I think, true remorse. Murderer as I am, I have, in that case, some moral worth still left in me. But, if I did *not* mean to kill the man — if his death was my misfortune as well as his — and if (as frequently happens) I am nevertheless troubled by remorse, the true cause lies in my own inability fairly to realise my own motives — before I look to results. I am the ignorant victim of false remorse; and if I will only ask myself boldly what has blinded me to the true state of the case, I shall find the mischief due to that misdirected appreciation

of my own importance which is nothing but egotism in disguise.'

'I entirely agree with you,' said Father Benwell; 'I have had occasion to say the same thing in the confessional.'

Mr Winterfield looked at his dog, and changed the subject. 'Do you like dogs, Mr Romayne?' he asked. 'I see my spaniel's eyes saying that he likes you, and his tail begging you to take some notice of him.'

Romayne caressed the dog rather absently.

His new friend had unconsciously presented to him a new view of the darker aspect of his own life. Winterfield's refined pleasant manners, his generous readiness in placing the treasures of his library at a stranger's disposal, had already appealed irresistibly to Romayne's sensitive nature. The favourable impression was now greatly strengthened by the briefly bold treatment which he had just heard of a subject in which he was seriously interested. 'I must see more of this man,' was his thought, as he patted the companionable spaniel.

Father Benwell's trained observation followed the vivid changes of expression on Romayne's face, and marked the eager look in his eyes, as he lifted his head from the dog to the dog's master. The priest saw his opportunity, and took it.

'Do you remain long at Ten Acres Lodge?' he said to Romayne.

'I hardly know as yet. We have no other plans at present.'

'You inherit the place, I think, from your late aunt, Lady Berrick?'

'Yes.'

The tone of the reply was not encouraging; Romayne felt no interest in talking of Ten Acres Lodge. Father Benwell persisted.

'I was told by Mrs Eyrecourt,' he went on, 'that Lady Berrick had some fine pictures. Are they still at the Lodge?'

'Certainly. I couldn't live in a house without pictures.'

Father Benwell looked at Winterfield. 'Another taste in common between you and Mr Romayne,' he said, 'besides your liking for dogs.'

This at once produced the desired result. Romayne eagerly invited Winterfield to see his pictures. 'There are not many of them,' he said. 'But they are really worth looking at. When will you come?'

'The sooner the better,' Winterfield answered, cordially. 'Will to-morrow do — by the noonday light?'

'Whenever you please. Your time is mine.'

Among his other accomplishments, Father Benwell was a chess-player. If his thoughts at that moment had been expressed in language, they would have said, 'Check to the queen.'

4

The End of the Honeymoon

On the next morning, Winterfield arrived alone at Romayne's house.

Having been included, as a matter of course, in the invitation to see the pictures, Father Benwell had made an excuse, and had asked leave to defer the proposed visit. From his point of view, he had nothing further to gain by being present at a second meeting between the two men — in the absence of Stella. He had it, on Romayne's own authority, that she was in constant attendance on her mother, and that her husband was alone. 'Either Mrs Eyrecourt will get better, or she will die,' Father Benwell reasoned. 'I shall make constant inquiries after her health, and, in either case, I shall know when Mrs Romayne returns to Ten Acres Lodge. After that domestic event, the next time Mr Winterfield visits Mr Romayne, I shall go and see the pictures.'

It is one of the defects of a super-subtle intellect to trust too implicitly to calculation, and to leave nothing to chance. Once or twice already Father Benwell had been (in the popular phrase) a little too clever — and chance had thrown him out. As events happened, chance was destined to throw him out once more.

Of the most modest pretensions, in regard to numbers and size, the pictures collected by the late Lady Berrick were masterly works of modern art. With few exceptions, they had been produced by the matchless English landscape painters of half a century since. There was no formal gallery here. The pictures were so few that they could be hung in excellent lights in the different living-rooms of the villa. Turner, Constable, Collins, Danby, Callcott, Linnell — the master of Beaupark House passed from one to the other with the enjoyment of a man who thoroughly appreciated the truest and finest landscape art that the world has yet seen.

'You had better not have asked me here,' he said to Romayne, in his quaintly good-humoured way. 'I can't part with those pictures when I say good-bye to-day. You will find me calling here again and again, till you are perfectly sick of me. Look at this sea piece. Who thinks of the brushes and palette of *that* painter? There, truth to nature and poetical feeling go hand in hand together. It is absolutely lovely — I could kiss that picture.'

They were in Romayne's study when this odd outburst of enthusiasm escaped Winterfield. He happened to look towards the writing-table next. Some pages of manuscript, blotted and interlined with corrections, at once attracted his attention.

'Is that the forthcoming history?' he asked. 'You are not one of the authors who perform the process of correction mentally — you revise and improve with the pen in your hand.'

Romayne looked at him in surprise. 'I suspect, Mr Winterfield, you have used your pen for other purposes than writing letters.'

'No, indeed; you pay me an undeserved compliment. When you come to see me in Devonshire, I can show you some manuscripts, and corrected proofs, left by our great writers, collected by my father. My knowledge of the secrets of the craft has been gained by examining those literary treasures. If the public only knew that every writer worthy of the name is the severest critic of his own book before it ever gets into the hands of the reviewers, how surprised they would be! The man who has worked in the full fervour of composition yesterday is the same man who sits in severe and merciless judgment to-day on what he has himself produced. What a fascination there must be in the Art which exacts and receives such double labour as this!'

Romayne thought — not unkindly — of his wife. Stella had once asked him how long a time he was usually occupied in writing one page. The reply had filled her with pity and wonder. 'Why do you take all that trouble?' she had gently remonstrated. 'It would be just the same to the people, darling, if you did it in half the time.'

By way of changing the topic, Romayne led his visitor into another room. 'I have a picture here,' he said, 'which belongs to a newer school of painting. You have been talking of hard work in one Art; there it is in another.'

'Yes,' said Winterfield; 'there it is — the misdirected hard work, which has been guided

225

by no critical faculty, and which doesn't know where to stop. I try to admire it; and I end in pitying the poor artist. Look at that leafless felled tree, in the middle distance. Every little twig, on the smallest branch, is conscientiously painted — and the result is like a coloured photograph. You don't look at a landscape as a series of separate parts; you don't discover every twig on a tree; you see the whole in Nature, and you want to see the whole in a picture. That canvas presents a triumph of patience and pains, produced exactly as a piece of embroidery is produced, all in little separate bits, worked with the same mechanically complete care. I turn away from it to your shrubbery there, with an ungrateful sense of relief.'

He walked to the window as he spoke. It looked out on the grounds in front of the house. At the same moment the noise of rolling wheels became audible on the drive. An open carriage appeared at the turn in the road. Winterfield called Romayne to the window. 'A visitor,' he began — and suddenly drew back, without saying a word more.

Romayne looked out, and recognised his wife.

'Excuse me for one moment,' he said, 'it is Mrs Romayne.'

On that morning an improvement in the fluctuating state of Mrs Eyrecourt's health had given Stella another of those opportunities of passing an hour or two with her husband, which she so highly prized. Romayne withdrew, to meet her at the door — too hurriedly to notice

226

Winterfield standing, in the corner to which he had retreated, like a man petrified.

Stella had got out of the carriage, when her husband reached the porch. She ascended the few steps that led to the hall as slowly and painfully as if she had been an infirm old woman. The delicately-tinted colour in her face had faded to an ashy white. She had seen Winterfield at the window.

For the moment, Romayne looked at her in speechless consternation. He led her into the nearest room that opened out of the hall, and took her in his arms. 'My love, this nursing of your mother has completely broken you down!' he said, with the tenderest pity for her. 'If you won't think of yourself, you must think of me. For my sake remain here, and take the rest that you need. I will be a tyrant, Stella, for the first time; I won't let you go back.'

She roused herself, and tried to smile — and hid the sad result from him in a kiss. 'I do feel the anxiety and fatigue,' she said. 'But my mother is really improving; and, if it only continues, the blessed sense of relief will make me strong again.' She paused, and roused all her courage, in anticipation of the next words — so trivial and so terrible — that must, sooner or later, be pronounced. 'You have a visitor,' she said.

'Did you see him at the window? A really delightful man — I know you will like him. Under any other circumstances, I should have introduced him. You are not well enough to see strangers to-day.'

She was too determined to prevent Winterfield from ever entering the house again to shrink from the meeting. 'I am not so ill as you think, Lewis,' she said bravely. 'When you go to your new friend, I will go with you. I am a little tired — that's all.'

Romayne looked at her anxiously. 'Let me get you a glass of wine,' he said.

She consented — she really felt the need of it. As he turned away to ring the bell, she put the question which had been in her mind from the moment when she had seen Winterfield.

'How did you become acquainted with this gentleman?'

'Through Father Benwell.'

She was not surprised by the answer — her suspicion of the priest had remained in her mind from the night of Lady Loring's ball. The future of her married life depended on her capacity to check the growing intimacy between the two men. In that conviction she found the courage to face Winterfield.

How should she meet him? The impulse of the moment pointed to the shortest way out of the dreadful position in which she was placed — it was to treat him like a stranger. She drank her glass of wine, and took Romayne's arm. 'We mustn't keep your friend waiting any longer,' she resumed. 'Come!'

As they crossed the hall, she looked suspiciously towards the house-door. Had he taken the opportunity of leaving the villa? At any other time she would have remembered that the plainest laws of good breeding compelled him to

wait for Romayne's return. His own knowledge of the world would tell him that an act of gross rudeness, committed by a well-bred man, would inevitably excite suspicion of some unworthy motive — and might, perhaps, connect that motive with her unexpected appearance at the house. Romayne opened the door, and they entered the room together.

'Mr Winterfield, let me introduce you to Mrs Romayne.'

They bowed to each other; they spoke the conventional words proper to the occasion — but the effort that it cost them showed itself. Romayne perceived an unusual formality in his wife's manner, and a strange disappearance of Winterfield's easy grace of address. Was he one of the few men, in these days, who are shy in the presence of women? And was the change in Stella attributable, perhaps, to the state of her health? The explanation might, in either case, be the right one. He tried to set them at their ease.

'Mr Winterfield is so pleased with the pictures, that he means to come and see them again,' he said to his wife. 'And one of his favourites happens to be your favourite, too.'

She tried to look at Winterfield, but her eyes sank. She could turn towards him, and that was all. 'Is it the sea-piece in the study?' she said to him faintly.

'Yes,' he answered, with formal politeness; 'it seems to me to be one of the painter's finest works.'

Romayne looked at him in unconcealed

wonder. To what flat commonplace Winterfield's lively enthusiasm had sunk in Stella's presence! She perceived that some unfavourable impression had been produced on her husband, and interposed with a timely suggestion. Her motive was not only to divert Romayne's attention from Winterfield, but to give him a reason for leaving the room.

'The little water-colour drawing in my bedroom is by the same artist,' she said. 'Mr Winterfield might like to see it. If you will ring the bell, Lewis, I will send my maid for it.'

Romayne had never allowed the servants to touch his works of art, since the day when a zealous housemaid had tried to wash one of his plaster casts. He made the reply which his wife had anticipated.

'No! no!' he said. 'I will fetch the drawing myself.' He turned gaily to Winterfield. 'Prepare yourself for another work that you would like to kiss.' He smiled, and left the room.

The instant the door was closed, Stella approached Winterfield. Her beautiful face became distorted by a mingled expression of rage and contempt. She spoke to him in a fierce peremptory whisper.

'Have you any consideration for me left?'

His look at her, as she put that question, revealed the most complete contrast between his face and hers. Compassionate sorrow was in his eyes, tender forbearance and respect spoke in his tones, as he answered her.

'I have more than consideration for you, Stella — '

She angrily interrupted him. 'How dare you call me by my Christian name?'

He remonstrated, with a gentleness that might have touched the heart of any woman. 'Do you still refuse to believe that I never deceived you? Has time not softened your heart to me yet?'

She was more contemptuous towards him than ever. 'Spare me your protestations,' she said; 'I heard enough of them two years since. Will you do what I ask of you?'

'You know that I will.'

'Put an end to your acquaintance with my husband. Put an end to it,' she repeated vehemently, 'from this day, at once and for ever! Can I trust you to do it?'

'Do you think I would have entered this house if I had known he was your husband?' He made that reply with a sudden change in him — with a rising colour, and in firm tones of indignation. In a moment more, his voice softened again, and his kind blue eyes rested on her sadly and devotedly. 'You may trust me to do more than you ask,' he resumed. 'You have made a mistake.'

'What mistake?'

'When Mr Romayne introduced us, you met me like a stranger — and you left me no choice but to do as you did.'

'I wish you to be a stranger.'

Her sharpest replies made no change in his manner. He spoke as kindly and as patiently as ever.

'You forget that you and your mother were my guests at Beaupark, two years ago — '

231

Stella understood what he meant — and more. In an instant she remembered that Father Benwell had been at Beaupark House. Had he heard of the visit? She clasped her hands in speechless terror.

Winterfield gently reassured her. 'You must not be frightened,' he said. 'It is in the last degree unlikely that Mr Romayne will ever find out that you were at my house. If he does — and if you deny it — I will do for you what I would do for no other human creature; I will deny it too. You are safe from discovery. Be happy — and forget me.'

For the first time she showed signs of relenting — she turned her head away, and sighed. Although her mind was full of the serious necessity of warning him against Father Benwell, she had not even command enough over her own voice to ask how he had become acquainted with the priest. His manly devotion, the perfect and pathetic sincerity of his respect, pleaded with her, in spite of herself. For a moment she paused to recover her composure. In that moment Romayne returned to them with the drawing in his hand.

'There!' he said. 'It's nothing, this time, but some children gathering flowers on the outskirts of a wood. What do you think of it?'

'What I thought of the larger work,' Winterfield answered. 'I could look at it by the hour together.' He consulted his watch. 'But time is a hard master, and tells me that my visit must come to an end. Thank you, most sincerely.'

He bowed to Stella. Romayne thought his

guest might have taken the English freedom of shaking hands. 'When will you come and look at the pictures again?' he asked. 'Will you dine with us, and see how they bear the lamp light?'

'I am sorry to say I must beg you to excuse me. My plans are altered since we met yesterday. I am obliged to leave London.'

Romayne was unwilling to part with him on these terms. 'You will let me know when you are next in town?' he said.

'Certainly!'

With that short answer he hurried away.

Romayne waited a little in the hall before he went back to his wife. Stella's reception of Winterfield, though not positively ungracious, was, nevertheless, the reverse of encouraging. What extraordinary caprice had made her insensible to the social attractions of a man so unaffectedly agreeable? It was not wonderful that Winterfield's cordiality should have been chilled by the cold welcome that he had received from the mistress of the house. At the same time, some allowance was to be made for the influence of Stella's domestic anxieties, and some sympathy was claimed by the state of her health. Although her husband shrank from distressing her by any immediate reference to her reception of his friend, he could not disguise from himself that she had disappointed him. When he went back to the room, Stella was lying on the sofa, with her face turned towards the wall. She was in tears, and she was afraid to let him see it. 'I won't disturb you,' he said, and withdrew to his

study. The precious volume which Winterfield had so kindly placed at his disposal was on the table, waiting for him.

Father Benwell had lost little by not being present at the introduction of Winterfield to Stella. He had witnessed a plainer betrayal of emotion when they met unexpectedly in Lord Loring's picture gallery. But if he had seen Romayne reading in his study, and Stella crying secretly on the sofa, he might have written to Rome by that day's post, and might have announced that he had sown the first seeds of disunion between husband and wife.

5

Father Benwell's Correspondence

To the Secretary, S.J., Rome.

I

In my last few hasty lines I was only able to inform you of the unexpected arrival of Mrs Romayne while Winterfield was visiting her husband. If you remember, I warned you not to attach any undue importance to my absence on that occasion. My present report will satisfy my reverend brethren that the interests committed to me are as safe as ever in my hands.

I have paid three visits, at certain intervals. The first to Winterfield (briefly mentioned in my last letter); the second to Romayne; the third to the invalid lady, Mrs Eyrecourt. In every case I have been rewarded by important results.

We will revert to Winterfield first. I found him at his hotel, enveloped in clouds of tobacco smoke. Having led him, with some difficulty, into talking of his visit to Ten Acres Lodge, I asked how he liked Romayne's pictures.

'I envy him his pictures.' That was the only answer.

'And how do you like Mrs Romayne?' I inquired next.

He laid down his pipe, and looked at me

attentively. My face (I flatter myself) defied discovery. He inhaled another mouthful of tobacco, and began to play with his dog. 'If I must answer your question,' he burst out suddenly, 'I didn't get a very gracious reception from Mrs Romayne.' There he abruptly stopped. He is a thoroughly transparent man; you see straight into his mind, through his eyes. I perceived that he was only telling me a part (perhaps a very small part) of the truth.

'Can you account for such a reception as you describe?' I asked. He answered shortly, 'No.'

'Perhaps I can account for it,' I went on. 'Did Mr Romayne tell his wife that I was the means of introducing you to him?'

He fixed another searching look on me. 'Mr Romayne might have said so when he left me to receive his wife at the door.'

'In that case, Mr Winterfield, the explanation is as plain as the sun at noonday. Mrs Romayne is a strong Protestant, and I am a Catholic priest.'

He accepted this method of accounting for his reception with an alacrity that would not have imposed on a child. You see I had relieved him from all further necessity of accounting for the conduct of Mrs Romayne!

'A lady's religious prejudices,' I proceeded in the friendliest way, 'are never taken seriously by a sensible man. You have placed Mr Romayne under obligations to your kindness — he is eager to improve his acquaintance with you. You will go again to Ten Acres Lodge?'

He gave me another short answer. 'I think not.'

I said I was sorry to hear it. 'However,' I added, 'you can always see him here, when you are in London.' He puffed out a big volume of smoke, and made no remark. I declined to be put down by silence and smoke. 'Or perhaps,' I persisted, 'you will honour me by meeting him at a simple little dinner at my lodgings?' Being a gentleman, he was of course obliged to answer this. He said, 'You are very kind; I would rather not. Shall we talk of something else, Father Benwell?'

We talked of something else. He was just as amiable as ever — but he was not in good spirits. 'I think I shall run over to Paris before the end of the month,' he said. 'To make a long stay?' I asked. 'Oh, no! Call in a week or ten days — and you will find me here again.'

When I got up to go, he returned of his own accord to the forbidden subject. He said, 'I must beg you to do me two favours. The first is, not to let Mr Romayne know that I am still in London. The second is, not to ask me for any explanations.'

The result of our interview may be stated in very few words. It has advanced me one step nearer to discovery. Winterfield's voice, look, and manner satisfied me of this — the true motive for his sudden change of feeling towards Romayne is jealousy of the man who has married Miss Eyrecourt. Those compromising circumstances which baffled the inquiries of my agent are associated, in plain English, with a

love affair. Remember all that I have told you of Romayne's peculiar disposition — and imagine, if you can, what the consequences of such a disclosure will be when we are in a position to enlighten the master of Vange Abbey!

As to the present relations between the husband and wife, I have only to tell you next what passed, when I visited Romayne a day or two later. I did well to keep Penrose at our disposal. We shall want him again.

On arriving at Ten Acres Lodge, I found Romayne in his study. His manuscript lay before him — but he was not at work. He looked worn and haggard. To this day I don't know from what precise nervous malady he suffers; I could only guess that it had been troubling him again since he and I last met.

My first conventional civilities were dedicated, of course, to his wife. She is still in attendance on her mother. Mrs Eyrecourt is now considered to be out of danger. But the good lady (who is ready enough to recommend doctors to other people) persists in thinking that she is too robust a person to require medical help herself. The physician in attendance trusts entirely to her daughter to persuade her to persevere with the necessary course of medicine. Don't suppose that I trouble you by mentioning these trumpery circumstances without a reason. We shall have occasion to return to Mrs Eyrecourt and her doctor.

Before I had been five minutes in his company, Romayne asked me if I had seen Winterfield

since his visit to Ten Acres Lodge.

I said I had seen him, and waited, anticipating the next question. Romayne fulfilled my expectations. He inquired if Winterfield had left London.

There are certain cases (as I am told by medical authorities) in which the dangerous system of bleeding a patient still has its advantages. There are other cases in which the dangerous system of telling the truth becomes equally judicious. I said to Romayne, 'If I answer you honestly, will you consider it as strictly confidential? Mr Winterfield, I regret to say, has no intention of improving his acquaintance with you. He asked me to conceal from you that he is still in London.'

Romayne's face plainly betrayed that he was annoyed and irritated. 'Nothing that you say to me, Father Benwell, shall pass the walls of this room.' he replied. 'Did Winterfield give any reason for not continuing his acquaintance with me?'

I told the truth once more, with courteous expressions of regret. 'Mr Winterfield spoke of an ungracious reception on the part of Mrs Romayne.'

He started to his feet, and walked irritably up and down the room. 'It is beyond endurance!' he said to himself.

The truth had served its purpose by this time. I affected not to have heard him. 'Did you speak to me?' I asked.

He used a milder form of expression. 'It is most unfortunate,' he said. 'I must

immediately send back the valuable book which Mr Winterfield has lent to me. And that is not the worst of it. There are other volumes in his library which I have the greatest interest in consulting — and it is impossible for me to borrow them now. At this time, too, when I have lost Penrose, I had hoped to find in Winterfield another friend who sympathised with my pursuits. There is something so cheering and attractive in his manner — and he has just the boldness and novelty of view in his opinions that appeal to a man like me. It was a pleasant future to look forward to; and it must be sacrificed — and to what? To a woman's caprice.'

From our point of view this was a frame of mind to be encouraged. I tried the experiment of modestly taking the blame on myself. I suggested that I might be (quite innocently) answerable for Romayne's disappointment.

He looked at me, thoroughly puzzled. I repeated what I had said to Winterfield. 'Did you mention to Mrs Romayne that I was the means of introducing you — ?'

He was too impatient to let me finish the sentence. 'I did mention it to Mrs Romayne,' he said. 'And what of it?'

'Pardon me for reminding you that Mrs Romayne has Protestant prejudices,' I rejoined. 'Mr Winterfield would, I fear, not be very welcome to her as the friend of a Catholic priest.'

He was almost angry with me for suggesting the very explanation which had proved so acceptable to Winterfield.

'Nonsense!' he cried. 'My wife is far too well-bred a woman to let her prejudices express themselves in *that* way. Winterfield's personal appearance must have inspired her with some unreasonable antipathy, or — '

He stopped, and turned away thoughtfully to the window. Some vague suspicion had probably entered his mind, which he had only become aware of at that moment, and which he was not quite able to realise as yet. I did my best to encourage the new train of thought.

'What other reason *can* there be?' I asked.

He turned on me sharply. 'I don't know. Do you?'

I ventured on a courteous remonstrance. 'My dear sir! if you can't find another reason, how can I? It must have been a sudden antipathy, as you say. Such things do happen between strangers. I suppose I am right in assuming that Mrs Romayne and Mr Winterfield are strangers?'

His eyes flashed with a sudden sinister brightness — the new idea had caught light in his mind. 'They *met* as strangers,' he said.

There he stopped again, and returned to the window. I felt that I might lose the place I had gained in his confidence if I pressed the subject any farther. Besides, I had my reasons for saying a word about Penrose next. As it happened, I had received a letter from him, relating to his present employment, and sending kindest regards to his dear friend and master in a postscript.

I gave the message. Romayne looked round,

with an instant change in his face. The mere sound of Penrose's name seemed to act as a relief to the gloom and suspicion that had oppressed him the moment before. 'You don't know how I miss the dear gentle little fellow,' he said sadly.

'Why not write to him?' I suggested. 'He would be so glad to hear from you again.'

'I don't know where to write.'

'Did I not send you his address when I forwarded your letter to him?'

'No.'

'Then let me atone for my forgetfulness at once.'

I wrote down the address, and took my leave.

As I approached the door I noticed on a side table the Catholic volumes which Penrose left with Romayne. One of them was open, with a pencil lying beside it. I thought that a good sign — but I said nothing.

Romayne pressed my hand at parting. 'You have been very kind and friendly, Father Benwell,' he said. 'I shall be glad to see you again.'

Don't mention it in quarters where it might do me harm. Do you know, I really pitied him. He has sacrificed everything to his marriage — and his marriage has disappointed him. He was even reduced to be friendly with Me.

Of course when the right time comes I shall give Penrose leave of absence. Do you foresee, as I do, the speedy return of 'the dear gentle little fellow' to his old employment; the resumed

work of conversion advancing more rapidly than ever; and the jealousy of the Protestant wife aggravating the false position in which she is already placed by her equivocal reception of Winterfield? You may answer this by reminding me of the darker side of the prospect. An heir may be born; and the heir's mother, backed by general opinion, may insist — if there is any hesitation in the matter — on asserting the boy's natural right to succeed his father.

Patience, my reverend colleague! There is no threatening of any such calamity yet. And, even if it happens, don't forget that Romayne has inherited a second fortune. The Vange estate has an estimated value. If the act of restitution represented that value in ready money, do you think the Church would discourage a good convert by refusing his cheque? You know better than that — and so do I.

The next day I called to inquire how Mrs Eyrecourt was getting on. The report was favourable. Three days later I called again. The report was still more encouraging. I was also informed that Mrs Romayne had returned to Ten Acres Lodge.

Much of my success in life has been achieved by never being in a hurry. I was not in a hurry now. Time sometimes brings opportunities — and opportunities are worth waiting for.

Let me make this clear by an example.

A man of headlong disposition, in my place, would have probably spoken of Miss Eyrecourt's marriage to Romayne at his first meeting with

Winterfield, and would have excited their distrust, and put them respectively on their guard, without obtaining any useful result. I can, at any time, make the disclosure to Romayne which informs him that his wife had been Winterfield's guest in Devonshire, when she affected to meet her former host on the footing of a stranger. In the meanwhile, I give Penrose ample opportunity for innocently widening the breach between husband and wife.

You see, I hope, that if I maintain a passive position, it is not from indolence or discouragement. Now we may get on.

After an interval of a few days more I decided on making further inquiries at Mrs Eyrecourt's house. This time, when I left my card, I sent a message, asking if the lady could receive me. Shall I own my weakness? She possesses all the information that I want, and she has twice baffled my inquiries. Under these humiliating circumstances, it is part of the priestly pugnacity of my disposition to inquire again.

I was invited to go upstairs.

The front and back drawing-rooms of the house were thrown into one. Mrs Eyrecourt was being gently moved backwards and forwards in a chair on wheels, propelled by her maid; two gentlemen being present, visitors like myself. In spite of rouge and loosely folded lace and flowing draperies, she presented a deplorable spectacle. The bodily part of her looked like a dead woman, painted and revived — while the moral part, in the strongest contrast, was just as lively as ever.

'So glad to see you again, Father Benwell, and so much obliged by your kind inquiries. I am quite well, though the doctor won't admit it. Isn't it funny to see me being wheeled about, like a child in a perambulator? Returning to first principles, I call it. You see it's a law of my nature that I must go about. The doctor won't let me go about outside the house, so I go about inside the house. Matilda is the nurse, and I am the baby who will learn to walk some of these days. Are you tired, Matilda? No? Then give me another turn, there's a good creature. Movement, perpetual movement, is a law of nature. Oh, dear no, doctor; I didn't make that discovery for myself. Some eminent scientific person mentioned it in a lecture. The ugliest man I ever saw. Now back again, Matilda. Let me introduce you to my friends, Father Benwell. Introducing is out of fashion, I know. But I am one of the few women who can resist the tyranny of fashion. I like introducing people. Sir John Drone — Father Benwell. Father Benwell — Doctor Wybrow. Ah, yes, you know the doctor by reputation? Shall I give you his character? Personally charming; professionally detestable. Pardon my impudence, doctor; it is one of the consequences of the overflowing state of my health. Another turn, Matilda — and a little faster this time. Oh, how I wish I was travelling by railway.'

There, her breath failed her. She reclined in her chair, and fanned herself silently — for awhile.

I was now able to turn my attention to the two

visitors. Sir John Drone, it was easy to see, would be no obstacle to confidential conversation with Mrs Eyrecourt. An excellent country gentleman, with the bald head, the ruddy complexion, and the inexhaustible capacity for silence, so familiar to us in English society — there you have the true description of Sir John. But the famous physician was quite another sort of man. I had only to look at him, and to feel myself condemned to small talk while *he* was in the room.

You have always heard of it in my correspondence, whenever I have been in the wrong. I was in the wrong again now — I had forgotten the law of chances. Capricious Fortune, after a long interval, was about to declare herself again in my favour, by means of the very woman who had twice already got the better of me. What a recompense for my kind inquiries after Mrs Eyrecourt! She recovered breath enough to begin talking again.

'Dear me, how dull you are!' she said to us. 'Why don't you amuse a poor prisoner confined to the house? Rest a little, Matilda, or you will be falling ill next. Doctor! is this your last professional visit?'

'Promise to take care of yourself, Mrs Eyrecourt, and I will confess that the professional visits are over. I come here today only as a friend.'

'You best of men! Do me another favour. Enliven our dullness. Tell us some interesting story about a patient. These great doctors, Sir John, pass their lives in a perfect atmosphere of romance. Dr Wybrow's consulting-room is like

your confessional, Father Benwell. The most fascinating sins and sorrows are poured into his ears. What is the last romance in real life, doctor, that has asked you to treat it medically? We don't want names and places — we are good children; we only want a story.'

Dr Wybrow looked at me with a smile.

'It is impossible to persuade ladies,' he said, 'that we, too, are father-confessors in our way. The first duty of a doctor, Mrs Eyrecourt — '

'Is to cure people, of course,' she interposed in her smartest manner.

The doctor answered seriously. 'No, indeed. That is only the second duty. Our first duty is invariably to respect the confidence of our patients. However,' he resumed in his easier tone. 'I happen to have seen a patient to-day, under circumstances which the rules of professional honour do not forbid me to mention. I don't know, Mrs Eyrecourt, whether you will quite like to be introduced to the scene of the story. The scene is in a madhouse.'

Mrs Eyrecourt burst out with a coquettish little scream, and shook her fan at the doctor. 'No horrors!' she cried. 'The bare idea of a madhouse distracts me with terror. Oh, fie, fie! I won't listen to you — I won't look at you — I positively refuse to be frightened out of my wits. Matilda! wheel me away to the farthest end of the room. My vivid imagination, Father Benwell, is my rock ahead in life. I declare I can *smell* the odious madhouse. Go straight to

the window, Matilda; I want to bury my nose among the flowers.'

Sir John, upon this, spoke for the first time. His language consisted entirely of beginnings of sentences, mutely completed by a smile. 'Upon my word, you know. Eh, Doctor Wybrow? A man of your experience. Horrors in madhouses. A lady in delicate health. No, really. Upon my honour, now, I cannot. Something funny, oh yes. But such a subject, oh no.'

He rose to leave us. Doctor Wybrow gently stopped him. 'I had a motive, Sir John,' he said, 'but I won't trouble you with needless explanations. There is a person, unknown to me, whom I want to discover. You are a great deal in society when you are in London. May I ask if you have ever met with a gentleman named Winterfield?'

I have always considered the power of self-control as one of the strongest points in my character. For the future I shall be more humble. When I heard that name, my surprise so completely mastered me that I sat self-betrayed to Dr Wybrow, as the man who could answer his question.

In the meanwhile, Sir John took his time to consider, and discovered that he had never heard of a person named Winterfield. Having acknowledged his ignorance, in his own eloquent language, he drifted away to the window-box in the next room, and gravely contemplated Mrs Eyrecourt, with her nose buried in flowers.

The doctor turned to me. 'Am I wrong, Father Benwell, in supposing that I had better have

addressed myself to *you*?'

I admitted that I knew a gentleman named Winterfield.

Dr Wybrow got up directly. 'Have you a few minutes to spare?' he asked. It is needless to say that I was at the doctor's disposal. 'My house is close by, and my carriage is at the door,' he resumed. 'When you feel inclined to say good-bye to our friend Mrs Eyrecourt, I have something to say to you which I think you ought to know.'

We took our departure at once. Mrs Eyrecourt (leaving some of the colour of her nose among the flowers) patted me encouragingly with her fan, and told the doctor that he was forgiven, on the understanding that he would 'never do it again.' In five minutes more we were in Dr Wybrow's study.

My watch tells me that I cannot hope to finish this letter by post time. Accept what I have written thus far — and be assured that the conclusion of my report shall follow a day later.

II

The Doctor began cautiously. 'Winterfield is not a very common name.' he said. 'But it may not be amiss, Father Benwell, to discover, if we can, whether *your* Winterfield is the man of whom I am in search. Do you only know him by name? or are you a friend of his?'

I answered, of course, that I was a friend.

Doctor Wybrow went on. 'Will you pardon

me if I venture on an indiscreet question? When you are acquainted with the circumstances, I am sure you will understand and excuse me. Are you aware of any — what shall I call it? — any romantic incident in Mr Winterfield's past life?'

This time — feeling myself, in all probability, on the brink of discovery — I was careful to preserve my composure. I said, quietly, 'Some such incident as you describe has occurred in Mr Winterfield's past life.' There I stopped discreetly, and looked as if I knew all about it.

The doctor showed no curiosity to hear more. 'My object,' he went on, 'was merely to be reasonably sure that I was speaking to the right person, in speaking to you. I may now tell you that I have no personal interest in trying to discover Mr Winterfield; I only act as the representative of an old friend of mine. He is the proprietor of a private asylum at Sandsworth — a man whose integrity is beyond dispute, or he would not be my friend. You understand my motive in saying this?'

Proprietors of private asylums are, in these days, the objects of very general distrust in England. I understood the doctor's motive perfectly.

He proceeded. 'Yesterday evening, my friend called upon me, and said that he had a remarkable case in his house, which he believed would interest me. The person to whom he alluded was a French boy, whose mental powers had been imperfectly developed from his childhood. The mischief had been

aggravated, when he was about thirteen years old, by a serious fright. When he was placed in my asylum, he was not idiotic, and not dangerously mad — it was a case (not to use technical language) of deficient intelligence, tending sometimes towards acts of unreasoning mischief and petty theft, but never approaching to acts of downright violence. My friend was especially interested in the lad — won his confidence and affection by acts of kindness — and so improved his bodily health as to justify some hope of also improving the state of his mind, when a misfortune occurred which has altered the whole prospect. The poor creature has fallen ill of a fever, and the fever has developed to typhus. So far, there has been little to interest you — I am coming to a remarkable event at last. At the stage of the fever when delirium usually occurs in patients of sound mind, this crazy French boy has become perfectly sane and reasonable!'

I looked at him, when he made this amazing assertion, with a momentary doubt of his being in earnest. Doctor Wybrow understood me.

'Just what I thought, too, when I first heard it!' he said. 'My friend was neither offended nor surprised. After inviting me to go to his house, and judge for myself, he referred me to a similar case, publicly cited in the 'Cornhill Magazine,' for the month of April, 1879, in an article entitled 'Bodily Illness as a Mental Stimulant.' The article is published anonymously; but the character of the periodical in which it appears is a sufficient guarantee of the trustworthiness

251

of the statement. I was so far influenced by the testimony thus cited, that I drove to Sandsworth and examined the case myself.'

'Did the examination satisfy you?'

'Thoroughly. When I saw him last night, the poor boy was as sane as I am. There is, however, a complication in this instance, which is not mentioned in the case related in print. The boy appears to have entirely forgotten every event in his past life, reckoning from the time when the bodily illness brought with it the strange mental recovery which I have mentioned to you.'

This was a disappointment. I had begun to hope for some coming result, obtained by the lad's confession.

'Is it quite correct to call him sane, when his memory is gone?' I ventured to ask.

'In this case there is no necessity to enter into the question,' the Doctor answered. 'The boy's lapse of memory refers, as I told you, to his past life — that is to say, his life when his intellect was deranged. During the extraordinary interval of sanity that has now declared itself, he is putting his mental powers to their first free use; and none of them fail him, so far as I can see. His new memory (if I may call it so) preserves the knowledge of what has happened since his illness. You may imagine how this problem in brain disease interests me; and you will not wonder that I am going back to Sandsworth to-morrow afternoon, when I have done with my professional visits. But you may be reasonably surprised at my troubling *you* with details which are mainly interesting to a medical man.'

Was he about to ask me to go with him to the asylum? I replied very briefly, merely saying that the details were interesting to every student of human nature. If he could have felt my pulse at that moment, I am afraid he might have thought I was in a fair way of catching the fever too.

'Prepare yourself,' he resumed, 'for another surprising circumstance. Mr Winterfield is, by some incomprehensible accident, associated with one of the mischievous tricks played by the French boy, before he was placed under my friend's care. There, at any rate, is the only explanation by which we can account for the discovery of an envelope (with enclosures) found sewn up in the lining of the lad's waistcoat, and directed to Mr Winterfield — without any place of address.'

I leave you to imagine the effect which those words produced on me.

'Now,' said the doctor, 'you will understand why I put such strange questions to you. My friend and I are both hardworking men. We go very little into society, as the phrase is; and neither he nor I had ever heard the name of Winterfield. As a certain proportion of my patients happen to be people with a large experience of society, I undertook to make inquiries, so that the packet might be delivered, if possible, to the right person. You heard how Mrs Eyrecourt (surely a likely lady to assist me?) received my unlucky reference to the madhouse; and you saw how I puzzled Sir John. I consider myself most fortunate,

Father Benwell, in having had the honour of meeting you. Will you accompany me to the asylum to-morrow? And can you add to the favour by bringing Mr Winterfield with you?'

This last request it was out of my power — really out of my power — to grant. Winterfield had left London that morning on his visit to Paris. His address there was, thus far, not known to me.

'Well, you must represent your friend,' the Doctor said. 'Time is every way of importance in this case. Will you kindly call here at five tomorrow afternoon?'

I was punctual to my appointment. We drove together to the asylum.

There is no need for me to trouble you with a narrative of what I saw — favoured by Doctor Wybrow's introduction — at the French boy's bedside. It was simply a repetition of what I had already heard. There he lay, at the height of the fever, asking, in the intervals of relief, intelligent questions relating to the medicines administered to him, and perfectly understanding the answers. He was only irritable when we asked him to take his memory back to the time before his illness; and then he answered in French, 'I haven't got a memory.'

But I have something else to tell you, which is deserving of your best attention. The envelope and its enclosures (addressed to 'Bernard Winterfield, Esqre.') are in my possession. The Christian name sufficiently

identifies the inscription with the Winterfield whom I know.

The circumstances under which the discovery was made were related to me by the proprietor of the asylum.

When the boy was brought to the house, two French ladies (his mother and sister) accompanied him, and mentioned what had been their own domestic experience of the case. They described the wandering propensities which took the lad away from home, and the odd concealment of his waistcoat, on the last occasion when he had returned from one of his vagrant outbreaks.

On his first night at the asylum he became excited by finding himself in a strange place. It was necessary to give him a composing draught. On going to bed, he was purposely not prevented from hiding his waistcoat under the pillow, as usual.

When the sedative had produced its effect, the attendant easily possessed himself of the hidden garment. It was the plain duty of the master of the house to make sure that nothing likely to be turned to evil uses was concealed by a patient. The seal which had secured the envelope was found, on examination, to have been broken.

'I would not have broken the seal myself,' our host added. 'But, as things were, I thought it my duty to look at the enclosures. They refer to private affairs of Mr Winterfield, in which he is deeply interested, and they ought to have been long since placed in his possession. I need hardly say that I consider myself bound

to preserve the strictest silence as to what I have read. An envelope, containing some blank sheets of paper, was put back in the boy's waistcoat, so that he might feel it in its place under the lining, when he woke. The original envelope and enclosures (with a statement of circumstances signed by my assistant and myself) have been secured under another cover, sealed with my own seal. I have done my best to discover Mr Bernard Winterfield. He appears not to live in London. At least I failed to find his name in the Directory. I wrote next, mentioning what had happened, to the English gentleman to whom I send reports of the lad's health. He couldn't help me. A second letter to the French ladies only produced the same result. I own I should be glad to get rid of my responsibility on honourable terms.'

All this was said in the boy's presence. He lay listening to it as if it had been a story told of someone else. I could not resist the useless desire to question him. Not speaking French myself (although I can read the language), I asked Doctor Wybrow and his friend to interpret for me.

My questions led to nothing. The French boy knew no more about the stolen envelope than I did.

There was no discoverable motive, mind, for suspecting him of imposing on us. When I said, 'Perhaps you stole it?' he answered quite composedly, 'Very likely; they tell me I have been mad; I don't remember it myself; but

mad people do strange things.' I tried him again. 'Or, perhaps, you took it away out of mischief?' 'Yes.' 'And you broke the seal, and looked at the papers?' 'I dare say.' 'And then you kept them hidden, thinking they might be of some use to you? Or perhaps feeling ashamed of what you had done, and meaning to restore them if you got the opportunity?' 'You know best, sir.' The same result followed when we tried to find out where he had been, and what people had taken care of him, during his last vagrant escape from home. It was a new revelation to him that he had been anywhere. With evident interest, he applied to *us* to tell him where he had wandered to, and what people he had seen!

So our last attempts at enlightenment ended. We came to the final question of how to place the papers, with the least possible loss of time, in Mr Winterfield's hands.

His absence in Paris having been mentioned, I stated plainly my own position towards him at the present time.

'Mr Winterfield has made an appointment with me to call at his hotel, on his return to London,' I said. 'I shall probably be the first friend who sees him. If you will trust me with your sealed packet, in consideration of these circumstances, I will give you a formal receipt for it in Doctor Wybrow's presence — and I will add any written pledge that you may require on my part, acting as Mr Winterfield's representative and friend. Perhaps you would like a reference, as well?'

He made a courteous reply. 'A friend of Doctor Wybrow's,' he said, 'requires no other reference.'

'Excuse me,' I persisted. 'I had the honour of meeting Doctor Wybrow, for the first time, yesterday. Permit me to refer you to Lord Loring, who has long known me as his spiritual director and friend.'

This account of myself settled the matter. I drew out the necessary securities — and I have all the papers lying before me on my desk at this moment.

You remember how seals were broken, and impressed again, at the Roman post-office, in the revolutionary days when we were both young men? Thanks to the knowledge then obtained, the extraordinary events which once associated Mr Winterfield and Miss Eyrecourt are at last plainly revealed to me. Copies of the papers are in my possession, and the originals are sealed again, with the crest of the proprietor of the asylum, as if nothing had happened. I make no attempt to excuse myself. You know our motto: — THE END JUSTIFIES THE MEANS.

I don't propose to make any premature use of the information which I have obtained. The first and foremost necessity, as I have already reminded you, is to give Penrose the undisturbed opportunity of completing the conversion of Romayne. During this interval, my copies of the papers are at the disposal of my reverend brethren at headquarters.

THE STOLEN PAPERS. — (COPIES.)

Number One. — From Emma Winterfield to Bernard Winterfield.

4, Maidwell Buildings, Belhaven.

How shall I address you? Dear Bernard, or Sir? It doesn't matter. I am going to do one of the few good actions of my life; and familiarities or formalities matter nothing to a woman who lies on her deathbed.

Yes — I have met with another accident. Shortly after the date of our separation, you heard, I think, of the fall in the circus that fractured my skull? On that occasion a surgical operation, and a bit of silver plate in place of the bone, put me right again. This time it has been the kick of a horse, in the stables. Some internal injury is the consequence. I may die to-morrow, or live till next week. Anyway, the doctor has confessed it, — my time has come.

Mind one thing. The drink — that vile habit which lost me your love and banished me from your house — the drink is not to blame for this last misfortune. Only the day before it happened I had taken the pledge, under persuasion of the good rector here, the Reverend Mr Fennick. It is he who has brought me to make this confession, and who takes it down in writing at my bedside. Do you remember how I once hated the very name of a parson — and when you proposed, in joke, to marry me before the registrar, how I took it in downright earnest, and kept you to

your word? We poor horseriders and acrobats only knew clergymen as the worst enemies we had — always using their influence to keep the people out of our show, and the bread out of our mouths. If I had met with Mr Fennick in my younger days, what a different woman I might have been!

Well, regrets of that kind are useless now. I am truly sorry, Bernard, for the evil that I have done to you; and I ask your pardon with a contrite heart.

You will at least allow it in my favour that your drunken wife knew she was unworthy of you. I refused to accept the allowance that you offered to me. I respected your name. For seven years from the time of our separation I returned to my profession under an assumed name, and never troubled you. The one thing I could not do was to forget you. If you were infatuated by my unlucky beauty, I loved devotedly on my side. The well-born gentleman who had sacrificed everything for my sake, was something more than mortal in my estimation; he was — no! I won't shock the good man who writes this by saying what he was. Besides, what do you care for my thoughts of you now?

If you had only been content to remain as I left you — or if I had not found out that you were in love with Miss Eyrecourt, and were likely to marry her, in the belief that death had released you from me — I should have lived and died, doing you no other injury than the first great injury of consenting to be your wife.

But I made the discovery — it doesn't matter

how. Our circus was in Devonshire at the time. My jealous rage maddened me, and I had a wicked admirer in a man who was old enough to be my father. I let him suppose that the way to my favour lay through helping my revenge on the woman who was about to take my place. He found the money to have you watched at home and abroad; he put the false announcement of my death in the daily newspapers, to complete your delusion; he baffled the inquiries made through your lawyers to obtain positive proof of my death. And last, and (in those wicked days) best service of all he took me to Brussels and posted me at the door of the English Church, so that your lawful wife (with her marriage certificate in her hand) was the first person who met you and the mock Mrs Winterfield on your way from the altar to the wedding breakfast.

I own it, to my shame. I triumphed in the mischief I had done.

But I had deserved to suffer; and I did suffer, when I heard that Miss Eyrecourt's mother and her two friends took her away from you — with her own entire approval — at the church door, and restored her to society, without a stain on her reputation. How the Brussels marriage was kept a secret, I could not find out. And when I threatened them with exposure, I got a lawyer's letter, and was advised in my own interests to hold my tongue. The rector has since told me that your marriage to Miss Eyrecourt could be lawfully declared null and void, and that the circumstances would excuse *you*, before any

judge in England. I can now well understand that people, with rank and money to help them, can avoid exposure to which the poor, in their places, must submit.

One more duty (the last) still remains to be done.

I declare solemnly, on my deathbed, that you acted in perfect good faith when you married Miss Eyrecourt. You have not only been a man cruelly injured by me, but vilely insulted and misjudged by the two Eyrecourts, and by the lord and lady who encouraged them to set you down as a villain guilty of heartless and shameless deceit.

It is my conviction that these people might have done more than misinterpret your honourable submission to the circumstances in which you were placed. They might have prosecuted you for bigamy — if they could have got me to appear against you. I am comforted when I remember that I did make some small amends. I kept out of their way and yours, from that day to this.

I am told that I owe it to you to leave proof of my death behind me.

When the doctor writes my certificate, he will mention the mark by which I may be identified, if this reaches you (as I hope and believe it will) between the time of my death and my burial. The rector, who will close and seal these lines, as soon as the breath is out of my body, will add what he can to identify me; and the landlady of this house is ready to answer any questions that may be put to her. This time you may be

really assured that you are free. When I am buried, and they show you my nameless grave in the churchyard, I know your kind heart — I die, Bernard, in the firm belief that you will forgive me.

There was one thing more that I had to ask of you, relating to a poor lost creature who is in the room with us at this moment. But, oh, I am so weary! Mr Fennick will tell you what it is. Say to yourself sometimes — perhaps when you have married some lady who is worthy of you — There was good as well as bad in poor Emma. Farewell.

Number Two — From the Reverend Charles Fennick to Bernard Winterfield

The Rectory, Belhaven.

Sir, — It is my sad duty to inform you that Mrs Emma Winterfield died this morning, a little before five o'clock. I will add no comment of mine to the touching language in which she has addressed you. God has, I most sincerely believe, accepted the poor sinner's repentance. Her contrite spirit is at peace, among the forgiven ones in the world beyond the grave.

In consideration of her wish that you should see her in death, the coffin will be kept open until the last moment. The medical man in attendance has kindly given me a copy of his certificate, which I enclose. You will see that the remains are identified by the description of

a small silver plate on the right parietal bone of the skull.

I need hardly add that all the information I can give you is willingly at your service.

She mentions, poor soul, something which she had to ask of you. I prefer the request which, in her exhausted state, she was unable to address to you in her own words.

While the performances of the circus were taking place in the next county to ours, a wandering lad, evidently of deficient intelligence, was discovered, trying to creep under the tent to see what was going on. He could give no intelligible account of himself. The late Mrs Winterfield (who was born and brought up, as I understand, in France) discovered that the boy was French, and felt interested in the unfortunate creature, from former happy association with kind friends of his nation. She took care of him, from that time to the day of her death — and he appeared to be gratefully attached to her.

I say 'appeared,' because an inveterate reserve marks one of the peculiarities of the mental affliction from which he suffers. Even his benefactress never could persuade him to take her into his confidence. In other respects, her influence (so far as I can learn) had been successfully exerted in restraining certain mischievous propensities in him, which occasionally showed themselves. The effect of her death has been to intensify that reserve to which I have already alluded. He is sullen and irritable — and the good landlady at the lodgings

does not disguise that she shrinks from taking care of him, even for a few days. Until I hear from you, he will remain under the charge of my housekeeper at the rectory.

You have, no doubt, anticipated the request which the poor sufferer wished to address to you but a few hours before her death. She hoped that you might be willing to place this friendless and helpless creature under competent protection. Failing your assistance, I shall have no alternative, however I may regret it, but to send him to the workhouse of this town, on his way, probably, to the public asylum.

<div style="text-align: right">Believe me, sir, your faithful servant,
CHARLES FENNICK.</div>

P.S. — I fear my letter and its enclosures may be delayed in reaching you.

Yesterday evening, I had returned to my house, before it occurred to me that Mrs Winterfield had not mentioned your address. My only excuse for this forgetfulness is, that I was very much distressed while I was writing by her bedside. I at once went back to the lodgings, but she had fallen asleep, and I dare not disturb her. This morning, when I returned to the house, she was dead. There is an allusion to Devonshire in her letter, which suggests that your residence may be in that county; and I think she once spoke of you as a person of rank and fortune. Having failed to find your name in a London directory, I am now about to search our free library here for a country history of Devon, on the chance that it may assist me. Let me add,

for your own satisfaction, that no eyes but mine will see these papers. For security's sake, I shall seal them at once, and write your name on the envelope.

Added by Father Benwell.

How the boy contrived to possess himself of the sealed packet, we shall probably never discover. Anyhow, we know that he must have escaped from the rectory, with the papers in his possession, and that he did certainly get back to his mother and sister in London.

With such complete information as I now have at my disposal, the prospect is as clear again as we can desire. The separation of Romayne from his wife, and the alteration of his will in favour of the Church, seem to be now merely questions of time.

Book The Fourth

1

The Breach is Widened

A fortnight after Father Benwell's discovery, Stella followed her husband one morning into his study. 'Have you heard from Mr Penrose?' she inquired.

'Yes. He will be here to-morrow.'

'To make a long visit?'

'I hope so. The longer the better.'

She looked at him with a mingled expression of surprise and reproach. 'Why do you say that?' she asked. 'Why do you want him so much — when you have got Me?'

Thus far, he had been sitting at his desk, resting his head on his hand, with his downcast eyes fixed on an open book. When she put her last question to him, he suddenly looked up. Through the large window at his side, the morning light fell on his face. The haggard look of suffering, which Stella remembered on the day when they met on the deck of the steamboat, was again visible — not softened and chastened now by the touching resignation of the bygone time, but intensified by the dogged and despairing endurance of a man weary of himself and his life. Her heart ached for him. She said softly,

'I don't mean to reproach you.'

'Are you jealous of Penrose?' he asked, with a bitter smile.

She desperately told him the truth. 'I am afraid of Penrose,' she answered.

He eyed her with a strange expression of suspicious surprise. 'Why are you afraid of Penrose?'

It was no time to run the risk of irritating him. The torment of the Voice had returned in the past night. The old gnawing remorse of the fatal day of the duel had betrayed itself in the wild words that had escaped him, when he sank into a broken slumber as the morning dawned. Feeling the truest pity for him, she was still resolute to assert herself against the coming interference of Penrose. She tried her ground by a dangerous means — the means of an indirect reply.

'I think you might have told me,' she said, 'that Mr Penrose was a Catholic priest.'

He looked down again at his book.

'How did you know Penrose was a Catholic priest?'

'I had only to look at the direction on your letters to him.'

'Well, and what is there to frighten you in his being a priest? You told me at the Lorings' ball that you took an interest in Penrose because I liked him.'

'I didn't know then, Lewis, that he had concealed his profession from us. I can't help distrusting a man who does that.'

He laughed — not very kindly. 'You might as well say you distrust a man who conceals

268

that he is an author, by writing an anonymous book. What Penrose did, he did under orders from his superior — and, moreover, he frankly owned to me that he was a priest. If you blame anybody, you had better blame me for respecting his confidence.'

She drew back from him, hurt by the tone in which he spoke to her. 'I remember the time, Lewis,' she said, 'when you would have been more indulgent towards my errors — even if I am wrong.'

That simple appeal touched his better nature. 'I don't mean to be hard on you, Stella,' he answered. 'It is a little irritating to hear you say that you distrust the most devoted and most affectionate friend that man ever had. Why can't I love my wife, and love my friend, too? You don't know, when I am trying to get on with my book, how I miss the help and sympathy of Penrose. The very sound of his voice used to encourage me. Come, Stella, give me a kiss — and let us, as the children say, make it up!'

He rose from his writing-table. She met him more than half way, and pressed all her love — and perhaps a little of her fear — on his lips. He returned the kiss as warmly as it was given and then, unhappily for both of them, he went back to the subject.

'My own love,' he said, 'try to like my friend for my sake; and be tolerant of other forms of Christianity besides the form which happens to be yours.'

Her smiling lips closed; she turned from him. With the sensitive selfishness of a woman's love,

she looked on Penrose as a robber who had stolen the sympathies which should have been wholly hers. As she moved away, her quick observation noticed the open book on the desk, with notes and lines in pencil on the margin of the page. What had Romayne been reading which interested him in *that* way? If he had remained silent, she would have addressed the inquiry to him openly. But he was hurt, on his side, by the sudden manner of her withdrawal from him. He spoke — and his tone was colder than ever.

'I won't attempt to combat your prejudices,' he said. 'But one thing I must seriously ask of you. When my friend Penrose comes here tomorrow, don't treat him as you treated Mr Winterfield.'

There was a momentary paleness in her face which looked like fear, but it passed away again. She confronted him firmly with steady eyes.

'Why do you refer again to that?' she asked. 'Is — ' (she hesitated, and recovered herself) — 'is Mr Winterfield another devoted friend of yours?'

He walked to the door, as if he could hardly trust his temper if he answered her — stopped — and, thinking better of it, turned towards her again.

'We won't quarrel, Stella,' he rejoined; 'I will only say I am sorry you don't appreciate my forbearance. Your reception of Mr Winterfield has lost me the friendship of a man whom I sincerely liked, and who might have assisted my literary labours. You were ill at the time,

270

and anxious about Mrs Eyrecourt. I respected your devotion to your mother. I remembered your telling me, when you first went away to nurse her, that your conscience accused you of having sometimes thoughtlessly neglected your mother in her days of health and good spirits, and I admired the motive of atonement which took you to her bedside. For those reasons I shrank from saying a word that might wound you. But, because I was silent, it is not the less true that you surprised and disappointed me. Don't do it again! Whatever you may privately think of Catholic priests, I once more seriously request you not to let Penrose see it.'

He left the room.

She stood, looking after him as he closed the door, like a woman thunderstruck. Never yet had he looked at her as he looked when he spoke his last warning words. With a heavy sigh she roused herself. The vague dread with which his tone rather than his words had inspired her, strangely associated itself with the momentary curiosity which she had felt on noticing the annotated book that lay on his desk.

She snatched up the volume, and looked at the open page. It contained the closing paragraphs of an eloquent attack on Protestantism, from the Roman Catholic point of view. With trembling hands she turned back to the title page. It presented this written inscription: — 'To Lewis Romayne from his attached friend and servant, Arthur Penrose.'

'God help me!' she said to herself, 'the priest has got between us already!'

271

2

A Christian Jesuit

On the next day Penrose arrived on his visit to Romayne.

The affectionate meeting between the two men tested Stella's self-control as it had never been tried yet. She submitted to the ordeal with the courage of a woman whose happiness depended on her outward graciousness of manner towards her husband's friend. Her reception of Penrose, viewed as an act of refined courtesy, was beyond reproach. When she found her opportunity of leaving the room, Romayne gratefully opened the door for her. 'Thank you!' he whispered, with a look which was intended to reward her.

She only bowed to him, and took refuge in her own room.

Even in trifles, a woman's nature is degraded by the falsities of language and manner which the artificial condition of modern society exacts from her. When she yields herself to more serious deceptions, intended to protect her dearest domestic interests, the mischief is increased in proportion. Deceit, which is the natural weapon of defence used by the weak creature against the strong, then ceases to be confined within the limits assigned by the sense of self-respect and by the restraints of education. A woman in this position will descend, self-blinded, to acts of

meanness which would be revolting to her if they were related of another person. Stella had already begun the process of self-degradation by writing secretly to Winterfield. It was only to warn him of the danger of trusting Father Benwell — but it was a letter, claiming him as her accomplice in an act of deception. That morning she had received Penrose with the outward cordialities of welcome which are offered to an old and dear friend. And now in the safe solitude of her room, she had fallen to a lower depth still. She was deliberately considering the safest means of acquainting herself with the confidential conversation which Romayne and Penrose would certainly hold when she left them together. 'He will try to set my husband against me; and I have a right to know what means he uses, in my own defence.' With that thought she reconciled herself to an action which she would have despised if she had heard of it as the action of another woman.

It was a beautiful autumn day, brightened by clear sunshine, enlivened by crisp air. Stella put on her hat, and went out for a stroll in the grounds.

While she was within view from the windows of the servants' offices she walked away from the house. Turning the corner of a shrubbery, she entered a winding path, on the other side, which led back to the lawn under Romayne's study window. Garden chairs were placed here and there. She took one of them, and seated herself — after a last moment of honourable hesitation — where she could hear the men's

voices through the open window above her.

Penrose was speaking at the time.

'Yes. Father Benwell has granted me a holiday,' he said; 'but I don't come here to be an idle man. You must allow me to employ my term of leave in the pleasantest of all ways. I mean to be your secretary again.'

Romayne sighed. 'Ah, if you knew how I have missed you!'

(Stella waited, in breathless expectation for what Penrose would say to this. Would he speak to *her*? No. There was a natural tact and delicacy in him which waited for the husband to introduce the subject.)

Penrose only said, 'How is the great work getting on?'

The answer was sternly spoken in one word — 'Badly!'

'I am surprised to hear that, Romayne.'

'Why? Were you as innocently hopeful as I was? Did you expect my experience of married life to help me in writing my book?'

Penrose replied after a pause, speaking a little sadly. 'I expected your married life to encourage you in all your highest aspirations,' he said.

(Stella turned pale with suppressed anger. He had spoken with perfect sincerity. The unhappy woman believed that he lied, for the express purpose of rousing irritation against her, in her husband's irritable mind. She listened anxiously for Romayne's answer.)

He made no answer. Penrose changed the subject. 'You are not looking very well,' he gently resumed. 'I am afraid your health has

interfered with your work. Have you had any return — ?'

It was still one of the characteristics of Romayne's nervous irritability that he disliked to hear the terrible delusion of the Voice referred to in words. 'Yes,' he interposed bitterly, 'I have heard it again and again. My right hand is as red as ever, Penrose, with the blood of a fellow-creature. Another destruction of my illusions when I married!'

'Romayne! I don't like to hear you speak of your marriage in that way.'

'Oh, very well. Let us go back to my book. Perhaps I shall get on better with it now you are here to help me. My ambition to make a name in the world has never taken so strong a hold on me (I don't know why, unless other disappointments have had something to do with it) as at this time, when I find I can't give my mind to my work. We will make a last effort together, my friend! If it fails, we will put my manuscripts into the fire, and I will try some other career. Politics are open to me. Through politics, I might make my mark in diplomacy. There is something in directing the destinies of nations wonderfully attractive to me in my present state of feeling. I hate the idea of being indebted for my position in the world, like the veriest fool living, to the accidents of birth and fortune. Are *you* content with the obscure life that you lead? Did you not envy that priest (he is no older than I am) who was sent the other day as the Pope's ambassador to Portugal?'

Penrose spoke out at last without hesitation.

275

'You are in a thoroughly unwholesome state of mind,' he said.

Romayne laughed recklessly. 'When was I ever in a healthy state of mind?' he asked.

Penrose passed the interruption over without notice. 'If I am to do you any good,' he resumed, 'I must know what is really the matter with you. The very last question that I ought to put, and that I wish to put, is the question which you force me to ask.'

'What is it?'

'When you speak of your married life,' said Penrose, 'your tone is the tone of a disappointed man. Have you any serious reason to complain of Mrs Romayne?'

(Stella rose to her feet, in her eagerness to hear what her husband's answer would be.)

'Serious reason?' Romayne repeated. 'How can such an idea have entered your head? I only complain of irritating trifles now and then. Even the best of women is not perfect. It's hard to expect it from any of them.'

(The interpretation of this reply depended entirely on the tone in which it was spoken. What was the animating spirit in this case? Irony or Indulgence? Stella was ignorant of the indirect methods of irritation, by means of which Father Benwell had encouraged Romayne's doubts of his wife's motive for the reception of Winterfield. Her husband's tone, expressing this state of mind, was new to her. She sat down again, divided between hope and fear, waiting to hear more. The next words, spoken by Penrose, astounded her. The priest, the Jesuit, the wily

spiritual intruder between man and wife, actually took the wife's side!)

'Romayne,' he proceeded quietly, 'I want you to be happy.'

'How am I to be happy?'

'I will try and tell you. I believe your wife to be a good woman. I believe she loves you. There is something in her face that speaks for her — even to an inexperienced person like myself. Don't be impatient with her! Put away from you that besetting temptation to speak in irony — it is so easy to take that tone, and sometimes so cruel. I am only a looker-on, I know. Domestic happiness can never be the happiness of *my* life. But I have observed my fellow-creatures of all degrees — and this, I tell you, is the result. The largest number of happy men are the husbands and fathers. Yes; I admit that they have terrible anxieties — but they are fortified by unfailing compensations and encouragements. Only the other day I met with a man who had suffered the loss of fortune and, worse still, the loss of health. He endured those afflictions so calmly that he surprised me. 'What is the secret of your philosophy?' I asked. He answered, 'I can bear anything while I have my wife and my children.' Think of that, and judge for yourself how much happiness you may have left yet ungathered in your married life.'

(Those words touched Stella's higher nature, as the dew touches the thirsty ground. Surely they were nobly spoken! How would her husband receive them?)

'I must think with your mind, Penrose, before

I can do what you ask of me. Is there any method of transformation by which I can change natures with you?' That was all he said — and he said it despondingly.

Penrose understood, and felt for him.

'If there is anything in my nature, worthy to be set as an example to you,' he replied, 'you know to what blessed influence I owe self-discipline and serenity of mind. Remember what I said when I left you in London, to go back to my friendless life. I told you that I found, in the Faith I held, the one sufficient consolation which helped me to bear my lot. And — if there came a time of sorrow in the future — I entreated you to remember what I had said. Have you remembered it?'

'Look at the book here on my desk — look at the other books, within easy reach, on that table — are you satisfied?'

'More than satisfied. Tell me — do you feel nearer to an understanding of the Faith to which I have tried to convert you?'

There was a pause. 'Say that I do feel nearer,' Romayne resumed — 'say that some of my objections are removed — are you really as eager as ever to make a Catholic of me, now that I am a married man?'

'I am even more eager,' Penrose answered. 'I have always believed that your one sure way to happiness lay through your conversion. Now, when I know, from what I have seen and heard in this room, that you are not reconciled, as you should be, to your new life, I am doubly confirmed in my belief. As

278

God is my witness, I speak sincerely. Hesitate no longer! Be converted, and be happy.'

'Have you not forgotten something, Penrose?'

'What have I forgotten?'

'A serious consideration, perhaps. I have a Protestant wife.'

'I have borne that in mind, Romayne, throughout our conversation.'

'And you still say — what you have just said?'

'With my whole heart, I say it! Be converted, and be happy. Be happy, and you will be a good husband. I speak in your wife's interest as well as in yours. People who are happy in each other's society, will yield a little on either side, even on questions of religious belief. And perhaps there may follow a more profitable result still. So far as I have observed, a good husband's example is gladly followed by his wife. Don't think that I am trying to persuade you against your will! I am only telling you, in my own justification, from what motives of love for yourself, and of true interest in your welfare, I speak. You implied just now that you had still some objections left. If I can remove them — well and good. If I fail — if you cannot act on purely conscientious conviction — I not only advise, I entreat you, to remain as you are. I shall be the first to acknowledge that you have done right.'

(This moderation of tone would appeal irresistibly, as Stella well knew, to her husband's ready appreciation of those good qualities in others which he did not himself possess. Once more her suspicion wronged Penrose. Had he his

279

own interested motives for pleading her cause? At the bare thought of it, she left her chair, and, standing under the window, boldly interrupted the conversation by calling to Romayne.)

'Lewis!' she cried, 'why do you stay indoors on this beautiful day? I am sure Mr Penrose would like a walk in the grounds.'

Penrose appeared alone at the window. 'You are quite right, Mrs Romayne,' he said, 'we will join you directly.'

In a few minutes he turned the corner of the house, and met Stella on the lawn. Romayne was not with him. 'Is my husband not coming with us?' she asked.

'He will follow us,' Penrose answered. 'I believe he has some letters to write.'

Stella looked at him, suspecting some under-hand exercise of influence on her husband.

If she had been able to estimate the noble qualities in the nature of Penrose, she might have done him the justice to arrive at a truer conclusion. It was he who had asked leave (when Stella had interrupted them) to take the opportunity of speaking alone with Mrs Romayne. He had said to his friend, 'If I am wrong in my anticipation of the effect of your change of religion on your wife, let me find it out from herself. My one object is to act justly towards you and towards her. I should never forgive myself if I made mischief between you, no matter how innocent of any evil intention I might be.' Romayne had understood him. It was Stella's misfortune ignorantly to misinterpret everything that Penrose said or

did, for the all-sufficient reason that he was a Catholic priest. She had drawn the conclusion that her husband had deliberately left her alone with Penrose, to be persuaded or deluded into giving her sanction to aid the influence of the priest. 'They shall find they are mistaken,' she thought to herself.

'Have I interrupted an interesting conversation?' she inquired abruptly. 'When I asked you to come out, were you talking to my husband about his historical work?'

'No, Mrs Romayne; we were not speaking at that time of the book.'

'May I ask an odd question, Mr Penrose?'

'Certainly!'

'Are you a very zealous Catholic?'

'Pardon me. I am a priest. Surely my profession speaks for me?'

'I hope you have not been trying to convert my husband?'

Penrose stopped and looked at her attentively. 'Are you strongly opposed to your husband's conversation?' he asked.

'As strongly,' she answered, 'as a woman can be.'

'By religious conviction, Mrs Romayne?'

'No. By experience.'

Penrose started. 'Is it indiscreet,' he said gently, 'to inquire what your experience may have been?'

'I will tell you what my experience has been,' Stella replied. 'I am ignorant of theological subtleties, and questions of doctrine are quite beyond me. But this I do know. A well-meaning

281

and zealous Catholic shortened my father's life, and separated me from an only sister whom I dearly loved. I see I shock you — and I daresay you think I am exaggerating?'

'I hear what you say, Mrs Romayne, with very great pain — I don't presume to form any opinion thus far.'

'My sad story can be told in a few words,' Stella proceeded. 'When my elder sister was still a young girl, an aunt of ours (my mother's sister) came to stay with us. She had married abroad, and she was, as I have said, a zealous Catholic. Unknown to the rest of us, she held conversations on religion with my sister — worked on the enthusiasm which was part of the girl's nature — and accomplished her conversion. Other influences, of which I know nothing, were afterwards brought to bear on my sister. She declared her intention of entering a convent. As she was under age, my father had only to interpose his authority to prevent this. She was his favourite child. He had no heart to restrain her by force — he could only try all that the kindest and best of fathers could do to persuade her to remain at home. Even after the years that have passed, I cannot trust myself to speak of it composedly. She persisted; she was as hard as stone. My aunt, when she was entreated to interfere, called her heartless obstinacy 'a vocation.' My poor father's loving resistance was worn out; he slowly drew nearer and nearer to death, from the day when she left us. Let me do her justice, if I can. She has not only never regretted entering the convent — she

282

is so happily absorbed in her religious duties, that she has not the slightest wish to see her mother or me. My mother's patience was soon worn out. The last time I went to the convent, I went by myself. I shall never go there again. She could not conceal her sense of relief when I took my leave of her. I need say no more. Arguments are thrown away on me, Mr Penrose, after what I have seen and felt. I have no right to expect that the consideration of *my* happiness will influence you — but I may perhaps ask you, as a gentleman, to tell me the truth. Do you come here with the purpose of converting my husband?'

Penrose owned the truth, without an instant's hesitation.

'I cannot take your view of your sister's pious devotion of herself to a religious life,' he said. 'But I can, and will, answer you truly. From the time when I first knew him, my dearest object has been to convert your husband to the Catholic Faith.'

Stella drew back from him, as if he had stung her, and clasped her hands in silent despair.

'But I am bound as a Christian,' he went on, 'to do to others as I would they should do to me.'

She turned on him suddenly, her beautiful face radiant with hope, her hand trembling as it caught him by the arm.

'Speak plainly!' she cried.

He obeyed her to the letter.

'The happiness of my friend's wife, Mrs Romayne, is sacred to me for his sake. Be the

283

good angel of your husband's life. I abandon the purpose of converting him.'

He lifted her hand from his arm, and raised it respectfully to his lips. Then, when he had bound himself by a promise that was sacred to him, the terrible influence of the priesthood shook even that brave and lofty soul. He said to himself, as he left her, 'God forgive me if I have done wrong!'

284

3

Winterfield Returns

Twice Father Benwell called at Derwent's Hotel, and twice he was informed that no news had been received there of Mr Winterfield. At the third attempt, his constancy was rewarded. Mr Winterfield had written, and was expected to arrive at the hotel by five o'clock.

It was then half-past four. Father Benwell decided to wait the return of his friend.

He was as anxious to deliver the papers which the proprietor of the asylum had confided to him, as if he had never broken a seal or used a counterfeit to hide the betrayal of a trust. The re-sealed packet was safe in the pocket of his long black frock-coat. His own future proceedings depended, in some degree, on the course which Winterfield might take, when he had read the confession of the unhappy woman who had once been his wife.

Would he show the letter to Stella, at a private interview, as an unanswerable proof that she had cruelly wronged him? And would it in this case be desirable — if the thing could be done — so to handle circumstances as that Romayne might be present, unseen, and might discover the truth for himself? In the other event — that is to say, if Winterfield abstained from communicating the confession to Stella — the responsibility

of making the necessary disclosure must remain with the priest.

Father Benwell walked softly up and down the room, looking about him with quietly-observant eyes. A side table in a corner was covered with letters, waiting Winterfield's return. Always ready for information of any sort, he even looked at the addresses on the letters.

The handwritings presented the customary variety of character. All but three of the envelopes showed the London district post-marks. Two of the other letters (addressed to Winterfield at his club) bore foreign postmarks; and one, as the altered direction showed, had been forwarded from Beaupark House to the hotel.

This last letter especially attracted the priest's attention.

The address was apparently in a woman's handwriting. And it was worthy of remark that she appeared to be the only person among Winterfield's correspondents who was not acquainted with the address of his hotel or of his club. Who could the person be? The subtly-inquiring intellect of Father Benwell amused itself by speculating even on such a trifling problem as this. He little thought that he had a personal interest in the letter. The envelope contained Stella's warning to Winterfield to distrust no less a person than Father Benwell himself!

It was nearly half-past five before quick footsteps were audible outside. Winterfield entered the room.

'This is friendly indeed!' he said. 'I expected to return to the worst of all solitudes — solitude in a hotel. You will stay and dine with me? That's right. You must have thought I was going to settle in Paris. Do you know what has kept me so long? The most delightful theatre in the world — the Opera Comique. I am so fond of the bygone school of music, Father Benwell — the flowing graceful delicious melodies of the composers who followed Mozart. One can only enjoy that music in Paris. Would you believe that I waited a week to hear Nicolo's delightful Joconde for the second time. I was almost the only young man in the stalls. All round me were the old men who remembered the first performances of the opera, beating time with their wrinkled hands to the tunes which were associated with the happiest days of their lives. What's that I hear? My dog! I was obliged to leave him here, and he knows I have come back!'

He flew to the door, and called down the stairs to have the dog set free. The spaniel rushed into the room and leaped into his master's outstretched arms. Winterfield returned his caresses, and kissed him as tenderly as a woman might have kissed her pet.

'Dear old fellow! it's a shame to have left you — I won't do it again. Father Benwell, have *you* many friends who would be as glad to see you as *this* friend? I haven't one. And there are fools who talk of a dog as an inferior being to ourselves! *This* creature's faithful love is mine, do what I may. I might be disgraced in

the estimation of every human creature I know, and he would be as true to me as ever. And look at his physical qualities. What an ugly thing, for instance, — I won't say your ear — I will say, my ear is; crumpled and wrinkled and naked. Look at the beautiful silky covering of *his* ear! What are our senses of smelling and hearing compared to his? We are proud of our reason. Could we find our way back, if they shut us up in a basket, and took us to a strange place away from home? If we both want to run down stairs in a hurry, which of us is securest against breaking his neck — I on my poor two legs, or he on his four? Who is the happy mortal who goes to bed without unbuttoning, and gets up again without buttoning? Here he is, on my lap, knowing I am talking about him, and too fond of me to say to himself, 'What a fool my master is!' '

Father Benwell listened to this rhapsody — so characteristic of the childish simplicity of the man — with an inward sense of impatience, which never once showed itself on the smiling surface of his face.

He had decided not to mention the papers in his pocket until some circumstance occurred which might appear to remind him naturally that he had such things about him. If he showed any anxiety to produce the envelope, he might expose himself to the suspicion of having some knowledge of the contents. When would Winterfield notice the side table, and open his letters?

The tick-tick of the clock on the mantelpiece

steadily registered the progress of time, and Winterfield's fantastic attentions were still lavished on his dog.

Even Father Benwell's patience was sorely tried when the good country-gentleman proceeded to mention not only the spaniel's name, but the occasion which had suggested it. 'We call him Traveller, and I will tell you why. When he was only a puppy he strayed into the garden at Beaupark, so weary and footsore that we concluded he had come to us from a great distance. We advertised him, but he was never claimed — and here he is! If you don't object, we will give Traveller a treat to-day. He shall have dinner with us.'

Perfectly understanding those last words, the dog jumped off his master's lap, and actually forwarded the views of Father Benwell in less than a minute more. Scampering round and round the room, as an appropriate expression of happiness, he came into collision with the side-table, and directed Winterfield's attention to the letters by scattering them on the floor.

Father Benwell rose politely, to assist in picking up the prostrate correspondence. But Traveller was beforehand with him. Warning the priest, with a low growl, not to interfere with another person's business, the dog picked up the letters in his mouth, and carried them by instalments to his master's feet. Even then, the exasperating Winterfield went no further than patting Traveller. Father Benwell's endurance reached its limits. 'Pray don't stand on ceremony with me,' he said. 'I will look at the newspaper

while you read your letters.'

Winterfield carelessly gathered the letters together, tossed them on the dining-table at his side, and took the uppermost one of the little heap.

Fate was certainly against the priest on that evening. The first letter that Winterfield opened, led him off to another subject of conversation before he had read it to the end. Father Benwell's hand, already in his coat pocket, appeared again — empty.

'Here's a proposal to me to go into Parliament,' said the Squire. 'What do you think of representative institutions, Father Benwell? To my mind, representative institutions are on their last legs. Honourable Members vote away more of our money every year. They have no alternative between suspending liberty of speech, or sitting helpless while half a dozen impudent idiots stop the progress of legislation from motives of the meanest kind. And they are not even sensitive enough to the national honour to pass a social law among themselves which makes it as disgraceful in a gentleman to buy a seat by bribery as to cheat at cards. I declare I think the card-sharper the least degraded person of the two. *He* doesn't encourage his inferiors to be false to a public trust. In short, my dear sir, everything wears out in this world — and why should the House of Commons be an exception to the rule?'

He picked up the next letter from the heap. As he looked at the address, his face changed.

The smile left his lips, the gaiety died out of his eyes. Traveller, entreating for more notice with impatient fore paws applied to his master's knees, saw the alteration, and dropped into a respectfully recumbent position. Father Benwell glanced sidelong off the columns of the newspaper, and waited for events with all the discretion, and none of the good faith, of the dog.

'Forwarded from Beaupark,' Winterfield said to himself. He opened the letter — read it carefully to the end — thought over it — and read it again.

'Father Benwell!' he said suddenly.

The priest put down the newspaper. For a few moments more nothing was audible but the steady tick-tick of the clock.

'We have not been very long acquainted,' Winterfield resumed. 'But our association has been a pleasant one, and I think I owe to you the duty of a friend. I don't belong to your Church; but I hope you will believe me when I say that ignorant prejudice against the Catholic priesthood is not one of *my* prejudices.'

Father Benwell bowed, in silence.

'You are mentioned,' Winterfield proceeded, 'in the letter which I have just read.'

'Are you at liberty to tell me the name of your correspondent?' Father Benwell asked.

'I am not at liberty to do that. But I think it due to you, and to myself, to tell you what the substance of the letter is. The writer warns me to be careful in my intercourse

with you. Your object (I am told) is to make yourself acquainted with events in my past life, and you have some motive which my correspondent has thus far failed to discover. I speak plainly, but I beg you to understand that I also speak impartially. I condemn no man unheard — least of all, a man whom I have had the honour of receiving under my own roof.'

He spoke with a certain simple dignity. With equal dignity, Father Benwell answered. It is needless to say that he now knew Winterfield's correspondent to be Romayne's wife.

'Let me sincerely thank you, Mr Winterfield, for a candour which does honour to us both,' he said. 'You will hardly expect me — if I may use such an expression — to condescend to justify myself against an accusation, which is an anonymous accusation so far as I am concerned. I prefer to meet that letter by a plain proof; and I leave you to judge whether I am still worthy of the friendship to which you have so kindly alluded.'

With this preface he briefly related the circumstances under which he had become possessed of the packet, and then handed it to Winterfield — with the seal uppermost.

'Decide for yourself,' he concluded, 'whether a man bent on prying into your private affairs, with that letter entirely at his mercy, would have been true to the trust reposed in him.'

He rose and took his hat, ready to leave the room, if his honour was profaned by the slightest expression of distrust. Winterfield's genial and

unsuspicious nature instantly accepted the offered proof as conclusive. 'Before I break the seal,' he said, 'let me do you justice. Sit down again, Father Benwell, and forgive me if my sense of duty has hurried me into hurting your feelings. No man ought to know better than I do how often people misjudge and wrong each other.'

They shook hands cordially. No moral relief is more eagerly sought than relief from the pressure of a serious explanation. By common consent, they now spoke as lightly as if nothing had happened. Father Benwell set the example.

'You actually believe in a priest!' he said gaily. 'We shall make a good Catholic of you yet.'

'Don't be too sure of that,' Winterfield replied, with a touch of his quaint humour. 'I respect the men who have given to humanity the inestimable blessing of quinine — to say nothing of preserving learning and civilisation — but I respect still more my own liberty as a free Christian.'

'Perhaps a free thinker, Mr Winterfield?'

'Anything you like to call it, Father Benwell, so long as it *is* free.'

They both laughed. Father Benwell went back to his newspaper. Winterfield broke the seal of the envelope and took out the enclosures.

The confession was the first of the papers at which he happened to look. At the opening lines he turned pale. He read more, and his eyes filled with tears. In low broken tones he said to the priest, 'You have innocently brought me most

distressing news. I entreat your pardon if I ask to be left alone.'

Father Benwell said a few well-chosen words of sympathy, and immediately withdrew. The dog licked his master's hand, hanging listlessly over the arm of the chair.

Later in the evening, a note from Winterfield was left by messenger at the priest's lodgings. The writer announced, with renewed expressions of regret, that he would be again absent from London on the next day, but that he hoped to return to the hotel and receive his guest on the evening of the day after.

Father Benwell rightly conjectured that Winterfield's destination was the town in which his wife had died.

His object in taking the journey was not, as the priest supposed, to address inquiries to the rector and the landlady, who had been present at the fatal illness and the death — but to justify his wife's last expression of belief in the mercy and compassion of the man whom she had injured. On that 'nameless grave,' so sadly and so humbly referred to in the confession, he had resolved to place a simple stone cross, giving to her memory the name which she had shrunk from profaning in her lifetime. When he had written the brief inscription which recorded the death of 'Emma, wife of Bernard Winterfield,' and when he had knelt for awhile by the low turf mound, his errand had come to its end. He thanked the good rector; he left gifts with the landlady and her children, by which he was gratefully remembered for many a year

afterwards; and then, with a heart relieved, he went back to London.

Other men might have made their sad little pilgrimage alone. Winterfield took his dog with him. 'I must have something to love,' he said to the rector, 'at such a time as this.'

4

Father Benwell's Correspondence

To the Secretary, S.J., Rome.

When I wrote last, I hardly thought I should trouble you again so soon. The necessity has, however, arisen. I must ask for instructions, from our Most Reverend General, on the subject of Arthur Penrose.

I believe I informed you that I decided to defer my next visit to Ten Acres Lodge for two or three days, in order that Winterfield (if he intended to do so) might have time to communicate with Mrs Romayne, after his return from the country. Naturally enough, perhaps, considering the delicacy of the subject, he has not taken me into his confidence. I can only guess that he has maintained the same reserve with Mrs Romayne.

My visit to the Lodge was duly paid this afternoon.

I asked first, of course, for the lady of the house, and hearing she was in the grounds, joined her there. She looked ill and anxious, and she received me with rigid politeness. Fortunately, Mrs Eyrecourt (now convalescent) was staying at Ten Acres, and was then taking the air in her chair on wheels. The good lady's nimble and discursive tongue offered me an

opportunity of referring, in the most innocent manner possible, to Winterfield's favourable opinion of Romayne's pictures. I need hardly say that I looked at Romayne's wife when I mentioned the name. She turned pale — probably fearing that I had some knowledge of her letter warning Winterfield not to trust me. If she had already been informed that he was not to be blamed, but to be pitied, in the matter of the marriage at Brussels, she would have turned red. Such, at least, is my experience, drawn from recollections of other days.[1]

The ladies having served my purpose, I ventured into the house, to pay my respects to Romayne.

He was in the study, and his excellent friend and secretary was with him. After the first greetings, Penrose left us. His manner told me plainly that there was something wrong. I asked no questions — waiting on the chance that Romayne might enlighten me.

'I hope you are in better spirits, now that you have your old companion with you,' I said.

'I am very glad to have Penrose with me,'

[1] Father Benwell's experience had, in this case, not misled him. If Stella had remained unmarried, Winterfield might have justified himself. But he was honourably unwilling to disturb her relations with her husband, by satisfying her that he had never been unworthy of the affection which had once united them.

he answered. And then he frowned, and looked out of the window at the two ladies in the grounds.

It occurred to me that Mrs Eyrecourt might be occupying the customary false position of a mother-in-law. I was mistaken. He was not thinking of his wife's mother — he was thinking of his wife.

'I suppose you know that Penrose had an idea of converting me?' he said suddenly.

I was perfectly candid with him — I said I knew it, and approved of it. 'May I hope that Arthur has succeeded in convincing you?' I ventured to add.

'He might have succeeded, Father Benwell, if he had chosen to go on.'

This reply, as you may easily imagine, took me by surprise.

'Are you really so obdurate that Arthur despairs of your conversion?' I asked.

'Nothing of the sort! I have thought and thought of it — and I can tell you I was more than ready to meet him half way.'

'Then where is the obstacle!' I exclaimed.

He pointed through the window to his wife. 'There is the obstacle,' he said, in a tone of ironical resignation.

Knowing Arthur's character as I knew it, I at last understood what had happened. For a moment I felt really angry. Under these circumstances, the wise course was to say nothing, until I could be sure of speaking with exemplary moderation. It doesn't do for a man in my position to show anger.

Romayne went on.

'We talked of my wife, Father Benwell, the last time you were here. You only knew, then, that her reception of Mr Winterfield had determined him never to enter my house again. By way of adding to your information on the subject of 'petticoat government,' I may now tell you that Mrs Romayne has forbidden Penrose to proceed with the attempt to convert me. By common consent, the subject is never mentioned between us.' The bitter irony of his tone, thus far, suddenly disappeared. He spoke eagerly and anxiously. 'I hope you are not angry with Arthur?' he said.

By this time my little fit of ill-temper was at an end. I answered — and it was really in a certain sense true — 'I know Arthur too well to be angry with him.'

Romayne seemed to be relieved. 'I only troubled you with this last domestic incident,' he resumed, 'to bespeak your indulgence for Penrose. I am getting learned in the hierarchy of the Church, Father Benwell! You are the superior of my dear little friend, and you exercise authority over him. Oh, he is the kindest and best of men! It is not his fault. He submits to Mrs Romayne — against his own better conviction — in the honest belief that he consults the interests of our married life.'

I don't think I misinterpret the state of Romayne's mind, and mislead you, when I express my belief that this second indiscreet interference of his wife between his friend and himself will produce the very result which she

299

dreads. Mark my words, written after the closest observation of him — this new irritation of Romayne's sensitive self-respect will hasten his conversion.

You will understand that the one alternative before me, after what has happened, is to fill the place from which Penrose has withdrawn. I abstained from breathing a word of this to Romayne. It is he, if I can manage it, who must invite me to complete the work of conversion — and, besides, nothing can be done until the visit of Penrose has come to an end. Romayne's secret sense of irritation may be safely left to develop itself, with time to help it.

I changed the conversation to the subject of his literary labours.

The present state of his mind is not favourable to work of that exacting kind. Even with the help of Penrose to encourage him, he does not get on to his satisfaction — and yet, as I could plainly perceive, the ambition to make a name in the world exercises a stronger influence over him than ever. All in our favour, my reverend friend — all in our favour!

I took the liberty of asking to see Penrose alone for a moment; and, this request granted, Romayne and I parted cordially. I can make most people like me, when I choose to try. The master of Vange Abbey is no exception to the rule. Did I tell you, by-the-bye, that the property has a little declined of late in value? It is now not worth more than six thousand a year. We will improve it, when it returns to the Church.

My interview with Penrose was over in two minutes. Dispensing with formality, I took his arm, and let him into the front garden.

'I have heard all about it,' I said; 'and I must not deny that you have disappointed me. But I know your disposition, and I make allowances. You have qualities, dear Arthur, which perhaps put you a little out of place among Us. I shall be obliged to report what you have done — but you may trust me to put it favourably. Shake hands, my son, and while we are still together, let us be as good friends as ever.'

You may think that I spoke in this way with a view to my indulgent language being repeated to Romayne, and so improving the position which I have already gained in his estimation. Do you know, I really believe I meant it at the time! The poor fellow gratefully kissed my hand when I offered it to him — he was not able to speak. I wonder whether I am weak about Arthur? Say a kind word for him, when his conduct comes under notice — but pray don't mention this little frailty of mine; and don't suppose I have any sympathy with his weak-minded submission to Mrs Romayne's prejudices. If I ever felt the smallest consideration for *her* (and I cannot call to mind any amiable emotion of that sort), her letter to Winterfield would have effectually extinguished it. There is something quite revolting to me in a deceitful woman.

In closing this letter, I may quiet the minds of our reverend brethren, if I assure them that my former objection to associating myself directly

with the conversion of Romayne no longer exists.

Yes! even at my age, and with my habits, I am now resigned to hearing, and confuting, the trivial arguments of a man who is young enough to be my son. I shall write a carefully-guarded letter to Romayne, on the departure of Penrose; and I shall send him a book to read, from the influence of which I expect gratifying results. It is not a controversial work (Arthur has been beforehand with me there) — it is Wiseman's 'Recollections of the Popes.' I look to that essentially readable book to excite Romayne's imagination, by vivid descriptions of the splendours of the Church, and the vast influence and power of the higher priesthood. Does this sudden enthusiasm of mine surprise you? And are you altogether at a loss to know what it means?

It means, my friend, that I see our position towards Romayne in a new light. Forgive me, if I say no more for the present. I prefer to be silent, until my audacity is justified by events.

5

Bernard Winterfield's Correspondence

I

From Mrs Romayne to Mr Winterfield.

Has my letter failed to reach you? I directed it (as I direct this) to Beaupark, not knowing your London address.

Yesterday, Father Benwell called at Ten Acres Lodge. He first saw my mother and myself, and he contrived to mention your name. It was done with his usual adroitness, and I might perhaps have passed it over if he had not looked at me. I hope, and pray, it may be only my fancy — but I thought I saw, in his eyes, that he was conscious of having me in his power, and that he might betray me to my husband at any moment.

I have no sort of claim on you. And, heaven knows, I have little reason to trust you. But I thought you meant fairly by me when we spoke together at this house. In that belief, I entreat you to tell me if Father Benwell has intruded himself into your confidence — or even if you have hinted anything to him which gives him a hold over me.

II

From Mr Winterfield to Mrs Romayne.

Both your letters have reached me.

I have good reason for believing that you are entirely mistaken in your estimate of Father Benwell's character. But I know, by sad experience, how you hold to your opinions when they are once formed; and I am eager to relieve you of all anxiety, so far as I am concerned. I have not said one word — I have not even let slip the slightest hint — which could inform Father Benwell of that past event in our lives to which your letter alludes. Your secret is a sacred secret to me; and it has been, and shall be, sacredly kept.

There is a sentence in your letter which has given me great pain. You reiterate the cruel language of the bygone time. You say, 'Heaven knows I have little reason to trust you.'

I have reasons, on my side, for not justifying myself — except under certain conditions. I mean under conditions which might place me in a position to serve and advise you as a friend or brother. In that case, I undertake to prove, even to you, that it was a cruel injustice ever to have doubted me, and that there is no man living whom you can more implicitly trust than myself.

My address, when I am in London, is at the head of this page.

III

From Doctor Wybrow to Mr Winterfield.

Dear Sir, — I have received your letter, mentioning that you wish to accompany me, at my next visit to the asylum, to see the French boy, so strangely associated with the papers delivered to you by Father Benwell.

Your proposal reaches me too late. The poor creature's troubled life has come to an end. He never rallied from the exhausting effect of the fever. To the last he was attended by his mother. I write with true sympathy for that excellent lady — but I cannot conceal from you or from myself that this death is not to be regretted. In a case of the same extraordinary kind, recorded in print, the patient recovered from the fever, and his insanity returned with his returning health. — Faithfully yours,

JOSEPH WYBROW.

6

The Saddest of all Words

On the tenth morning, dating from the despatch of Father Benwell's last letter to Rome, Penrose was writing in the study at Ten Acres Lodge, while Romayne sat at the other end of the room, looking listlessly at a blank sheet of paper, with the pen lying idle beside it. On a sudden he rose, and, snatching up paper and pen, threw them irritably into the fire.

'Don't trouble yourself to write any longer,' he said to Penrose. 'My dream is over. Throw my manuscripts into the waste paper basket, and never speak to me of literary work again.'

'Every man devoted to literature has these fits of despondency,' Penrose answered. 'Don't think of your work. Send for your horse, and trust to fresh air and exercise to relieve your mind.'

Romayne barely listened. He turned round at the fireplace, and studied the reflection of his face in the glass.

'I look worse and worse,' he said thoughtfully to himself.

It was true. His flesh had fallen away; his face had withered and whitened; he stooped like an old man. The change for the worse had been steadily proceeding from the time when he left Vange Abbey.

'It's useless to conceal it from me!' he burst out, turning towards Penrose. 'I believe I am in some way answerable — though you all deny it — for the French boy's death. Why not? His voice is still in my ears, and the stain of his brother's blood is on me. I am under a spell! Do you believe in the witches — the merciless old women who made wax images of the people who injured them, and stuck pins in their mock likenesses, to register the slow wasting away of their victims day after day? People disbelieve it in these times, but it has never been disproved.' He stopped, looked at Penrose, and suddenly changed his tone. 'Arthur! what is the matter with you? have you had a bad night? Has anything happened?'

For the first time in Romayne's experience of him, Penrose answered evasively.

'Is there nothing to make me anxious,' he said, 'when I hear you talk as you are talking now? The poor French boy died of a fever. Must I remind you again that he owed the happiest days of his life to you and your good wife?'

Romayne still looked at him, without attending to what he said.

'Surely you don't think I am deceiving you?' Penrose remonstrated.

'No; I was thinking of something else. I was wondering whether I really know you as well as I thought I did. Am I mistaken in supposing that you are not an ambitious man?'

'My only ambition is to lead a worthy life, and to be as useful to my fellow-creatures as I can. Does this satisfy you?'

Romayne hesitated. 'It seems strange — ' he began.

'What seems strange?'

'I don't say it seems strange that you should be a priest,' Romayne explained. 'I am only surprised that a man of your simple way of thinking should have attached himself to the Order of the Jesuits.'

'I can quite understand that,' said Penrose. 'But you should remember that circumstances often influence a man in his choice of a vocation. It has been so with me. I am a member of a Roman Catholic family. A Jesuit College was near our place of abode, and a near relative of mine — since dead — was one of the resident priests.' He paused, and added, in a lower tone. 'When I was little more than a lad I suffered a disappointment, which altered my character for life. I took refuge in the College, and I have found patience and peace of mind since that time. Oh, my friend, you might have been a more contented man — ' He stopped again. His interest in the husband had all but deceived him into forgetting his promise to the wife.

Romayne held out his hand. 'I hope I have not thoughtlessly hurt you?' he said.

Penrose took the offered hand, and pressed it fervently. He tried to speak — and suddenly shuddered, like a man in pain. 'I am not very well this morning,' he stammered; 'a turn in the garden will do me good.'

Romayne's doubts were confirmed by the manner in which Penrose left him. Something had unquestionably happened, which his friend

shrank from communicating to him. He sat down again at his desk, and tried to read. The time passed — and he was still left alone. When the door was at last opened, it was only Stella who entered the room.

'Have you seen Penrose?' he asked.

The estrangement between them had been steadily widening of late. Romayne had expressed his resentment at his wife's interference between Penrose and himself, by that air of contemptuous endurance which is the hardest penalty that a man can inflict on the woman who loves him. Stella had submitted with a proud and silent resignation — the most unfortunate form of protest that she could have adopted towards a man of Romayne's temper. When she now appeared, however, in her husband's study, there was a change in her expression which he instantly noticed. She looked at him with eyes softened by sorrow. Before she could answer his first question, he hurriedly added another. 'Is Penrose really ill?'

'No, Lewis. He is distressed.'

'About what?'

'About you, and about himself.'

'Is he going to leave us?'

'Yes.'

'But he will come back again?'

Stella took a chair by her husband's side. 'I am truly sorry for you, Lewis,' she said. 'It is even a sad parting for Me. If you will let me say it, I have a sincere regard for dear Mr Penrose.'

Under other circumstances, this confession of feeling for the man who had sacrificed his

dearest aspiration to the one consideration of her happiness, might have provoked a sharp reply. But by this time Romayne had really become alarmed. 'You speak as if Arthur was going to leave England,' he said.

'He leaves England this afternoon,' she answered, 'for Rome.'

'Why does he tell this to you, and not to me?' Romayne asked.

'He cannot trust himself to speak of it to you. He begged me to prepare you — '

Her courage failed her. She paused. Romayne beat his hand impatiently on the desk before him. 'Speak out!' he cried. 'If Rome is not the end of the journey — what is?'

Stella hesitated no longer.

'He goes to Rome,' she said, 'to receive his instructions, and to become personally acquainted with the missionaries who are associated with him. They will leave Leghorn in the next vessel which sets sail for a port in Central America. And the dangerous duty entrusted to them is to re-establish one of the Jesuit missions destroyed by the savages years since. They will find their church a ruin, and not a vestige left of the house once inhabited by the murdered priests. It is not concealed from them that they may be martyred too. They are soldiers of the Cross; and they go — willingly go — to save the souls of the Indians, at the peril of their lives.'

Romayne rose, and advanced to the door. There, he turned, and spoke to Stella. 'Where is Arthur?' he said.

Stella gently detained him.

'There was one word more he entreated me to say — pray wait and hear it,' she pleaded. 'His one grief is at leaving You. Apart from that, he devotes himself gladly to the dreadful service which claims him. He has long looked forward to it, and has long prepared himself for it. Those, Lewis, are his own words.'

There was a knock at the door. The servant appeared, to announce that the carriage was waiting.

Penrose entered the room as the man left it.

'Have you spoken for me?' he said to Stella.

She could only answer him by a gesture. He turned to Romayne, with a faint smile.

'The saddest of all words must be spoken,' he said. 'Farewell!'

Pale and trembling Romayne took his hand. 'Is this Father Benwell's doing?' he asked.

'No!' Penrose answered, firmly. 'In Father Benwell's position it might have been his doing, but for his goodness to me. For the first time since I have known him, he has shrunk from a responsibility. For my sake he has left it to Rome. And Rome has spoken. Oh, my more than friend — my brother in love — !'

His voice failed him. With a resolution which was nothing less than heroic in a man of his affectionate nature, he recovered his composure.

'Let us make it as little miserable as it *can* be,' he said. 'At every opportunity we will write to each other. And, who knows — I may yet come back to you? God has preserved his servants in dangers as great as any that I

shall encounter. May that merciful God bless and protect you. Oh, Romayne, what happy days we have had together!' His last powers of resistance were worn out. Tears of noble sorrow dimmed the friendly eyes which had never once looked unkindly on the brother of his love. He kissed Romayne. 'Help me out!' he said, turning blindly towards the hall, in which the servant was waiting. That last act of mercy was not left to a servant. With sisterly tenderness, Stella took his hand and led him away. 'I shall remember you gratefully as long as I live,' she said to him when the carriage door was closed. He waved his hand at the window, and she saw him no more.

She returned to the study.

The relief of tears had not come to Romayne. He had dropped into a chair when Penrose left him. In stony silence he sat there, his head down, his eyes dry and staring. The miserable days of their estrangement were forgotten by his wife in the moment when she looked at him. She knelt by his side, and lifted his head a little, and laid it on her bosom. Her heart was full — she let the caress plead for her silently. He felt it; his cold fingers pressed her hand thankfully; but he said nothing. After a long interval, the first outward expression of sorrow that fell from his lips showed that he was still thinking of Penrose.

'Every blessing falls away from me,' he said, 'I have lost my best friend.'

Years afterwards, Stella remembered those words, and the tone in which he had spoken them.

7

The Impulsive Sex

After a lapse of a few days, Father Benwell was again a visitor at Ten Acres Lodge — by Romayne's invitation. The priest occupied the very chair, by the study fireside, in which Penrose had been accustomed to sit.

'It is really kind of you to come to me,' said Romayne, 'so soon after receiving my acknowledgment of your letter. I can't tell you how I was touched by the manner in which you wrote of Penrose. To my shame I confess it, I had no idea that you were so warmly attached to him.'

'I hardly knew it myself, Mr Romayne, until our dear Arthur was taken away from us.'

'If you used your influence, Father Benwell, is there no hope that you might yet persuade him — ?'

'To withdraw from the Mission? Oh, Mr Romayne, don't you know Arthur's character better than that! Even his gentle temper has its resolute side. The zeal of the first martyrs to Christianity is the zeal that burns in that noble nature. The Mission has been the dream of his life — it is endeared to him by the very dangers which we dread. Persuade Arthur to desert the dear and devoted colleagues who have opened their arms to him? I might as soon persuade

313

that statue in the garden to desert its pedestal, and join us in this room. Shall we change the sad subject? Have you received the book which I sent you with my letter?'

Romayne took up the book from his desk. Before he could speak of it someone called out briskly, on the other side of the door, 'May I come in?' — and came in, without waiting to be asked. Mrs Eyrecourt, painted and robed for the morning — wafting perfumes as she moved — appeared in the study. She looked at the priest, and lifted her many-ringed hands with a gesture of coquettish terror.

'Oh, dear me! I had no idea you were here, Father Benwell. I ask ten thousand pardons. Dear and admirable Romayne, you don't look as if you were pleased to see me. Good gracious! I am not interrupting a confession, am I?'

Father Benwell (with his paternal smile in perfect order) resigned his chair to Mrs Eyrecourt. The traces of her illness still showed themselves in an intermittent trembling of her head and her hands. She had entered the room, strongly suspecting that the process of conversion might be proceeding in the absence of Penrose, and determined to interrupt it. Guided by his subtle intelligence, Father Benwell penetrated her motive as soon as she opened the door. Mrs Eyrecourt bowed graciously, and took the offered chair. Father Benwell sweetened his paternal smile, and offered to get a footstool.

'How glad I am,' he said, 'to see you in your customary good spirits! But wasn't it just a little malicious to talk of interrupting a confession? As

314

if Mr Romayne was one of Us! Queen Elizabeth herself could hardly have said a sharper thing to a poor Catholic priest!'

'You clever creature!' said Mrs Eyrecourt. 'How easily you see through a simple woman like me! There — I give you my hand to kiss; and I will never try to deceive you again. Do you know, Father Benwell, a most extraordinary wish has suddenly come to me. Please don't be offended. I wish you were a Jew.'

'May I ask why?' Father Benwell inquired, with an apostolic suavity worthy of the best days of Rome.

Mrs Eyrecourt explained herself with the modest self-distrust of a maiden of fifteen. 'I am really so ignorant, I hardly know how to put it. But learned persons have told me that it is the peculiarity of the Jews — may I say, the amiable peculiarity? — never to make converts. It would be so nice if you would take a leaf out of their book, when we have the happiness of receiving you here. My lively imagination pictures you in a double character. Father Benwell everywhere else; and — say, the patriarch Abraham at Ten Acres Lodge.'

Father Benwell lifted his persuasive hands in courteous protest. 'My dear lady! pray make your mind easy. Not one word on the subject of religion has passed between Mr Romayne and myself — '

'I beg your pardon,' Mrs Eyrecourt interposed, 'I am afraid I fail to follow you. My silent son-in-law looks as if he longed to smother me, and my

attention is naturally distracted. You were about to say — ?'

'I was about to say, dear Mrs Eyrecourt, that you are alarming yourself without any reason. Not one word, on any controversial subject, has passed — '

Mrs Eyrecourt cocked her head, with the artless vivacity of a bird. 'Ah, but it might though!' she suggested slily.

Father Benwell once more remonstrated in dumb show, and Romayne lost his temper.

'Mrs Eyrecourt!' he cried sternly.

Mrs Eyrecourt screamed, and lifted her hands to her ears. 'I am not deaf, dear Romayne, and I am not to be put down by any ill-timed exhibition of, what I may call, domestic ferocity. Father Benwell sets you an example of Christian moderation. Do, please, follow it.'

Romayne refused to follow it.

'Talk on any other topic that you like, Mrs Eyrecourt. I request you — don't oblige me to use a harder word — I request you to spare Father Benwell and myself any further expression of your opinion on controversial subjects.'

A son-in-law may make a request, and a mother-in-law may decline to comply. Mrs Eyrecourt declined to comply.

'No, Romayne, it won't do. I may lament your unhappy temper, for my daughter's sake — but I know what I am about, and you can't provoke me. Our reverend friend and I understand each other. He will make allowances for a sensitive woman, who has had sad experience

of conversions in her own household. My eldest daughter, Father Benwell — a poor foolish creature — was converted into a nunnery. The last time I saw her (she used to be sweetly pretty; my dear husband quite adored her) — the last time I saw her, she had a red nose, and, what is even more revolting at her age, a double chin. She received me with her lips pursed up, and her eyes on the ground, and she was insolent enough to say that she would pray for me. I am not a furious old man with a long white beard, and I don't curse my daughter and rush out into a thunderstorm afterwards — but *I* know what King Lear felt, and *I* have struggled with hysterics just as he did. With your wonderful insight into human nature, I am sure you will sympathise with and forgive me. Mr Penrose, as my daughter tells me, behaved in the most gentlemanlike manner. I make the same appeal to your kind forbearance. The bare prospect of our dear friend here becoming a Catholic — '

Romayne's temper gave way once more.

'If anything can make me a Catholic,' he said, 'your interference will do it.'

'Out of sheer perversity, dear Romayne?'

'Not at all, Mrs Eyrecourt. If I became a Catholic, I might escape from the society of ladies, in the refuge of a monastery.'

Mrs Eyrecourt hit him back again with the readiest dexterity.

'Remain a Protestant, my dear, and go to your club. There is a refuge for you from the ladies — a monastery, with nice little dinners, and all the newspapers and periodicals.' Having

launched this shaft, she got up, and recovered her easy courtesy of look and manner. 'I am so much obliged to you, Father Benwell. I have not offended you, I hope and trust?'

'You have done me a service, dear Mrs Eyrecourt. But for your salutary caution I *might* have drifted into controversial subjects. I shall be on my guard now.'

'How very good of you! We shall meet again, I hope, under more agreeable circumstances. After that polite allusion to a monastery, I understand that my visit to my son-in-law may as well come to an end. Please don't forget five o'clock tea at my house.'

As she approached the door, it was opened from the outer side. Her daughter met her half-way. 'Why are you here, Mama?' Stella asked.

'Why indeed, my love! You had better leave the room with me. Our amiable Romayne's present idea is to relieve himself of our society by retiring to a monastery. Don't you see Father Benwell?'

Stella coldly returned the priest's bow — and looked at Romayne. She felt a vague forewarning of what had happened. Mrs Eyrecourt proceeded to enlighten her, as an appropriate expression of gratitude. 'We are indeed indebted to Father Benwell, my dear. He has been most considerate and kind — '

Romayne interrupted her without ceremony. 'Favour me,' he said, addressing his wife, 'by inducing Mrs Eyrecourt to continue her narrative in some other room.'

Stella was hardly conscious of what her mother or her husband had said. She felt that the priest's eyes were on her. Under any other circumstances, Father Benwell's good breeding and knowledge of the world would have impelled him to take his departure. As things were, he knew perfectly well that the more seriously Romayne was annoyed, in his presence, the better his own private interest would be served. Accordingly, he stood apart, silently observant of Stella. In spite of Winterfield's reassuring reply to her letter, Stella instinctively suspected and dreaded the Jesuit. Under the spell of those watchful eyes she trembled inwardly; her customary tact deserted her; she made an indirect apology to the man whom she hated and feared.

'Whatever my mother may have said to you, Father Benwell, has been without my knowledge.'

Romayne attempted to speak, but Father Benwell was too quick for him.

'Dear Mrs Romayne, nothing has been said which needs any disclaimer on your part.'

'I should think not!' Mrs Eyrecourt added. 'Really, Stella, I don't understand you. Why may I not say to Father Benwell what you said to Mr Penrose? You trusted Mr Penrose as your friend. I can tell you this — I am quite sure you may trust Father Benwell.'

Once more Romayne attempted to speak. And, once more, Father Benwell was beforehand with him.

'May I hope,' said the priest, with a finely

ironical smile, 'that Mrs Romayne agrees with her excellent mother?'

With all her fear of him, the exasperating influence of his tone and his look was more than Stella could endure. Before she could restrain them, the rash words flew out of her lips.

'I am not sufficiently well acquainted with you, Father Benwell, to express an opinion.'

With that answer, she took her mother's arm, and left the room.

The moment they were alone, Romayne turned to the priest, trembling with anger. Father Benwell, smiling indulgently at the lady's little outbreak, took him by the hand, with peace-making intentions. 'Now don't — pray don't excite yourself!'

Romayne was not to be pacified in that way. His anger was trebly intensified by the long-continued strain on his nerves of the effort to control himself.

'I must, and will, speak out at last!' he said. 'Father Benwell, the ladies of my household have inexcusably presumed on the consideration which is due to women. No words can say how ashamed I am of what has happened. I can only appeal to your admirable moderation and patience to accept my apologies, and the most sincere expression of my regret.'

'No more, Mr Romayne! As a favour to Me, I beg and entreat you will say no more. Sit down and compose yourself.'

But Romayne was impenetrable to the influence of friendly and forgiving demonstrations.

'I can never expect you to enter my house again!' he exclaimed.

'My dear sir, I will come and see you again, with the greatest pleasure, on any day that you may appoint — the earlier day the better. Come! come! let us laugh. I don't say it disrespectfully, but poor dear Mrs Eyrecourt has been more amusing than ever. I expect to see our excellent Archbishop to-morrow, and I must really tell him how the good lady felt insulted when her Catholic daughter offered to pray for her. There is hardly anything more humorous, even in Moliére. And the double chin, and the red nose — all the fault of those dreadful Papists. Oh, dear me, you still take it seriously. How I wish you had my sense of humour! When shall I come again, and tell you how the Archbishop likes the story of the nun's mother?'

He held out his hand with irresistible cordiality. Romayne took it gratefully — still bent, however, on making atonement.

'Let me first do myself the honour of calling on You,' he said. 'I am in no state to open my mind — as I might have wished to open it to you — after what has happened. In a day or two more — '

'Say the day after to-morrow,' Father Benwell hospitably suggested. 'Do me a great favour. Come and eat your bit of mutton at my lodgings. Six o'clock, if you like — and some remarkably good claret, a present from one of the Faithful. You will? That's hearty! And do promise me to think no more of our little domestic comedy. Relieve your mind. Look at

321

Wiseman's Recollections of the Popes. Good-bye — God bless you!'

The servant who opened the house door for Father Benwell was agreeably surprised by the Papist's cheerfulness. 'He isn't half a bad fellow,' the man announced among his colleagues. 'Gave me half-a-crown, and went out humming a tune.'

8

Father Benwell's Correspondence

To the Secretary, S.J., Rome.

I

I beg to acknowledge the receipt of your letter.

You mention that our Reverend Fathers are discouraged at not having heard from me for more than six weeks, since I reported the little dinner given to Romayne at my lodgings.

I am sorry for this, and more than sorry to hear that my venerated brethren are beginning to despair of Romayne's conversion. Grant me a delay of another week — and, if the prospects of the conversion have not sensibly improved in that time, I will confess myself defeated. Meanwhile, I bow to superior wisdom, without venturing to add a word in my own defence.

II

The week's grace granted to me has elapsed. I write with humility. At the same time I have something to say for myself.

Yesterday, Mr Lewis Romayne, of Vange Abbey, was received into the community of the Holy Catholic Church. I enclose an

accurate newspaper report of the ceremonies which attended the conversion.

Be pleased to inform me, by telegraph, whether our Reverend Fathers wish me to go on, or not.

Book The Fifth

1

Mrs Eyrecourt's Discovery

The leaves had fallen in the grounds at Ten Acres Lodge, and stormy winds told drearily that winter had come.

An unchanging dullness pervaded the house. Romayne was constantly absent in London, attending to his new religious duties under the guidance of Father Benwell. The litter of books and manuscripts in the study was seen no more. Hideously rigid order reigned in the unused room. Some of Romayne's papers had been burnt; others were imprisoned in drawers and cupboards — the history of the Origin of Religions had taken its melancholy place among the suspended literary enterprises of the time. Mrs Eyrecourt (after a superficially cordial reconciliation with her son-in-law) visited her daughter every now and then, as an act of maternal sacrifice. She yawned perpetually; she read innumerable novels; she corresponded with her friends. In the long dull evenings, the once-lively lady sometimes openly regretted that she had not been born a man — with the three masculine resources of smoking, drinking, and swearing placed at her disposal. It was a dreary

existence, and happier influences seemed but little likely to change it. Grateful as she was to her mother, no persuasion would induce Stella to leave Ten Acres and amuse herself in London. Mrs Eyrecourt said, with melancholy and metaphorical truth, 'There is no elasticity left in my child.'

On a dim grey morning, mother and daughter sat by the fireside, with another long day before them.

'Where is that contemptible husband of yours?' Mrs Eyrecourt asked, looking up from her book.

'Lewis is staying in town,' Stella answered listlessly.

'In company with Judas Iscariot?'

Stella was too dull to immediately understand the allusion. 'Do you mean Father Benwell?' she inquired.

'Don't mention his name, my dear. I have re-christened him on purpose to avoid it. Even his name humiliates me. How completely the fawning old wretch took me in — with all my knowledge of the world, too! He was so nice and sympathetic — such a comforting contrast, on that occasion, to you and your husband — I declare I forgot every reason I had for not trusting him. Ah, we women are poor creatures — we may own it among ourselves. If a man only has nice manners and a pleasant voice, how many of us can resist him? Even Romayne imposed upon me — assisted by his property, which in some degree excuses my folly. There is nothing to be done now, Stella,

326

but to humour him. Do as that detestable priest does, and trust to your beauty (there isn't as much of it left as I could wish) to turn the scale in your favour. Have you any idea when the new convert will come back? I heard him ordering a fish dinner for himself, yesterday — because it was Friday. Did you join him at dessert-time, profanely supported by meat? What did he say?'

'What he has said more than once already, Mama. His peace of mind is returning, thanks to Father Benwell. He was perfectly gentle and indulgent — but he looked as if he lived in a different world from mine. He told me he proposed to pass a week in, what he called, Retreat. I didn't ask him what it meant. Whatever it is, I suppose he is there now.'

'My dear, don't you remember your sister began in the same way? *she* retreated. We shall have Romayne with a red nose and a double chin, offering to pray for us next! Do you recollect that French maid of mine — the woman I sent away, because she would spit, when she was out of temper, like a cat? I begin to think I treated the poor creature harshly. When I hear of Romayne and his Retreat, I almost feel inclined to spit, myself. There! let us go on with our reading. Take the first volume — I have done with it.'

'What is it, Mama?'

'A very remarkable work, Stella, in the present state of light literature in England — a novel that actually tells a story. It's quite incredible, I know. Try the book. It has another extraordinary

merit — it isn't written by a woman.'

Stella obediently received the first volume, turned over the leaves, and wearily dropped the wonderful novel on her lap. 'I can't attend to it,' she said. 'My mind is too full of my own thoughts.'

'About Romayne?' said her mother.

'No. When I think of my husband now. I almost wish I had his confidence in Priests and Retreats. The conviction grows on me, Mama, that my worst troubles are still to come. When I was younger, I don't remember being tormented by presentiments of any kind. Did I ever talk of presentiments to you, in the bygone days?'

'If you had done anything of the sort, my love (excuse me, if I speak plainly), I should have said, 'Stella, your liver is out of order;' and I should have opened the family medicine-chest. I will only say now send for the carriage; let us go to a morning concert, dine at a restaurant, and finish the evening at the play.'

This characteristic proposal was entirely thrown away on Stella. She was absorbed in pursuing her own train of thought. 'I almost wish I had told Lewis,' she said to herself absently.

'Told him of what, my dear?'

'Of what happened to me with Winterfield.'

Mrs Eyrecourt's faded eyes opened wide in astonishment.

'Do you really mean it?' she asked.

'I do, indeed.'

'Are you actually simple enough, Stella, to think that a man of Romayne's temper would

328

have made you his wife if you had told him of the Brussels marriage?'

'Why not?'

'Why not! Would Romayne — would any man — believe that you really did part from Winterfield at the church door? Considering that you are a married woman, your innocence, my sweet child, is a perfect phenomenon! It's well there were wiser people than you to keep your secret.'

'Don't speak too positively, Mama. Lewis may find it out yet.'

'Is that one of your presentiments?'

'Yes.'

'How is he to find it out, if you please?'

'I am afraid, through Father Benwell. Yes! yes! I know you only think him a fawning old hypocrite — you don't fear him as I do. Nothing will persuade me that zeal for his religion is the motive under which that man acts in devoting himself to Romayne. He has some abominable object in view, and his eyes tell me that I am concerned in it.'

Mrs Eyrecourt burst out laughing.

'What is there to laugh at?' Stella asked.

'I declare, my dear, there is something absolutely provoking in your utter want of knowledge of the world! When you are puzzled to account for anything remarkable in a clergyman's conduct (I don't care, my poor child, to what denomination he belongs) you can't be wrong in attributing his motive to — Money. If Romayne had turned Baptist or Methodist, the reverend gentleman in charge

of his spiritual welfare would not have forgotten
— as you have forgotten, you little goose — that
his convert was a rich man. His mind would have
dwelt on the chapel, or the mission, or the infant
school, in want of funds; and — with no more
abominable object in view than I have, at this
moment, in poking the fire — he would have
ended in producing his modest subscription list,
and would have betrayed himself (just as our
odious Benwell will betray himself) by the two
amiable little words, Please contribute. Is there
any other presentiment, my dear, on which
you would like to have your mother's candid
opinion?'

Stella resignedly took up the book again.

'I dare say you are right,' she said. 'Let us
read our novel.'

Before she had reached the end of the first
page, her mind was far away again from the
unfortunate story. She was thinking of that
'other presentiment,' which had formed the
subject of her mother's last satirical inquiry.
The vague fear that had shaken her when she
had accidentally touched the French boy, on
her visit to Camp's Hill, still from time to
time troubled her memory. Even the event of
his death had failed to dissipate the delusion,
which associated him with some undefined
evil influence that might yet assert itself. A
superstitious forewarning of this sort was a
weakness new to her in her experience of herself.
She was heartily ashamed of it — and yet, it
kept its hold. Once more the book dropped on
her lap. She laid it aside, and walked wearily to

the window to look at the weather.

Almost at the same moment Mrs Eyrecourt's maid disturbed her mistress over the second volume of the novel by entering the room with a letter.

'For me?' Stella asked, looking round from the window.

'No, ma'am — for Mrs Eyrecourt.'

The letter had been brought to the house by one of Lady Loring's servants. In delivering it he had apparently given private instructions to the maid. She laid her finger significantly on her lips when she gave the letter to her mistress.

In these terms Lady Loring wrote:-

'If Stella happens to be with you, when you receive my note, don't say anything which will let her know that I am your correspondent. She has always, poor dear, had an inveterate distrust of Father Benwell; and, between ourselves, I am not sure that she is quite so foolish as I once thought. The Father has unexpectedly left us — with a well-framed excuse which satisfied Lord Loring. It fails to satisfy Me. Not from any wonderful exercise of penetration on my part, but in consequence of something I have just heard in course of conversation with a Catholic friend. Father Benwell, my dear, turns out to be a Jesuit; and, what is more, a person of such high authority in the Order, that his concealment of his rank, while he was with us, must have been a matter of necessity. He must have had some very serious motive for occupying a position so entirely beneath him as his position in our house. I have not the shadow of a reason for associating

this startling discovery with dear Stella's painful misgivings — and yet there is something in my mind which makes me want to hear what Stella's mother thinks. Come and have a talk about it as soon as you possibly can.'

Mrs Eyrecourt put the letter in her pocket, smiling quietly to herself.

Applying to Lady Loring's letter the infallible system of solution which she had revealed to her daughter, Mrs. Eyrecourt solved the mystery of the priest's conduct without a moment's hesitation. Lord Loring's cheque, in Father Benwell's pocket, representing such a liberal subscription that my lord was reluctant to mention it to my lady — there was the reading of the riddle, as plain as the sun at noonday! Would it be desirable to enlighten Lady Loring as she had already enlightened Stella? Mrs Eyrecourt decided in the negative. As Roman Catholics, and as old friends of Romayne, the Lorings naturally rejoiced in his conversion. But, as old friends also of Romayne's wife, they were bound not to express their sentiments too openly. Feeling that any discussion of the priest's motives would probably lead to the delicate subject of the conversion, Mrs Eyrecourt prudently determined to let the matter drop. As a consequence of this decision, Stella was left without the slightest warning of the catastrophe which was now close at hand.

Mrs Eyrecourt joined her daughter at the window.

'Well, my dear, is it clearing up? Shall we take a drive before luncheon?'

'If you like, Mama.'

She turned to her mother as she answered. The light of the clearing sky, at once soft and penetrating, fell full on her. Mrs Eyrecourt, looking at her as usual, suddenly became serious: she studied her daughter's face with an eager and attentive scrutiny.

'Do you see any extraordinary change in me?' Stella asked, with a faint smile.

Instead of answering, Mrs Eyrecourt put her arm round Stella with a loving gentleness, entirely at variance with any ordinary expression of her character. The worldly mother's eyes rested with a lingering tenderness on the daughter's face. 'Stella!' she said softly — and stopped, at a loss for words for the first time in her life.

After a while, she began again. 'Yes; I see a change in you,' she whispered — 'an interesting change which tells me something. Can you guess what it is?'

Stella's colour rose brightly, and faded again. She laid her head in silence on her mother's bosom. Worldly, frivolous, self-interested, Mrs Eyrecourt's nature was the nature of a woman — and the one great trial and triumph of a woman's life, appealing to her as a trial and triumph soon to come to her own child, touched fibres under the hardened surface of her heart which were still unprofaned. 'My poor darling,' she said, 'have you told the good news to your husband?'

'No.'

'Why not?'

'He doesn't care, now, for anything that I can tell him.'

'Nonsense, Stella! You may win him back to you by a word — and do you hesitate to say the word? *I* shall tell him!'

Stella suddenly drew herself away from her mother's caressing arm. 'If you do,' she cried, 'no words can say how inconsiderate and how cruel I shall think you. Promise — on your word of honour — promise you will leave it to me!'

'Will you tell him, yourself — if I leave it to you?'

'Yes — at my own time. Promise!'

'Hush, hush! don't excite yourself, my love; I promise. Give me a kiss. I declare I am agitated myself!' she exclaimed, falling back into her customary manner. 'Such a shock to my vanity, Stella — the prospect of becoming a grandmother! I really must ring for Matilda, and take a few drops of red lavender. Be advised by me, my poor dear, and we will turn the priest out of the house yet. When Romayne comes back from his ridiculous Retreat — after his fasting and flagellation, and Heaven knows what besides — *then* bring him to his senses; then is the time to tell him. Will you think of it?'

'Yes; I will think of it.'

'And one word more, before Matilda comes in. Remember the vast importance of having a male heir to Vange Abbey. On these occasions you may practise with perfect impunity on the ignorance of the men. Tell him you're sure it's going to be a boy!'

2

The Seed is Sown

Situated in a distant quarter of the vast western suburb of London, the house called The Retreat stood in the midst of a well-kept garden, protected on all sides by a high brick wall. Excepting the grand gilt cross on the roof of the chapel, nothing revealed externally the devotional purpose to which the Roman Catholic priesthood (assisted by the liberality of 'the Faithful') had dedicated the building.

But the convert privileged to pass the gates left Protestant England outside, and found himself, as it were, in a new country. Inside The Retreat, the paternal care of the Church took possession of him; surrounded him with monastic simplicity in his neat little bedroom; and dazzled him with devotional splendour when his religious duties called him into the chapel. The perfect taste — so seldom found in the modern arrangement and decoration of convents and churches in southern countries — showed itself here, pressed into the service of religion, in every part of the house. The severest discipline had no sordid and hideous side to it in The Retreat. The inmates fasted on spotless table cloths, and handled knives and forks (the humble servants of half-filled stomachs) without a speck on their decent brightness. Penitents who

kissed the steps of the altar (to use the expressive Oriental phrase), 'eat no dirt.' Friends, liberal friends, permitted to visit the inmates on stated days, saw copies of famous Holy Families in the reception room which were really works of Art; and trod on a carpet of studiously modest pretensions, exhibiting pious emblems beyond reproach in colour and design. The Retreat had its own artesian well; not a person in the house drank impurity in his water. A faint perfume of incense was perceptible in the corridors. The soothing and mysterious silence of the place was intensified rather than disturbed by soft footsteps, and gentle opening and closing of doors. Animal life was not even represented by a cat in the kitchen. And yet, pervaded by some inscrutable influence, the house was not dull. Heretics, with lively imaginations, might have not inappropriately likened it to an enchanted castle. In one word, the Catholic system here showed to perfection its masterly knowledge of the weakness of human nature, and its inexhaustible dexterity in adapting the means to the end.

On the morning when Mrs Eyrecourt and her daughter held their memorable interview by the fireside at Ten Acres, Father Benwell entered one of the private rooms at The Retreat, devoted to the use of the priesthood. The demure attendant, waiting humbly for instructions, was sent to request the presence of one of the inmates of the house, named Mortleman.

Father Benwell's customary serenity was a little ruffled, on this occasion, by an appearance

of anxiety. More than once he looked impatiently towards the door, and he never even noticed the last new devotional publications laid invitingly on the table.

Mr Mortleman made his appearance — a young man, and a promising convert. The wild brightness of his eyes revealed that incipient form of brain disease which begins in fanaticism, and ends not infrequently in religious madness. His manner of greeting the priest was absolutely servile. He cringed before the illustrious Jesuit.

Father Benwell took no notice of these demonstrations of humility. 'Be seated, my son,' he said. Mr Mortleman looked as if he would have preferred going down on his knees — but he yielded, and took a chair.

'I think you have been Mr Romayne's companion for a few days, in the hours of recreation?' the priest began.

'Yes, Father.'

'Does he appear to be at all weary of his residence in this house?'

'Oh, far from it! He feels the benign influence of The Retreat; we have had some delightful hours together.'

'Have you anything to report?'

Mr Mortleman crossed his hands on his breast, and bowed profoundly. 'I have to report of myself, Father, that I have committed the sin of presumption. I presumed that Mr Romayne was, like myself, not married.'

'Have I spoken to you on that subject?'

'No, Father.'

'Then you have committed no sin. You have

337

only made an excusable mistake. How were you led into error?'

'In this way, Father. Mr Romayne had been speaking to me of a book which you had been so good as to send to him. He had been especially interested by the memoir therein contained of the illustrious Englishman, Cardinal Acton. The degrees by which his Eminence rose to the rank of a Prince of the Church seemed, as I thought, to have aroused in my friend a new sense of vocation. He asked me if I myself aspired to belong to the holy priesthood. I answered that this was indeed my aspiration, if I might hope to be found worthy. He appeared to be deeply affected. I ventured to ask if he too had the same prospect before him. He grieved me indescribably. He sighed and said, 'I have no such hope; I am married.' Tell me, Father, I entreat you, have I done wrong?'

Father Benwell considered for a moment. 'Did Mr Romayne say anything more?' he asked.

'No, Father.'

'Did you attempt to return to the subject?'

'I thought it best to be silent.'

Father Benwell held out his hand. 'My young friend, you have not only done no wrong — you have shown the most commendable discretion. I will detain you no longer from your duties. Go to Mr Romayne, and say that I wish to speak with him.'

Mr Mortleman dropped on one knee, and begged for a blessing. Father Benwell lifted the traditional two fingers, and gave the blessing. The conditions of human happiness are easily

fulfilled if we rightly understand them. Mr Mortleman retired perfectly happy.

Left by himself again, Father Benwell paced the room rapidly from end to end. The disturbing influence visible in his face had now changed from anxiety to excitement. 'I'll try it today!' he said to himself — and stopped, and looked round him doubtfully. 'No, not here,' he decided; 'it may get talked about too soon. It will be safer in every way at my lodgings.' He recovered his composure, and returned to his chair.

Romayne opened the door.

The double influence of the conversion, and of the life in The Retreat, had already changed him. His customary keenness and excitability of look had subsided, and had left nothing in their place but an expression of suave and meditative repose. All his troubles were now in the hands of his priest. There was a passive regularity in his bodily movements and a beatific serenity in his smile.

'My dear friend,' said Father Benwell, cordially shaking hands, 'you were good enough to be guided by my advice in entering this house. Be guided by me again, when I say that you have been here long enough. You can return, after an interval, if you wish it. But I have something to say to you first — and I beg to offer the hospitality of my lodgings.'

The time had been when Romayne would have asked for some explanation of this abrupt notice of removal. Now, he passively accepted the advice of his spiritual director. Father

Benwell made the necessary communication to the authorities, and Romayne took leave of his friends in The Retreat. The great Jesuit and the great landowner left the place, with becoming humility, in a cab.

'I hope I have not disappointed you?' said Father Benwell.

'I am only anxious,' Romayne answered, 'to hear what you have to say.'

3

The Harvest is reaped

On their way through the streets, Father Benwell talked as persistently of the news of the day as if he had nothing else in his thoughts. To keep his companion's mind in a state of suspense was, in certain emergencies, to exert a useful preparatory influence over a man of Romayne's character. Even when they reached his lodgings, the priest still hesitated to approach the object that he had in view. He made considerate inquiries, in the character of a hospitable man.

'They breakfast early at The Retreat,' he said. 'What may I offer you?'

'I want nothing, thank you,' Romayne answered, with an effort to control his habitual impatience of needless delay.

'Pardon me — we have a long interview before us, I fear. Our bodily necessities, Romayne (excuse me if I take the friendly liberty of suppressing the formal 'Mr') — our bodily necessities are not to be trifled with. A bottle of my famous claret, and a few biscuits, will not hurt either of us.' He rang the bell, and gave the necessary directions. 'Another damp day!' he went on cheerfully. 'I hope you don't pay the rheumatic penalties of a winter residence in England? Ah, this glorious country would be

too perfect if it possessed the delicious climate of Rome!'

The wine and biscuits were brought in. Father Benwell filled the glasses, and bowed cordially to his guest.

'Nothing of this sort at The Retreat!' he said gaily. 'Excellent water, I am told — which is a luxury in its way, especially in London. Well, my dear Romayne, I must begin by making my apologies. You no doubt thought me a little abrupt in running away with you from your retirement at a moment's notice?'

'I believed that you had good reasons, Father — and that was enough for me.'

'Thank you — you do me justice — it was in your best interests that I acted. There are men of phlegmatic temperament, over whom the wise monotony of discipline at The Retreat exercises a wholesome influence — I mean an influence which may be prolonged with advantage. You are not one of those persons. Protracted seclusion and monotony of life are morally and mentally unprofitable to a man of your ardent disposition. I abstained from mentioning these reasons, at the time, out of a feeling of regard for our excellent resident director, who believes unreservedly in the institution over which he presides. Very good! The Retreat has done all that it could usefully do in your case. We must think next of how to employ that mental activity which, rightly developed, is one of the most valuable qualities that you possess. Let me ask, first, if you have in some degree recovered your tranquillity?'

'I feel like a different man, Father Benwell.'

'That's right! And your nervous sufferings — I don't ask what they are; I only want to know if you experience a sense of relief?'

'A most welcome sense of relief,' Romayne answered, with a revival of the enthusiasm of other days. 'The complete change in all my thoughts and convictions, which I owe to you — '

'And to dear Penrose,' Father Benwell interposed, with the prompt sense of justice which no man could more becomingly assume. 'We must not forget Arthur.'

'Forget him?' Romayne repeated. 'Not a day passes without my thinking of him. It is one of the happy results of the change in me that my mind does not dwell bitterly on the loss of him now. I think of Penrose with admiration, as of one whose glorious life, with all its dangers, I should like to share!'

He spoke with a rising colour and brightening eyes. Already, the absorbent capacity of the Roman Church had drawn to itself that sympathetic side of his character which was also one of its strongest sides. Already, his love for Penrose — hitherto inspired by the virtues of the man — had narrowed its range to sympathy with the trials and privileges of the priest. Truly and deeply indeed had the physician consulted, in bygone days, reasoned on Romayne's case! That 'occurrence of some new and absorbing influence in his life,' of which the doctor had spoken — that 'working of some complete change in his habits of thought' — had found its way to him at last, after the wife's

343

simple devotion had failed, through the subtler ministrations of the priest.

Some men, having Father Benwell's object in view, would have taken instant advantage of the opening offered to them by Romayne's unguarded enthusiasm. The illustrious Jesuit held fast by the wise maxim which forbade him to do anything in a hurry.

'No,' he said, 'your life must not be the life of our dear friend. The service on which the Church employs Penrose is not the fit service for you. You have other claims on us.'

Romayne looked at his spiritual adviser with a momentary change of expression — a relapse into the ironical bitterness of the past time.

'Have you forgotten that I am, and can be, only a layman?' he asked. 'What claims can I have, except the common claim of all faithful members of the Church on the good offices of the priesthood?' He paused for a moment, and continued with the abruptness of a man struck by a new idea. 'Yes! I have perhaps one small claim of my own — the claim of being allowed to do my duty.'

'In what respect, dear Romayne?'

'Surely you can guess? I am a rich man; I have money lying idle, which it is my duty (and my privilege) to devote to the charities and necessities of the Church. And, while I am speaking of this, I must own that I am a little surprised at your having said nothing to me on the subject. You have never yet pointed out to me the manner in which I might devote my money to the best and noblest uses. Was it

forgetfulness on your part?'

Father Benwell shook his head. 'No,' he replied; 'I can't honestly say that.'

'Then you had a reason for your silence?'

'Yes.'

'May I not know it?'

Father Benwell got up and walked to the fireplace. Now there are various methods of getting up and walking to a fireplace, and they find their way to outward expression through the customary means of look and manner. We may feel cold, and may only want to warm ourselves. Or we may feel restless, and may need an excuse for changing our position. Or we may feel modestly confused, and may be anxious to hide it. Father Benwell, from head to foot, expressed modest confusion, and polite anxiety to hide it.

'My good friend,' he said, 'I am afraid of hurting your feelings.'

Romayne was a sincere convert, but there were instincts still left in him which resented their expression of regard, even when it proceeded from a man whom he respected and admired. 'You will hurt my feelings,' he answered a little sharply, 'if you are not plain with me.'

'Then I *will* be plain with you,' Father Benwell rejoined. 'The Church — speaking through me, as her unworthy interpreter — feels a certain delicacy in approaching You on the subject of money.'

'Why?'

Father Benwell left the fireplace, without immediately answering. He opened a drawer,

345

and took out of it a flat mahogany box. His gracious familiarity became transformed, by some mysterious process of congelation, into a dignified formality of manner. The priest took the place of the man.

'The Church, Mr Romayne, hesitates to receive, as benevolent contributions, money derived from property of its own, arbitrarily taken from it, and placed in a layman's hands. No!' he cried, interrupting Romayne, who instantly understood the allusion to Vange Abbey — 'No! I must beg you to hear me out. I state the case plainly, at your own request. At the same time, I am bound to admit that the lapse of centuries has, in the eye of the law, sanctioned the deliberate act of robbery perpetrated by Henry the Eighth. You have lawfully inherited Vange Abbey from your ancestors. The Church is not unreasonable enough to assert a merely moral right against the law of the country. It may feel the act of spoliation — but it submits.' He unlocked the flat mahogany box, and gently dropped his dignity: the man took the place of the priest. 'As the master of Vange,' he said, 'you may be interested in looking at a little historical curiosity which we have preserved. The title-deeds, dear Romayne, by which the monks held your present property, in *their* time. Take another glass of wine.'

Romayne looked at the title-deeds, and laid them aside unread.

Father Benwell had roused his pride, his sense of justice, his wild and lavish instincts of generosity. He, who had always despised

346

money — except when it assumed its only estimable character, as a means for the attainment of merciful and noble ends — *he* was in possession of property to which he had no moral right: without even the poor excuse of associations which attached him to the place.

'I hope I have not offended you?' said Father Benwell.

'You have made me ashamed of myself,' Romayne answered warmly. 'On the day when I became a Catholic, I ought to have remembered Vange. Better late than never. I refuse to take shelter under the law — I respect the moral right of the Church. I will at once restore the property which I have usurped.'

Father Benwell took both Romayne's hands in his, and pressed them fervently.

'I am proud of you!' he said. 'We shall all be proud of you, when I write word to Rome of what has passed between us. But — no, Romayne! — this must not be. I admire you, I feel with you; and I refuse. On behalf of the Church, I say it — I refuse the gift.'

'Wait a little, Father Benwell! You don't know the state of my affairs. I don't deserve the admiration which you feel for me. The loss of the Vange property will be no pecuniary loss, in my case. I have inherited a fortune from my aunt. My income from that source is far larger than my income from the Yorkshire property.'

'Romayne, it must not be!'

'Pardon me, it must be. I have more money than I can spend — without Vange. And I have painful associations with the house which

347

disincline me ever to enter it again.'

Even this confession failed to move Father Benwell. He obstinately crossed his arms, obstinately tapped his foot on the floor. 'No!' he said. 'Plead as generously as you may, my answer is No.'

Romayne only became more resolute on his side. 'The property is absolutely my own,' he persisted. 'I am without a near relation in the world. I have no children. My wife is already provided for at my death, out of the fortune left me by my aunt. It is downright obstinacy — forgive me for saying so — to persist in your refusal.'

'It is downright duty, Romayne. If I gave way to you, I should be the means of exposing the priesthood to the vilest misinterpretation. I should be deservedly reprimanded, and your proposed deed of gift would, without a moment's hesitation, be torn up. If you have any regard for me, drop the subject.'

Romayne refused to yield, even to this unanswerable appeal.

'Very well,' he said, 'there is one document you can't tear up. You can't interfere with my making another will. I shall leave the Vange property to the Church, and I shall appoint you one of the trustees. You can't object to that.'

Even rigorous Father Benwell was now at a loss for any further expression of honourable protest. He could only plead sadly and submissively for an immediate change of subject. 'No more, dear Romayne — you distress me! What were we talking of, before

this unfortunate topic turned up?'

He filled the glasses; he offered more biscuits — he was really, and even perceptibly, agitated by the victory that he had won.

Refusing a deed of gift in Romayne's lifetime, in the fear that it might lead to a public scandal, he had gained the Vange property for the Church by the safer means of a legacy, which (especially in the absence of an heir) would be an unassailable proof of the testator's attachment to the Catholic Faith. But one last necessity now confronted him — the necessity of placing a serious obstacle in the way of any future change of purpose on the part of Romayne. As to the choice of that obstacle, Father Benwell's mind had been made up for some time past.

For a few minutes he walked up and down the room, without looking at his guest.

'What *was* it I had to say to you?' he resumed. 'Surely, I was speaking on the subject of your future life, and the right employment of your energies?'

'You are very kind, Father Benwell. The subject has little interest for me. My future life is shaped out — domestic retirement, ennobled by religious duties.'

Still pacing the room, Father Benwell stopped at that reply, and put his hand kindly on Romayne's shoulder.

'We don't allow a good Catholic to drift into domestic retirement, who is worthy of better things,' he said. 'The Church, Romayne, wishes to make use of you. I never flattered anyone in my life, but I may say before your face what I

have said behind your back. A man of your strict sense of honour — of your intellect — of your high aspirations — of your personal charm and influence — is not a man whom we can allow to run to waste. Open your mind, my friend, fairly to me, and I will open my mind fairly to you. Let me set the example. I say it, with authority; an enviable future is before you.'

Romayne's pale cheeks flushed with excitement. 'What future?' he asked eagerly. 'Am I free to choose? Must I remind you that a man with a wife cannot think only of himself.'

'Suppose you were *not* a man with a wife.'

'What do you mean?'

'Romayne; I am trying to break my way through that inveterate reserve which is one of the failings in your character. Unless you can prevail on yourself to tell me those secret thoughts, those unexpressed regrets, which you can confide to no other man, this conversation must come to an end. Is there no yearning, in your inmost soul, for anything beyond the position which you now occupy?'

There was a pause. The flush on Romayne's face faded away. He was silent.

'You are not in the confessional,' Father Benwell reminded him, with melancholy submission to circumstances. 'You are under no obligation to answer me.'

Romayne roused himself. He spoke in low reluctant tones. 'I am afraid to answer you,' he said.

That apparently discouraging reply armed Father Benwell with the absolute confidence

of success, which he had thus far failed to feel. He wound his way deeper and deeper into Romayne's mind, with the delicate ingenuity of penetration, of which the practice of years had made him master.

'Perhaps I have failed to make myself clearly understood,' he said. 'I will try to put it more plainly. You are no half-hearted man, Romayne. What you believe, you believe fervently. Impressions are not dimly and slowly produced on *your* mind. As the necessary result, your conversion being once accomplished, your whole soul is given to the Faith that is in you. Do I read your character rightly?'

'So far as I know it — yes.'

Father Benwell went on.

'Bear in mind what I have just said,' he resumed; 'and you will understand why I feel it my duty to press the question which you have not answered yet. You have found in the Catholic Faith the peace of mind which you have failed to obtain by other means. If I had been dealing with an ordinary man, I should have expected from the change no happier result than this. But I ask You, has that blessed influence taken no deeper and nobler hold on your heart? Can you truly say to me, 'I am content with what I have gained; I wish for no more?' '

'I cannot truly say it,' Romayne answered.

The time had now come for speaking plainly. Father Benwell no longer advanced to his end under cover of a cloud of words.

'A little while since,' he said, 'you spoke of Penrose, as of a man whose lot in life you longed

351

to share. The career which has associated him with an Indian mission is, as I told you, only adapted to a man of his special character and special gifts. But the career which has carried him into the sacred ranks of the priesthood is open to every man who feels the sense of divine vocation, which has made Penrose one of Us.'

'No, Father Benwell! Not open to every man.'

'I say, Yes!'

'It is not open to Me!'

'I say it is open to You. And more — I enjoin, I command, you to dismiss from your mind all merely human obstacles and discouragements. They are beneath the notice of a man who feels himself called to the priesthood. Give me your hand, Romayne! Does your conscience tell you that you are that man?'

Romayne started to his feet, shaken to the soul by the solemnity of the appeal.

'I can't dismiss the obstacles that surround me!' he cried passionately. 'To a man in my position, your advice is absolutely useless. The ties that bind me are beyond the limit of a priest's sympathies.'

'Nothing is beyond the limit of a priest's sympathies.'

'Father Benwell, I am married!'

Father Benwell folded his arms over his breast — looked with immovable resolution straight in Romayne's face — and struck the blow which he had been meditating for months past.

'Rouse your courage,' he said sternly. 'You are no more married than I am.'

352

4

On the Road to Rome

There was not a sound in the room. Romayne stood, looking at the priest.

'Did you hear what I said?' Father Benwell asked.

'Yes.'

'Do you understand that I really mean what I said?'

He made no reply — he waited, like a man expecting to hear more.

Father Benwell was alive to the vast importance, at such a moment, of not shrinking from the responsibility which he had assumed. 'I see how I distress you,' he said; 'but, for your sake, I am bound to speak out. Romayne! the woman whom you have married is the wife of another man. Don't ask me how I know it — I do know it. You shall have positive proof, as soon as you have recovered. Come! rest a little in the easy chair.'

He took Romayne's arm, and led him to the chair, and made him drink some wine. They waited awhile. Romayne lifted his head, with a heavy sigh.

'The woman whom I have married is the wife of another man.' He slowly repeated the words to himself — and then looked at Father Benwell.

'Who is the man?' he asked.

'I introduced you to him, when I was as ignorant of the circumstances as you are,' the priest answered. 'The man is Mr Bernard Winterfield.'

Romayne half raised himself from the chair. A momentary anger glittered in his eyes, and faded out again, extinguished by the nobler emotions of grief and shame. He remembered Winterfield's introduction to Stella.

'Her husband!' he said, speaking again to himself. 'And she let me introduce him to her. And she received him like a stranger.' He paused, and thought of it. 'The proofs, if you please, sir,' he resumed with sudden humility. 'I don't want to hear any particulars. It will be enough for me if I know beyond all doubt that I have been deceived and disgraced.'

Father Benwell unlocked his desk and placed two papers before Romayne. He did his duty with a grave indifference to all minor considerations. The time had not yet come for expressions of sympathy and regret.

'The first paper,' he said, 'is a certified copy of the register of the marriage of Miss Eyrecourt to Mr Winterfield, celebrated (as you will see) by the English chaplain at Brussels, and witnessed by three persons. Look at the names.'

The bride's mother was the first witness. The two names that followed were the names of Lord and Lady Loring. '*They*, too, in the conspiracy to deceive me!' Romayne said as he laid the paper back on the table.

'I obtained that piece of written evidence,'

Father Benwell proceeded, 'by the help of a reverend colleague of mine, residing at Brussels. I will give you his name and address, if you wish to make further inquiries.'

'Quite needless. What is this other paper?'

'This other paper is an extract from the shorthand writer's notes (suppressed in the reports of the public journals) of proceedings in an English court of law, obtained at my request by my lawyer in London.'

'What have I to do with it?'

He put the question in a tone of passive endurance — resigned to the severest moral martyrdom that could be inflicted on him.

'I will answer you in two words,' said Father Benwell. 'In justice to Miss Eyrecourt, I am bound to produce her excuse for marrying you.'

Romayne looked at him in stern amazement.

'Excuse!' he repeated.

'Yes — excuse. The proceedings to which I have alluded declare Miss Eyrecourt's marriage to Mr Winterfield to be null and void — by the English law — in consequence of his having been married at the time to another woman. Try to follow me. I will put it as briefly as possible. In justice to yourself, and to your future career, you must understand this revolting case thoroughly, from beginning to end.'

With those prefatory words, he told the story of Winterfield's first marriage; altering nothing; concealing nothing; doing the fullest justice to Winterfield's innocence of all evil motive, from first to last. When the plain truth served his

purpose, as it most assuredly did in this case, the man has never yet been found who could match Father Benwell at stripping himself of every vestige of reserve, and exhibiting his naked heart to the moral admiration of mankind.

'You were mortified, and I was surprised,' he went on, 'when Mr Winterfield dropped his acquaintance with you. We now know that he acted like an honourable man.'

He waited to see what effect he had produced. Romayne was in no state of mind to do justice to Winterfield or to any one. His pride was mortally wounded; his high sense of honour and delicacy writhed under the outrage inflicted on it.

'And mind this,' Father Benwell persisted, 'poor human nature has its right to all that can be justly conceded in the way of excuse and allowance. Miss Eyrecourt would naturally be advised by her friends, would naturally be eager, on her own part, to keep hidden from you what happened at Brussels. A sensitive woman, placed in a position so horribly false and degrading, must not be too severely judged, even when she does wrong. I am bound to say this — and more. Speaking from my own knowledge of all the parties, I have no doubt that Miss Eyrecourt and Mr Winterfield did really part at the church door.'

Romayne answered by a look — so disdainfully expressive of the most immovable unbelief, that it absolutely justified the fatal advice by which Stella's worldly-wise friends had encouraged her to conceal the truth. Father Benwell prudently closed his lips. He had put the case with perfect

356

fairness — his bitterest enemy could not have denied that.

Romayne took up the second paper, looked at it, and threw it back again on the table with an expression of disgust.

'You told me just now,' he said, 'that I was married to the wife of another man. And there is the judge's decision, releasing Miss Eyrecourt from her marriage to Mr Winterfield. May I ask you to explain yourself?'

'Certainly. Let me first remind you that you owe religious allegiance to the principles which the Church has asserted, for centuries past, with all the authority of its divine institution. You admit that?'

'I admit it.'

'Now, listen! In *our* Church, Romayne, marriage is even more than a religious institution — it is a sacrament. We acknowledge no human laws which profane that sacrament. Take two examples of what I say. When the great Napoleon was at the height of his power, Pius the Seventh refused to acknowledge the validity of the Emperor's second marriage to Maria Louisa — while Josephine was living, divorced by the French Senate. Again, in the face of the Royal Marriage Act, the Church sanctioned the marriage of Mrs Fitzherbert to George the Fourth, and still declares, in justice to her memory, that she was the King's lawful wife. In one word, marriage, to *be* marriage at all, must be the object of a purely religious celebration — and, this condition complied with, marriage is only to be dissolved by death. You

remember what I told you of Mr Winterfield?'

'Yes. His first marriage took place before the registrar.'

'In plain English, Romayne, Mr Winterfield and the woman-rider in the circus pronounced a formula of words before a layman in an office. That is not only no marriage, it is a blasphemous profanation of a holy rite. Acts of Parliament which sanction such proceedings are acts of infidelity. The Church declares it, in defence of religion.'

'I understand you,' said Romayne. 'Mr Winterfield's marriage at Brussels — '

'Which the English law,' Father Benwell interposed, 'declares to be annulled by the marriage before the registrar, stands good, nevertheless, by the higher law of the Church. Mr Winterfield is Miss Eyrecourt's husband, as long as they both live. An ordained priest performed the ceremony in a consecrated building — and Protestant marriages, so celebrated, are marriages acknowledged by the Catholic Church. Under those circumstances, the ceremony which afterwards united you to Miss Eyrecourt — though neither you nor the clergyman were to blame — was a mere mockery. Need I say any more? Shall I leave you for awhile by yourself?'

'No! I don't know what I may think, I don't know what I may do, if you leave me by myself.'

Father Benwell took a chair by Romayne's side. 'It has been my hard duty to grieve and humiliate you,' he said. 'Do you bear me no

ill-will?' He held out his hand.

Romayne took it — as an act of justice, if not as an act of gratitude.

'Can I be of any use in advising you?' Father Benwell asked.

'Who can advise a man in my position?' Romayne bitterly rejoined.

'I can at least suggest that you should take time to think over your position.'

'Time? take time? You talk as if my situation was endurable.'

'Everything is endurable, Romayne!'

'It may be so to you, Father Benwell. Did you part with your humanity when you put on the black robe of the priest?'

'I parted, my son, with those weaknesses of *our* humanity on which women practise. You talk of your position. I will put it before you at its worst.'

'For what purpose?'

'To show you exactly what you have now to decide. Judged by the law of England, Mrs Romayne is your wife. Judged by the principles held sacred among the religious community to which you belong, she is not Mrs Romayne — she is Mrs Winterfield, living with you in adultery. If you regret your conversion — '

'I don't regret it, Father Benwell.'

'If you renounce the holy aspirations which you have yourself acknowledged to me, return to your domestic life. But don't ask us, while you are living with that lady, to respect you as a member of our communion.'

Romayne was silent. The more violent

emotions aroused in him had, with time, subsided into calm. Tenderness, mercy, past affection found their opportunity, and pleaded with him. The priest's bold language had missed the object at which it aimed. It had revived in Romayne's memory the image of Stella in the days when he had first seen her. How gently her influence had wrought on him for good; how tenderly, how truly, she had loved him. 'Give me some more wine!' he cried. 'I feel faint and giddy. Don't despise me, Father Benwell — I was once so fond of her!'

The priest poured out the wine. 'I feel for you,' he said. 'Indeed, indeed, I feel for you.'

It was not all a lie — there were grains of truth in that outburst of sympathy. Father Benwell was not wholly merciless. His far-seeing intellect, his daring duplicity, carried him straight on to his end in view. But, that end once gained — and, let it be remembered, not gained, in this case, wholly for himself — there were compassionate impulses left in him which sometimes forced their way to the surface. A man of high intelligence — however he may misuse it, however unworthy he may be of it — has a gift from Heaven. When you want to see unredeemed wickedness, look for it in a fool.

'Let me mention one circumstance,' Father Benwell proceeded, 'which may help to relieve you for the moment. In your present state of mind, you cannot return to The Retreat.'

'Impossible!'

'I have had a room prepared for you in this house. Here, free from any disturbing influence,

you can shape the future course of your life. If you wish to communicate with your residence at Highgate — '

'Don't speak of it!'

Father Benwell sighed. 'Ah, I understand!' he said, sadly. 'The house associated with Mr Winterfield's visit — '

Romayne again interrupted him — this time by gesture only. The hand that had made the sign clenched itself, when it rested afterwards on the table. His eyes looked downward, under frowning brows. At the name of Winterfield, remembrances that poisoned every better influence in him rose venomously in his mind. Once more he loathed the deceit that had been practised on him. Once more the detestable doubt of that asserted parting at the church door renewed its stealthy torment, and reasoned with him as if in words: — She has deceived you in one thing; why not in another?

'Can I see my lawyer here?' he asked, suddenly.

'My dear Romayne, you can see any one whom you like to invite.'

'I shall not trouble you by staying very long, Father Benwell.'

'Do nothing in a hurry, my son. Pray do nothing in a hurry!'

Romayne paid no attention to this entreaty. Shrinking from the momentous decision that awaited him, his mind instinctively took refuge in the prospect of change of scene. 'I shall leave England!' he said, impatiently.

'Not alone,' Father Benwell remonstrated.

'Who will be my companion?'

'I will,' the priest answered.

Romayne's weary eyes brightened faintly. In his desolate position, Father Benwell was the one friend on whom he could rely. Penrose was far away; the Lorings had helped to keep him deceived; Major Hynd had openly pitied and despised him as a victim to priestcraft.

'Can you go with me at any time?' he asked. 'Have you no duties that keep you in England?'

'My duties, Romayne, are already confided to other hands.'

'Then you have foreseen this?'

'I have thought it possible. Your journey may be long, or may be short — you shall not go away alone.'

'I can think of nothing yet; my mind is a blank,' Romayne confessed sadly. 'I don't know where I shall go.'

'I know where you ought to go — and where you *will* go,' said Father Benwell, emphatically.

'Where?'

'To Rome.'

Romayne understood the true meaning of that brief reply. A vague sense of dismay began to rise in his mind. While he was still tortured by doubt, it seemed as if Father Benwell had, by some inscrutable process of prevision, planned out his future beforehand. Had the priest foreseen events?

No — he had only foreseen possibilities, on the day when it first occurred to him

that Romayne's marriage was assailable, before the court of Romayne's conscience, from the Roman Catholic point of view. By this means, the misfortune of Romayne's marriage having preceded his conversion might be averted; and the one certain obstacle in the way of any change of purpose on his part — the obstacle of the priesthood — might still be set up, by the voluntary separation of the husband from the wife. Thus far the Jesuit had modestly described himself to his reverend colleagues, as regarding his position towards Romayne in a new light. His next letter might boldly explain to them what he had really meant. The triumph was won. Not a word more passed between his guest and himself that morning.

Before post-time, on the same day, Father Benwell wrote his last report to the Secretary of the Society of Jesus, in these lines:-

'Romayne is free from the domestic ties that bound him. He bequeaths Vange Abbey as a legacy to the Church; and he acknowledges a vocation for the priesthood. Expect us at Rome in a fortnight's time.'

After The Story

Extracts From Bernard Winterfield's Diary

I

Winterfield Defends Himself

Beaupark House. June 17th, 18—.

You and I, Cousin Beeminster, seldom meet. But I occasionally hear of you, from friends acquainted with both of us.

I have heard of you last at Sir Philip's rent-day dinner, a week since. My name happened to be mentioned by one of the gentlemen present, a guest like yourself. You took up the subject of your own free will, and spoke of me in these terms:

'I am sorry to say it of the existing head of the family — but Bernard is really unfit for the position which he holds. He has, to say the least of it, compromised himself and his relatives on more than one occasion. He began as a young man by marrying a circus-rider. He got into some other scrape, after that, which he has contrived to keep a secret from us. We only know how disgraceful it must have been by the results — he was a voluntary exile from England

for more than a year. And now, to complete the list, he has mixed himself up in that miserable and revolting business of Lewis Romayne and his wife.'

If any other person had spoken of me in this manner, I should have set him down as a mischievous idiot — to be kicked perhaps, but not to be noticed in any other way.

With you, the case is different. If I die without male offspring, the Beaupark estate goes to you, as next heir.

I don't choose to let a man in this position slander me, and those dear to me, without promptly contradicting him. The name I bear is precious to me, in memory of my father. Your unanswered allusion to my relations with 'Lewis Romayne and his wife,' coming from a member of the family, will be received as truth. Rather than let this be, I reveal to you, without reserve, some of the saddest passages of my life. I have nothing to be ashamed of — and, if I have hitherto kept certain events in the dark, it has been for the sake of others, not for my own sake. I know better now. A woman's reputation — if she is a good woman — is not easily compromised by telling the truth. The person of whom I am thinking, when I write this, knows what I am going to do — and approves of it.

You will receive, with these lines, the most perfectly candid statement that I can furnish, being extracts cut out of my own private Diary. They are accompanied (where plain necessity seems to call for it) by the written evidence of other persons.

There has never been much sympathy between us. But you have been brought up like a gentleman — and, when you have read my narrative, I expect that you will do justice to me, and to others — even though you think we acted indiscreetly under trying and critical circumstances.

B.W.

II

Winterfield Makes Extracts

First Extract.

April 11 *th*, 1859. — Mrs Eyrecourt and her daughter have left Beaupark to-day for London. Have I really made any impression on the heart of the beautiful Stella? In my miserable position — ignorant whether I am free or not — I have shrunk from formally acknowledging that I love her.

12 *th*. — I am becoming superstitious! In the Obituary of to-day's 'Times' the death is recorded of that unhappy woman whom I was mad enough to marry. After hearing nothing of her for seven years — I am free! Surely this is a good omen? Shall I follow the Eyrecourts to London, and declare myself? I have not confidence enough in my own power of attraction to run the risk. Better to write first, in strictest confidence, to Mrs Eyrecourt.

14 *th*. — An enchanting answer from my angel's mother, written in great haste. They are on the point of leaving for Paris. Stella

is restless and dissatisfied; she wants change of scene; and Mrs Eyrecourt adds, in so many words: — 'It is you who have upset her; why did you not speak while we were at Beaupark?' I am to hear again from Paris. Good old Father Newbliss said all along that she was fond of me, and wondered, like Mrs Eyrecourt, why I failed to declare myself. How could I tell them of the hideous fetters which bound me in those days?

18 *th, Paris.* — She has accepted me! Words are useless to express my happiness.

19 *th.* — A letter from my lawyer, full of professional subtleties and delays. I have no patience to enumerate them. We move to Belgium tomorrow. Not on our way back to England — Stella is so little desirous of leaving the Continent that we are likely to be married abroad. But she is weary of the perpetual gaiety and glitter of Paris, and wants to see the old Belgian cities. Her mother leaves Paris with regret. The liveliest woman of her age that I ever met with.

Brussels, May 7. — My blessing on the old Belgian cities. Mrs Eyrecourt is so eager to get away from them that she backs me in hurrying the marriage, and even consents, sorely against the grain, to let the wedding be celebrated at Brussels in a private and unpretending way. She has only stipulated that Lord and Lady Loring (old friends) shall be present. They are to arrive to-morrow, and two days afterwards we are to be married.

★ ★ ★

(An enclosure is inserted in this place. It consists of the death-bed confession of Mr Winterfield's wife, and of the explanatory letter written by the rector of Belhaven. The circumstances related in these documents, already known to the reader, are left to speak for themselves, and the Extracts from the Diary are then continued.)

★ ★ ★

Bingen, on the Rhine, May 19. — Letters from Devonshire at last, which relieve my wretchedness in some small degree. The frightful misfortune at Brussels will at least be kept secret, so far as I am concerned. Beaupark House is shut up, and the servants are dismissed, 'in consequence of my residence abroad.' To Father Newbliss I have privately written. Not daring to tell him the truth, I leave him to infer that my marriage-engagement has been broken off; he writes back a kind and comforting letter. Time will, I suppose, help me to bear my sad lot. Perhaps a day may come when Stella and her friends will know how cruelly they have wronged me.

London, November 18, 1860. — The old wound has been opened again. I met her accidentally in a picture gallery. She turned deadly pale, and left the place. Oh, Stella! Stella!

London, August 12, 1861. — Another meeting with her. And another shock to endure, which I

368

might not have suffered if I had been a reader of the marriage announcements in the newspapers. Like other men, I am in the habit of leaving the marriage announcements to the women.

I went to visit an agreeable new acquaintance, Mr Romayne. His wife drove up to the house while I was looking out of the window. I recognised Stella! After two years, she has made use of the freedom which the law has given to her. I must not complain of that, or of her treating me like a stranger, when her husband innocently introduced us. But, when we were afterwards left together for a few minutes — no! I cannot write down the merciless words she said to me. Why am I fool enough to be as fond of her as ever?

Beaupark, November 16. — Stella's married life is not likely to be a happy one. To-day's newspaper announces the conversion of her husband to the Roman Catholic Faith. I can honestly say I am sorry for her, knowing how she has suffered, among her own relatives, by these conversions. But I so hate *him*, that this proof of his weakness is a downright consolation to me.

Beaupark, January 27, 1862. — A letter from Stella, so startling and deplorable that I cannot remain away from her after reading it. Her husband has deliberately deserted her. He has gone to Rome, to serve his term of probation for the priesthood. I travel to London by to-day's train.

London, January 27. — Short as it is, I looked at Stella's letter again and again on the journey. The tone of the closing sentences is still studiously cold. After informing me that she is staying with her mother in London, she concludes her letter in these terms:-

'Be under no fear that the burden of my troubles will be laid on your shoulders. Since the fatal day when we met at Ten Acres, you have shown forbearance and compassion towards me. I don't stop to inquire if you are sincere — it rests with you to prove that. But I have some questions to ask, which no person but you can answer. For the rest, my friendless position will perhaps plead with you not to misunderstand me. May I write again?'

Inveterate distrust in every sentence! If any other woman had treated me in this way, I should have put her letter into the fire, and should not have stirred from my comfortable house.

January 29. — A day missed out of my Diary. The events of yesterday unnerved me for the time.

Arriving at Derwent's Hotel on the evening of the 27th, I sent a line to Stella by messenger, to ask when she could receive me.

It is strange how the merest trifles seem to touch women! Her note in reply contains the first expression of friendly feeling towards me which has escaped her since we parted at Brussels. And this expression proceeds from her ungovernable surprise and gratitude, at my

taking the trouble to travel from Devonshire to London on her account!

For the rest, she proposed to call on me at the hotel the next morning. She and her mother, it appeared, differed in opinion on the subject of Mr Romayne's behaviour to her; and she wished to see me, in the first instance, unrestrained by Mrs Eyrecourt's interference.

There was little sleep for me that night. I passed most of the time in smoking and walking up and down the room. My one relief was afforded by Traveller — he begged so hard to go to London with me, I could not resist him. The dog always sleeps in my room. His surprise at my extraordinary restlessness (ending in downright anxiety and alarm) was expressed in his eyes, and in his little whinings and cries, quite as intelligibly as if he had put his meaning into words. Who first called a dog a dumb creature? It must have been a man, I think — and a thoroughly unlovable man, too, from a dog's point of view.

Soon after ten, on the morning of the 28th, she entered my sitting-room.

In her personal appearance, I saw a change for the worse; produced, I suppose, by the troubles that have tried her sorely, poor thing. There was a sad loss of delicacy in her features, and of purity in her complexion. Even her dress — I should certainly not have noticed it in any other woman — seemed to be loose and slovenly. In the agitation of the moment, I forgot the long estrangement between us; I half lifted my hand to take hers, and checked myself. Was I

mistaken in supposing that she yielded to the same impulse, and resisted it as I did? She concealed her embarrassment, if she felt any, by patting the dog.

'I am ashamed that you should have taken the journey to London in this wintry weather — ' she began.

It was impossible, in her situation, to let her assume this commonplace tone with me. 'I sincerely feel for you,' I said, 'and sincerely wish to help you, if I can.'

She looked at me for the first time. Did she believe me? or did she still doubt? Before I could decide, she took a letter from her pocket, opened it, and handed it to me.

'Women often exaggerate their troubles,' she said. 'It is perhaps an unfair trial of your patience — but I should like you to satisfy yourself that I have not made the worst of my situation. That letter will place it before you in Mr Romayne's own words. Read it, except where the page is turned down.'

It was her husband's letter of farewell.

The language was scrupulously delicate and considerate. But to my mind it entirely failed to disguise the fanatical cruelty of the man's resolution, addressed to his wife. In substance, it came to this:-

'He had discovered the marriage at Brussels, which she had deliberately concealed from him when he took her for his wife. She had afterwards persisted in that concealment, under circumstances which made it impossible that he could ever trust her again.' (This no

doubt referred to her ill-advised reception of me, as a total stranger, at Ten Acres Lodge.) 'In the miserable break-up of his domestic life, the church to which he now belonged offered him, not only her divine consolation, but the honour, above all earthly distinctions, of serving the cause of religion in the sacred ranks of the priesthood. Before his departure for Rome he bade her a last farewell in this world, and forgave her the injuries that she had inflicted on him. For her sake he asked leave to say some few words more. In the first place, he desired to do her every justice, in a worldly sense. Ten Acres Lodge was offered to her as a free gift for her lifetime, with a sufficient income for all her wants. In the second place, he was anxious that she should not misinterpret his motives. Whatever his opinion of her conduct might be, he did not rely on it as affording his only justification for leaving her. Setting personal feeling aside, he felt religious scruples (connected with his marriage) which left him no other alternative than the separation on which he had resolved. He would briefly explain those scruples, and mention his authority for entertaining them, before he closed his letter.'

There the page was turned down, and the explanation was concealed from me.

A faint colour stole over her face as I handed the letter back to her.

'It is needless for you to read the end,' she said. 'You know, under his own hand, that he has left me; and (if such a thing pleads with you in his favour), you also know that he is liberal in providing for his deserted wife.'

I attempted to speak. She saw in my face how I despised him, and stopped me.

'Whatever you may think of his conduct,' she continued, 'I beg that you will not speak of it to me. May I ask your opinion (now you have read his letter) on another matter, in which my own conduct is concerned? In former days — '

She paused, poor soul, in evident confusion and distress.

'Why speak of those days?' I ventured to say.

'I must speak of them. In former days, I think you were told that my father's will provided for my mother and for me. You know that we have enough to live on?'

I had heard of it, at the time of our betrothal — when the marriage-settlement was in preparation. The mother and daughter had each a little income of a few hundreds a year. The exact amount had escaped my memory.

After answering her to this effect, I waited to hear more.

She suddenly became silent; the most painful embarrassment showed itself in her face and manner. 'Never mind the rest,' she said, mastering her confusion after an interval. 'I have had some hard trials to bear; I forget things — ' she made an effort to finish the sentence, and gave it up, and called to the dog to come to her. The tears were in her eyes, and that was the way she took to hide them from me.

In general, I am not quick at reading the minds of others — but I thought I understood

374

Stella. Now that we were face to face, the impulse to trust me had, for the moment, got the better of her caution and her pride; she was half ashamed of it, half inclined to follow it. I hesitated no longer. The time for which I had waited — the time to prove, without any indelicacy on my side, that I had never been unworthy of her — had surely come at last.

'Do you remember my reply to your letter about Father Benwell?' I asked.

'Yes — every word of it.'

'I promised, if you ever had need of me, to prove that I had never been unworthy of your confidence. In your present situation, I can honourably keep my promise. Shall I wait till you are calmer? or shall I go on at once?'

'At once!'

'When your mother and your friends took you from me,' I resumed, 'if you had shown any hesitation — '

She shuddered. The image of my unhappy wife, vindictively confronting us on the church steps, seemed to be recalled to her memory. 'Don't go back to it!' she cried. 'Spare me, I entreat you.'

I opened the writing-case in which I keep the papers sent to me by the Rector of Belhaven, and placed them on the table by which she was sitting. The more plainly and briefly I spoke now, the better I thought it might be for both of us.

'Since we parted at Brussels,' I said, 'my wife has died. Here is a copy of the medical certificate of her death.'

Stella refused to look at it. 'I don't understand such things,' she answered faintly. 'What is this?'

She took up my wife's death-bed confession. 'Read it,' I said.

She looked frightened. 'What will it tell me?' she asked.

'It will tell you, Stella, that false appearances once led you into wronging an innocent man.'

Having said this, I walked away to a window behind her, at the farther end of the room, so that she might not see me while she read.

After a time — how much longer it seemed to be than it really was! — I heard her move. As I turned from the window, she ran to me, and fell on her knees at my feet. I tried to raise her; I entreated her to believe that she was forgiven. She seized my hands, and held them over her face — they were wet with her tears. 'I am ashamed to look at you,' she said. 'Oh, Bernard, what a wretch I have been!'

I never was so distressed in my life. I don't know what I should have said, what I should have done, if my dear old dog had not helped me out of it. He, too, ran up to me, with the loving jealousy of his race, and tried to lick my hands, still fast in Stella's hold. His paws were on her shoulder; he attempted to push himself between us. I think I successfully assumed a tranquillity which I was far from really feeling. 'Come, come!' I said, 'you mustn't make Traveller jealous.' She let me raise her. Ah, if she could have kissed *me* — but that was not to be done; she kissed the dog's head, and then she spoke

to me. I shall not set down what she said in these pages. While I live, there is no fear of my forgetting those words.

I led her back to her chair. The letter addressed to me by the Rector of Belhaven still lay on the table, unread. It was of some importance to Stella's complete enlightenment, as containing evidence that the confession was genuine. But I hesitated, for her sake, to speak of it just yet.

'Now you know that you have a friend to help and advise you — ' I began.

'No,' she interposed; 'more than a friend; say a brother.'

I said it. 'You had something to ask of me,' I resumed, 'and you never put the question.'

She understood me.

'I meant to tell you,' she said, 'that I had written a letter of refusal to Mr Romayne's lawyers. I have left Ten Acres, never to return; and I refuse to accept a farthing of Mr Romayne's money. My mother — though she knows that we have enough to live on — tells me I have acted with inexcusable pride and folly. I wanted to ask if you blame me, Bernard, as she does?'

I dare say I was inexcusably proud and foolish, too. It was the second time she had called me by my Christian name since the happy bygone time, never to come again. Under whatever influence I acted, I respected and admired her for that refusal, and I owned it in so many words. This little encouragement seemed to relieve her. She

was so much calmer that I ventured to speak of the Rector's letter.

She wouldn't hear of it. 'Oh, Bernard, have I not learnt to trust you yet? Put away those papers. There is only one thing I want to know. Who gave them to you? The Rector?'

'No.'

'How did they reach you, then?'

'Through Father Benwell.'

She started at that name like a woman electrified.

'I knew it!' she cried. 'It *is* the priest who has wrecked my married life — and he got his information from those letters, before he put them into your hands.' She waited awhile, and recovered herself. 'That was the first of the questions I wanted to put to you,' she said. 'I am answered. I ask no more.'

She was surely wrong about Father Benwell? I tried to show her why.

I told her that my reverend friend had put the letters into my hand, with the seal which protected them unbroken. She laughed disdainfully. Did I know him so little as to doubt for a moment that he could break a seal and replace it again? This view was entirely new to me; I was startled, but not convinced. I never desert my friends — even when they are friends of no very long standing — and I still tried to defend Father Benwell. The only result was to make her alter her intention of asking me no more questions. I innocently roused in her a new curiosity. She was eager to know how I had first become acquainted with the priest, and how he

had contrived to possess himself of papers which were intended for my reading only.

There was but one way of answering her.

It was far from easy to a man like myself, unaccustomed to state circumstances in their proper order — but I had no other choice than to reply, by telling the long story of the theft and discovery of the Rector's papers. So far as Father Benwell was concerned, the narrative only confirmed her suspicions. For the rest, the circumstances which most interested her were the circumstances associated with the French boy.

'Anything connected with that poor creature,' she said, 'has a dreadful interest for me now.'

'Did you know him?' I asked, with some surprise.

'I knew him and his mother — you shall hear how, at another time. I suppose I felt a presentiment that the boy would have some evil influence over me. At any rate, when I accidentally touched him, I trembled as if I had touched a serpent. You will think me superstitious — but, after what you have said, it is certainly true that he has been the indirect cause of the misfortune that has fallen on me. How came he to steal the papers? Did you ask the Rector, when you went to Belhaven?'

'I asked the Rector nothing. But he thought it his duty to tell me all that he knew of the theft.'

She drew her chair nearer to me. 'Let me hear every word of it!' she pleaded eagerly.

I felt some reluctance to comply with the request.

'Is it not fit for me to hear?' she asked.

This forced me to be plain with her. 'If I repeat what the Rector told me,' I said, 'I must speak of my wife.'

She took my hand. 'You have pitied and forgiven her,' she answered. 'Speak of her, Bernard — and don't, for God's sake, think that my heart is harder than yours.'

I kissed the hand that she had given to me — even her 'brother' might do that!

'It began,' I said, 'in the grateful attachment which the boy felt for my wife. He refused to leave her bedside on the day when she dictated her confession to the Rector. As he was entirely ignorant of the English language, there seemed to be no objection to letting him have his own way. He became inquisitive as the writing went on. His questions annoyed the Rector — and, as the easiest way of satisfying his curiosity, my wife told him that she was making her will. He knew just enough, from what he had heard at various times, to associate making a will with gifts of money — and the pretended explanation silenced and satisfied him.'

'Did the Rector understand it?' Stella asked.

'Yes. Like many other Englishmen in his position, although he was not ready at speaking French, he could read the language, and could fairly well understand it, when it was spoken. After my wife's death, he kindly placed the boy, for a few days, under the care of his housekeeper. Her early life had been passed in the island of Martinique, and she was able to communicate with the friendless foreigner in

380

his own language. When he disappeared, she was the only person who could throw any light on his motive for stealing the papers. On the day when he entered the house, she caught him, peeping through the key-hole of the study door. He must have seen where the confession was placed, and the colour of the old-fashioned blue paper, on which it was written, would help him to identify it. The next morning, during the Rector's absence, he brought the manuscript to the housekeeper, and asked her to translate it into French, so that he might know how much money was left to him in 'the will.' She severely reproved him, made him replace the paper in the desk from which he had taken it, and threatened to tell the Rector if his misconduct was repeated. He promised amendment, and the good-natured woman believed him. On that evening the papers were sealed, and locked up. In the morning the lock was found broken, and the papers and the boy were both missing together.'

'Do you think he showed the confession to any other person?' Stella asked. 'I happen to know that he concealed it from his mother.'

'After the housekeeper's reproof,' I replied, 'he would be cunning enough, in my opinion, not to run the risk of showing it to strangers. It is far more likely that he thought he might learn English enough to read it himself.'

There the subject dropped. We were silent for awhile. She was thinking, and I was looking at her. On a sudden, she raised her head. Her eyes rested on me gravely.

'It is very strange!' she said.

'What is strange?'

'I have been thinking of the Lorings. They encouraged me to doubt you. They advised me to be silent about what happened at Brussels. And they too are concerned in my husband's desertion of me. He first met Father Benwell at their house.' Her head drooped again; her next words were murmured to herself. 'I am still a young woman,' she said. 'Oh, God, what is my future to be?'

This morbid way of thinking distressed me. I reminded her that she had dear and devoted friends.

'Not one,' she answered, 'but you.'

'Have you not seen Lady Loring?' I asked.

'She and her husband have written most kindly, inviting me to make their house my home. I have no right to blame them — they meant well. But after what has happened, I can't go back to them.'

'I am sorry to hear it,' I said.

'Are you thinking of the Lorings?' she asked.

'I don't even know the Lorings. I can think of nobody but you.'

I was still looking at her — and I am afraid my eyes said more than my words. If she had doubted it before, she must have now known that I was as fond of her as ever. She looked distressed rather than confused. I made an awkward attempt to set myself right.

'Surely your brother may speak plainly,' I pleaded.

She agreed to this. But nevertheless she rose to go — with a friendly word, intended (as

382

I hoped) to show me that I had got my pardon for that time. 'Will you come and see us to-morrow?' she said. 'Can you forgive my mother as generously as you have forgiven me? I will take care, Bernard, that she does you justice at last.'

She held out her hand to take leave. How could I reply? If I had been a resolute man, I might have remembered that it would be best for me not to see too much of her. But I am a poor weak creature — I accepted her invitation for the next day.

January 30. — I have just returned from my visit.

My thoughts are in a state of indescribable conflict and confusion — and her mother is the cause of it. I wish I had not gone to the house. Am I a bad man, I wonder? and have I only found it out now?

Mrs Eyrecourt was alone in the drawing-room when I went in. Judging by the easy manner in which she got up to receive me, the misfortune that has befallen her daughter seemed to have produced no sobering change in this frivolous woman.

'My dear Winterfield,' she began, 'I have behaved infamously. I won't say that appearances were against you at Brussels — I will only say I ought not to have trusted to appearances. You are the injured person; please forgive me. Shall we go on with the subject? or shall we shake hands, and say no more about it?'

I shook hands of course. Mrs Eyrecourt perceived that I was looking for Stella.

'Sit down,' she said; 'and be good enough to put up with no more attractive society than mine. Unless I set things straight, my good friend, you and my daughter — oh, with the best intentions! — will drift into a false position. You won't see Stella to-day. Quite impossible — and I will tell you why. I am the worldly old mother; I don't mind what I say. My innocent daughter would die before she would confess what I am going to tell you. Can I offer you anything? Have you had lunch?'

I begged her to continue. She perplexed — I am not sure that she did not even alarm me.

'Very well,' she proceeded. 'You may be surprised to hear it — but I don't mean to allow things to go on in this way. My contemptible son-in-law shall return to his wife.'

This startled me, and I suppose I showed it.

'Wait a little,' said Mrs Eyrecourt. 'There is nothing to be alarmed about. Romayne is a weak fool; and Father Benwell's greedy hands are (of course) in both his pockets. But he has, unless I am entirely mistaken, some small sense of shame, and some little human feeling still left. After the manner in which he has behaved, these are the merest possibilities, you will say. Very likely. I have boldly appealed to those possibilities, nevertheless. He has already gone away to Rome; and I need hardly add — Father Benwell would take good care of that — he has left us no address. It doesn't in the least matter. One of the advantages of being so much in Society as I am is that I have nice acquaintances everywhere, always ready to

oblige me, provided I don't borrow money of them. I have written to Romayne, under cover to one of my friends living in Rome. Wherever he may be, there my letter will find him.'

So far, I listened quietly enough, naturally supposing that Mrs Eyrecourt trusted to her own arguments and persuasions. I confess it, even to myself, with shame. It was a relief to me to feel that the chances (with such a fanatic as Romayne) were a hundred to one against her.

This unworthy way of thinking was instantly checked by Mrs Eyrecourt's next words.

'Don't suppose that I am foolish enough to attempt to reason with him,' she went on. 'My letter begins and ends on the first page. His wife has a claim on him, which no newly-married man can resist. Let me do him justice. He knew nothing of it before he went away. My letter — my daughter has no suspicion that I have written it — tells him plainly what the claim is.'

She paused. Her eyes softened, her voice sank low — she became quite unlike the Mrs Eyrecourt whom I knew.

'In a few months more, Winterfield,' she said, 'my poor Stella will be a mother. My letter calls Romayne back to his wife — *and his child.*'

Mrs Eyrecourt paused, evidently expecting me to offer an opinion of some sort. For the moment I was really unable to speak. Stella's mother never had a very high opinion of my abilities. She now appeared to consider me the stupidest person in the circle of her acquaintance.

'Are you a little deaf, Winterfield?' she asked.

'Not that I know of.'

'Do you understand me?'

'Oh, yes.'

'Then why can't you say something? I want a man's opinion of our prospects. Good gracious, how you fidget! Put yourself in Romayne's place, and tell me this. If you had left Stella — '

'I should never have left her, Mrs Eyrecourt.'

'Be quiet. You don't know what you would have done. I insist on your supposing yourself to be a weak, superstitious, conceited, fanatical fool. You understand? Now, tell me, then. Could you keep away from your wife, when you were called back to her in the name of your first-born child? Could you resist that?'

'Most assuredly not!'

I contrived to reply with an appearance of tranquillity. It was not very easy to speak with composure. Envious, selfish, contemptible — no language is too strong to describe the turn my thoughts now took. I never hated any human being as I hated Romayne at that moment. 'Damn him, he will come back!' There was my inmost feeling expressed in words.

In the meantime, Mrs Eyrecourt was satisfied. She dashed at the next subject as fluent and as confident as ever.

'Now, Winterfield, it is surely plain to your mind that you must not see Stella again — except when I am present to tie the tongue of scandal. My daughter's conduct must not allow her husband — if you only knew how I detest that man! — must not, I say, allow her husband the slightest excuse for keeping away from her. If we

give that odious old Jesuit the chance, he will make a priest of Romayne before we know where we are. The audacity of these Papists is really beyond belief. You remember how they made Bishops and Archbishops here, in flat defiance of our laws? Father Benwell follows that example, and sets our other laws at defiance — I mean our marriage laws. I am so indignant I can't express myself as clearly as usual. Did Stella tell you that he actually shook Romayne's belief in his own marriage? Ah, I understand — she kept that to herself, poor dear, and with good reason too.'

I thought of the turned-down page in the letter. Mrs Eyrecourt readily revealed what her daughter's delicacy had forbidden me to read — including the monstrous assumption which connected my marriage before the registrar with her son-in-law's scruples.

'Yes,' she proceeded, 'these Catholics are all alike. My daughter — I don't mean my sweet Stella; I mean the unnatural creature in the nunnery — sets herself above her own mother. Did I ever tell you she was impudent enough to say she would pray for me? Father Benwell and the Papal Aggression over again! Now tell me, Winterfield, don't you think — taking the circumstances into consideration — that you will act like a thoroughly sensible man if you go back to Devonshire while we are in our present situation? What with foot-warmers in the carriage, and newspapers and magazines to amuse you, it isn't such a very long journey. And then Beaupark — dear Beaupark — is such

a remarkably comfortable house in the winter; and you, you enviable creature, are such a popular man in the neighbourhood. Oh, go back! go back!'

I got up and took my hat. She patted me on the shoulder. I could have throttled her at that moment. And yet she was right.

'You will make my excuses to Stella?' I said.

'You dear good fellow, I will do more than make your excuses; I will sing your praises — as the poet says.' In her ungovernable exultation at having got rid of me, she burst into extravagant language, 'I feel like a mother to you,' she went on, as we shook hands at parting. 'I declare I could almost let you kiss me.'

There was not a single kissable place about Mrs Eyrecourt, unpainted, undyed, or unpowdered. I resisted temptation, and opened the door. There was still one last request that I could not help making.

'Will you let me know,' I said, 'when you hear from Rome?'

'With the greatest pleasure,' Mrs Eyrecourt answered briskly. 'Goodbye, you best of friends — goodbye.'

I write these lines while the servant is packing my portmanteau. Traveller knows what that means. My dog is glad, at any rate, to get away from London. I think I shall hire a yacht, and try what a voyage round the world will do for me. I wish to God I had never seen Stella!

Second Extract.

Beaupark: February 10. — News at last from Mrs Eyrecourt.

Romayne has not even read the letter that she addressed to him — it has actually been returned to her by Father Benwell. Mrs Eyrecourt writes, naturally enough, in a state of fury. Her one consolation, under this insulting treatment, is that her daughter knows nothing of the circumstances. She warns me (quite needlessly) to keep the secret — and sends me a copy of Father Benwell's letter:-

'Dear Madam, — Mr Romayne can read nothing that diverts his attention from his preparation for the priesthood, or that recalls past associations with errors which he has renounced for ever. When a letter reaches him, it is his wise custom to look at the signature first. He has handed your letter to me, *unread* — with a request that I will return it to you. In his presence, I instantly sealed it up. Neither he, nor I, know, or wish to know, on what subject you have addressed him. We respectfully advise you not to write again.'

This is really too bad; but it has one advantage, so far as I am concerned. It sets my own unworthy doubts and jealousies before me in a baser light than ever. How honestly I defended Father Benwell! and how completely he has deceived me! I wonder whether I shall live long enough to see the Jesuit caught in one of his own traps?

11 *th*. — I was disappointed at not hearing from Stella yesterday. This morning has made amends; it has brought me a letter from her.

She is not well; and her mother's conduct sadly perplexes her. At one time, Mrs Eyrecourt's

389

sense of injury urges her to indulge in violent measures — she is eager to place her deserted daughter under the protection of the law; to insist on a restitution of conjugal rights or on a judicial separation. At another time she sinks into a state of abject depression; declares that it is impossible for her, in Stella's deplorable situation, to face Society; and recommends immediate retirement to some place on the Continent in which they can live cheaply. This latter suggestion Stella is not only ready, but eager, to adopt. She proves it by asking for my advice, in a postscript; no doubt remembering the happy days when I courted her in Paris, and the many foreign friends of mine who called at our hotel.

The postscript gave me the excuse that I wanted. I knew perfectly well that it would be better for me not to see her — and I went to London, for the sole purpose of seeing her, by the first train.

London, February 12. — I found mother and daughter together in the drawing-room. It was one of Mrs Eyrecourt's days of depression. Her little twinkling eyes tried to cast on me a look of tragic reproach; she shook her dyed head, and said, 'Oh, Winterfield, I didn't think you would have done this! Stella, fetch me my smelling-bottle.'

But Stella refused to take the hint. She almost brought the tears into my eyes, she received me so kindly. If her mother had not been in the room — but her mother *was* in the room; I had no other choice than to enter on my business, as if I had been the family lawyer.

Mrs Eyrecourt began by reproving Stella for asking my advice, and then assured me that she had no intention of leaving London. 'How am I to get rid of my house?' she asked, irritably enough. I knew that 'her house' (as she called it) was the furnished upper part of a house belonging to another person, and that she could leave it at a short notice. But I said nothing. I addressed myself to Stella.

'I have been thinking of two or three places which you might like,' I went on. 'The nearest place belongs to an old French gentleman and his wife. They have no children, and they don't let lodgings; but I believe they would be glad to receive friends of mine, if their spare rooms are not already occupied. They live at St Germain — close to Paris.'

I looked at Mrs Eyrecourt as I said those last words — I was as sly as Father Benwell himself. Paris justified my confidence; the temptation was too much for her. She not only gave way, but actually mentioned the amount of rent which she could afford to pay. Stella whispered her thanks to me as I went out. 'My name is not mentioned, but my misfortune is alluded to in the newspapers,' she said. 'Well-meaning friends are calling and condoling with me already. I shall die, if you don't help me to get away among strangers!'

I start for Paris, by the mail train, tonight.

Paris, February 13. — It is evening. I have just returned from St Germain. Everything is settled — with more slyness on my part. I begin to think I am a born Jesuit; there must have

391

been some detestable sympathy between Father Benwell and me.

My good friends, Monsieur and Madame Villeray, will be only too glad to receive English ladies, known to me for many years. The spacious and handsome first floor of their house (inherited from once wealthy ancestors by Madame Villeray) can be got ready to receive Mrs Eyrecourt and her daughter in a week's time. Our one difficulty related to the question of money. Monsieur Villeray, living on a Government pension, was modestly unwilling to ask terms; and I was too absolutely ignorant of the subject to be of the slightest assistance to him. It ended in our appealing to a houseagent at St Germain. His estimate appeared to me to be quite reasonable. But it exceeded the pecuniary limit mentioned by Mrs Eyrecourt. I had known the Villerays long enough to be in no danger of offending them by proposing a secret arrangement which permitted me to pay the difference. So that difficulty was got over in due course of time.

We went into the large garden at the back of the house, and there I committed another act of duplicity.

In a nice sheltered corner I discovered one of those essentially French buildings called a 'pavilion,' a delightful little toy house of three rooms. Another private arrangement made me the tenant of this place. Madame Villeray smiled. 'I bet you,' she said to me in her very best English, 'one of these ladies is in her fascinating first youth.' The good lady little knows what a

hopeless love affair mine is. I must see Stella sometimes — I ask, and hope for, no more. Never have I felt how lonely my life is, as I feel it now.

Third Extract.

London, March 1. — Stella and her mother have set forth on their journey to St Germain this morning, without allowing me, as I had hoped and planned, to be their escort.

Mrs Eyrecourt set up the old objection of the claims of propriety. If that were the only obstacle in my way, I should have set it aside by following them to France. Where is the impropriety of my seeing Stella, as her friend and brother — especially when I don't live in the same house with her, and when she has her mother, on one side, and Madame Villeray, on the other, to take care of her?

No! the influence that keeps me away from St Germain is the influence of Stella herself.

'I will write to you often,' she said; 'but I beg you, for my sake, not to accompany us to France.' Her look and tone reduced me to obedience. Stupid as I am, I think (after what passed between me and her mother) I can guess what she meant.

'Am I never to see you again?' I asked.

'Do you think I am hard and ungrateful?' she answered. 'Do you doubt that I shall be glad, more than glad, to see you, when — ?' She turned away from me and said no more.

It was time to take leave. We were under

her mother's superintendence; we shook hands — and that was all.

Matilda (Mrs Eyrecourt's maid) followed me downstairs to open the door. I suppose I looked, as I felt, wretchedly enough. The good creature tried to cheer me. 'Don't be anxious about them,' she said; 'I am used to travelling, sir — and I'll take care of them.' She is a woman to be thoroughly depended on, a faithful and attached servant. I made her a little present at parting, and I asked her if she would write to me from time to time.

Some people might consider this to be rather an undignified proceeding on my part. I can only say it came naturally to me. I am not a dignified man; and, when a person means kindly towards me, I don't ask myself whether that person is higher or lower, richer or poorer, than I am. We are, to my mind, on the same level when the same sympathy unites us. Matilda was sufficiently acquainted with all that had passed to foresee, as I did, that there would be certain reservations in Stella's letters to me. 'You shall have the whole truth from Me, sir, don't doubt it,' she whispered. I believed her. When my heart is sore, give me a woman for my friend. Whether she is lady or lady's-maid, she is equally precious to me.

Cowes, March 2. — I am in treaty with an agent for the hire of a yacht.

I must do something, and go somewhere. Returning to Beaupark is out of the question. People with tranquil minds can find pleasure in the society of their country neighbours. I

am a miserable creature, with a mind in a state of incessant disturbance. Excellent fathers of families talking politics to me; exemplary mothers of families offering me matrimonial opportunities with their daughters — that is what society means, if I go back to Devonshire. No. I will go for a cruise in the Mediterranean; and I will take one friend with me whose company I never weary of — my dog.

The vessel is discovered — a fine schooner of three hundred tons, just returned from a cruise to Madeira. The sailing-master and crew only ask for a few days on shore. In that time the surveyor will have examined the vessel, and the stores will be on board.

March 3. — I have written to Stella, with a list of addresses at which letters will reach me; and I have sent another list to my faithful ally the maid. When we leave Gibraltar, our course will be to Naples — thence to Civita Vecchia, Leghorn, Genoa, Marseilles. From any of those places, I am within easy travelling distance of St Germain.

March 7. *At Sea.* — It is half-past six in the evening. We have just passed the Eddystone Lighthouse, with the wind abeam. The log registers ten knots.

Fourth Extract.

Naples, May 10. — The fair promise at the beginning of my voyage has not been fulfilled. Owing to contrary winds, storms, and delay at Cadiz in repairing damages, we have only arrived at Naples this evening. Under trying

circumstances of all sorts, the yacht has behaved admirably. A stouter and finer sea-boat never was built.

We are too late to find the post office open. I shall send ashore for letters the first thing to-morrow morning. My next movements will depend entirely on the news I get from St Germain. If I remain for any length of time in these regions, I shall give my crew the holiday they have well earned at Civita Vecchia. I am never weary of Rome — but I always did, and always shall, dislike Naples.

May 11. — My plans are completely changed. I am annoyed and angry; the further I get away from France, the better I shall be pleased.

I have heard from Stella, and heard from the maid. Both letters inform me that the child is born, and that it is a boy. Do they expect me to feel any interest in the boy? He is my worst enemy before he is out of his long clothes.

Stella writes kindly enough. Not a line in her letter, however, invites me, or holds out the prospect of inviting me, to St Germain. She refers to her mother very briefly, merely informing me that Mrs Eyrecourt is well, and is already enjoying the gaieties of Paris. Three-fourths of the letter are occupied with the baby. When I wrote to her I signed myself 'yours affectionately.' Stella signs 'yours sincerely.' It is a trifle, I dare say — but I feel it, for all that.

Matilda is faithful to her engagement; Matilda's letter tells me the truth.

'Since the birth of the baby,' she writes, 'Mrs Romayne has never once mentioned your name;

396

she can talk of nothing, and think of nothing, but her child. I make every allowance, I hope, for a lady in her melancholy situation. But I do think it is not very grateful to have quite forgotten Mr Winterfield, who has done so much for her, and who only asks to pass a few hours of his day innocently in her society. Perhaps, being a single woman, I write ignorantly about mothers and babies. But I have my feelings; and (though I never liked Mr Romayne) I feel for *you*, sir — if you will forgive the familiarity. In my opinion this new craze about the baby will wear out. He is already a cause of difference of opinion. My good mistress, who possesses knowledge of the world, and a kind heart as well, advises that Mr Romayne should be informed of the birth of a son and heir. Mrs Eyrecourt says, most truly, that the hateful old priest will get possession of Mr Romayne's property, to the prejudice of the child, unless steps are taken to shame him into doing justice to his own son. But Mrs Romayne is as proud as Lucifer; she will not hear of making the first advances, as she calls it. 'The man who has deserted me,' she says, 'has no heart to be touched either by wife or child.' My mistress does not agree with her. There have been hard words already, and the nice old French gentleman and his wife try to make peace. You will smile when I tell you that they offer sugar-plums as a sort of composing gift. My mistress accepts the gift, and has been to the theatre at Paris, with Monsieur and Madame Villeray, more than once already. To conclude, sir, if I might venture to advise you,

I should recommend trying the effect on Mrs R. of absence and silence.'

A most sensibly written letter. I shall certainly take Matilda's advice. My name is never mentioned by Stella — and not a day has passed without my thinking of her!

Well, I suppose a man can harden his heart if he likes. Let me harden *my* heart, and forget her.

The crew shall have three days ashore at Naples, and then we sail for Alexandria. In that port the yacht will wait my return. I have not yet visited the cataracts of the Nile; I have not yet seen the magnificent mouse-coloured women of Nubia. A tent in the desert, and a dusky daughter of Nature to keep house for me — there is a new life for a man who is weary of the vapid civilisation of Europe! I shall begin by letting my beard grow.

Fifth Extract.
Civita Vecchia, February 28, 1863. — Back again on the coast of Italy — after an absence, at sea and ashore, of nine months!

What have my travels done for me? They have made me browner and thinner; they have given me a more patient mind, and a taste for mild tobacco. Have they helped me to forget Stella? Not the least in the world — I am more eager than ever to see her again. When I look back at my diary I am really ashamed of my own fretfulness and impatience. What miserable vanity on my part to expect her to think of me, when she was absorbed in the first cares and joys

of maternity; especially sacred to her, poor soul, as the one consolation of her melancholy life! I withdraw all that I wrote about her — and from the bottom of my heart I forgive the baby.

Rome, March 1. — I have found my letters waiting for me at the office of my banker.

The latest news from St Germain is all that I could wish. In acknowledging the receipt of my last letter from Cairo (I broke my rash vow of silence when we got into port, after leaving Naples) Stella sends me the long-desired invitation. 'Pray take care to return to us, dear Bernard, before the first anniversary of my boy's birthday, on the twenty-seventh of March.' After those words she need feel no apprehension of my being late at my appointment. Traveller — the dog has well merited his name by this time — will have to bid good-bye to the yacht (which he loves), and journey homeward by the railway (which he hates). No more risk of storms and delays for me. Goodbye to the sea for one while.

I have sent the news of my safe return from the East, by telegraph. But I must not be in too great a hurry to leave Rome, or I shall commit a serious error — I shall disappoint Stella's mother.

Mrs Eyrecourt writes to me earnestly, requesting, if I return by way of Italy, that I will get her some information about Romayne. She is eager to know whether they have made him a priest yet. I am also to discover, if I can, what are his prospects — whether he is as miserable as he deserves to be — whether he has been

disappointed in his expectations, and is likely to be brought back to his senses in that way — and, above all, whether Father Benwell is still at Rome with him. My idea is that Mrs Eyrecourt has not given up her design of making Romayne acquainted with the birth of his son.

The right person to apply to for information is evidently my banker. He has been a resident in Rome for twenty years — but he is too busy a man to be approached, by an idler like myself, in business hours. I have asked him to dine with me tomorrow.

March 2. — My guest has just left me. I am afraid Mrs Eyrecourt will be sadly disappointed when she hears what I have to tell her.

The moment I mentioned Romayne's name, the banker looked at me with an expression of surprise. 'The man most talked about in Rome,' he said; 'I wonder you have not heard of him already.'

'Is he a priest?'

'Certainly! And, what is more, the ordinary preparations for the priesthood were expressly shortened by high authority on his account. The Pope takes the greatest interest in him; and as for the people, the Italians have already nicknamed him 'the young cardinal.' Don't suppose, as some of our countrymen do, that he is indebted to his wealth for the high position which he has already attained. His wealth is only one of the minor influences in his favour. The truth is, he unites in himself two opposite qualities, both of the greatest value to the Church, which are very rarely found combined in the same man. He

has already made a popular reputation here, as a most eloquent and convincing preacher — '

'A preacher!' I exclaimed. 'And a popular reputation! How do the Italians understand him?'

The banker looked puzzled.

'Why shouldn't they understand a man who addresses them in their own language?' he said. 'Romayne could speak Italian when he came here — and since that time he has learnt by constant practice to think in Italian. While our Roman season lasts, he preaches alternately in Italian and in English. But I was speaking of the two opposite accomplishments which this remarkable man possesses. Out of the pulpit, he is capable of applying his mind successfully to the political necessities of the Church. As I am told, his intellect has had severe practical training, by means of historical studies, in the past years of his life. Anyhow, in one of the diplomatic difficulties here between the Church and the State, he wrote a memorial on the subject, which the Cardinal-Secretary declared to be a model of ability in applying the experience of the past to the need of the present time. If he doesn't wear himself out, his Italian nickname may prove prophetically true. We may live to see the new convert, Cardinal Romayne.'

'Are you acquainted with him yourself?' I asked.

'No Englishman is acquainted with him,' the banker answered. 'There is a report of some romantic event in his life which has led to his

401

leaving England, and which makes him recoil from intercourse with his own nation. Whether this is true or false, it is certain that the English in Rome find him unapproachable. I have even heard that he refuses to receive letters from England. If you wish to see him, you must do what I have done — you must go to church and look at him in the pulpit. He preaches in English — I think for the last time this season — on Thursday evening next. Shall I call here and take you to the church?'

If I had followed my inclinations, I should have refused. I feel no sort of interest in Romayne — I might even say I feel a downright antipathy towards him. But I have no wish to appear insensible to the banker's kindness, and my reception at St Germain depends greatly on the attention I show to Mrs Eyrecourt's request. So it was arranged that I should hear the great preacher — with a mental reservation on my part, which contemplated my departure from the church before the end of his sermon.

But, before I see him, I feel assured of one thing — especially after what the banker has told me. Stella's view of his character is the right one. The man who has deserted her has no heart to be touched by wife or child. They are separated for ever.

March 3. — I have just seen the landlord of the hotel; he can help me to answer one of Mrs Eyrecourt's questions. A nephew of his holds some employment at the Jesuit head-quarters here, adjoining their famous church *Il Gesù*. I have requested the young man to ascertain

402

if Father Benwell is still in Rome — without mentioning me. It would be no small trial to my self-control if we met in the street.

March 4. — Good news this time for Mrs Eyrecourt, so far as it goes. Father Benwell has long since left Rome, and has returned to his regular duties in England. If he exercises any further influence over Romayne, it must be done by letter.

March 5. — I have returned from Romayne's sermon. This double renegade — has he not deserted his religion and his wife? — has failed to convince my reason. But he has so completely upset my nerves, that I ordered a bottle of champagne (to the great amusement of my friend the banker) the moment we got back to the hotel.

We drove through the scantily lighted streets of Rome to a small church in the neighbourhood of the Piazza Navona. To a more imaginative man than myself, the scene when we entered the building would have been too impressive to be described in words — though it might perhaps have been painted. The one light in the place glimmered mysteriously from a great wax candle, burning in front of a drapery of black cloth, and illuminating dimly a sculptured representation, in white marble, of the crucified Christ, wrought to the size of life. In front of this ghastly emblem a platform projected, also covered with black cloth. We could penetrate no further than to the space just inside the door of the church. Everywhere else the building was filled with standing, sitting, and kneeling figures, shadowy

and mysterious, fading away in far corners into impenetrable gloom. The only sounds were the low wailing notes of the organ, accompanied at intervals by the muffled thump of fanatic worshippers penitentially beating their breasts. On a sudden the organ ceased; the self-inflicted blows of the penitents were heard no more. In the breathless silence that followed, a man robed in black mounted the black platform, and faced the congregation. His hair had become prematurely grey; his face was of the ghastly paleness of the great crucifix at his side. The light of the candle, falling on him as he slowly turned his head, cast shadows into the hollows of his cheeks, and glittered in his gleaming eyes. In tones low and trembling at first, he stated the subject of his address. A week since, two noteworthy persons had died in Rome on the same day. One of them was a woman of exemplary piety, whose funeral obsequies had been celebrated in that church. The other was a criminal charged with homicide under provocation, who had died in prison, refusing the services of the priest — impenitent to the last. The sermon followed the spirit of the absolved woman to its eternal reward in heaven, and described the meeting with dear ones who had gone before, in terms so devout and so touching that the women near us, and even some of the men, burst into tears. Far different was the effect produced when the preacher, filled with the same overpowering sincerity of belief which had inspired his description of the joys of heaven, traced the downward progress of

404

the lost man, from his impenitent death-bed to his doom in hell. The dreadful superstition of everlasting torment became doubly dreadful in the priest's fervent words. He described the retributive voices of the mother and the brother of the murdered man ringing incessantly in the ears of the homicide. 'I, who speak to you, hear the voices,' he cried. 'Assassin! assassin! where are you? I see him — I see the assassin hurled into his place in the sleepless ranks of the damned — I see him, dripping with the flames that burn for ever, writhing under the torments that are without respite and without end.' The climax of this terrible effort of imagination was reached when he fell on his knees and prayed with sobs and cries of entreaty — prayed, pointing to the crucifix at his side — that he and all who heard him might die the death of penitent sinners, absolved in the divinely atoning name of Christ. The hysterical shrieks of women rang through the church. I could endure it no longer. I hurried into the street, and breathed again freely, when I looked up at the cloudless beauty of the night sky, bright with the peaceful radiance of the stars.

And this man was Romayne! I had last met with him among his delightful works of art; an enthusiast in literature; the hospitable master of a house filled with comforts and luxuries to its remotest corner. And now I had seen what Rome had made of him.

'Yes,' said my companion, 'the Ancient Church not only finds out the men who can best serve it, but develops qualities

405

in those men of which they have been themselves unconscious. The advance which Roman Catholic Christianity has been, and is still, making has its intelligible reason. Thanks to the great Reformation, the papal scandals of past centuries have been atoned for by the exemplary lives of servants of the Church, in high places and low places alike. If a new Luther arose among us, where would he now find abuses sufficiently wicked and widely spread to shock the sense of decency in Christendom? He would find them nowhere — and he would probably return to the respectable shelter of the Roman sheepfold.'

I listened, without making any remark. To tell the truth, I was thinking of Stella.

March 6. — I have been to Civita Vecchia, to give a little farewell entertainment to the officers and crew before they take the yacht back to England.

In a few words I said at parting I mentioned that it was my purpose to make an offer for the purchase of the vessel, and that my guests should hear from me again on the subject. This announcement was received with enthusiasm. I really like my crew — and I don't think it is vain in me to believe that they return the feeling, from the sailing-master to the cabin-boy. My future life, after all that has passed, is likely to be a roving life, unless — No! I may think sometimes of that happier prospect, but I had better not put my thoughts into words. I have a fine vessel; I have plenty of money; and I like the sea. There are three good reasons for buying the yacht.

Returning to Rome in the evening, I found waiting for me a letter from Stella.

She writes (immediately on the receipt of my telegram) to make a similar request to the request addressed to me by her mother. Now that I am at Rome, she too wants to hear news of a Jesuit priest. He is absent on a foreign mission, and his name is Penrose. 'You shall hear what obligations I owe to his kindness,' she writes, 'when we meet. In the meantime, I will only say that he is the exact opposite of Father Benwell, and that I should be the most ungrateful of women if I did not feel the truest interest in his welfare.'

This is strange, and, to my mind, not satisfactory. Who is Penrose? and what has he done to deserve such strong expressions of gratitude? If anybody had told me that Stella could make a friend of a Jesuit, I am afraid I should have returned a rude answer. Well, I must wait for further enlightenment, and apply to the landlord's nephew once more.

March 7. — There is small prospect, I fear, of my being able to appreciate the merits of Mr Penrose by personal experience. He is thousands of miles away from Europe, and he is in a situation of peril, which makes the chance of his safe return doubtful in the last degree.

The Mission to which he is attached was originally destined to find its field of work in Central America. Rumours of more fighting to come, in that revolutionary part of the world, reached Rome before the missionaries had sailed from the port of Leghorn. Under

these discouraging circumstances, the priestly authorities changed the destination of the Mission to the territory of Arizona, bordering on New Mexico, and recently purchased by the United States. Here, in the valley of Santa Cruz, the Jesuits had first attempted the conversion of the Indian tribes two hundred years since, and had failed. Their mission-house and chapel are now a heap of ruins, and the ferocious Apache Indians keep the fertile valley a solitude by the mere terror of their name. To this ill-omened place Penrose and his companions have made their daring pilgrimage; and they are now risking their lives in the attempt to open the hearts of these bloodthirsty savages to the influence of Christianity. Nothing has been yet heard of them. At the best, no trustworthy news is expected for months to come.

What will Stella say to this? Anyhow, I begin to understand her interest in Penrose now. He is one of a company of heroes. I am already anxious to hear more of him.

To-morrow will be a memorable day in my calendar. To-morrow I leave Rome for St Germain.

If any further information is to be gained for Mrs Eyrecourt and her daughter, I have made the necessary arrangements for receiving it. The banker has promised to write to me, if there is a change in Romayne's life and prospects. And my landlord will take care that I hear of it, in the event of news reaching Rome from the Mission at Arizona.

St Germain, March 14. — I arrived yesterday. Between the fatigue of the journey and the pleasurable agitation caused by seeing Stella again, I was unfit to make the customary entry in my diary when I retired for the night.

She is more irresistibly beautiful than ever. Her figure (a little too slender as I remember it) has filled out. Her lovely face has lost its haggard, careworn look; her complexion has recovered its delicacy; I see again in her eyes the pure serenity of expression which first fascinated me, years since. It may be due to the consoling influence of the child — assisted, perhaps, by the lapse of time and the peaceful life which she now leads — but this at least is certain, such a change for the better I never could have imagined as the change I find in Stella after a year's absence.

As for the baby, he is a bright, good-humoured little fellow; and he has one great merit in my estimation — he bears no resemblance to his father. I saw his mother's features when I first took him on my knee, and looked at his face, lifted to mine in grave surprise. The baby and I are certain to get on well together.

Even Mrs Eyrecourt seems to have improved in the French air, and under the French diet. She has a better surface to lay the paint on; her nimble tongue runs faster than ever; and she has so completely recovered her good spirits, that Monsieur and Madame Villeray declare she must have French blood in her veins. They were all so unaffectedly glad to see me (Matilda

409

included), that it was really like returning to one's home. As for Traveller, I must interfere (in the interests of his figure and his health) to prevent everybody in the house from feeding him with every eatable thing, from plain bread to *pâté de foie gras*.

My experience of to-day will, as Stella tells me, be my general experience of the family life at St Germain.

We begin the morning with the customary cup of coffee. At eleven o'clock I am summoned from my 'pavilion' of three rooms to one of those delicious and artfully-varied breakfasts which are only to be found in France and in Scotland. An interval of about three hours follows, during which the child takes his airing and his siesta, and his elders occupy themselves as they please. At three o'clock we all go out — with a pony chaise which carries the weaker members of the household — for a ramble in the forest. At six o'clock we assemble at the dinner-table. At coffee time, some of the neighbours drop in for a game at cards. At ten, we all wish each other goodnight.

Such is the domestic programme, varied by excursions in the country and by occasional visits to Paris. I am naturally a man of quiet stay-at-home habits. It is only when my mind is disturbed that I get restless and feel longings for change. Surely the quiet routine at St Germain ought to be welcome to me now? I have been looking forward to this life through a long year of travel. What more can I wish for?

Nothing more, of course.

And yet — and yet — Stella has innocently made it harder than ever to play the part of her 'brother'. The recovery of her beauty is a subject for congratulation to her mother and her friends. How does it affect Me?

I had better not think of my hard fate. Can I help thinking of it? Can I dismiss from memory the unmerited misfortunes which have taken from me, in the prime of her charms, the woman whom I love? At least I can try.

The good old moral must be *my* moral:-'Be content with such things as ye have.'

March 15. — It is eight in the morning — and I hardly know how to employ myself. Having finished my coffee, I have just looked again at my diary.

It strikes me that I am falling into a bad habit of writing too much about myself. The custom of keeping a journal certainly has this drawback — it encourages egotism. Well! the remedy is easy. From this date, I lock up my book — only to open it again when some event has happened which has a claim to be recorded for its own sake. As for myself and my feelings, they have made their last appearance in these pages.

Seventh Extract.

June 7. — The occasion for opening my diary once more has presented itself this morning.

News has reached me of Romayne, which is too important to be passed over without notice. He has been appointed one of the Pope's Chamberlains. It is also reported, on

411

good authority, that he will be attached to a Papal embassy when a vacancy occurs. These honours, present and to come, seem to remove him farther than ever from the possibility of a return to his wife and child.

June 8. — In regard to Romayne, Mrs Eyrecourt seems to be of my opinion.

Being in Paris to-day, at a morning concert, she there met with her old friend, Doctor Wybrow. The famous physician is suffering from overwork, and is on his way to Italy for a few months of rest and recreation. They took a drive together, after the performance, in the Bois de Boulogne; and Mrs Eyrecourt opened her mind to the doctor, as freely as usual, on the subject of Stella and the child. He entirely agreed (speaking in the future interests of the boy) that precious time has been lost in informing Romayne of the birth of an heir; and he has promised, no matter what obstacles may be placed in his way, to make the announcement himself, when he reaches Rome.

June 9. — Madame Villeray has been speaking to me confidentially on a very delicate subject.

I am pledged to discontinue writing about myself. But in these private pages I may note the substance of what my good friend said to me. If I only look back often enough at this little record, I may gather the resolution to profit by her advice. In brief, these were her words:-

'Stella has spoken to me in confidence, since she met you accidentally in the garden yesterday. She cannot be guilty of the poor affectation of concealing what you must have already

discovered for yourself. But she prefers to say the words that must be said to you, through me. Her husband's conduct to her is an outrage that she can never forget. She now looks back with sentiments of repulsion, which she dare not describe, to that 'love at first sight' (as you call it in England), conceived on the day when they first met — and she remembers regretfully that other love, of years since, which was love of steadier and slower growth. To her shame she confesses that she failed to set you the example of duty and self-restraint when you two happened to be alone yesterday. She leaves it to my discretion to tell you that you must see her for the future, always in the presence of some other person. Make no reference to this when you next meet; and understand that she has only spoken to me instead of to her mother, because she fears that Mrs Eyrecourt might use harsh words, and distress you again, as she once distressed you in England. If you will take my advice, you will ask permission to go away again on your travels.'

It matters nothing what I said in reply. Let me only relate that we were interrupted by the appearance of the nursemaid at the pavilion door.

She led the child by the hand. Among his first efforts at speaking, under his mother's instruction, had been the effort to call me Uncle Bernard. He had now got as far as the first syllable of my Christian name, and he had come to me to repeat his lesson. Resting his little hands on my knees, he looked up at me

413

with his mother's eyes, and said, 'Uncle Ber'. A trifling incident, but, at that moment, it cut me to the heart. I could only take the boy in my arms, and look at Madame Villeray. The good woman felt for me. I saw tears in her eyes.

No! no more writing about myself. I close the book again.

Eighth Extract.

July 3. — A letter has reached Mrs Eyrecourt this morning, from Doctor Wybrow. It is dated, 'Castel Gandolpho, near Rome.' Here the doctor is established during the hot months — and here he has seen Romayne, in attendance on the 'Holy Father,' in the famous summer palace of the Popes. How he obtained the interview Mrs Eyrecourt is not informed. To a man of his celebrity, doors are no doubt opened which remain closed to persons less widely known.

'I have performed my promise,' he writes, 'and I may say for myself that I spoke with every needful precaution. The result a little startled me. Romayne was not merely unprepared to hear of the birth of his child — he was physically and morally incapable of sustaining the shock of the disclosure. For the moment, I thought he had been seized with a fit of catalepsy. He moved, however, when I tried to take his hand to feel the pulse — shrinking back in his chair, and feebly signing to me to leave him. I committed him to the care of his servant. The next day I received a letter from one of his priestly colleagues, informing me that he was slowly recovering after the

shock that I had inflicted, and requesting me to hold no further communication with him, either personally or by letter. I wish I could have sent you a more favourable report of my interference in this painful matter. Perhaps you or your daughter may hear from him.'

July 4 – 9. — No letter has been received. Mrs Eyrecourt is uneasy. Stella, on the contrary, seems to be relieved.

July 10. — A letter has arrived from London, addressed to Stella by Romayne's English lawyers. The income which Mrs Romayne has refused for herself is to be legally settled on her child. Technical particulars follow, which it is needless to repeat here.

By return of post, Stella has answered the lawyers, declaring that, so long as she lives, and has any influence over her son, he shall not touch the offered income. Mrs Eyrecourt, Monsieur and Madame Villeray — and even Matilda — entreated her not to send the letter. To my thinking, Stella acted with becoming spirit. Though there is no entail, still Vange Abbey is morally the boy's birthright — it is a cruel wrong to offer him anything else.

July 11. — For the second time I have proposed to leave St Germain. The presence of the third person, whenever I am in her company, is becoming unendurable to me. She still uses her influence to defer my departure. 'Nobody sympathises with me,' she said, 'but you.'

I am failing to keep my promise to myself, not to write about myself. But there is some little excuse this time. For the relief of my own

conscience, I may surely place it on record that I have tried to do what is right. It is not my fault if I remain at St Germain, insensible to Madame Villeray's warning.

Ninth Extract.

September 13. — Terrible news from Rome of the Jesuit Mission to Arizona.

The Indians have made a night attack on the new mission-house. The building is burnt to the ground, and the missionaries have been massacred — with the exception of two priests, carried away captive. The names of the priests are not known. News of the atrocity has been delayed four months on its way to Europe, owing partly to the civil war in the United States, and partly to disturbances in Central America.

Looking at the 'Times' (which we receive regularly at St Germain), I found this statement confirmed in a short paragraph — but here also the names of the two prisoners failed to appear.

Our one present hope of getting any further information seems to me to depend on our English newspaper. The 'Times' stands alone as the one public journal which has the whole English nation for volunteer contributors. In their troubles at home, they appeal to the Editor. In their travels abroad, over civilised and savage regions alike, if they meet with an adventure worth mentioning they tell it to the Editor. If any one of our countrymen knows anything of this dreadful massacre, I foresee with certainty where we shall find the information in print.

Soon after my arrival here, Stella had told me of her memorable conversation with Penrose in the garden at Ten Acres Lodge. I was well acquainted with the nature of her obligation to the young priest, but I was not prepared for the outbreak of grief which escaped her when she had read the telegram from Rome. She actually went the length of saying, 'I shall never enjoy another happy moment till I know whether Penrose is one of the two living priests!'

The inevitable third person with us, this morning, was Monsieur Villeray. Sitting at the window with a book in his hand — sometimes reading, sometimes looking at the garden with the eye of a fond horticulturist — he discovered a strange cat among his flower beds. Forgetful of every other consideration, the old gentleman hobbled out to drive away the intruder, and left us together.

I spoke to Stella, in words which I would now give everything I possess to recall. A detestable jealousy took possession of me. I meanly hinted that Penrose could claim no great merit (in the matter of Romayne's conversion) for yielding to the entreaties of a beautiful woman who had fascinated him, though he might be afraid to own it. She protested against my unworthy insinuation — but she failed to make me ashamed of myself. Is a woman ever ignorant of the influence which her beauty exercises over a man? I went on, like the miserable creature that I was, from bad to worse.

'Excuse me,' I said, 'if I have unintentionally made you angry. I ought to have known that I

was treading on delicate ground. Your interest in Penrose may be due to a warmer motive than a sense of obligation.'

She turned away from me — sadly, not angrily — intending, as it appeared, to leave the room in silence. Arrived at the door, she altered her mind, and came back.

'Even if you insult me, Bernard, I am not able to resent it,' she said, very gently. '*I* once wronged *you* — I have no right to complain of your now wronging me. I will try to forget it.'

She held out her hand. She raised her eyes — and looked at me.

It was not her fault; I alone am to blame. In another moment she was in my arms. I held her to my breast — I felt the quick beating of her heart on me — I poured out the wild confession of my sorrow, my shame, my love — I tasted again and again and again the sweetness of her lips. She put her arms round my neck, and drew her head back with a long sigh. 'Be merciful to my weakness,' she whispered. 'We must meet no more.'

She pushed me back from her, with a trembling hand, and left the room.

I have broken my resolution not to write about myself — but there is no egotism, there is a sincere sense of humiliation in me, when I record this confession of misconduct. I can make but one atonement — I must at once leave St Germain. Now, when it is too late, I feel how hard for me this life of constant repression has been.

418

Thus far I had written, when the nursemaid brought me a little note, addressed in pencil. No answer was required.

The few lines were in Stella's handwriting:-
'You must not leave us too suddenly, or you may excite my mother's suspicions. Wait until you receive letters from England, and make them the pretext for your departure. — S.'

I never thought of her mother. She is right. Even if she were wrong, I must obey her.

September 14. — The letters from England have arrived. One of them presents me with the necessary excuse for my departure, ready made. My proposal for the purchase of the yacht is accepted. The sailing-master and crew have refused all offers of engagement, and are waiting at Cowes for my orders. Here is an absolute necessity for my return to England.

The newspaper arrived with the letters. My anticipations have been realised. Yesterday's paragraph has produced another volunteer contributor. An Englishman just returned from Central America, after travelling in Arizona, writes to the 'Times.' He publishes his name and address — and he declares that he has himself seen the two captive priests.

The name of this correspondent carries its own guarantee with it. He is no less a person than Mr Murthwaite — the well-known traveller in India, who discovered the lost diamond called 'The Moonstone,' set in the forehead of a Hindoo idol. He writes to the editor as follows:-

'Sir, — I can tell you something of the two

Jesuit priests who were the sole survivors of the massacre in the Santa Cruz Valley four months since.

'I was travelling at the time in Arizona, under the protection of an Apache chief, bribed to show me his country and his nation (instead of cutting my throat and tearing off my scalp) by a present tribute of whisky and gunpowder, and by the promise of more when our association came to an end.

'About twelve miles northward of the little silver-mining town of Tubac we came upon an Apache encampment. I at once discovered two white men among the Indians. These were the captive priests.

'One of them was a Frenchman, named L'Herbier. The other was an Englishman, named Penrose. They owed their lives to the influence of two powerful considerations among the Indians. Unhappy L'Herbier lost his senses under the horror of the night massacre. Insanity, as you may have heard, is a sacred thing in the estimation of the American savages: they regard this poor madman as a mysteriously-inspired person. The other priest, Penrose, had been in charge of the mission medicine-chest, and had successfully treated cases of illness among the Apaches. As a 'great medicine-man,' he too is a privileged person — under the strong protection of their interest in their own health. The lives of the prisoners are in no danger, provided they can endure the hardship of their wandering existence among the Indians. Penrose spoke to me with the resignation of a true hero. 'I am in the hands

of God,' he said; 'and if I die, I die in God's service.' '

'I was entirely unprovided with the means of ransoming the missionaries — and nothing that I could say, or that I could promise, had the smallest effect on the savages. But for severe and tedious illness, I should long since have been on my way back to Arizona with the necessary ransom. As it is, I am barely strong enough to write this letter. But I can head a subscription to pay expenses; and I can give instructions to any person who is willing to attempt the deliverance of the priests.'

So the letter ended.

Before I had read it, I was at a loss to know where to go, or what to do, when I leave St Germain. I am now at no loss. I have found an object in life, and a means of making atonement to Stella for my own ungracious and unworthy words. Already I have communicated by telegraph with Mr Murthwaite and with my sailing-master. The first is informed that I hope to be with him, in London, to-morrow morning. The second is instructed to have the yacht fitted out immediately for a long voyage. If I can save these men — especially Penrose — I shall not have lived in vain.

London, September 15. — No. I have resolution enough to go to Arizona, but I have no courage to record the parting scene when it was time to say goodbye.

I had intended to keep the coming enterprise a secret, and only to make the disclosure in

421

writing when the vessel was ready to sail. But, after reading the letter to the 'Times,' Stella saw something in my face (as I suppose) that betrayed me. Well, it's over now. I do my best to keep myself from thinking of it — and, for this reason, I abstain from dwelling on the subject here.

Mr Murthwaite has not only given me valuable instructions — he has provided me with letters of introduction to persons in office, and to the *padres* (or priests) in Mexico, which will be of incalculable use in such an expedition as mine. In the present disturbed condition of the United States, he recommends me to sail for a port on the eastern coast of Mexico, and then to travel northward overland, and make my first inquiries in Arizona at the town of Tubac. Time is of such importance, in his opinion, that he suggests making inquiries in London and Liverpool for a merchant vessel under immediate sailing orders for Vera Cruz or Tampico. The fitting-out of the yacht cannot be accomplished, I find, in less than a fortnight or three weeks. I have therefore taken Mr Murthwaite's advice.

September 16. — No favourable answer, so far as the port of London is concerned. Very little commerce with Mexico, and had harbours in that country when you do trade. Such is the report.

September 17. — A Mexican brig has been discovered at Liverpool, under orders for Vera Cruz. But the vessel is in debt, and the date of departure depends on expected remittances! In this state of things I may wait, with my

conscience at ease, to sail in comfort on board my own schooner.

September 18 – 30. — I have settled my affairs; I have taken leave of my friends (good Mr Murthwaite included); I have written cheerfully to Stella; and I sail from Portsmouth to-morrow, well provided with the jars of whisky and the kegs of gunpowder which will effect the release of the captives.

It is strange, considering the serious matters I have to think of, but it is also true, that I feel out of spirits at the prospect of leaving England without my travelling companion, the dog. I am afraid to take the dear old fellow with me, on such a perilous expedition as mine may be. Stella takes care of him — and, if I don't live to return, she will never part with him, for his master's sake. It implies a childish sort of mind, I suppose — but it is a comfort to me to remember that I have never said a hard word to Traveller, and never lifted my hand on him in anger.

All this about a dog! And not a word about Stella? Not a word. *Those* thoughts are not to be written.

I have reached the last page of my diary. I shall lock it, and leave it in charge of my bankers, on my way to the Portsmouth train. Shall I ever want a new diary? Superstitious people might associate this coming to the end of the book with coming to an end of another kind. I have no imagination, and I take my leap in the dark hopefully — with Byron's glorious lines in my mind:

Here's a sigh to those who love me,
And a smile to those that hate;
And whatever sky's above me,
Here's heart for every fate!

(An enclosure is inserted here, marking a lapse of seven months, before the entries in the diary are resumed. It consists of two telegrams, despatched respectively on the 1st and 2nd of May, 1864.)

1. 'From Bernard Winterfield, Portsmouth, England. To Mrs Romayne, care of M. Villeray, St Germain, near Paris. — Penrose is safe on board my yacht. His unfortunate companion has died of exhaustion, and he is himself in a feeble state of health. I at once take him with me to London for medical advice. We are eager for news of you. Telegraph to Derwent's Hotel.'

2. 'From Mrs Eyrecourt, St Germain. To Bernard Winterfield, Derwent's Hotel, London. — Your telegram received with joy, and sent on to Stella in Paris. All well. But strange events have happened. If you cannot come here at once, go to Lord Loring. He will tell you everything.'

Tenth Extract.
London, 2nd May, 1864. — Mrs Eyrecourt's telegram reached me just after Doctor Wybrow had paid his first professional visit to Penrose, at the hotel. I had hardly time to feel relieved by the opinion of the case which he expressed, before my mind was upset by Mrs Eyrecourt. Leaving Penrose under the charge of our excellent

landlady, I hurried away to Lord Loring.

It was still early in the day: his lordship was at home. He maddened me with impatience by apologising at full length for 'the inexcusable manner in which he had misinterpreted my conduct on the deplorable occasion of the marriage ceremony at Brussels.' I stopped his flow of words (very earnestly spoken, it is only right to add), and entreated him to tell me, in the first place, what Stella was doing in Paris.

'Stella is with her husband,' Lord Loring replied.

My head turned giddy, my heart beat furiously. Lord Loring looked at me — ran to the luncheon table in the next room — and returned with a glass of wine. I really don't know whether I drank the wine or not. I know I stammered out another inquiry in one word.

'Reconciled?' I said.

'Yes, Mr Winterfield — reconciled, before he dies.'

We were both silent for a while.

What was he thinking of? I don't know. What was I thinking of? I daren't write it down.

Lord Loring resumed by expressing some anxiety on the subject of my health. I made the best excuse for myself that I could, and told him of the rescue of Penrose. He had heard of my object in leaving England, and heartily congratulated me. 'This will be welcome news indeed,' he said, 'to Father Benwell.'

Even the name of Father Benwell now excites my distrust. 'Is *he* in Paris too?' I inquired.

'He left Paris last night,' Lord Loring

answered; 'and he is now in London, on important business (as I understand) connected with Romayne's affairs.'

I instantly thought of the boy.

'Is Romayne in possession of his faculties?' I asked.

'In complete possession.'

'While justice is in his power, has he done justice to his son?'

Lord Loring looked a little confused. 'I have not heard,' was all he said in reply.

I was far from satisfied. 'You are one of Romayne's oldest friends,' I persisted. 'Have you not seen him yourself?'

'I have seen him more than once. But he has never referred to his affairs.' Having said this he hastily changed the subject. 'Is there any other information that I can give you?' he suggested.

I had still to learn under what circumstances Romayne had left Italy for France, and how the event of his illness in Paris had been communicated to his wife. Lord Loring had only to draw on his own recollections to enlighten me.

'Lady Loring and I passed the last winter in Rome,' he said. 'And, there, we saw Romayne. You look surprised. Perhaps you are aware that we had offended him, by advice which we thought it our duty to offer to Stella before her marriage?'

I was certainly thinking of what Stella had said of the Lorings on the memorable day when she visited me at the hotel.

'Romayne would probably have refused to

426

receive us,' Lord Loring resumed, 'but for the gratifying circumstance of my having been admitted to an interview with the Pope. The Holy Father spoke of him with the most condescending kindness; and, hearing that I had not yet seen him, gave instructions, commanding Romayne to present himself. Under these circumstances it was impossible for him to refuse to receive Lady Loring and myself on a later occasion. I cannot tell you how distressed we were at the sad change for the worse in his personal appearance. The Italian physician, whom he occasionally consulted, told me that there was a weakness in the action of his heart, produced, in the first instance, by excessive study and the excitement of preaching, and aggravated by the further drain on his strength due to insufficient nourishment. He would eat and drink just enough to keep him alive, and no more; and he persistently refused to try the good influence of rest and change of scene. My wife, at a later interview with him, when they were alone, induced him to throw aside the reserve which he had maintained with me, and discovered another cause for the deterioration in his health. I don't refer to the return of a nervous misery, from which he has suffered at intervals for years past; I speak of the effect produced on his mind by the announcement — made no doubt with the best intentions by Doctor Wybrow — of the birth of his child. This disclosure (he was entirely ignorant of his wife's situation when he left her) appears to have affected him far more

seriously than the English doctor supposed. Lady Loring was so shocked at what he said to her on the subject, that she has only repeated it to me with a certain reserve. 'If I could believe I did wrong,' he said, 'in dedicating myself to the service of the Church, after the overthrow of my domestic happiness, I should also believe that the birth of this child was the retributive punishment of my sin, and the warning of my approaching death. I dare not take this view. And yet I have it not in me, after the solemn vows by which I am bound, to place any more consoling interpretation on an event which, as a priest, it disturbs and humiliates me even to think of.' That one revelation of his tone of thought will tell you what is the mental state of this unhappy man. He gave us little encouragement to continue our friendly intercourse with him. It was only when we were thinking of our return to England that we heard of his appointment to the vacant place of first attaché to the embassy at Paris. The Pope's paternal anxiety on the subject of Romayne's health had chosen this wise and generous method of obliging him to try a salutary change of air, as well as a relaxation from his incessant employments in Rome. On the occasion of his departure we met again. He looked like a worn-out old man. We could now only remember his double claim on us — as a priest of our religion, and as a once dear friend — and we arranged to travel with him. The weather at the time was mild; our progress was made by easy stages. We left him at Paris, apparently the better for his journey.'

I asked if they had seen Stella on that occasion.

'No,' said Lord Loring. 'We had reason to doubt whether Stella would be pleased to see us, and we felt reluctant to meddle, unasked, with a matter of extreme delicacy. I arranged with the Nuncio (whom I have the honour to know) that we should receive written information of Romayne's state of health, and on that understanding we returned to England. A week since, our news from the Embassy was so alarming that Lady Loring at once returned to Paris. Her first letter informed me that she had felt it her duty to tell Stella of the critical condition of Romayne's health. She expressed her sense of my wife's kindness most gratefully and feelingly, and at once removed to Paris, to be on the spot if her husband expressed a wish to see her. The two ladies are now staying at the same hotel. I have thus far been detained in London by family affairs. But, unless I hear of a change for the better before evening, I follow Lady Loring to Paris by the mail train.'

It was needless to trespass further on Lord Loring's time. I thanked him, and returned to Penrose. He was sleeping when I got to the hotel.

On the table in the sitting-room I found a telegram waiting for me. It had been sent by Stella, and it contained these lines:-

'I have just returned from his bedside, after telling him of the rescue of Penrose. He desires to see you. There is no positive suffering — he is sinking under a complete prostration of the

forces of life. That is what the doctors tell me. They said, when I spoke of writing to you, 'Send a telegram; there is no time to lose.' '

Towards evening Penrose awoke. I showed him the telegram. Throughout our voyage, the prospect of seeing Romayne again had been the uppermost subject in his thoughts. In the extremity of his distress, he declared that he would accompany me to Paris by the night train. Remembering how severely he had felt the fatigue of the short railway journey from Portsmouth, I entreated him to let me go alone. His devotion to Romayne was not to be reasoned with. While we were still vainly trying to convince each other, Doctor Wybrow came in.

To my amazement he sided with Penrose.

'Oh, get up by all means,' he said; 'we will help you to dress.' We took him out of bed and put on his dressing-gown. He thanked us; and saying he would complete his toilette by himself, sat down in an easy chair. In another moment he was asleep again, so soundly asleep that we put him back in his bed without waking him. Doctor Wybrow had foreseen this result: he looked at the poor fellow's pale peaceful face with a kindly smile.

'There is the treatment,' he said, 'that will set our patient on his legs again. Sleeping, eating, and drinking — let that be his life for some weeks to come, and he will be as good a man as ever. If your homeward journey had been by land, Penrose would have died on the way. I will take care of him while you are in Paris.'

At the station I met Lord Loring. He understood that I too had received bad news, and gave me a place in the *coupé* carriage which had been reserved for him. We had hardly taken our seats when we saw Father Benwell among the travellers on the platform, accompanied by a grey-haired gentleman who was a stranger to both of us. Lord Loring dislikes strangers. Otherwise, I might have found myself travelling to Paris with that detestable Jesuit for a companion.

Paris, 3rd May. — On our arrival at the hotel I was informed that no message had yet been received from the Embassy.

We found Lady Loring alone at the breakfast table, when we had rested after our night-journey.

'Romayne still lives,' she said. 'But his voice has sunk to a whisper, and he is unable to breathe if he tries to rest in bed. Stella has gone to the Embassy; she hopes to see him today for the second time.'

'Only for the second time!' I exclaimed.

'You forget, Mr Winterfield, that Romayne is a priest. He was only consecrated on the customary condition of an absolute separation from his wife. On her side — never let her know that I told you this — Stella signed a formal document, sent from Rome, asserting that she consented of her own free will to the separation. She was relieved from the performance of another formality (which I need not mention more particularly) by a special dispensation. Under these circumstances — communicated to

431

me while Stella and I have been together in this house — the wife's presence at the bedside of her dying husband is regarded by the other priests at the Embassy as a scandal and a profanation. The kindhearted Nuncio is blamed for having exceeded his powers in yielding (even under protest) to the last wishes of a dying man. He is now in communication with Rome, waiting for the final instructions which are to guide him.'

'Has Romayne seen his child?' I asked.

'Stella has taken the child with her today. It is doubtful in the last degree whether the poor little boy will be allowed to enter his father's room. *That* complication is even more serious than the other. The dying Romayne persists in his resolution to see the child. So completely has his way of thinking been altered by the approach of death, and by the closing of the brilliant prospect which was before him, that he even threatens to recant, with his last breath, if his wishes are not complied with. How it will end I cannot even venture to guess.'

'Unless the merciful course taken by the Nuncio is confirmed,' said Lord Loring, 'it may end in a revival of the protest of the Catholic priests in Germany against the prohibition of marriage to the clergy. The movement began in Silesia in 1826, and was followed by unions (or Leagues, as we should call them now) in Baden, Wurtemberg, Bavaria, and Rhenish Prussia. Later still, the agitation spread to France and Austria. It was only checked by a papal bull issued in 1847, reiterating the final decision of the famous Council of Trent

432

in favour of the celibacy of the priesthood. Few people are aware that this rule has been an institution of slow growth among the clergy of the Church of Rome. Even as late as the twelfth century, there were still priests who set the prohibition of marriage at defiance.'

I listened, as one of the many ignorant persons alluded to by Lord Loring. It was with difficulty that I fixed my attention on what he was saying. My thoughts wandered to Stella and to the dying man. I looked at the clock.

Lady Loring evidently shared the feeling of suspense that had got possession of me. She rose, and walked to the window.

'Here is the message!' she said, recognising her travelling-servant, as he entered the hotel door.

The man appeared, with a line written on a card. I was requested to present the card at the Embassy, without delay.

4th May. — I am only now able to continue my record of the events of yesterday.

A silent servant received me at the Embassy, looked at the card, and led the way to an upper floor of the house. Arrived at the end of a long passage, he opened a door, and retired.

As I crossed the threshold Stella met me. She took both my hands in hers, and looked at me in silence. All that was true and good and noble expressed itself in that look.

The interval passed, and she spoke — very sadly, very quietly.

'One more work of mercy, Bernard. Help him to die with a heart at rest.'

She drew back — and I approached him.

He reclined, propped up with pillows, in a large easy chair; it was the one position in which he could still breathe with freedom. The ashy shades of death were on his wasted face. In the eyes alone, as they slowly turned on me, there still glimmered the waning light of life. One of his arms hung down over the chair; the other was clasped round his child, sitting on his knee. The boy looked at me wonderingly, as I stood by his father. Romayne signed to me to stoop, so that I might hear him.

'Penrose?' he asked, faintly whispering. 'Dear Arthur! Not dying, like me?'

I quieted *that* anxiety. For a moment there was even the shadow of a smile on his face, as I told him of the effort that Penrose had vainly made to be the companion of my journey. He asked me, by another gesture, to bend my ear to him once more.

'My last grateful blessing to Penrose. And to you. May I not say it? You have saved Arthur' — his eyes turned towards Stella — 'you have been *her* best friend.' He paused to recover his feeble breath; looking round the large room, without a creature in it but ourselves. Once more the melancholy shadow of a smile passed over his face — and vanished. I listened, nearer to him still.

'Christ took a child on his knee. The priests call themselves ministers of Christ. They have left me, because of *this* child, here on my knee. Wrong, wrong, wrong. Winterfield, Death is a great teacher. I know how I have erred — what I have lost. Wife and child. How poor and barren

434

all the rest of it looks now.'

He was silent for a while. Was he thinking? No: he seemed to be listening — and yet there was no sound in the room. Stella, anxiously watching him, saw the listening expression as I did. Her face showed anxiety, but no surprise.

'Does it torture you still?' she asked.

'No,' he said; 'I have never heard it plainly, since I left Rome. It has grown fainter and fainter from that time. It is not a Voice now. It is hardly a whisper: my repentance is accepted, my release is coming. — Where is Winterfield?'

She pointed to me.

'I spoke of Rome just now. What did Rome remind me of?' He slowly recovered the lost recollection. 'Tell Winterfield,' he whispered to Stella, 'what the Nuncio said when he knew that I was going to die. The great man reckoned up the dignities that might have been mine if I had lived. From my place here in the Embassy — '

'Let me say it,' she gently interposed, 'and spare your strength for better things. From your place in the Embassy you would have mounted a step higher to the office of Vice-Legate. Those duties wisely performed, another rise to the Auditorship of the Apostolic Chamber. That office filled, a last step upward to the highest rank left, the rank of a Prince of the Church.'

'All vanity!' said the dying Romayne. He looked at his wife and his child. 'The true happiness was waiting for me here. And I only know it now. Too late. Too late.'

He laid his head back on the pillow, and

435

closed his weary eyes. We thought he was composing himself to sleep. Stella tried to relieve him of the boy. 'No,' he whispered; 'I am only resting my eyes to look at him again.' We waited. The child stared at me, in infantine curiosity. His mother knelt at his side, and whispered in his ear. A bright smile irradiated his face; his clear brown eyes sparkled; he repeated the forgotten lesson of the bygone time, and called me once more, 'Uncle Ber.'

Romayne heard it. His heavy eyelids opened again. 'No,' he said. 'Not uncle. Something better and dearer. Stella, give me your hand!'

Still kneeling, she obeyed him. He slowly raised himself on the chair. 'Take her hand,' he said to me. I too knelt. Her hand lay cold in mine. After a long interval he spoke to me. 'Bernard Winterfield,' he said, 'love them, and help them, when I am gone.' He laid his weak hand on our hands, clasped together. 'May God protect you! may God bless you!' he murmured. 'Kiss me, Stella.'

I remember no more. As a man, I ought to have set a better example; I ought to have preserved my self-control. It was not to be done. I turned away from them — and burst out crying.

The minutes passed. Many minutes or few minutes, I don't know which.

A soft knock at the door aroused me. I dashed away the useless tears. Stella had retired to the farther end of the room. She was sitting by the fireside, with the child in her arms. I withdrew to the same part of the room, keeping far enough

away not to disturb them.

Two strangers came in, and placed themselves on either side of Romayne's chair. He seemed to recognise them unwillingly. From the manner in which they examined him, I inferred that they were medical men. After a consultation in low tones, one of them went out.

He returned again almost immediately, followed by the grey-headed gentleman whom I had noticed on the journey to Paris — and by Father Benwell.

The Jesuit's vigilant eyes discovered us instantly, in our place near the fireside. I thought I saw suspicion as well as surprise in his face. But he recovered himself so rapidly, that I could not feel sure. He bowed to Stella. She made no return; she looked as if she had not even seen him.

One of the doctors was an Englishman. He said to Father Benwell, 'Whatever your business may be with Mr Romayne, we advise you to enter on it without delay. Shall we leave the room?'

'Certainly not,' Father Benwell answered. 'The more witnesses are present, the more relieved I shall feel.' He turned to his travelling companion. 'Let Mr Romayne's lawyer,' he resumed, 'state what our business is.'

The grey-headed gentleman stepped forward.

'Are you able to attend to me, sir?' he asked.

Romayne, reclining in his chair, apparently lost to all interest in what was going on, heard and answered. The weak tones of his voice failed

to reach my ear at the other end of the room. The lawyer, seeming to be satisfied so far, put a formal question to the doctors next. He inquired if Mr Romayne was in full possession of his faculties.

Both the physicians answered without hesitation in the affirmative. Father Benwell added *his* attestation. 'Throughout Mr Romayne's illness,' he said firmly, 'his mind has been as clear as mine is.'

While this was going on, the child had slipped off his mother's lap with the natural restlessness of his age. He walked to the fireplace, and stopped — fascinated by the bright red glow of the embers of burning wood. In one corner of the low fender lay a loose little bundle of sticks, left there in case the fire might need re-lighting. The boy, noticing the bundle, took out one of the sticks and threw it experimentally into the grate. The flash of flame, as the stick caught fire, delighted him. He went on burning stick after stick. The new game kept him quiet: his mother was content to be on the watch, to see that no harm was done.

In the meantime, the lawyer briefly stated his case.

'You remember, Mr Romayne, that your will was placed, for safe keeping, in our office,' he began. 'Father Benwell called upon us, and presented an order, signed by yourself, authorising him to convey the will from London to Paris. The object was to obtain your signature to a codicil, which has been considered a necessary addition to secure the validity of

the will. — Are you favouring me with your attention, sir?'

Romayne answered by a slight bending of his head. His eyes were fixed on the boy — still absorbed in throwing his sticks, one by one, into the fire.

'At the time when your will was executed,' the lawyer went on, 'Father Benwell obtained your permission to take a copy of it. Hearing of your illness, he submitted the copy to a high legal authority. The written opinion of this competent person declares the clause, bequeathing the Vange estate to the Roman Church, to be so imperfectly expressed, that the will might be made a subject of litigation after the testator's death. He has accordingly appended a form of codicil amending the defect, and we have added it to the will. I thought it my duty, as one of your legal advisers, to accompany Father Benwell on his return to Paris in charge of the will — in case you might feel disposed to make any alteration.' He looked towards Stella and the child, as he completed that sentence. Father Benwell's keen eyes took the same direction. 'Shall I read the will, sir?' the lawyer resumed; 'or would you prefer to look at it yourself?'

Romayne held out his hand for the will, in silence. He was still watching his son. There were but few more sticks now left to be thrown in the fire.

Father Benwell interfered, for the first time.

'One word, Mr Romayne, before you examine that document,' he said. 'The Church receives back from you the property which was once its

439

own. Beyond that, it authorises and even desires you (by my voice) to make any changes which you or your trusted legal adviser may think right. I refer to the clauses of the will which relate to the property you have inherited from the late Lady Berrick — and I beg the persons present to bear in memory the few plain words that I have now spoken.'

He bowed with dignity, and drew back. Even the lawyer was favourably impressed. The doctors looked at each other with silent approval. For the first time, the sad repose of Stella's face was disturbed — I could see that it cost her an effort to repress her indignation. The one unmoved person was Romayne. The sheet of paper on which the will was written lay unregarded upon his lap; his eyes were still riveted on the little figure at the fireplace.

The child had thrown his last stick into the glowing red embers. He looked about him for a fresh supply, and found nothing. His fresh young voice rose high through the silence in the room.

'More!' he cried. 'More!'

His mother held up a warning finger. 'Hush!' she whispered. He shrank away from her, as she tried to take him on her knee, and looked across the room at his father. 'More!' he burst out, louder than ever.

Romayne beckoned to me, and pointed to the boy.

I led him across the room. He was quite willing to go with me — he reiterated his petition, standing at his father's knees.

'Lift him to me,' said Romayne.

I could barely hear the words: even his strength to whisper seemed to be fast leaving him. He kissed his son — with a panting fatigue under that trifling exertion, pitiable to see. As I placed the boy on his feet again, he looked up at his dying father, with the one idea still in his mind.

'More, papa! More!'

Romayne put the will into his hand.

The child's eyes sparkled. 'Burn?' he asked eagerly.

'Yes!'

Father Benwell sprang forward, with outstretched hands. I stopped him. He struggled with me. I forgot the privilege of the black robe. I took him by the throat.

The boy threw the will into the fire. 'Oh!' he shouted in high delight, and clapped his chubby hands as the bright little blaze flew up the chimney. I released the priest.

In a frenzy of rage and despair, he looked round at the persons in the room. 'I take you all to witness,' he cried, 'this is an act of madness!'

'You yourself declared just now,' said the lawyer, 'that Mr Romayne was in perfect possession of his faculties.'

The baffled Jesuit turned furiously on the dying man. They looked at each other.

For one awful moment Romayne's eyes brightened. Romayne's voice rallied its power, as if life was returning to him. Frowning darkly, the priest put his question.

'What did you do it for?'

Quietly and firmly the answer came.

'Wife and child.'

The last long-drawn sigh rose and fell. With those sacred words on his lips, Romayne died.

London, 6th May. — At Stella's request, I have returned to Penrose — with but one fellow-traveller. My dear old companion, the dog, is coiled up, fast asleep at my feet, while I write these lines. Penrose has gained strength enough to keep me company in the sitting-room. In a few days more he will see Stella again.

What instructions reached the Embassy from Rome — whether Romayne received the last sacrament at the earlier period of his illness — we never heard. No objection was made, when Lord Loring proposed to remove the body to England, to be buried in the family vault at Vange Abbey.

I had undertaken to give the necessary directions for the funeral, on my arrival in London. Returning to the hotel, I met Father Benwell in the street. I tried to pass on. He deliberately stopped me.

'How is Mrs Romayne?' he asked — with that infernal suavity which he seems always to have at command. 'Fairly well, I hope? And the boy? Ah, he little thought how he was changing his prospects for the better, when he made that blaze in the fire! Pardon me, Mr Winterfield, you don't seem to be quite so cordial as usual. Perhaps you are thinking of your inconsiderate assault on my throat? Let us forgive and forget.

Or, perhaps, you object to my having converted poor Romayne, and to my being ready to accept from him the restoration of the property of the Church. In both cases I only did my duty as a priest. You are a liberal-minded man. Surely I deserve a favourable construction of my conduct?'

I really could not endure this. 'I have my own opinion of what you deserve,' I answered. 'Don't provoke me to mention it.'

He eyed me with a sinister smile.

'I am not so old as I look,' he said; 'I may live another twenty years!'

'Well?' I asked.

'Well,' he answered, 'much may happen in twenty years!'

With that, he left me. If he means any further mischief, I can tell him this — he will find Me in his way.

To turn to a more pleasant subject. Reflecting on all that had passed at my memorable interview with Romayne, I felt some surprise that one of the persons present had made no effort to prevent the burning of the will. It was not to be expected of Stella — or of the doctors, who had no interest in the matter — but I was unable to understand the passive position maintained by the lawyer. He enlightened my ignorance in two words.

'The Vange property and the Berrick property were both absolutely at the disposal of Mr Romayne,' he said. 'If he died without leaving a will, he knew enough of the law to foresee that houses, lands, and money would go to his

443

'nearest of kin.' In plainer words, his widow and his son.'

When Penrose can travel, he accompanies me to Beaupark. Stella and her little son and Mrs Eyrecourt will be the only other guests in my house. Time must pass, and the boy will be older, before I may remind Stella of Romayne's last wishes on that sad morning when we two knelt on either side of him. In the meanwhile, it is almost happiness enough for me to look forward to the day —

NOTE. — The next leaf of the Diary is missing. By some accident, a manuscript page has got into its place, bearing a later date, and containing elaborate instructions for executing a design for a wedding dress. The handwriting has since been acknowledged as her own, by no less a person than — Mrs Eyrecourt.

THE END

We do hope that you have enjoyed reading this large print book.

Did you know that all of our titles are available for purchase?

We publish a wide range of high quality large print books including:
Romances, Mysteries, Classics
General Fiction
Non Fiction and Westerns

Special interest titles available in large print are:
The Little Oxford Dictionary
Music Book
Song Book
Hymn Book
Service Book

Also available from us courtesy of Oxford University Press:
Young Readers' Dictionary
(large print edition)
Young Readers' Thesaurus
(large print edition)

For further information or a free brochure, please contact us at:
Ulverscroft Large Print Books Ltd.,
The Green, Bradgate Road, Anstey,
Leicester, LE7 7FU, England.
Tel: (00 44) **0116 236 4325**
Fax: (00 44) **0116 234 0205**

STORY OF THE
WRECK OF THE TITANIC

Marshall Everett (editor)

This is a graphic and thrilling account of the sinking of the greatest floating palace ever built, carrying down to watery graves more than one thousand five hundred souls. The story is set forth clearly, giving the facts about the ship and the voyage, the passengers, and the pathetic details of the wreck. There are first-hand accounts of the survivors, telling of exciting escapes from death and acts of heroism not equalled in ancient or modern times.

MALICE

Danielle Steel

At seventeen, on the night of her mother's funeral, Grace Adams is attacked. With secrets too horrible to tell, with hurts so deep they may never heal, Grace withholds the truth about the attack. In healing her own pain, she reaches out to battered women and children who live a nightmare she knows only too well. When Grace meets Charles Mackenzie, a New York lawyer, she has found a man who wants nothing from her — except to heal her, to hear her secrets. But with happiness finally within her grasp, Grace is at her most vulnerable — in danger of losing everything to an enemy from her past, bent on malice.

SUNSTROKE

Madge Swindells

A fund manager for a London merchant
bank, Nina Ogilvie vowed that love would
struggle to have a place in her life. She
has reaped the rewards and become one
of the City's most brilliant — and most
heartless — operators. When her firm decides
a sojourn in South Africa is just the break she
needs, Nina finds the Cape's beauty piercing
her professional defences. Caught up in a
romantic whirlwind with Wolf Moller, a
wealthy German, she becomes pregnant and
sacrifices her career for a man she deeply
loves — but barely knows. Two years later,
Wolf disappears with her beloved son, Nicky,
exposing the reality of a man wanted by both
Interpol and the CIA . . .